AUSTIN S. BELANGER

In the Shadow of the Great White Wall

Facebook: facebook.com/bardofthesand/

Twitter: @bardofthesand

Gmail: bardofthesands@gmail.com

First edition

Editing by Hillary Crawford
Cover art by Naiha Raza

This book was professionally typeset on Reedsy.
Find out more at reedsy.com

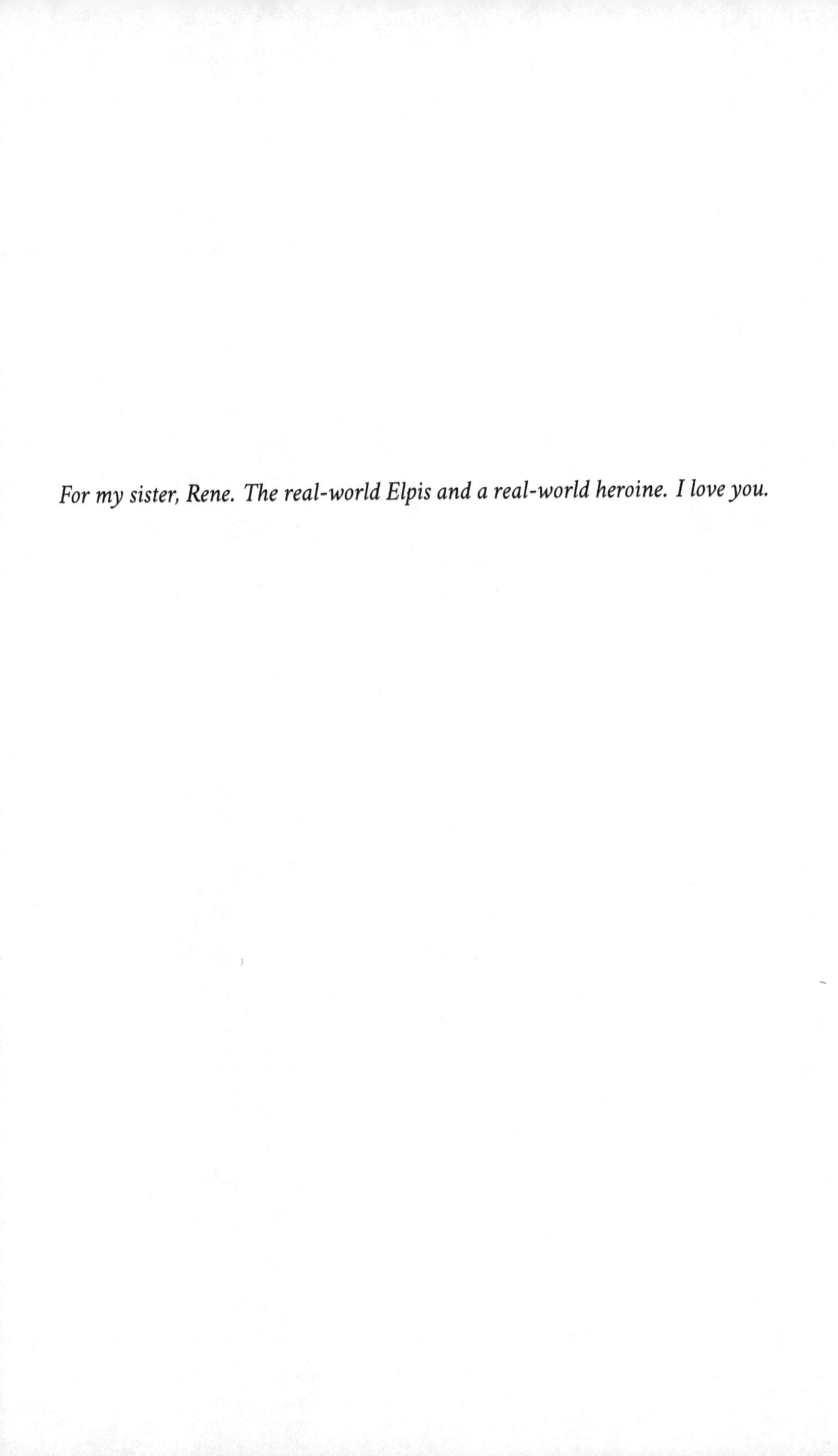

For my sister, Rene. The real-world Elpis and a real-world heroine. I love you.

"It has been written and proven time and time again, through trials of man and Gods, that all things return in a circle, and all things have their season under the sky, and great deeds tend to turn into dusty scrolls that sit on a darkened shelf in some great library, when fools forget their past and are doomed to repeat its folly."

– An unknown Eden Scholar

Contents

Acknowledgement

Karen, Mark, Donna, Matt, Nate, Nate Jr., Barry, Richard, Jeff, and Ron –
"The Party"

Hillary Crawford – Editor

Naiha Raza – Cover Art

Prologue

Fickle Gods watched the mortals of the Ert. As the blood stopped flowing, the dust began to settle, and those who had survived the carnage, surveyed what remained of their lives. Haeldrun scoffed at the failure of his creatures. Annoyed, the God turned his back on the dark army of his creation, leaving the few who managed to survive to their own devices. Many of the Underlord's children scurried in terror of the dragons, to cracks within the Ert, to find safety, bewildered at what they had done to anger their God so.

Soon, all who lived upon the Ert, crawled from their holes, witnessing the promise of a new age of light. King Swyk, the hero, was sent off to Aeternum, with many tears shed and much ceremonial fanfare, as was the Champion Sir Ontak. A new King now sat on the throne of Yslandeth, and the Alliances held with Hodan, Torith and Dornat Al Ar. The people of the Ert fully expected an immediate return to life as it was before the invasion, and when it did not happen, they wondered what the holdup was.

When that sun rose on the first day, many believed the Goddess herself would descend from the sky and take up all of their troubles, but after several weeks of the same routine, it began to sink in that Haya had no intention of letting her creations off that easy. There would be no magical rescue from Aeternum, as some had envisioned. People would have to work and cooperate in rebuilding. People who had once been foes, would need to aid each other to survive. The lack of divine intervention angered some, but the wise knew that it was by design. The unwise began to dissent in many remote, lawless locales.

While the smoke of many fires still burned in villages far from the Great White Wall, the first grumblings began to be voiced. The Goddess Haya lamented the selfishness and short-sightedness of her creations. Her daughter, the Goddess Aluia, interceded for mortals, arguing for her mother's mercy, saying, "The days of mortals are short and full of pain and trials below the golden sun, while they tread upon the green." Haya reluctantly agreed. Still, the older Goddess tested her creation, and Aluia sat in quiet contemplation of current events.

Many mortals learned the cold truth in those dark days. The scourge of the Offlander invaders had scoured their civilizations off of the map. The cities of mortals lay in ruin, with a lucky few living within the rubble of yesterday's life. The survivors had little more than the rags they wore on their backs. Over time, their many tears washed away the ashes of war, much like the fires of the Underworld burned their dreams like chaff in a fireplace. Mortals now lived in a harsh world with little security and scarce resources. Memories of life before conflict faded, as if the past was just a mirage of lost aspirations. Still, mortals lived, and with life, there is always promise, and with that promise, hope.

Puryn dwelled in despair, unsure of himself. The shadow of the great leaders of his era loomed, imposing over his soul. He forever thought of what his Masters, both Human and Elfish, would do if placed in his boots. Asking their guidance, he was met with only silence. It was then, in the quiet of his meditations, where he finally realized that he was alone and that they were indeed gone. Many times, Haya sat and watched as her Champion was wracked with personal guilt and insecurity, as he sat beside Swyk and Ontak's monuments seeking answers. But they never spoke. His only solace was his love and the family she had given him. The young King and his beloved Priestess had inherited hot ash, blowing in the wind, and within that dusty legacy, a myriad of sad, hungry, dirty faces looking to them for deliverance. Puryn felt the weight of their stares as he sat in his castle in Erynseere and sipped mead with his advisors. The new King planned his responses carefully, seeking to reduce suffering, and not to cause more with rash decisions.

The Kingdom of Yslandeth remained the beacon on the hill for all the Ert to see, just as it had always been. Empyr was a tarnished and crumbling shadow of itself, but the Great White Wall still stood in many places. This monument was a symbol and testament to Swyk's steady hand in turbulent times. Now the people impatiently waited for the same from King Puryn. They needed a Champion to lead them back to the days of peace and prosperity. While the Gods remained silent, the new King and his Queen set out to feed the masses, rebuild the glory of the nations, and bring about real prosperity to all who lived upon the Ert.

Puryn thought long and hard about every decision, asking Adasser for her input on all things of importance. He could not bear to see the lifeless gaze of any more children. As King, he would not be the cause of more suffering. This hesitation resulted in a delay of recovery in many places, ironically creating many of the problems that he sought to avoid. The indecision was viewed as a hindrance to practical action, and had the effect of encouraging rebellious factions in the three southern Kingdoms.

Each region had its issues, and its own underground cast of dissenters. The parties to the South knew that Puryn could not deal with all of their threats over all of these dispersed areas. The factions to the South calculated that Yslandeth would allow them to work their disputes out among themselves. These leaders knew that the North would not interfere with events, unless things escalated to an all-out regional war.

Cinnog was in great turmoil. King Lorus has perished outside of his Citadel with his armies. They met the blackness of Haeldrun's minions alone, after foolishly declining to join forces with Puryn and Orus, at the beginning of the invasion. The Offlanders decimated Cinnog's Citadel, but the castle remained. These remains became a symbol of Cinnog's legacy, and pretenders used them to debate and banter as to whom the crown truly belonged. With no clear successor to assume the throne left by King Lorus, many pretenders sprung up, wooing young fools to arms, pitting them brother against brother.

These self-proclaimed Lords pursued control of fallen piles of bricks and burned out farms, while boys died for their causes and claims of nobility.

Puryn shook his head from afar and wondered what they were thinking. The King of Yslandeth often tried to visualize what Cinnog's factions felt was of so much value that they would deplete the only resource left to their kingdom—its people. The young Champion could not understand the wish for more war after what the Ert had just endured. Puryn thought of the tough answers that awaited his consideration, concerning the growing problems in Cinnog. He began the practice of deploying covert, elite "scout teams" throughout all of the lands of the Ert. They were sent out to observe—most of the time.

Sudenyag was only a country if you looked it up on a map. The Kingdom was no more, and the people of Suden reverted to the ancient system of nomadic clans and tribes. Offlander invaders wholly razed the Suden capital. What remained of the Port of Valent were a few piers and dock warehouses, which were not touched by the flames of war. The Offlander forces made sure to destroy all of the smaller cities and villages, down to their last buildings, killing or imprisoning all who resided there. This response was an answer to Captain Harun Il Arnat, and his marauding gaggle of insurgents, whose successful assault on the Offlander headquarters resulted in the beheading of two decorated Offlander war heroes. The Orcs and Goblins were not amused.

The destitute survivors of Sudenyag resorted to thievery and organized crime to make ends meet, as well as to protect themselves from outside threats of attack. "Guilds" recruited members from these desperate masses of transient homeless. Their leaders offered the destitute mobs dreams of self-determination, as they employed anyone capable of spying, stealing, or wielding a dagger to the tasks facing the guild. Children were trained to serve, from the time that they were old enough to stand on their own. Sudenyag quickly became a dangerous place to be if one was an outsider with no business being there. The Suden government no longer existed as it was once known. It was now a no-man's land, ruled by the guilds, tribes, and warlords.

Edenyag suffered a similar fate as Sudenyag, when the dark army arrived. Although its destruction was very similar, Eden's recovery was quite different. The Eden Scribes were eventually successful in reclaiming most of their capital city, known as The Great Library. Within these sacred buildings, the writers and mages maintained the lore, history, and sciences of the entirety of the Ert. Eden Scribes were known to travel far and wide, collecting bits of knowledge, much like some Kingdom's armies strove to gain gold and jewels for their treasuries. These sages recovered as much as they possibly could from their damaged library halls, salvaging much of their treasures, but sadly, many tales and magic scrolls were forever lost to time. That lost learning is now primarily remembered by elders, when told by word of mouth, as they strive to pass on traditions to the next generation. This informal instruction would many times merely entail the telling of old stories around a campfire, or the teaching of "the trick" you learned as a child to your own children.

Edenyag endured much during its time at war, due to its poor leadership and planning. The conflict was not a thing that the Edenyag monarchy felt needed attention. Edenyag's leadership foolishly believed that, because their nation remained a neutral party, they were somehow insulated from invasion. The Kingdom fielded a meager citizen militia, which was more for show than for any tactical use or effective defense. King Cathir of Edenyag, allied with King Swyk of Yslandeth, never considering that a foreign power would ever occupy his lands.

With the threat of the Offlanders eliminated, Edenyag now faced the political reality of a close alliance between Hodan and Yslandeth. A demilitarized zone was created by Yslan, using Hodan forces as peacekeepers. The official story from Yslan was that King Puryn wished to protect Edenyag from further invasions via Sudenyag. King Cathir knew that this was all for the show, and the façade of peacekeeping was merely a nod to Puryn's new brother in arms, Orus, who had his eyes on expanding Hodan into the anarchy that was now the three southern Kingdoms.

To add insult to injury, King Cathir was expected to quietly endure a Hodan presence on the very fields where Orus's Legion, years before the Offlanders arrived, slaughtered thousands of Eden civilian militia for King Jabir of Hodan, during the First War of the People. This slight was not lost on the people of Edenyag. The lack of objections by their King to Yslandeth, made Edenyag's people question their leader's resolve. Eden was ripe for a revolution, and King Cathir knew this.

Hodan remained Hodan. It restored its villages and small towns, designating Warrior's Crossing as the new capital of their rebuilding nation. The new capital city was the home of their King, Orus the Lion, and instantly became the central hub of all Hodan. Hodan's Alliance with Yslandeth allowed it to recover more quickly than its rivals, and although it sorely lacked the military might that it once had, Hodan could still assert its power at will over the other southern nations, which were protected by little more than militia, especially when those militias were in the process of killing each other over territory and resources.

Hodan was far from in its golden era, but its people lived well when compared with any of its three neighbors to the South. Yslandeth reaffirmed its alliance and commitment to Hodan, and Hodan reciprocated. The other Kingdoms of the Ert feared the alliance, knowing that if Puryn spoke, Orus would agree with him, and vice versa. The two Kings never disagreed in public, presenting an iron-clad message to anyone who thought to test their resolve. Nervous jokes were made in private circles, as the jokers pretended to be facetious, while saying that the Goddess had cut both Kings from the same cloth. Many people went even further, questioning Puryn's loyalties and declaring him as much a Hodan as Orus.

Adasser, High Priestess of the Elfish people, conversed with her trees once the threat of death and darkness was utterly defeated. She ordered her loyal forests to divide in half. Adasser kept half at Erynseere to defend against anything that came her way, and sent the rest to re-establish the tree ring around her homeland in Torith. The Elves were elated that their Priestess blessed them once again with their tree ring and rebuilt in the trees that Adasser afforded them.

The Elves recovered quickly, spending the majority of their time rebuilding their homes and infrastructure, while training new military forces and reestablishing trade with Dornat Al Ar. The majority of Elfish commerce and production over the first couple of years was strictly food.

Crops were in strong demand, and the Elves knew how to grow food quickly and plentifully. The threat of overt conflict was nil. King Glorin of the Elves, knew that his son-in-law, Puryn, Protector of the Elves, would respond swiftly and without mercy to anyone foolish enough to attack his second home, and if Puryn did not, Glorin's daughter, Adasser, would use the very nature of the Ert itself against the aggressors. Glorin and his wife, Hansu, slept securely within their trees, knowing that they possessed all of the deterrents required to provide security for their people.

The Dwarves immediately rebuilt their hillside settlements and replanted their forests. The Dwarfish King Bogrol knew that food would be his first concern. The Battle of Arondayre claimed all of the Dwarfish military forces, but Dornat Al Ar was located within a great fortress, built beneath the Altyr Mountains, and the Kingdom's gates were virtually unbreachable. Still, Bogrol sent emissaries to Glorin in Torith, and the elder races, once again, reaffirmed their friendship, trading goods freely between their Kingdoms. These two allies privately decided to allow Humans to work out their problems on their own.

A new development for the Elves and Dwarves was that of repatriation. Many Elves and Dwarves left their adopted homes in the lands of the Humans, returning to their Kingdoms of origin. Even between Dornat Al Ar and Torith, this seemed to be the new norm. Many felt obligated to move homeward to their people to aid in the rebuilding. Soon, there was a migration from every clime and place around the Ert. Many travelers logically looked around at their surroundings, and knew that life would be better in the lands of the Dwarves and Elves. Humans were still sorting out their quarrels. The elder races were already building schools, temples, and marketplaces.

The orderly and voluntary migration of the Elves and Dwarves, sparked resentment among the suffering Human nations, as many saw the elder races as abandoning those who accepted them openly when times were good. Many of the Human population experienced a shift toward nationalism. The Suden began to organize their underground guilds to expel invaders from the North and East. Cinnog's warring militias and armies started not only patrolling rival factions, but also began deporting those of neighboring nations that they saw as spies or invaders. Edenyag, for the first time since the war, was conscripting a militia for the defense of its lands.

Within all nations, new prejudices and biases fomented discord, as resentment toward repatriation continued and turned to blame and accusations. Many of the mixed races, who had up until now, resided peacefully within civilized nations, felt the brunt of this new social attitude. Humans now shunned them openly and sometimes even publicly persecuted them. Human-Elves, Human-Dwarves, and Dwarf-Elves of all nations became second-class citizens overnight. Occasionally, angry mobs would go as far as to attack mixed families, violently running them out of their villages and towns. So, out of necessity, the displaced created their own ethnic communities in remote locations, where they could openly congregate, organize, and cooperate, to survive without the constant threat of mob rule.

The Suden had it the worst among Humans, when it came to persecution. Their Kingdom had allowed the scourge in. Everyone outside of Sudenyag blamed them for their current plight, even though the common Suden subject had no more power to stop the will of their King, than did any subject of any other Kingdom. It was just easier to blame someone else for the troubles the Ert faced, and the Suden survivors were the personification of the Ert's scapegoat.

Suden were not welcome anywhere on the Ert outside of their own Kingdom. If a Suden person ventured outside of their borders, they lied and told whoever asked them who they were, that they were from some remote region of Cinnog or Edenyag. As a Suden, it was imperative to deny your heritage if you wished to remain safe within any outside city on the Ert. The term "Suden," became an insult that was thrown about coarsely, and on the same level as the vilest of Etah curse words. The wisest Suden let the abuses pass, as they knew there were very few Suden left alive, and many who wished to do them harm wherever they went.

The last segment of the Ert that, of necessity, went into hiding, was that of the women who were assaulted by the Offlander forces and survived. Truthfully, neither the Goddess Haya, nor her belligerent estranged husband, Haeldrun, had considered the possibility of the races of the Ert and Wargyrn mixing. Many pregnant women of all races took their own lives, rather than give birth to a half-Orc, half-Goblin, or hybrid-Todessen spawn. However, many did not.

By far, most of the victims were Suden and of Cinnog. There, the enemy was most potent, and took their time decimating and dominating the peoples of both of those nations. Later, when they hit Edenyag with a split force, they did not have the numbers required to rape and pillage with impunity, so Eden was mostly spared. Adasser's stand at the Battle of Erynseere bled them dearly, and by the time the forces reached Yslandeth, they were all about business, and left the debauchery for after the victory was won.

Still, there were hundreds of women who became impregnated with Offlander children against their will, and in true vile fashion, their own tribes and people persecuted them and ran them out of their communities. Many women in this condition were stoned to death, but those who could, ran from their villages to the trees, begging Haya or Alluia to protect them from the lynch mobs that were sure to follow. Most never materialized, but these women still hid in fear for their lives. Luckily for them, with so much chaos going on around the Ert, most people paid no attention to anything, aside from where their next meal was coming from. Under the camouflage of confusion, the victims found their way to safety.

Over time, women from every nation who carried Offlander offspring, made their way to the Alabaster Sands Canyon, where everyone knew that no one lived. There, they created their own settlement within the caves they found within the rocky terrain. A river ran through the interior of the canyon, providing fresh water and fish. With some work, and the help of some Elfish women refugees, the settlers also learned to grow root vegetables on the river banks. Reportedly, the women lived meager lives there, but they were safe from prying eyes, the mobs, and the pitchforks and torches.

Many old women in the surrounding villages told tales around the campfires of a vile evil that resided within the canyons. Those who dared to enter the canyons never seemed to return. Some blamed bandits or highwaymen, but many believed the new tales of demonic presences in the rocks, tearing travelers to pieces in the night. This served as a strong deterrent for most, and secured the canyons as a suitable place for the women seeking asylum. When scattered reports of evil spirits in the canyons reached Puryn in Erynseere, he rolled his eyes and put it on his list of things to look into, as soon as he was able. The issue was lost in a sea of other pressing problems never to be investigated.

So, the Ert was a smoky, charred mess of disorder, chaos, and violence, and despite the gilded words of a victor's scribes and heralds, real people suffered in those first few years after the great reckoning of the Goddess. The official truth is always skewed, and seldom bears a resemblance to the reality of what happened.

Humankind is known to tell a good tale when the drink is good, or the lady listening is fair, or when the truth is too ugly to remember. Many times, a scribe takes poetic license with the events of man, washing facts with cleansing waters of prose and legend. More often than not, fairy tales are not written for the children of men, but instead for adults seeking comfort in better memories of their past deeds. These prettier versions of the truth soothe the guilt of many past indiscretions.

This tale is not one of those stories. This account is of what happened next.

Chapter 1

It was an ordinary morning at the Castle Erynseere. Adasser was in the sanctuary, communing with nature and serving the Goddess, when her son, Illari, stormed into the chamber, uninvited. Immediately, he shrieked and turned about, facing the nearest wall with his eyes closed. It had happened again.

"Mother!" the young Prince shouted. "You are doing it again!"

Adasser looked at the back of her 10-year-old son and wondered for a moment what he was squawking about. Then she realized that she was completely nude. Reaching for the robe on a peg on the wall nearby, she slipped on the garment.

Cringing for a moment, she closed her eyes, angry at herself. "I am sorry, my son," she sighed. "I get so caught up in my duties that many trivial things of the mortal world are forgotten. Still, I have no excuse for offending you so. I am sorry."

"Are you clothed now?" the young boy asked as he shuddered, thinking of the awkwardness of the encounter.

"Yes, I am, son. It is safe to turn around," Adasser snorted.

"I wish you would stop doing that, mother. I mean, how am I supposed to know when it is safe to come in here and learn from you?" Illari wore an annoyed face.

"Perhaps, you should try knocking next time, young man," Adasser asserted sternly. "Then maybe you would not surprise me, nor would I offend you."

Illari knew that she was right. When his mother was in communion with the Goddess, all other things burned away. Many times, his mother would speak in a one-sided conversation, as if answering voices that no one else heard but her. Many thought that perhaps the young Queen had gone mad when she used the power of the Goddess to defeat so many at the Battle of Erynseere, but others were sure that she spoke directly to Haya herself. Illari knew that she was praying when she talked to herself. He wondered if Haya indeed spoke to his mother anymore, but he knew that there was a connection, because his mother had much too much power to be a common Priestess.

Adasser spoke with excitement. "Are you prepared to go to the Towers, as your father once did?"

"Why must I learn the ways of men? They are so ignorant and rash," Illari protested.

"Because you are half Human, my son. You should understand your heritage and your bloodline. There is no shame in being the son of the King." Adasser caressed her son's cheeks, brushing the golden locks behind his pointed ears. "You will always be your father's son."

"Very well, but I will not enjoy myself. It will be a long absence from home, and I will miss … everyone." Illari looked at his mother and frowned.

"I am as close as the nearest tree, my son." Adasser smiled and hugged her son. "Now, let us learn how to make that healing potion."

Illari groaned. "Not again. I am terrible at alchemy. The last time it smelled like a corpse in here for two days!"

Laughing, Adasser picked up the containers with the components for the potion and led her son to a table by a window. She opened the shutters.

"There. In case we spill the essences on the wood again." She smiled.

"Yes, mother," Illari moaned, dragging his feet to the table. "I will get it right one of these tries."

* * *

Puryn was in his war room, surrounded by Commanders of the Draj Erynseere. They were looking over the map on the table, and Puryn was carefully moving wooden representations of military forces to places he felt that they should be. Over the past five years of "peace," the Ert was more warlike than it had been before the invasion from the seas. Puryn was sick of war and annoyed that peace had not materialized.

The young leader's first priority was addressing new attacks inside of Yslandeth. The young King knew from past experiences, that if he were perceived as not being in control of his own lands, the consequences would be dangerous for all in general. Cinnog was already embroiled in a full-out civil war; Sudenyag's underground crime guilds had established firm control over everything that occurred within the Suden borders; and Edenyag was raising a formidable army of citizen warriors. Orus had come to Puryn earlier in the year, discussing the possibility that Hodan annex Sudenyag. Puryn protested, but eventually gave in to his friend's request. Suden was a simmering cauldron of anger and violence. Puryn reasoned that Hodan could get a handle on the lawlessness in the South, but with every passing day, he realized that another war was coming.

Now in Yslandeth, reports were coming in from the subjects of outlying villages. Brigands were now openly operating near the Raven's Pass and in other remote locations. A target of interest for Puryn was a small village of outcast half-Elves, which was established northwest of the mouth of the Raven's Pass. He wondered if these attacks were motivated by ethnicity. The half-Elves seemed to be the focus of the attacks.

Puryn was not tolerant of the discrimination that had grown rampant in his beloved land. He railed against it loudly from his throne, but many had stopped listening and let their baser selves take over. The enlightened attitude of earlier ages had given way to so many petty grievances and endless grudges. Feuds between the Human population of Yslandeth, and anyone considered an "outsider" or "half-blood," were taken personally by the King, because he was husband to an Elfish woman and father to three half-Elf children.

Puryn was angry. "So, Constable, what is the report from Empyr concerning the village known as Hero's Pass?"

The Constable cleared his throat and reported. "Your Majesty, the villagers report night raids of livestock and agriculture. Up until the last week or so, it was only food and petty theft. Now, there are reports of women and children disappearing from their homes or from the fields farther out from the village proper. No one reports seeing anything, but the Red-Hand is rumored to have a hideout somewhere in the Pass or near it."

Puryn looked around at his advisors. "The Red-Hand again? Wasn't I advised that the grand show of force last month had 'broken their will'?" Puryn paused, then looked at a nervous Commander, who looked away immediately.

Looking at the floor, the General answered, "Apparently they regrouped, Your Majesty?"

Puryn nodded. "Apparently so." The King sternly looked at his Commanders. "All of you present do realize that half-Elves are subjects of Yslandeth, and because they are my people, they are entitled to the same protections that any Human settlement would be afforded."

The Commanders answered in unison, "Yes, Your Majesty!"

"Let me be understood clearly, gentlemen. If I find out that my leadership is unconcerned with the lives of Yslandeth citizens …," Puryn inhaled deeply to compose himself, "… I would not want to be that Commander. All of Yslan is our concern. If a show of force will not quell these cowardly bastards, then I will send a scout team to locate, engage, and destroy them. If they surrender, they will be put on trial. I feel very intolerant of bigots today."

Some in the room murmured. "Your Majesty, do you think that a small group can handle a militia that is rumored to be significantly large?"

Puryn sipped mead from his tankard. "I shall go to Empyr and meet with Donick. He will know if we have any new recruits with the skills necessary to take on this task. A new wave of conscripts reported a month ago. Several thousand from all over the Ert. Our forces at the capital are being tested and sorted according to capabilities and education. I am encouraged by Donick's reports. We shall see what we have to work with. Perhaps we can assemble a team of specialists. If not, I will go in with a Draj Legion, burning their camps, and killing every last one of them, personally."

The room grunted affirmatively. Puryn dismissed his Generals and called for some food and drink. A girl entered the room, setting down a tray with meats, cheeses, bread, and more mead. Puryn thanked the girl, and she curtsied, backing out of the chamber quickly. There was a knock at the door.

"Enter! Who is it?" Puryn barked.

"It is only me, husband," the Queen answered sarcastically, rolling her eyes.

"Oh, I am sorry, My Love. Tough news southeast of Empyr. Missing women and children. Half-Elf." Puryn's voice began to betray his anger.

"I am sure that you will handle it appropriately, My King," the Queen said in almost a question.

"Oh, I am going to handle this, and several other issues that are smoldering around at our doorstep." Puryn stood and walked to his wife, cradling her face in his hands. "They will never hurt you or my children. I will send them all to Haeldrun personally." Adasser knew he meant it. She remembered another long past day when she was forced to flee from the danger of battle in her home Kingdom of Torith. A younger Draj warrior saw her off and watched her go as she cried. He was older now, but still her Champion. Of a truth, he reminded her more of Swyk every day. During their last visit to Torith, Adasser remembered that Falda had remarked that Puryn had begun to remind her of her deceased husband. The former Queen was not wrong.

"You are correct, my husband. The last time someone challenged our family, it went rather badly for them, if I remember correctly." She smirked. "We have a Goddess on our side, and if she is not available, at least she has loaned me her creations. We have more than we require to quell any threat against us. Be at peace, My Love."

Puryn smiled. "I agree. No one comes for us, because they know better.

Now, I must ensure that others in less fortunate situations are afforded similar security." Puryn paused thinking, then shook his head. "You would think after five years, this belligerence and chaos would quell itself, but apparently there is no end to the greed and ambition of some men. I am sending a reconnaissance team to Hero's Pass. The subjects there will know that I value them as much as any 'true-blood.'"

"They see you, husband. You have nothing to prove." She kissed his lips. "You love an Elf and raise three children who are a part of two worlds. The oppressed know what you stand for. They know that you will come."

* * *

Empyr was far from restored. The main hall of the monastery was repaired, and Donick supervised the old Order of Haya's dawn from an administrative office within the building. When he was not dealing with Order related business, he was at the old castle, attempting to direct an orderly restoration of the capital. Donick had several apprentices and liaisons who dealt directly with the military. Just inside the main gate of Empyr, the Yslan forces had set up a massive tent complex, in an attempt to house all of the new recruits who Puryn was conscripting. By all estimates, Puryn's army numbers were approaching fifty-thousand conscripts and five-thousand Draj forces. Other Kingdoms had not fared quite as well in fielding a military. Hodan recruited and trained twenty-five-thousand Elites, while Edenyag raised its twenty-thousand militia. Cinnog's twelve to fifteen-thousand comprised of several small militias who were fighting each other at the moment, and Sudenyag had an estimated three-thousand-five-hundred in its criminal underground, but its numbers were only estimated, because no one could tell who a member of the guild was and who was not.

The smell of mildewed canvas was ripe in the air. It had been raining for the past few days, and the camp was an organized mud pit with neat columns of dirty, once-white, wall tents. Donick had ordered that the civil engineers use the gravel left over from construction to shore up the paths between the tents, because the whole area was becoming impossible to navigate on foot. Somewhere off in the distance, the wind shifted, and the unmistakable smell of a burning latrine met the Master's nose.

"Ah, memories," he sarcastically quipped to himself, remembering living in Erynseere for almost two years without proper buildings and outhouses. Donick walked across the remnant of the original military parade deck to where the Guard Officer of the Day was stationed. There, he found a young soldier of around seventeen years old, according to his estimations.

"You there! Who is the Officer of the Guard on duty?" Donick demanded. He was a civilian, but all of the military leaders knew that this Master not only reported directly to the King, but he was also his childhood friend. Donick had the King's ear, and no one wanted to be on the wrong side of his reports.

The young Lieutenant stood smartly, saluting. "I am the duty Captain, Sir!"

"The King sends a message via his lady that we are to screen the new recruits for those suitable for 'special' duties. Do you understand, son?" Donick raised an eyebrow.

"Completely, Sir. We have been culling the herd for those who are better than average. They have been segregated according to skill-set. Exceptional warriors have been relocated to the red candidate tents. Mages are being housed in the blue candidate tents. We have contacted the local 'guild' to inquire about the availability of stealth and recon forces, and as you are aware, all priests are located in the green tents outside of the main building near the Towers." The Lieutenant paused, awaiting any questions from the Master.

"Excellent. Have the top ten percent of every group assemble in the Towers courtyard. Do this quietly. Spies are everywhere, and we need to keep this as hidden as possible. Have them slowly arrive, in small groups, a few at a time. They will report directly to me. This is the decree of King Puryn. Do you understand my orders?" Donick stared gravely at the young man in armor before him.

"I do, Sir. I will give the orders and have the platoon Commanders pick their brightest candidates for your approval. Have a great day, Sir!" The Lieutenant bowed, then saluted. Donick nodded in approval. The young man left to do as he was told.

Master Donick, the headmaster of the Order of Haya's Dawn, lit his pipe, as he looked out over the muddy field before him. The smell of burning Human waste was stronger now. He shook his head, puffing on his pipe in an unsuccessful attempt to mask that smell. He was unsure of what he would find in the morning, but he knew that it would be up to him to find the able teams that Puryn required for his missions. Donick only hoped that these teams would make it home, unlike countless others, who had died in undisclosed locations, while covertly fighting in an unofficial capacity. He did not like sending the young to their deaths. Donick hated war already, but apparently, the Ert had not yet had its fill.

Chapter 2

The sun rose, silently from behind the horizon and over the trees surrounding the Erynseere ring. It had been five years and several months, since Illari stood in the courtyard center and witnessed the full power of his mother's fury. The ten-year-old lad quietly sat on a bench, gruesomely recalling the spot where an Orc was torn in two by his mother's sheer will. Illari saw things, and in the moments of her incredible violence, he saw the Goddess's beauty. Through all of the carnage, he remembered seeing his mother bathed in pure white light, as if the sun was physically a part of her person. The young Prince smiled as he remembered the whole day. That was the day that the young Baroness of Erynseere changed the course of a war, single-handedly.

Then he looked at the small trunk by his feet, and came back to the realization that today was the day that he was to depart to Yslandeth's capital city of Empyr. He was to attend the Towers monastery for the next five years. His mother thought it right for him. His father knew Donick would be a good teacher and was not opposed.

As he waited, Illari's younger sister, Elpis, joined him in the courtyard. She was an impetuous young red-headed maiden who resembled her mother as a young lass. There were many occasions where Adasser would complain to her mother that she was never that bad as a child, but all her mother, Queen Hansu, would do is laugh at her protests. Elpis was a very strong-willed young one, and she inherited an Elfish magic power befitting her disposition. She could manipulate the elements around her. Fire, water, air, earth, and electricity were her tools. At eight years old, she was an annoyance to Illari, who tired of being pranked with shocking touches or flying rocks. He would not miss his sister, so he said anyway.

"What do you want?" Illari asked in a harsh tone. Elpis had a sad look on her face.

"What? I can't come to say goodbye to my brother?" Elpis frowned. "Who will I play with?"

"Perhaps you could shock Altwidus for a time!" Illari quipped.

Elpis began to cry, and Illari felt terrible for what he had said. "Come here," he said gently, and he hugged his sobbing younger sibling. Then it happened. ZAP! Elpis giggled between her sniffles as Illari yelped.

"You brat!" He kissed her on the forehead, and she laid her head on his shoulder.

"Will you come to visit?" Elpis asked.

"I do not think they allow us to leave," Illari replied gravely. He frowned.

"Then we shall come to see you!" Elpis smiled.

"During Winterfest!" Illari smiled at his sister. "You will come to me then!"

Adasser sat silently, watching her son with her daughter and was pleased with who her oldest son was becoming. War, hatred, and bigotry had been his whole life, but his heart was still in the right place. The Queen rose from her seat under the gazebo and walked to where her two children sat.

"And what are you two up to?" Adasser smiled.

"Nothing, mother, just waiting for the carriage to arrive and take me away," Illari sighed.

"Oh, for the love of Haya, you'd think we were sending you off to Sudenyag!" Adasser laughed. "You are only a two or three days ride away, boy. You will be fine!"

"Yes, mother," Illari droned.

A bit later on, two carriages and a contingent of twenty-five men on horseback arrived at the loading area where Adasser, Elpis, and Illari sat. Altwidus, Illari's brother, had come and gone to the stables, saying his farewells, but running to attend to his first love, horses. Puryn was on a new white warhorse. The horse was a massive steed with plate mail armor from head to tail. Puryn sat high in the saddle, his Elfish mail gleaming in the early morning light. As always, he carried the customary short glaive of the Draj and a shield. On the side of the horse, were an Elfish longbow and a quiver with many arrows. Puryn was dressed for war. The way the highways were now, it was not overkill.

"Good morning, husband. We are all packed and ready to depart." Adasser rose and touched Puryn's cuisse on his left side. He responded with a short bow.

"Well, we should get on the road, My Love. The faster we get from here to there, the better. Nothing good happens outside of a city's walls after dark. It is bad enough that we shall camp at least twice on our journey." Puryn barked out orders in Elfish to his Draj, who immediately complied with his requests. They had formed a perimeter around royal carriages and were ready to depart Erynseere for Empyr.

Adasser looked at her sad little girl. "Time to let him go, young one."

Elpis kissed her brother on the cheek. "Do not get in trouble like father did!"

"Oh really, young lady!" Puryn chuckled and blew a kiss to his daughter, who pretended to catch it and hug it to her chest. The King smiled. "We shall be back before you miss us. Behave for your grandmother!"

"Yes, da!" Elpis was waving furiously as Puryn's mother, Arla, picked her up so she could get a better view of the procession.

The carriages departed without fanfare. Puryn ordered a subdued departure to keep his movements as unknown as possible. Adasser and Illari sat alone in a carriage. In the other transport were four ladies-in-waiting and a load of supplies for the road. A supply cart followed closely behind.

After about an hour, the caravan navigated its way eastward out of the Erynseere ring and out into Yslandeth proper. Off to the northeast, one could see the immense community farms and the encircling hamlets that had sprung up around them. People were working in the fields and tending to livestock. Food was beginning to stabilize, and the infrastructure was being rebuilt. Yslandeth was coming together slowly, except in one aspect—the people.

Human villages seemed to be returning to prosperity, but they were the only ones seeing a healthy recovery. Ever since the repatriation of the elder races and the segregation imposed by the Human population against all "half-bloods," the mixed-race communities seemed to be floundering or struggling, because they always got the worst land and the last of anything the Kingdom had to offer. Still, the ethnic villages were proud people, and they persevered as best that they could.

On the road, it was not uncommon to see mobs of hungry people looking for food, shelter, or work. This day was no different. Puryn was disturbed by what he saw happening before him. One group had attacked the other over the baskets that they were carrying. The larger group was Human. The victims seemed to be half-Elfish.

Illari shouted. "Father! Do something!"

Puryn lit off at full gallop into the fray. He stopped after crushing an attacker, rearing his horse. Many of both sides ran toward opposite sides of the road.

"Cease this barbarity!" the King roared. As soon as the people realized who was addressing them, many knelt, averting their eyes. One woman stood crying over the crushed body of her husband. He appeared to be a gray-haired man in his forties.

"We are hungry, Your Majesty, and these traitors would not share. My poor love is now gone! You killed him over those filthy traitors! Oh, my poor Edris, you did not deserve to die." The woman wept, her face buried in the man's bloody clothing. Puryn was emotionless.

"Was I to let your mob beat, or worse yet, murder these, who are also my subjects?" Puryn's looked around angrily. He realized his Draj had assumed defensive positions around his wife, son, and the ladies-in-waiting. Two of his trusted guards now flanked him, weapons drawn.

"Would you choose them over your own kind?" she asked with a disgusted tone, then she saw Adasser and Illari and answered her own question. "Oh, of course, you would, Your Majesty." The woman's words were full of contempt, and everyone there heard them clearly. The guard to the left leveled his glaive at the woman's throat. She stood and stared at Puryn.

"Stand down, Draj," Puryn said softly in Elfish. The soldier relaxed his posture, but kept his guard up.

"Pass this to all who travel this road! This is one Kingdom, not many separate ones under one banner. All people are welcome here. If you have an issue with the Elves or Dwarves, resolve them peacefully or deal with the consequences. I will not tolerate violence or intimidation of anyone within my borders." The King looked at the shocked and terrified faces. Two more Draj came forward to assist their King. The people began to disperse, and a few of the half-Elves cheered their King.

"All hail King Puryn! Huzzah!" one victim cheered, but Puryn was in no mood for gratitude or praise. He stung from the hate of the woman who would now have to bury her husband due to his actions.

The royal caravan had been on the road for several hours, and it was getting to the tenth hour of the day when the incident occurred. One of the half-Elves spoke to a guard.

"My Lord, may I have permission to speak with His Majesty?" He looked up at the Human in the saddle of another sizeable white warhorse, clad in silver plate mail. It was an intimidating sight.

"Your Majesty, this subject requests an audience," the Draj projected loudly toward where Puryn now stood dismounted, mixing with the older half-Elf women, who were now picking up dirty loaves of bread from the road.

"Yes, yes, what is it?" Puryn replied, not really listening.

"Your Majesty," the half-Elf said bowing, "our village would be honored if you would camp with us this evening. It is late and traveling farther will put you in the rough. We can provide an open field with a bit of a fence in which to camp, or the main longhouse if you would rather sleep there."

Puryn thought for a moment. He could see Adasser consoling Illari, who was apparently distraught, but for what Puryn could not be sure. Was it the killing he had just witnessed, or the barbarity of Humans toward his own kind. Puryn did not care which it was, the effect was the same. His son should not be afraid for his safety or ashamed of who he is. Camping with the refugees sounded like a good plan.

"Thank you for your generous offer. We will accept." Puryn mounted his horse, trotting back to the carriage where Adasser and Illari were whispering. Illari had composed himself, but Puryn could see the redness in his eyes.

"Are you all right, boy?" he asked in an uncharacteristically tender voice. Adasser watched her husband with a smile and curiosity.

"Yes," Illari said, his voice cracking as he blew his nose into a handker-chief.

"It is good that you do not seek after death, my young son. Your heart is wise to shed tears when life is taken for little more than a crust of bread. It is never easy to kill a man." Puryn stared at his son, who was tearing up as he listened.

"They would kill us for a loaf? Do we kill them in return? Why do people hate so much? What do they hate? How can you sit there so calmly, father!?" Illari sniffled. "How are you so strong?"

"Sadly, I've had much practice at this art called war, my son. I hope you forever stay a novice in this discipline." Puryn rode close. Adasser stood and kissed her husband. Puryn reached out and messed up Illari's hair, getting a meek smile from him in return. "I love you both. Anyone who threatens my family takes their life into their own hands."

He looked to the road as the last of the Human attackers carried their wounded and dead back North, toward the field worker villages. Puryn wondered if some would take this as a cue to retaliate. He told his Draj as much. They knew that they would be on duty during the night and the Commander split the twenty-four into four, six-man teams that would rotate throughout the royal stay in the country.

Puryn spun his horse around, shouting out Elfish commands and the Draj instantly reformed their defense, riding at a walk with the villagers leading the way to a decent sized village that was named Midway, since it was near mid-way between Erynseere and Empyr. Puryn estimated that fifty people lived in the collective and he saw that they had their own crops growing. Puryn also saw evidence of raiding, but the half-Elves and half-Dwarves who lived in this village posted spearmen, who looked as if they could handle brigands, at least to some degree. Puryn nodded in approval.

"My Lord," the King said, addressing the half-Elf who had invited him to stay. "What is your name and what is the name of your village leader?"

"Oh, of course, Your Majesty, please excuse my rudeness," the young half-Elven man cleared his throat nervously. "I am Grelas, and my mother, Frega, is our Chieftain."

"I should like to meet her tonight around the fire, perhaps?" The King dismounted and handed his reins to one of the Draj, who bowed and took the horse to a holding place around the wagons.

"Of course, Your Majesty. Whatever you wish!" The young man beamed. He begged his leave and went to find his mother. Puryn figured the boy to be a young seventy years old in half-Elven years. He was in the prime of his young life, and Puryn envied him in some ways. The land was beautiful, and the Elves always knew how to make things grow.

After cleaning up, Puryn, Adasser, and young Illari approached the fire in the shared courtyard near the community well. The Elfish folks had a pretty good fire going, and one person was playing the lute, while another played a small drum. Many sang together. When the crowd saw the Draj guards coming with Puryn and his family in tow, they parted widely and let them enter.

"Please, be at ease, my people," Puryn said soothingly. "I only wish to participate. Please be at your leisure!"

One lady whistled and then the crowd erupted in three cheers for the royal family. Adasser smiled, raising her eyebrows and winking at her smiling husband. Illari was taking in everything around him. He had lived a very sheltered life up until today, and had no idea what the people had to contend with daily. Things were just provided for him, and he had become accustomed to being served. Tonight, it was different. He quietly observed and interacted with the other children. As he made his way back to where his mother and father sat, an Elf rose and read from a scroll.

"If you would not be offended, Your Majesty, I wish to read this scroll in your honor." The Elf bowed.

Puryn wondered what he was going to say, but agreed. "Please, go ahead."

The Elf said, in a bardic tone:

> "On the day when men bled crimson,
> Hope was lost on barren field,
> Below the mountain,
> Men did garrison,
> Dwarves retreated,
> Their gates did yield,
> The Elves did likewise,
> Ran and hid,
> And in the forest,
> Farewell, they bid.
> No quarter granted to men few,
> The evil came,
> It charged anew.
> But against the last of light's fair chance,
> A hero spoke and raised his lance,
> His men cheered loudly,
> Their horses reared,
> And died they should have,
> As they feared.
> But from Aeternum she rained down,
> Her golden visage and holy crown,
> With call her kindred,
> Who brought their doom,
> With fire and magic,
> And smoky gloom,
> She rent the evil with her clan,
> And saved the hero,
> This mortal man,

And shout they did,
With might and cheer,
The Queen they loved,
They did revere,
And she did turn and roar to go,
Up to the sky,
Man, down below.
Now on that day do all recall,
The deeds of Puryn and them all,
How honor moved the heart of One,
Who watches over man and son,
And granted man a new day, bright,
To stand with her,
And evil smite."

When the Elf had finished, all were standing and looking at Puryn. They bowed and then rose. Puryn stood and clapped politely. The Elf smiled, nodded, and sat down. Puryn knew the facts were a bit off, but he was not prepared to correct the Elf and to give him a history lesson. It was close enough for the official report and people loved the legend. The King simply smiled and sat.

"That was wonderful, Sir, but enough seriousness, more mirth!" Puryn smiled raising a tankard, and the crowd again erupted in a cheer as the musicians started up again.

The young half-Elf guide appeared a few moments later with a middle-aged Elfish woman. She was several hundred years old and looking every minute of it. Puryn was intrigued.

The King stood and kissed the older woman's hand. "Good evening, My Lady."

She smiled and looked at the Queen. "Oh he is a charmer, is he not, My Queen?"

"That he is!" Adasser said, laughing. Puryn smiled at the informal nature of this woman's interchange. She was apparently older than he thought she was, and clearly not impressed with pomp and circumstance. No one was insulted. Everyone sat.

"So, I am told that raids are occurring in my lands. I hear worse tales that they are targeting settlements, such as yours. Are these reports true?" The King leaned forward to hear her words over the din of the revelers.

"It is, Your Majesty. We are a larger settlement, so they avoid us in most cases, but Hero's Pass is a much smaller group. They have maybe thirty souls where we were counted recently at approximately eighty." Puryn's eyes opened wider at eighty.

"Is it brigands or bands from the farms to the North?" Puryn looked northward with disgust. He shook his head.

"Of a truth, Your Majesty, it is hard to tell in the darkness, but lately, the attacks have been more coordinated and effective, leading me to believe that someone is commanding a larger, more organized force. Maybe it could be those known as the Red-Hand." She looked at her spearmen. All were standing tall and vigilant. She nodded in approval.

"I seek to address these issues, My Lady. Rest assured, I will not allow these attacks to go unpunished." Puryn leaned back, sipping his mead. He did not want more conflict, but the battle was coming, wanted or not.

"The one puzzling thing, My King, is the disappearances." The old woman drew closer to the King, as if she was telling him a secret. "The Red-Hand, and those to the North, may be brigands and louts, but killers and kidnappers, they are not. Thieves and fools, oh yes!" She smiled and took a bite of an apple.

"I see," Puryn nodded. "That is an astute observation. I will take these words to my advisors in Empyr. There, we will devise a plan and draw the forces necessary to put it into action. Until then, you are wise to keep your guard sharp."

"As always, Draj-Manot. We will not sleep while the Protector and his Lady, our High Priestess, reside within our borders. We will stand with your Draj. It is our honor, Your Majesty."

"And I am honored by the gesture, my wise and hospitable host." Puryn helped the older lady to her feet, and her son took over for him. She bowed and then waved, smiling at Adasser as she left. Illari was asleep.

Adasser said, "Husband, it is late. We should retire and leave at sunrise to reach the gates of Empyr by nightfall tomorrow."

"Agreed, My Love. I will carry him," Puryn replied, smiling and picking up the sleeping Illari. "He is getting too big for me to carry!"

* * *

Puryn was up before the dawn. He stretched, did his monk forms, and then found a post on which to do a bit of pell work before the rest awoke. The village guards watched from time to time, and the Draj kept the King in view at all times. No threats were observed, and soon the entire encampment was awake and packing up. The villagers were also stirring from their night of revelry, and many waved to the camp as they headed out to the fields to harvest, while others tended sheep and pigs. It was a chilly morning at fifty degrees.

Adasser opened the flap of her tent, looking around for where her husband had run off to. She saw him in armor checking his horse's tack and harness. He was also looking over his equipment.

"That man never stops," she muttered, waking a protesting Illari. "Wake up, boy, and get clothed. This tent needs to come down very soon!"

Illari groaned, rolled out of bed, then slipped on a clean tunic and pants. He and Adasser went out to the supply cart where two ladies-in-waiting had tea and pastries awaiting them. They ate as the Draj, who were not guarding, broke down the encampment. It was down in less than an hour.

Frega and Grelas were there to bid the caravan farewell. "Safe journeys, to the entire royal family," Frega said waving.

"Do not worry, sister. I will not forget what we spoke about last night," Puryn said, buckling his helmet strap.

"I know that you will not, My King. Be well." Grelas helped his mother sit as she watched the family ride away. It was only the second hour of the morning.

On the King's road, many groups of homeless continued to travel East and West, in search of what they could find, but wherever the King's caravan was, peaceful interactions were the norm. Word had apparently spread overnight at fires throughout the region that Puryn was on the move and that he was not playing games with anyone, oppressing any group within Yslandeth.

By the twelfth hour of the day, the group reached the main gates of Empyr. It was late, but the guard verified the travelers were the royal family and allowed them to enter. Donick had prepared the throne room and two small bedrooms for the royal family to sleep in. The Draj set camp in the courtyard with two on duty at all times.

"We have much to discuss tomorrow morning, brother," Puryn said to Donick. "But first I must eat, cleanse my filthy body and get some sleep. The events outside in the settlements do not add up. There is something more sinister going on than brigand raids. A wise woman made some excellent points around a fire last night. We will discuss what her observation may mean tomorrow."

"As you wish, Your Majesty," Donick bowed.

"Oh, for the love of Haya, stop it!" Puryn smiled and hugged his friend.

Donick pulled out a couple of cups and a bottle. The two enjoyed a mead or two, while Adasser and Illari went to bed. There was much to accomplish at first light.

Chapter 3

Kairoth was an earnest young man. At sixteen years of age, he had found his way to Empyr, under the order of the King, for conscription into the Yslandeth military. He was less than enthused. It was his duty, but in reality, he knew that he had no other place to go. He sat in the segregated encampment in a red tent, waiting for the examiners. He knew what was coming. He had been chosen, and he was pleased to finally get his chance to prove himself.

Kairoth was born of an Yslan woman, but his father was Hodan. Before the Great War, he had lived just South of the Yslandeth border with his father and mother. He was now eighteen years of age, but remembered the attacks like they were yesterday. The young man's face turned to stone, as he remembered his father's valiant stand against overwhelming odds, recalling how the man single-handedly dispatched two Orcs, a Goblin, and two Todessen warriors, before the cowards surrounded him with spears and summarily executed him. He watched with his mother from a crack in the floorboards. Kairoth and his mother hid in the escape space under the floor of their house, as they hoped for a miracle that was not coming. When his father was killed, the two quietly crept out of the tunnel that was under their home to a hidden escape hatch that was fifty-feet from the house. There, they could see the entire countryside covered by the enemy. They waited as their house burned, breathing clean air from within the cover of the hidden door.

Much later, when an opening in the enemy forces was seen, Kairoth and his mother ran northward in an attempt to reach Yslan. They were not the only ones. The plan was to use the cover of darkness and terrain to covertly make their way, but the Hodan did not know that the dark army saw better in the night than in the light, and the majority of those fleeing perished or were captured and made slaves.

The mother of Kairoth would be no slave, nor would her son suffer that fate. She had trained to be a Hodan warrior, as all of the Hodan were required. In the end, she fought off two Goblin scouts and an Orc warrior before finally being subdued. Kairoth ran to assist, but his mother forbade him, shouting for him to run to the North. Spying a small copse of trees to the northwest, the young lad ran swiftly to the tree line, enemy in pursuit.

Kairoth was a fast runner and an agile scout at the age of thirteen. He was destined to become a Hodan Elite, according to his father. The enemy could not keep up, but as he entered the border of the trees, the boy turned to see the enemy almost upon him. Then he saw them in action for the first time.

Adasser's trees lashed out with fury after letting the Human pass freely within them. The Orcs and Goblins totaled maybe twenty or thirty pursuers. The trees swayed in unison, interlocking branches. They formed a bulwark, and the enemy was stopped in their tracks, unable to enter. As the evil tried to push their way into the barrier, they were met with a gauntlet of tree branch spears, choking vines, and pounding log-size boughs. The main enemy forces did not even miss those who died before the tree line, but Kairoth would never forget them.

* * *

The chattering of pretentious voices permeated the air. Young Elfish girls sat doing parlor tricks to impress their peers within the blue tents. Sal'iabac, a young Human woman from Edenyag, sat with her sister, Safiya. They were not impressed. Glancing over at the overt display of natural talent, the two mages were miffed. Elves could perform tricks from birth, but the two young women had worked their whole lives to perfect their art.

Sal'iabac was about twenty years old when she arrived in Empyr. She brought Safiya who was three years her junior along with her. The two had survived the war by use of their magic, and had made their way to Edenyag when the war was over to study more. There, they honed their skills until the call to arms in Empyr. Edenyag was gearing up for something, and both of the sisters wanted nothing to do with it, so they departed and headed North.

Sal'iabac was getting annoyed. The Elves were becoming loud and obnoxious, as they bragged about their superiority in the magic arts. One of them made an offhand remark in Elfish about Safiya being the spawn of a Troll. There was a twitter of giggling among several in the Elfish band, but Sal'iabac saw her sister frown and was not amused. The offender did not realize that both ladies were fluent in Elfish.

The elder sister responded in a scathing retort. "At least my sister is not one of their whores."

The Elfish circle was stunned to silence. "What did you say?" questioned the offender in Elfish.

Sal'iabac muttered words to herself, touching her sister's shoulder. "Guardus Maji Fortus." An invisible shield covered her and her sister. "I said, you are the evening sport of large, smelly Offlander invaders. I would wager that your mother may have been defiled by one, creating one such as yourself. Toad."

Toad was a derogatory term for Todessen. The Human race had names for everyone. The Elf was enraged. She faced the Human squarely, increasing the size of her fireball. Sal'iabac noted the increase, but acted as if she was not concerned in the least.

Again, the Human mage muttered something to herself. Safiya giggled, hearing the words. The Elf then cast her fireball. It hit Safiya squarely, then shattered, sending shards of burning matter in all directions. Everyone in the tent began running out of the front flap as the shelter started to glow.

"Pathetic," Safiya remarked, looking at her sister smugly.

"Agreed, sister," Sal'iabac responded, as she cast an energy bolt at the offending Elf. "I held back. No need to kill the fool."

The Elf was knocked off of her feet and disoriented. The tent was now engulfed in flames, but the two sisters calmly remained inside, seemingly immune. The Elf was not, and they both knew it.

Safiya sighed. "It would not be wise to let the Elf die, even if the fire was her fault." Safiya grabbed the Elf mage by her tunic vest and pulled her out of the door to a crowd of gathering onlookers.

Sal'iabac was now visibly annoyed. "Wonderful, there go our chances of getting out of the regular tents and into something more accommodating." She motioned to the Elves who now stood silent, tensely waiting for more.

"Take this person from me," Safiya droned as if bored. Two Elfish ladies complied, bowing awkwardly and leaving quickly.

Off in the distance, the commotion did not go unnoticed. Master Donick sat drinking his morning tea while looking out of the window toward the courtyard. He smelled the burning tent and rushed to see what the matter was. There, the Headmaster saw a testy exchange between two Human women and a group of Elves. One Elf was unconscious.

"Mages. What can you do with them? Time to order another tent to be dyed." Annoyed, he returned to his perch and sat down as he saw the morning guard showing up to restore order. "Be careful, gentlemen," the Headmaster remarked, chuckling to himself.

* * *

Down in the sanctuary, while the Headmaster lamented the loss of the tent, the monks and priests of the Order had gathered for morning prayers. The rhythm of rote prayer and responsive worship could be heard in the direct vicinity of the main sanctuary building, where the monastery was under reconstruction.

A young priest knelt facing the building. He was not of the Order, officially, having only been an apprentice to a local practitioner of the faith. He was a commoner and only the Elites, and those who found favor, were allowed within the walls of the Order of Haya's Dawn. Valtyr prayed alone outside. He was earnest and sincere in his worship, but to his annoyance, he was not alone in the green tent.

"Hey! Whatcha doin'?" a younger man spoke in an annoyingly loud tone.

Rolling his eyes, Valtyr responded, "Praying, what do you think that I'm doing, looking for worms?" He glared at the young man, who had a potted plant in his hand and was watering it.

"Well, at least worms are useful," the young man said with a half-smile. "Do you priests really think that the Goddess listens to all of your blathering, repetitive nonsense?" The young man poured water from a skin into the pot, talking lovingly to his little bush.

"Damn you, Reynir! Can you just afford me a short time of peace in the morning, without your incessant commentary on the priesthood?" Valtyr stood. The moment was gone. He was not amused.

"Hey, just saying … I worship Haya also, but sitting or kneeling, while pleading without actions to back it up? What is that? That is not true worship in my eyes." He was not looking at Valtyr. He was looking at his bush and pruning dead leaves and sprouts from the plant. "There, all better, my little green friend."

"Your only friend!" Valtyr quipped sarcastically.

"Oh, that hurts, brother," Reynir laughed hugging Valtyr.

Valtyr pushed him off gently, shaking his head, and entered the green tent looking for his rations. He had known Reynir since the younger man was born. They grew up playing together within the ring at Erynseere, living in relative peace. Despite their peaceful start, both remembered huddling in the castle basement fortress, while their Queen held off the dark invasion with a few Draj. Valtyr was fifteen years old at the time of the devastation and Reynir an impressionable twelve. From their births, both studied with the clergy, becoming literate, proficient apprentices, and very devout along the way. At twelve years old, however, Reynir would strike off on another path, leaving the priesthood to its own devices. He had witnessed her.

In the fortress darkness, awaiting their deaths, Reynir stood on a crate and watched as Adasser raised a dead girl while scolding her son's disobedience. He watched as she then tore an Orc apart without touching him. Wide-eyed, the young man remembered the shock of watching her command the trees, animals, and insects to her will. He knew this was the Order he wished to pursue. When he unexpectedly survived, he discovered that the Queen had only Prince Illari as her student. Boldly, he petitioned his Queen to take him as an apprentice, and, impressed with his courage and audacity, Adasser decided to take the twelve-year-old in as her charge.

In the beginning, he washed the chamber pots, cleaned the floors, and brought the Queen what she needed. As Valtyr mocked him, Adasser continued to test Reynir's resolve, and she was quietly pleased that her apprentice never waned in his fervor to learn, watching her every move, and noting everything that she did. Adasser could tell that her son, Illari, was a bit jealous, but the two boys got along well enough, and Reynir always seemed to know his place.

Valtyr emerged from the mildewed tent with two pieces of hardtack, a couple of slices of hard cheese, and a small decanter of hot tea. He motioned to Reynir to come over. Smiling, Reynir arrived.

"Oh no, this is for me, I just wanted you to see how proper tea is brewed," Valtyr said mockingly.

Reynir crossed his arms. "Truly, you are still offended. You, woman," Reynir said, suppressing a laugh.

"I was going to give you some, you, intolerable horse's ass, but not now!" Valtyr pretended to start picking up the food and leave, but then began laughing loudly. "Ass, sit down!" Reynir complied.

"Brother, perhaps today they will choose us to serve the Queen and her cause. There, we can put actions to both of our words and truly please the Goddess." Reynir stared off at the sky in an apparent dream of glory.

"Perhaps, we should be careful about what we wish, brother," Valtyr said, stuffing bread into his mouth. "It seldom results in what we expect!"

Reynir nodded and ate. Valtyr had never steered him wrong.

* * *

Puryn arrived at Donick's door by the third hour of the morning. The King was equipped in full battle dress. Donick knew that this was to make an impression. The King was an imposing soul in regular attire, but in armor, he could be downright terrifying, depending upon if you were on his side or not. Donick rose.

"Your Majesty, I was going to come to you!" He smiled, shaking the King's hand.

"You will never stop. We are not in public, brother. Formality is not required," Puryn replied, smiling.

"Still, you are armed. I am watching myself," Donick winked.

Puryn laughed, pulling up a chair. "So, what do we have, brother?" the King asked, getting down to business.

"Well, I'm just getting the list together. Apparently, there was a dispute among the Human and Elfish mages, and one Elf was sent to the infirmary while the tent was burned to the ground." Donick was mildly annoyed.

"Well, bring those offenders to the trials! They seem to be somewhat proficient," Puryn snorted. "No one died?"

"No deaths, just an Elfish ego squashed." Donick shook his head.

"Oooh! Human girls dispatched an Elfish girl. Yes, bring them to the trials. The Elf must be furious," Puryn smirked. "They are so proud of their gifts."

"She's not going anywhere for a while, brother. The Human woman defeated her pretty soundly, from what I'm told. It was in retaliation for the Elf's initial attack. Two Humans on one Elf, but reportedly, only one Human responded. They could be interesting." Donick raised an eyebrow.

"Definitely. Any Human who can beat an Elf at her own game … How old was the Elf?" Puryn inquired.

"Report says seventy years, Your Majesty."

"Old enough to know better," Puryn smiled. "What of warriors?"

"We have several. One who distinguishes himself. The man's name is

Kairoth of Hodan; a couple of rangers, another Hodan, and one lad from Empyr, then the usual lot. By far though, the Kairoth lad was the most impressive." Donick paused. "That boy sent five to the infirmary, using wooden practice weapons, and they are unsure if one of his opponents will live."

"No restraint. Well, he is of Hodan." Puryn sighed. "I hope the injured one survives. They're so young, Donick."

"That they are, My King," the Master remarked somberly. "Oh, and I found a 'specialist' as you requested."

"Oh excellent, where?" Puryn asked, sipping some tea.

"Where else? Tied to the post." Donick shook his head.

"Oh, splendid. That post. How I hate that post." Puryn grimaced angrily. "What did he or she do?"

"Stealing food from the military stores. He also assaulted a guard to get in, knocking him out, but not killing him. He could have. So, I decided that he only got three lashes." Donick waited for the King's reply.

"Is he still serviceable, or did they break him?" Puryn furrowed his brow.

"He is healing, Your Majesty. He will be well in a couple of days. That one is pretty tough. One of the reasons that I picked him. He says he is of Cinnog, but I'm not sure. Could be Suden." Donick wrinkled his nose at the word.

"Suden or Yslan matters not to me, as long as he is proficient and loyal to the cause," the King stated firmly, rising and finishing his tea.

"Understood, Your Majesty. I will assemble them later today for your inspection, if that is all right?" Donick rose and bowed.

Puryn shook his head. "You will never stop that, will you?"

"Never, Chosen One. You may be my brother and my King, but I am a monk and a priest, and you are touched by the Gods." Donick hugged his King. Puryn hugged him back. "Be well. I will see you later today."

"You as well, my oldest friend." Puryn left the room.

* * *

Donick sent out the writs, and the chosen were informed of their new status. Orders were given to each of the prospects to report to the courtyard at the tenth hour of the day, clean, in clean clothing, and ready for inspection. Each of the members went to their separate laundries and washed their clothing. The warriors and rangers tended to their weapons and armor, making last-minute repairs while cleaning them. All were prepared for the gathering by the eighth hour of the day. They spent the remainder of their free time collecting their pay from the quartermaster, and eating at the field kitchen in the main camp. Many of the regulars looked at the particular candidates with disdain, but everyone knew that they were the supposed best of the best, so they kept their distances and only made remarks out of the range of hearing.

At the tenth hour, all were gathered in the courtyard as ordered. There were divided into several nondescript teams, each with a variety of members of all races and skills. Kairoth looked around at his group in disappointment. Two women scribes, a priest, a druid, a couple of hunters, two warriors of unknown proficiency, and a squirrely little person he knew had to be a thief. The championship team this was not.

Sal'iabac picked up on his disapproval. "What are you looking at?" she snapped.

Kairoth just snorted and turned away from her scowl. "Nothing."

Safiya chimed in. "Likewise."

Kairoth turned and remarked. "Go back to scribbling in your little book, tiny person. I only fight men and Hodan women. You are not a worthy opponent."

Safiya reached into a pouch, but Sal'iabac grabbed her wrist. "There will be a time, but it is not now, sister." Safiya relented angrily, twisting her face and glaring at the Hodan warrior.

Reynir watched and had no inhibitions. "What's wrong, my companions? We are on an adventure to serve the needs of the Goddess! We're all on the same side! Why fight amongst ourselves?" he reasoned with the three.

Valtyr interjected. "Um, Reynir, can you come here for a minute, please?" Valtyr sensed the Hodan warrior was ready to crush his smaller friend.

Reynir smiled and turned, walking back to Valtyr. "What's the matter, brother?"

Valtyr pulled him close. "He's Hodan, so he's always going to be angry. They're probably mages, and he's too dim to see that, so angering them will end badly. I heard those women sent an Elf to the medical tents this morning."

Reynir's eyes widened with intrigue. "Human mages who can best an Elf? Excellent!" He looked at the ladies, saying the statement much too loud.

Valtyr put his face in his hands. "What am I going to do with you? Will you never shut up!?"

The other warrior members of the band sat quietly. The two rangers appeared to know each other, while the other warrior had gravitated over to Kairoth, and was conversing with him civilly. Apparently, he was of Hodan birth also. Off in the corner, a beaten, younger Human of around sixteen sat eating something. He was avoiding eye contact with anyone who looked his way.

Kairoth wondered where he had stolen it from. "You." The Hodan warrior pointed at the thief. "Why are you here? You are a criminal, aren't you?"

The young man looked up with a weathered stare. "What is it to you? I was ordered here just as you were. Mind your own business." He went back to eating his food. Kairoth began to advance to challenge the lad, when the horns started blowing.

As if by instinct, all of the groups became silent. Each group stood in circles of ten members. They all faced the stone platform that was raised ten feet above them. Very shortly after the horn blasts, Master Donick and the King appeared on the landing. All eyes were on the duo.

Donick spoke. "All of you here today, have shown promise in your arts. You have defeated your peers in every test. You stand here, chosen to take on the real work of the Kingdom. You will aid in the restoration of peace and prosperity for all of mortal-kind. Your Majesty ...," Donick bowed and gave the stage to Puryn, backing out of view.

The sun gleamed off of Puryn's Elfish mail, and his garb was a bright white with blue. He stood beside four standard bearers who held the four banners of Yslandeth, Hodan, Torith and Dornat Al Ar. The wind caught them, and they fluttered on cue, as if for effect. The King represented the interests of all of the Northern Alliance.

Puryn spoke with an authoritative voice. "All of you here are the best that our nation has to offer. There is a new evil in our lands and among our people. The scourge of the Underlord has been defeated, but now greed, avarice, and extortion rule the three nations to the South. Within our own borders, persecution of those who we once held as brothers and sisters is rampant, and travel is perilous, even during the daylight hours." Puryn looked at each face out before him. There were ten groups of ten. One-hundred more faces to add to the thousands he saw in his dreams every night. He frowned and composed himself. "We must work to preserve the light. We must restore security to our people from all backgrounds. We must put down the lawlessness that seeks to destroy what we are rebuilding. You will be the tools that build this future."

The groups around them cheered as the King saluted and then departed. Even the rangers and the other Hodan warrior of Kairoth's group lifted a fist in approval. Kairoth looked at the mages in his circle. They had the same look of apathy on their faces. All three chuckled as they realized that they were probably all thinking the same thing. Guards began escorting the other candidates to separate living quarters in another private tent complex nearer to the monastery. They would not get to their group for a while.

"Perhaps you are not as dim as I thought," Safiya stated, looking away from Kairoth.

Kairoth could see in her satchel. There were herbs and strange bits of this and that in small containers. Immediately, he realized that she was a mage. Smiling, he responded. "And apparently I misjudged your profession," he remarked, nodding at the reagents in the mage's sack. Safiya grabbed her bag and tied it securely, making a face at the warrior.

"Oh good, you're getting along!" Reynir remarked joyfully. Seemingly, the druid acted as if he thought that they were all going off to some retreat for a little holiday. This annoyed Valtyr to no end.

The three looked at the druid curiously. Safiya shook her head. "What is wrong with this one?"

"I am wrong? Why, because I choose not to be angry and disgruntled? I believe the Goddess has me right where she wants me to be! I believe that about all of us! Our adventure will prove our beliefs through our actions, and that is all I desire! I wish to serve the Goddess and not to just talk about it."

Valtyr interrupted. "My apologies, friends. He is very 'enthusiastic' at times, but he means no harm."

Reynir sighed. "I am not a doddering fool who requires you to make excuses for me, brother," he replied with annoyance. "I can speak for myself."

Valtyr waved him off with one hand. "As you wish."

Everyone went off to sit, and for a time, the group all sat silently, but when the introductions began, much to Valtyr's dismay, it was Reynir who spoke first. The priest started to worry less about surviving the 'adventures' ahead, and instead pondered whether or not they would survive their first day together.

Only time would tell, but no one was injured ... yet.

Chapter 4

The sun rose red on the horizon. Puryn sat with Donick as he had for the past two weeks. Looking out over the reconstruction, the pair could see the foundation of the old city materializing as if by magic, but both knew that thousands of souls, both military and civilian, were toiling day and night to raise the walls that they would one day inherit. The King resolved to not only resurrect the gray stones of his childhood, but also the dream that was Yslandeth's splendor.

"Well, that does it, Your Majesty," the Master said, adding a few jots to the text and rolling up the long scroll. "All teams have been matched to the missions that best suit their skill-set."

Puryn looked off at the color-coded tent complexes as a twinge of guilt hit. An old, familiar tightness was in his chest and throat as he contemplated sending his charges off to die in foreign lands. Watching as the teams practiced in specially created facilities, the King was torn about what he was setting out to do. The warriors, mages, priests and specialists were becoming coordinated. They would soon be instruments of their King's will, and the enemies of the light would not be happy to meet them.

"Be sure that we issue them all that they need, Donick," the King said, staring off in thought.

"Of course, Your Majesty. We will equip them with appropriate armor, weapons, and provisions." Donick wrote a note on the parchment to remind himself of the King's orders.

"Horses. Give them horses, Donick. We do have enough, don't we?" the King asked.

"Oh yes, Korin has the warhorses, Your Majesty, but may I suggest riding horses to maintain anonymity? They would be seen coming for miles if riding a Korinian warhorse. No commoner would be able to afford such a fine animal." The master looked at the King inquisitively.

"Yes, to maintain the illusion of normalcy, give them riding horses. Make sure that they are sturdy steeds. They may need them to travel far. One never knows." The King turned and smiled. "Donick, give them their best chance. Please."

"Of course, Your Majesty. I will do my best."

Puryn left the room at the monastery and made his way down to the throne room. There he sat and sipped a mug of mead. His guilt was eating away at him. He wondered, while looking out over the muddy tent city before him, whether Swyk had ever felt as he did now.

Nodding, he finished the last swallow. "Of course he did. It is my turn now."

* * *

The quartermaster was dismayed by the long line of rabble before him. One-hundred men, women, Elves, Dwarves and half-bloods were in line with scripts to draw gear. One by one, with the help of several duty guards, the sergeant issued each new conscript a backpack, provisions for two weeks, clothing, a small tent, field bedding, appropriate armor, and weapons. Then, checking the order twice, the steward shook his head as he issued a script to each for an average riding horse with all required tack, harness, and saddle bags. Each new team member stuffed everything into the pack and went to the stables chit-in-hand to get their horse.

After drawing their horses, the teams split up into their own groups. No group knew the other, and that was by design. Each team's objectives were also kept secret. One hand knew not what the other was up to. The groups all gathered and set their equipment in the appropriate places.

Kairoth and his team looked impressive once outfitted with their issued equipment. The warriors were all dressed in hauberks of chain, as was the priest. The druid preferred leather, and after many protests, he was issued what he asked for. The mages declined the bulky armor, but were given quality clothing instead. Kairoth knew that although the two women were not as proficient as his men in hand-to-hand combat, they had other ways of protecting themselves. No one questioned their ability to inflict mass casualties if given the opportunity.

Kairoth assumed leadership and no one in the group seemed to protest. He was a natural leader, and after a couple of weeks, he had shown the most tactical promise of any in the group. Surprisingly, the young Hodan warrior was not as hard-headed as the mages first thought, and he further surprised them by consulting his team concerning many decisions. All members were valued, and that led to a quick unification. The group became one entity, complimenting each other's strengths while covering each other's weaknesses.

"We are to leave immediately for Hero's Pass?" Valtyr questioned.

"Yes, that is what the orders are," Kairoth replied seriously. "Is that a problem?"

"Well, no, friend, but do any of you know where that village is?" Valtyr asked inquisitively.

Sal'iabac interrupted. "I believe it's somewhere southeast of the city. Somewhere near the Raven's Pass. I am told that it is a half-blood Elfish settlement. Relatively new, I do believe."

One of the rangers outside of the immediate conversation shook his head. "Half-blood Toads. What are their problems to us? Why do we saddle up to defend the very people who abandoned us when they were most needed?" Roland spat.

The other ranger nodded in agreement.

The thief sat up and spoke, which was a rarity. "They are people, you asses. They just want to live in peace, and they are being kidnapped. Perhaps by dimwitted bigots such as yourselves." The specialist was visibly annoyed and stood up. He was a good six inches shorter than either of the bowmen. "Besides, the King ordered us to go there. Apparently, he thinks they matter. Go tell Puryn to his face that they don't. Or shut your mouths and get in line like the rest of us."

Kairoth raised an eyebrow and stood as one of the rangers made a move toward the smaller thief. "There will be none of that, brothers, or you will answer to me."

Roland scowled, mumbling an unintelligible curse, sitting back down on the hay bale that he rose from. Kairoth looked over at Famlin with a grin on his face. The warrior shook his head. The specialist nodded back in appreciation for the warrior's backing.

"Any other objections? If so, let us get it out into the open. We do not have to like who we are saving or what our mission is. We simply need to get it done. Then we get paid and get to relax for a time, before we are called upon again." Kairoth looked at all of the faces around him. All nodded in unison, even the reluctant rangers, Roland and Brynd. Reynir had an overly cheery smile on his face, as usual.

"Kairoth, before we depart, I have been given leave to enter the sanctuary and pray. It is a great honor for a common priest, such as I. I cannot pass it up. Please do not be offended." Valtyr looked embarrassed.

"I understand. I will visit the monuments of Swyk and Ontak as you visit your holy place. All of us need to prepare and make our peace with the Gods and our lives. We know not what the future may hold. We meet back here in the seventh hour of the day." Kairoth stood and saluted his comrades, who acknowledged and returned the gesture, breaking the circle to attend to their personal needs.

* * *

Puryn ordered a metered dispersal of each group. Donick made sure to let three to five teams leave at a time, every group in a different direction. The dispersal looked to those on the outside as if the increased traffic was just a bunch of supply caravans, duty guard rotations, or travelers who had decided to travel in numbers. With the highwaymen and brigands that ran rampant on the King's highways, no one questioned the logic.

By the ninth hour of the day, Kairoth and his team were dispatched quietly southeast. The group was dressed as if they were common Yslan subjects, but most of them were on mounts and in armor, so despite the attempted ruse, the average person in Yslan thought them to be at least lesser nobility or part of the affluent merchant class. The most common theory of the average person encountering the team was that the two ladies in the center of the traveling group must be of some importance, because they had their own priest and a small contingent of private security. People on the road gave them a wide berth.

The team traveled for hours making it far enough away from Empyr that the fires of the city were a distant grayness on a tree-lined horizon. At the thirteenth hour of the day, the sun was dipping low, when the group looked for a place to hastily set up camp. Pulling fifty measures off the main road, the rangers found a suitable place to pitch the tents and start a small fire. Within an hour, the camp was set up.

"We need to set the watch schedule," Roland remarked to the other ranger. He had been in the rough many times before and knew that dangers would creep up in the darkness on an unguarded party.

"Yeah, good call, Roland," Brynd replied. The two grabbed forearms in a salute that only the Draj usually used.

The two had trained in Torith before the repatriation had begun. When the cultural reset started, they were both shunned, and quietly run out of the Kingdom of the Elves, making their ways back to Empyr, only to end up joining Puryn's crusade. They, too, knew what it felt like to be refugees. Being uprooted from the only home that either had ever known, the two resented the elder races for their own personal reasons.

"Kairoth, who do you want on watch?" Roland questioned.

"The women should sleep. Mages ...," Kairoth began.

Sal'iabac interrupted angrily, "The women?"

"Mages? Is that better? You are both women. For the love of the Gods.

Relax!" Kairoth shrugged. He did not understand what his mage's problem was.

Safiya rolled her eyes. "Fine, sister, who cares. We get to sleep? I'm fine with that, as long as these buffoons can keep a watch."

Brynd laughed loudly. "A fine trip this will be. Off to save Toads with a charming pair of ladies who never cease to speak like asps!"

"Perhaps I should stop speaking and seal your lips, permanently," Sal'iabac said with a scathing stare.

The ranger laughed again. "So pretty, but so angry!" He wisely walked away, disappearing into the darkness. The party could not see him within seconds. "I will take the first watch," he said from outside of sight of the camp.

"I will take the second, brother," Roland replied pulling out a bedroll.

"I will take the third," Kairoth said, watching the two with curiosity.

"I want to stand a watch!" Reynir said excitedly. "May I stand with you, Brynd?"

"Sure. Just shut up and stay out of sight, will you?" The ranger appeared as if from thin air, entering the camp. "You stay within the firelight. I will explore the darkness. Understood?"

"Sounds like a good plan! I am ready!" Reynir smiled like a boy who had just won a prize. The ranger sighed deeply and disappeared into the darkness from where he came. "How does he do that?"

Kairoth walked over to Roland. "Draj?"

"No. The Elves evicted us before we could test. We could have made it, I'm certain. It's all we ever wanted to be. Now we are hired men. So much for dreams of honor and glory." Roland turned to his small tent and grabbed a waterskin, drinking from it sparingly.

"There is always tomorrow, brother. Honor waits for you with the dawn. They cannot give it to you. You must take it for yourself." Kairoth looked as if he gained thirty years as he spoke, then he smiled and was eighteen again.

The ranger nodded smiling. "How are you not an ass? You are Hodan."

"We are more than our labels. We define ourselves by what we do and who we say that we are." Kairoth nodded and went to his tent to sleep.

"Where is the thief?" Valtyr asked, checking the horses.

"I don't know," Reynir said, looking furiously around the camp. "Did we lose him?"

"Hardly. That one is very sneaky. Well, I guess that's his job. I wonder what he is up to." Valtyr squinted, looking off in the gathering darkness.

After a couple of hours, the fire died down a bit, and the party went to sleep, except for two who were on the watch.

* * *

It was near midnight when Safiya inevitably felt the need to use the privy. She slipped out of her bedroll, shivering. It was a cold night of forty degrees. As she exhaled, the mage could see her breath misting before her. Grabbing her small spade, she made for the nearby tree line to find a secluded spot to do her business.

The moon was full, and Safiya could see the tent outline clearly against the fire's light. She smelled the crisp night air and burning wood. Finding the perfect spot, she sunk the blade into the soft Ert and dug a small hole. Squatting, she began.

While relieving herself, Safiya was startled, hearing something of size moving within the dark woods. "What was that?" she asked under her breath.

Without a torch, she could not see into the blackness. Safiya was frozen in vigilance. Fear was slowly making its presence known to her as she felt the adrenaline begin to pump into her breast. She was sure that she heard a deep panting and low growl, but could not see where it was coming from. It was close. Then she saw a dark blur run within the tree line in front of the background of the lit camp.

Pulling down her long tunic, she grabbed the shovel in one hand, looking for a hint of where the growling blur had gone. When she was sure that it was not in her immediate vicinity, Safiya bolted for the camp, screaming loudly.

"Help! Help me! Something is after me!" She looked like a pale specter floating across the field as she ran, shovel in hand.

"Valtyr!" Reynir shrieked as if he had seen a ghost. "The undead attack us!"

Valtyr sat up with a start. "What?" He ran out into the camp to see the running mage. Confused, he looked at Reynir, who was armed with his cudgel. "Wait! That's the mage. The younger one. Do not hit her, you dimwit!"

"Oh, well, I thought she was asleep in her tent, not off communing with nature at this time of night. What is she doing out here, and … what is that?" Reynir pointed at a dark, furry creature that now bounded across the field toward the mage and the camp. It was moving quickly and making a beeline for the fire pit.

Kairoth, now up, had his sword drawn. He was moving with purpose toward the charging black mass, as the mage sprinted into the firelight and ran to her tent to find her reagents.

Reynir's eyes opened wide, running toward Kairoth. "Waaaaiiiit!!!"

Kairoth turned to see the druid who was yelling at him, right about the time the furry man-sized creature knocked the Hodan warrior over, as it bounded toward one of the backpacks, tearing it open in one try. Kairoth ran to attack the brown bear that was in the team's camp. It was not an overly large creature, but definitely a threat and very unwelcome.

The druid ran up and stood in front of the warrior, pleading, "Wait! Hold for a moment! Let me try something first!"

"Out of my way, druid," the angry Hodan protested.

"Fine, kill the baby bear. You kill the baby bear; you anger the mother. Do you want the momma bear? That's how you get the momma bear. Maybe several …" Reynir spoke angrily, as if the warrior should know this.

Kairoth relaxed. "Fine. Do whatever it is that you do, but do it quickly. Oh, and you will replace my rations for the bear's life. You will do this. That damn thing ate all of my food."

Reynir smiled and turned to mutter words with his eyes closed, then he approached the bear and began to speak to it as if it were another person who he had met at the market. "Hello, my name is Reynir. Why are you here?"

The bear turned around, looking at the young druid, and then sat like a puppy with a growl.

"Well, we don't have much here to eat. Maybe in the woods, you can find more food. Where is your mother?" Reynir asked calmly.

The bear growled sadly, and then angrily.

Reynir looked at Kairoth. "He says that he is hungry and that hunters or something separated him from his mother. I should help him find his mother, or he will keep doing this sort of thing. I will be back later."

Kairoth looked curiously at the druid. "Be careful?" Then he turned and looked at Safiya. "I'm still taking half of your rations, Reynir. Stupid bear. And you, young lady—could you please let the watch know when you are leaving camp? It would be a good idea in the future."

Safiya nodded sheepishly. "Yeah, yeah. I understand. Won't happen again." Then she ducked into her tent clutching her shovel. "Goodnight."

Reynir tapped Brynd on the boot. "I might need your skill, friend. Would you be willing to come with me to find the mother?"

Brynd woke to sigh. "Well, after that racket, who can sleep? Let me get my bow."

The two let the bear lead back to where it lost its mother, while Reynir spoke with the bear all of the way there.

"Nice trick, priest!" Brynd remarked, following the surrounding terrain attentively. Then he picked up a trail. "I think that I can track her from here."

"Excellent!" Reynir exclaimed and related the message to his new furry friend.

* * *

The morning sun hung low and red in the sky. It was mildly humid, but clouds were beginning to arrive from the South as the wind pushed them quickly into the vicinity. It was cold, and now it looked like rain. Kairoth looked up and wondered what he had done to anger the Gods. Then he looked around for the druid and the ranger.

"Wonderful, where in the Underworld are those two?" the warrior complained. "We can't wait here all day."

The other Hodan warrior, called Danzu, reported in. "Nothing yet, brother, but I am watching on the tree line for anything coming our way. I will let you know if I see anything."

"Danzu! There, near the copse right below the tree line. Two on foot," Medadel shouted. Danzu ran over to the Yslan warrior looking where his watch partner now pointed. It was them.

"Thanks, brother," Danzu said to Medadel, who kept an eye on the two as they approached. They appeared to be running.

"Kairoth, they come," Danzu stated.

The Hodan leader nodded. "Well, it's about damned time."

Within moments, a winded pair of men entered a camp that was almost completely torn down. They had their hands on their knees and were sucking wind hard. Kairoth approached them in a disapproving manner.

"Well, druid, was that worth it?" he asked sarcastically.

"Actually, in my opinion, yes," the exhausted druid responded tersely.

Brynd immediately set about breaking down his tent and packing his belongings. Valtyr had taken the liberty of tearing down Reynir's camp and made sure to let him know about it.

"Nice of you to join us. Are you now an envoy to the bear population of the Ert?" Valtyr smirked and rolled his eyes.

"I reunited a child with its mother while you slept. I call that a win." Reynir grabbed his pack and threw it up on his horse, yawning. "Thanks for packing, by the way, but I can manage though. You are not my wife." He laughed as he saw a scowl on Valtyr's face, while the priest searched his mind for an appropriate response. Shaking his head, but not admitting defeat, Valtyr turned and mounted his horse, joining the others.

"Enough. Get the camp packed and let's get on the road. It's already the third hour of the morning. We are not on sabbatical here." Kairoth, hands on his hips, looked at the two clergy members with impatience.

The group of travelers made their last preparations and then left down the road, traveling southeast toward their objective, the village of Hero's Pass.

* * *

It was the twelfth hour of the day when Roland finally saw a small village to the South of the road. It was only a couple of miles away, but the ranger could already make out the night fires being lit. Smoke rose in small grey chalk lines into the darkening sky. This was definitely an organized settlement, vice a camp. He rode back to where Kairoth was.

"Settlement to the southeast. I think it is the place we are looking for." Roland pointed toward the now-obvious fires that were visible to all on the broad, open terrain of this part of the Kingdom.

"Agreed. Let's make haste to get there by nightfall. I do not want to camp in the rough again, if at all possible." Kairoth's statement met with instant approval from both mages.

Reynir was barely upright in the saddle. "I need some sleep."

Kairoth laughed. "I will bet that you do." He looked at Valtyr, sighing. Valtyr returned his sigh.

To the North of the road, a rider approached their position. The rangers readied their bows and Kairoth had a hand on his sword hilt. It was quickly determined that Famlin was rejoining the group after his overnight absence. Kairoth was interested.

"Where have you been, specialist?" Kairoth asked suspiciously.

"Relax, oh fearless leader, I was on reconnaissance," Famlin responded in an irritated manner. "I am doing my job."

"Well, let me know next time. Or someone else at least. Did you see anything interesting on your evening ride?" Kairoth waited.

"Well, actually, yes. On the North side of the Raven's Pass, there appear to be mid-sized camps of the militia." Famlin was now surrounded by interested party members. "I counted around fifty men, ages fifteen to fifty, some on horseback, but mostly on foot. Arms and armor look pretty substandard, so I'd say brigands for sure."

"You would know," Roland said with a sneer. Brynd chuckled softly.

Ignoring the slight, Famlin continued. "There is a beaten path into the ridge on the North side of the pass, but I lost it in the mountainous region. I could've used one of these wannabe Elves to track that."

The comment stung, and both of the rangers were not amused. One started to speak, but Famlin continued. "I did notice something strange up there. The trees looked dead, and no wildlife appeared to be within the area. I've never seen anything like it before."

Reynir looked puzzled. "No wildlife at all?"

"Nothing, not even a bird," Famlin responded.

"That is definitely not good. I should like to investigate that situation and report my findings to Her Holiness, the Queen." Reynir became oddly serious when talking about the forest and the Queen. No one mocked his demeanor.

"After we deal with these brigands, we can look at the forest, druid. Will that suffice?" Kairoth offered.

"Yes, thank you." Reynir was oddly silent and had a worried look on his face. Kairoth almost missed his cheerful banter, wondering what was wrong. He merely nodded, and Reynir responded in kind.

The team regrouped and continued on the dirt road. Within two hours, they were met by a farmer, claiming to be a sentry.

"Hold there! Who are you?" the half-Elf asked in as intimidating a voice as he could muster.

Kairoth stifled a desire to laugh. Before he could answer, Sal'iabac said, "My sister and I are ladies of moderate means who travel to Torith for magic reagents and training. These gentlemen are our traveling party." She pointed out each member. "We have clergy for spiritual guidance and healing if necessary, and of course, guides, and security personnel." Sal'iabac fanned herself pretentiously, eliciting a look of amusement from Kairoth. "It is so unsafe on the roads these days," she said batting her eyelids.

The guard leaned on his boar spear. "Agreed, My Lady. Perhaps you should stay the night at our small inn? It is but a common room, but warm and much more secure than sleeping in the rough."

"Is it true, what the rumors say?" Sal'iabac rode up to where the guard now relaxed his posture. She said to him in a loud whisper, "Are brigands operating in this locale?" She looked concerned for good measure.

"You have heard correctly, My Lady. The bastards hit us a few nights ago. They used to only target our crops and mead, but now it appears that they seek after slaves also. Our women and children are now also targeted. We keep them indoors or under guard now. It is a hard way to live." The guard frowned, looking toward the village. "Isn't it bad enough that everyone hates us so? Are these men so cruel as to tear our children and wives from us also?"

"That sounds atrocious!" Sal'iabac said in actual horror. She was not faking anymore. "Perhaps my men can be of assistance while we are here." She looked at Kairoth, daring him to contradict her.

"I consider all who are willing to stand the watch with us to be a friend." He whistled loudly, and two young boys arrived. "Take them to the inn. They are travelers."

The boys nodded and did as they were told. The horses were secured and cared for in the village corral as the travelers all walked into the small tavern and inn. It was a thirty measure by thirty measure mud building with a thatch roof and a hinged wooden door on the side of it. There was a bar to secure the door, but the building was essentially always open for business. A hole in the roof acted as a chimney, and a large round stone fire pit was located in the center of the room. The floor was lined with a thick layer of straw. It was warm and dry. There were only two others in the building at the time.

One of them spoke. "Welcome, My Lords and Ladies, may I get you something to eat or drink? A copper coin is all it costs!" The old lady smiled as she stood.

"Yes please," Kairoth responded. "Please bring out a mead or ale for each of my friends, and a serving of the evening fare."

He provided the old woman with the coin required, and a bit extra for her trouble, and she returned with a barley stew and the drinks. The party sat and ate their meal, quietly discussing the evening watch schedule. They kept the discussion of their mission quiet, because they did not know who was listening.

The two rangers drew the first watch. One remained indoors, the other positioned himself outside near the horses and grain storage. Brynd hid as the Elves do, in plain sight. None of the local guards knew of his presence.

* * *

The horns were blown sometime late into the first watch. Brynd slowly moved toward the sound of the trumpets. Looking toward the tavern, he could see Roland peeking around the open door. He was making hand signals to his partner. Brynd responded in kind. Roland gave a thumbs-up, acknowledging the order and ducked inside.

"Get up!" Roland whispered as he kicked each of the group's membership in their shoes. "The brigands are in the village. Brynd is out there, ready to engage."

Kairoth was up immediately and still in his armor. "Let's go, team. It is time to earn our paychecks."

The other warriors were up and ready within a moment. As the priest shook the druid awake, the mages began mixing components.

"Five more minutes," Reynir protested, then rolled over.

"Get your lazy behind up!" Valtyr said assertively, yanking Reynir's blanket off of him.

"What is your problem?" Reynir asked bleary-eyed. He had been working on three hours of sleep in two days.

"Brigands? Remember?" Valtyr looked at his friend expectantly.

"Oh yes! Time to work!" Reynir sprang to his feet, immediately energized and enthusiastic. "Let's get them!"

Outside, the sound of horses could be heard off in the distance. Guards were shouting in Elfish to each other. Brynd watched from his vantage point, nocking an arrow. As he saw his first marauder, he drew his Elfish bow and let the arrow fly. Without looking, he pulled another and let it fly. Then another and another. Horsemen were dropping from their horses and regrouping on the ground. The ranger had killed two, but three others were still very much alive.

The door to the inn burst open, as three shield men stepped out and to the front. Kairoth was in the middle, to his left was Medadel, and to his right, Danzu. Behind the wall were the two mages, with the druid on the right and the priest on the left. The specialist was nowhere to be seen. Kairoth looked around and shook his head. The unit moved as one, as they had trained in Empyr. The brigand leadership saw this and regrouped its forces. Their leader had at least ten horsemen left and twenty foot soldiers.

"Shields stay together. Stand by for a charge. Watch the horses on the left." Kairoth surveyed the field with enthusiasm. These foes were about to engage something that they hadn't bargained for. Kairoth yelled to Roland. "Go back up, Brynd. We have this over here."

When Kairoth had finished saying this, he felt the hair on the back of his neck stand up, "Duck!" The shield wall hit the ground instinctively, as Sal'iabac and Safiya let loose with a barrage of energy bolts, instantly killing five horsemen and three foot soldiers. Some turned to run away, but Roland and Brynd made their run a short trip.

"Reform!" Kairoth commanded and the shield wall reformed. "Forward at a walk, gentlemen," the Hodan warrior said. "Come and get it, scum!" he shouted toward fifteen or so brigands reforming for a charge.

Then they came. The brigands hit the shield wall in waves. The priest and the druid fought any flanking maneuvers, but the majority of the killing came from the three shield men at the front. The mages tried to get off another shot, but because of the mayhem, they were unable to concentrate and utter the proper incantations to make it happen. Both drew daggers and hoped that they would not be forced into physical combat. So far, so good.

Up front, the ill-equipped force of brigands crashed against two angry Hodan and one motivated Yslandeth warrior. The Yslan warrior made it a personal goal to kill as many as the other two, because he felt the honor of his homeland was at stake. Tearing through the rabble that presented itself, the trio left a gruesome trail of gore and death. A few in the distance ran back toward where their camp was reported to be. Just as the party thought that they would escape and bring reinforcements, three distinct screaming voices were heard out of sight. Then two. Then one. Then silence.

Brynd and Roland now surveyed the direction of the screams, their bows out and strings drawn back. Through the mist of the light evening fog, they saw a small man or boy advancing on the village. He was coming in fast and light. He looked as if he was a skilled scout. The rangers let loose their arrows. The figure disappeared.

"Damn you two!" a familiar voice screamed. "Are you both blind?"

"Who is that?" Roland remarked loudly to the invisible person.

"It's me, you horse's ass! Famlin! Your specialist. I need a doctor now, please!?" Famlin was frantic.

"Oh no!" Brynd said with concern. "I hope we didn't kill him."

"Yeah, that would not be ideal," Roland quipped. "We are coming to you. Do not shoot us … or do whatever it is that you do."

"Hurry up and bring the priest, you fools," Famlin pleaded.

Valtyr hurried out into the field. "I'm coming as fast as I can. Hang on!"

When Valtyr arrived, he could see that Famlin had two arrows in him, one in his belly, the other through his left thigh. He was in extreme pain and losing blood quickly. Valtyr called out to Reynir, who brought the medical kit. Carefully, the two removed the arrows from their friend, binding the wounds as best that they could along the way. Valtyr pulled out a green vial with an Elfish symbol on it and applied it to Famlin's abdominal injury, and then prayed. His prayers resulted in the expected healing, but they were still required to carry the thief back to the inn. He was in no condition to walk.

"Where did you go?" Kairoth demanded.

Groggily, Famlin responded, "I set traps in the field where I thought they would come. I set caltrops out for their horses. When they tried to run, they were ensnared, and I dealt with them personally. I was returning when the two asses shot me."

"How in the Underworld were we supposed to know it was you, you damned fool?" Roland protested. Brynd nodded in agreement.

"I don't know, but I didn't have time to check out with all of you when the action started. I did what I do. I killed five in total. The fallen are in the field where you shot me, unless the enemy carries off their dead, but I don't think that there were enough left to carry anyone off. We did a fine job!" Famlin coughed.

"Enough talk. Rest and heal. Priest, give him a potion. We need him on his feet tomorrow at the latest. The enemy will come here for retaliation. We need to travel down Raven's Pass and try to draw them out. They will try to ambush us there, and that is when we will have them where we want them." Kairoth looked almost maniacal when he thought about the battle to come.

Valtyr raised a hand.

"What is it, priest?" Kairoth responded with irritation.

"So, we're going to intentionally walk into an ambush, to draw THEM out? Are you sure you didn't get hit on the head?" Valtyr was perplexed.

"I am sure. It is a sound plan. We move to the side that the enemy is weakest, and then we divide their forces and conquer them. Easy day." Kairoth seemed a bit overconfident after the evening's rout of the enemy.

"Never underestimate your foe, brother," Valtyr asserted. "You do so at your own peril, and also at ours."

Kairoth was annoyed. He immediately recognized that Valtyr had quoted that from the Book of Hodan Wisdom. He looked at Valtyr with a grave face.

"Don't you worry about that. The plan is sound. Now, everyone get some sleep. I will take the watch with Reynir." Kairoth turned from Valtyr's judging stare and began patrolling.

Reynir groaned. He was exhausted. Valtyr laughed at him. "Serves you right, bear lover."

Reynir made a face, then a profane gesture at his brother. "Go and get your beauty sleep you, Ogre. Gods know you need it more than I!"

The group went back to their bedrolls. Reynir bolted the inn door. Kairoth sat on a bench beside the fire with mead that the lady of the establishment handed him, free of charge. The team was not as bad as he once thought. In fact, they were much more lethal than he had ever imagined possible.

Maybe they would survive to retire, perhaps not, but if tonight was any indication of what was to come, many would know their names. That was more than any Hodan could ever ask for. Retirement would be a bonus.

Chapter 5

The rain fell in sheets. Thunder woke the team as they slept in the common room. The old woman who was the innkeeper, was behind her bar, making the morning mush, with a concerned look on her face. The door was barred to the inn, and that was a rare occurrence. She heard a loud, rapid knock on the door, and bent down behind the counter to hide. Kairoth rose immediately, drawing his sword.

"It is only me!" a subdued voice said from the other side of the door. It was Roland reporting in.

Brynd cracked the door, instinctively putting his foot behind it, in case Roland was not alone. He was alone. Brynd stepped back his bow at the ready. "Get in here, quickly!" he yelled.

Roland entered. He was soaked. His tunic stuck to him, and he was shivering. It had to be in the forties outside, but the ranger never faltered while on duty. Kairoth beckoned for him to come near the fire. "Get warm, brother. What do you have to report?"

Roland replied, teeth chattering a bit, staring at the fire. "Small unit moving northwest of the road. Twenty to thirty more men. Most on horseback. I was able to see one fancy-looking gent on an armored steed." He looked at Kairoth with a look of disgust. "I would wager that he is their leader."

"Then they come for retribution as I had feared. Tell the village leader to pull their people inside if they are out in this maelstrom. We will use the weather to hide and ambush this scum. They are trifling with the King's best. They will pay for it dearly."

On the other side of the room, Valtyr tended to Famlin. He looked under the bandages and could see that the Elfish potions had done their magic. The thief's wounds were sealed on the outside, but as Famlin tried to sit up, it was apparent that the insides were still on the mend.

Valtyr helped the thief up to a chair. "Take it slow, friend," he ordered. "You still have a day or two before the magic is complete. Do not re-injure yourself."

The mages were up and reading their books. When they had finished, they set up small bundles of reagents that were necessary to practice their arts. Safiya looked up at Famlin and knew that he was in no condition to fight. She walked over to the priest attending him, handing him a pouch of herbs.

"Give him this," she said, dropping the small sack into Valtyr's hand. "It should aid his healing greatly. I learned it in Edenyag."

"Thank you," Valtyr responded, and went about getting some hot water to steep the mixture in.

Famlin smiled at the younger mage,and she began to blush, pulling her hood up over her head and turning away abruptly. "Yes, thank you very much, My Lady," the thief said, bowing slightly and holding his side.

Sal'iabac raised an eyebrow and shook her head. "Always a ruffian with you, sister. What is your issue with normal men?" The older sister glared at Famlin with squinting eyes. The thief was now openly staring at Safiya with a wide grin.

The warriors were now up. They attended to their weapons and put on their armor, preparing for battle. Once everyone was ready, the older woman supplied a large pot of oatmeal for the group to eat before they went into action.

"Something warm before you face the weather—and them." She trailed off with a frown, looking at the young group before her. "You are all too young for this sort of life."

She left them all at the table and returned to her kitchen. Kairoth noticed that the woman had a giant meat cleaver near her at all times, even though there was no meat to cleave. He nodded in approval, grinning.

"All right, we split into two teams. Warriors and priests in the open to draw them in. You priests keep the rest of us upright with your prayers and healing, and if you can, kill a few for Runnir and Gunnir." Kairoth looked at Valtyr and Reynir, who for once, seemed to be in agreement.

"What of the rest of us?" Sal'iabac asked.

"I thought that you both could pick a nearby stable or shed to hide in. When the fools attack us with the majority of their forces, you hit them with whatever magic you can muster. A lot of what you did yesterday would be excellent."

Sal'iabac blushed at Kairoth's approval. She looked down humbly, and replied, "As you wish." Her face was red, and Safiya picked up on her demeanor immediately.

"Really? *I pick the ruffians?*" Safiya rolled her eyes and slapped her sister on the back of the head lightly. The two snorted for a second then composed themselves. All of the group was looking at them.

"What?" the sisters answered in unison.

"So, what about the two Draj?" Medadel asked Kairoth. "Where do they fit in? I mean, after that one is unfrozen, that is." The warrior gestured toward Roland, who waved to the group, nodding sarcastically.

"I am not a Draj, you damned fool. Stop calling me that." Roland was not amused. "They stole that from me. To the Underworld with the Elves."

The old lady looked up in alarm from behind the counter. Roland relented. "Fine to the Underworld with THOSE Elves. You have done no wrong to me, My Lady. I apologize for being rude."

The mages nodded in approval of Roland's apology, and the old lady waved him off, going back to her duties. Kairoth drew a crude diagram in the dust on a platter.

"Village center. Inn. Shed. Barn. Well." The Hodan warrior looked around, then continued. "Fighters and priests, here, at the well, in this formation. Mages in the barn. It's bigger and allows a higher vantage if you wish to go into the loft. One ranger with the mages for support and the other ranger pick a good sniper vantage. I will leave that up to your decision. You have the training there that I do not."

"What about me?" Famlin asked in an offended tone.

"You will sit this one out and heal, my friend. No need to die unnecessarily. If we are defeated, you will travel to Empyr and give a report to Master Donick and the King." Kairoth looked at the thief with sincerity. "This is not a consolation prize, my friend, it is a reality. We may not win. If we do not, your mission must be a success. You will tell them that you are a homeless person looking for work if they make it past us. Then slip away into the night as only you are capable."

"Yeah. Understood, but whatever. If we make it out of here, I will prove myself another way," the thief said muttering.

As the plan was set in stone, and the comrades finished their meal, the guard was heard shouting. Then a distant bell rang six or seven times and went silent. Kairoth knew that it was the watch, warning the village of incoming invaders. He called for his group to dispatch to their previously agreed upon locations. The inn door opened for a second at a time to the now torrential downpour that seemed to worsen with the hour. First, the mages ran to the community storehouse barn with Roland, who complained, because he had just finally gotten warm and dry. Then Brynd left and disappeared into the driving rain, as Draj often do. After that, the warrior waited until they could hear the horse hooves pounding into the mud of the common area. All were in armor, shields in hand, swords drawn, and helmets strapped on tight. That is when the plan went south.

Kairoth heard a shriek of an onlooking woman. It was getting louder and more apparent as she wailed in Etah and Elfish. The warrior looked out of a knothole in the door and beheld a well-dressed man on horseback as he threw a lifeless body from his horse onto the ground. The woman was beside herself with grief and laid in the mud covering what appeared to be a boy of around twelve years old. Kairoth could barely make out his pointed ears. He was a villager.

"Probably the one who hit the bell," he remarked to no one in particular. The warriors looked at their leader. He was uncharacteristically cold.

From outside the door, the woman screamed at the mounted man. "He was a child retrieving sheep in the rains, you despicable excuse for a pig's ass!" She stood and attacked the man futilely, receiving the butt of his sword hilt as a reward for actions. Kairoth was stone silent.

The group was looking at one another in confusion when Danzu spoke. "Prepare yourself. I don't think he's thinking of the 'plan' right now."

Medadel nodded. "We will play this by ear. Priests on me. Watch out and stay out of his way. I've seen this one berserk before."

As Medadel finished his words, Kairoth nearly tore the door from its hinges. He burst out into the courtyard and into the torrential rain. No one could see his tears.

"You will not be a slave to the likes of this," Kairoth roared.

"Fan out on the flanks," Medadel barked out loudly, and the rest of the warriors and priests fanned out to the sides of their leader.

Valtyr began praying, as did Reynir. Valtyr smiled at the dull glow of his war hammer. Reynir greeted the vines that now wove their way around the men in his circle.

"Let us begin to serve the Queen," Reynir said to Valtyr in a strange voice.

"Agreed, brother," Valtyr answered him in a similar tone. The warriors looked at each other, wondering which God was present. They hoped for the warring brothers.

"Luck in battle, brother," Danzu said to Medadel, and the two tapped each other on the shield.

The battle began with a roar and a crazed blur. Kairoth, without warning, leaped forward, mounting the horse of the nobleman in question. Throwing his shield at the nearest lackey, he knocked the lad off of his horse. With his newly freed hand, he grabbed fast to the rider, as his horse reared back, then proceeded to sever the rider's head from his shoulder with his sword. To the onlookers, both enemy and friend, it appeared as if Kairoth flew up and executed this maneuver in one motion. Kairoth threw the body on the ground beside the young boy.

He roared as if Gunnir spoke from Aeternum. "What are you waiting for, gentlemen!? Kill them all!"

The half-Elfish woman kissed her son's cold cheek and stood. Then she bowed to Kairoth as he reared his new horse and turned to the field of the oncoming militia. Kairoth only nodded, covered in blood and hidden tears.

"Not again, mother," he said in his helmet. "Not without every one of them dying for it."

* * *

"What in the Underworld is he doing!?" shrieked Sal'iabac, as she watched Kairoth go. The hair on the back of her neck stood up as she witnessed the immediate and unbridled rage he displayed, as he dispatched the leader of the enemy band, and then turned to kill more.

"Being a ruffian," Safiya mocked, "and a Hodan. They are not known to be 'philosophers.'"

Sal'iabac glared angrily. "Now is not the time for jokes, sister." She was genuinely concerned for Kairoth's safety and was no longer reluctant to show it.

"Let us go and assist," Safiya said, her eyes glowing as if filled with fire.

"Let's go, ranger! It looks like the plan went down the drain with all of this damned water." Sal'iabac looked back to see Brynd nod and hop up, running out into the rain and disappearing.

The ladies waded out into the muck, and were not happy with the fact that they now resembled two drown street urchins. Safiya said words and touched her sister. A faint glow encapsulated both mages, and they walked to within range of their desired targets. Then they let loose.

Kairoth was in the thick of the fight, as were the other non-mounted warriors. He was out of range of healing and had sustained one arrow in his shoulder and one in his left hip area. Still, he rode as if unimpeded, chasing down the archers and killing six or seven more militia as he continued his rampage.

From behind the Hodan leader, a specialist appeared on a rooftop. The enemy sniper stood and was taking aim at Kairoth, when Roland noticed him from his hiding spot and summarily dispatched him with two arrows from his Elfish longbow. Kairoth never saw the exchange, never stopping his charge, crushing the skull of another young attacker with one blow. Roland quietly, and with stealth, dispatched two other warriors who he felt were maneuvering too close to his leader for his liking. He hit both marauders with headshots while running across a rooftop at a range of seventy yards. Arriving on the scene, he searched the specialist for information.

"Poison. Damned assassins. Suden dung." The ranger carefully searched, but only found a few coins, and a favor with a black field with a Red-Hand emblazoned upon it. "Red-Hand. You should have stayed afraid, fools."

Off in the distance, the battle began to turn on Kairoth, and this fact was not lost on Reynir, who bolted from the relative safety of the other two warriors. As he did, he saw Kairoth hit by a third arrow and a spear thrust, knocking him from his mount and onto the ground. The warrior was rolling over to respond, when the druid arrived on the scene. The Hodan was surrounded by five mounted spearmen, who were about to make a pin cushion out of their foe.

Kairoth had gotten to his knees. He was bleeding from two stab wounds to his sides. The arrows were still in him, but the shafts were broken off. He was using his sword to brace himself to stand. Reynir had seen enough.

"Stop!" the lanky, young druid commanded, bellowing in a voice much too big for his small frame. All, including Kairoth, looked at the leather-clad man with wonder. Kairoth grinned. He was hoping for some trees to intercede. He was close.

"Step away from my friend, gentlemen, and I will not have to become violent," the druid asserted angrily. Kairoth could not remember when he'd ever seen the boy angry.

"And if we do not? What will you do?" the eldest attacker responded by mocking the druid. "You will die as he does, half-breed."

"As you wish," Reynir said, making a hand gesture and then looking down.

The druid then spoke in a language no one there recognized, raising his hands above his head. As he did these things, the grasses and vines in the immediate area began to shoot out and grab the five attackers. First, the grass caught the horses' hooves. The horses tried to bolt and fell as the grass then hobbled the horses, tethering them on top of their riders and to the muck that was the ground.

"What is this!?" the eldest attacker screamed. "Help us! Brothers, come to help us!"

But there was no reply in the murky rain, as Reynir commanded the vines to bind them further. The faces of the men around Kairoth became red, then turned a pale blue, as Reynir squeezed the life out of the attackers he had ensnared within the grasses of the field. Kairoth stood in awe and horror at what he was witnessing. When the last pleading attacker had gurgled his last breath, Reynir released his hold on nature and calmly walked over to Kairoth extending his hand.

"Sorry about the gruesome nature of, well … nature," Reynir said helping Kairoth up.

As the warrior stood up, he immediately swooned from his injuries, and Reynir steadied him. "I will carry you this time, hero. Someday, you will carry me, no doubt," the druid said, as a matter of fact, hoisting the warrior over his shoulder and carrying him back toward the inn.

"You are stronger than you look, in more ways than one," Kairoth said smiling. "I will buy the ale tonight!"

"I will hold you to that," replied the druid. "Valtyr, a little help here, brother!"

Valtyr had just patched up Medadel and healed Danzu, who had held off another ten or twelve horsemen with the assistance of the mages, who let loose with bolts of energy, as if they were shooting bolts from Dwarven crossbows. There was an almost perfect circle of dead horses and men around the well in the shared courtyard. Valtyr looked up at the sisters, who waved him off and dragged themselves back into the barn to hide. They looked exhausted, and he knew that they had given all that they had.

In the inn, the priest saw that the druid had set the Hodan leader on the main dining table and was attempting to carefully remove the arrow from the Kairoth's shoulder. The Hodan warrior was in extreme pain, and the innkeeper brought Dwarven ale to the table to assist with the surgery.

"We never see Dwarves anymore. No one will touch the stuff. Drink this, boy, you will feel nothing in a moment."

"What of the battle?" Kairoth asked groaning. "The mages? The rangers? Where are they? Are they safe?"

"Calm yourself, brother," Valtyr said soothingly. "The mages are spent, but they waved to me, saying that they were fine. They are in the barn resting."

"What of the battle? How many are left?" Kairoth looked at Danzu.

"At least twelve ride away. They retreat. Cowards!" Danzu spat.

"That will not do! They will escape and come back." Kairoth tried to sit up, but Valtyr held him down.

"The rangers are dealing with them. Two almost-Draj against twelve horses' asses. The enemy is done for." Medadel laughed.

The constant, peaceful, white noise of the rain against the rooftop was rudely interrupted by loud explosions, off in the distance, near the edge of the village. Everyone in the room turned to look. The thief was gone.

"That little bastard," Kairoth laughed. "He is good for something after all." Then Kairoth lost consciousness. After a quick check, Valtyr determined that he was only feeling the effects of a Dwarven ale that he had just downed to dull the pain. The mages appeared in the door.

"Where is he!?" Safiya shrieked, looking toward the bedroll that once contained Famlin.

"Out there! Causing the enemy a loud and painful death I am guessing," Danzu replied, looking on the horizon.

"How is Kairoth?" Sal'iabac asked with genuine concern looking at the bloodied warrior. She wore a frown.

Safiya put her hand on her sister's shoulder. "He is Hodan, sister. They have hard heads and strong bodies. He will survive. Let him rest."

Sal'iabac nodded, sitting in the corner, sipping an ale the old innkeeper handed her, but never taking her eyes off of Kairoth, as the priest and druid worked their type of magic to save him.

Valtyr removed the arrows successfully, packing the wounds with herbs and binding them with clean linen bandages. Reynir said prayers to Aluia and secured as much divine healing as he could muster. Valtyr did similarly. Kairoth slept. The bleeding had stopped. The bruises were healing. He was lucky to have survived, and the healers knew it, but they said nothing.

An hour later, Roland and Brynd arrived, carrying Famlin back to the inn. The specialist had another arrow in his other leg this time. The rangers were laughing and making jokes with their younger passenger.

"You need plate mail, lad. You seem to attract arrows!" Roland joked loudly.

"At least some chain or something! For the love of the Gods—or learn to take cover for Runnir's sake!" Brynd bantered.

Safiya stood up immediately and rushed to the door. "What in the Underworld, do you think you were doing!? You were told to stay here! You are not ready to fight!"

She was so close that Famlin could smell the mead on her breath. Smiling, he kissed her lips. Shocked, Safiya jerked backward, slapping his face, but only half-heartedly, "How dare you!?"

Famlin smiled and touched the spot she had slapped him. "I rarely do what I am supposed to." He turned from her to face the rest, as the rangers set him down next to the sleeping Kairoth. "He needs a nap. He nearly scared them all away, single-handedly! Your specialist reports that the rest died on the plains in fire and arrows from these two." He gestured toward the two rangers, who lifted their own mugs of mead and went about drinking. "I'm rather glad that they showed up when they did." Valtyr cut the arrow shaft, pulling through the thief's leg. He let out a yelp and then took a long pull of what was left of the Dwarven ale near Kairoth. The priest then packed the wounds with herbs, bound them in linen and prayed once again.

"Now go to bed and stay there!" Valtyr said emphatically to Famlin.

Famlin raised his eyebrows, looking at Safiya. He patted a spot near him on the bedroll. Safiya feigned offense, but the smirk on her face said otherwise. Famlin smiled. Safiya turned away from him to a judgmental look from her sister.

"What?" she asked in defiance, looking over at Kairoth and then making a face toward Sal'iabac. The elder sister snorted and then rolled out her bedding, laughing.

"Who's got first watch?" Reynir asked, looking out at the setting sun. It had been a long and painful day.

The rangers looked at each other. "We've got it," Brynd responded. "Better that you magic-types sleep. Be ready at dawn for anything. Good night, heroes."

Chapter 6

It was a week before the Yslandeth regulars showed up in Hero's Pass. The King's men arrived to little fanfare. Of a truth, the villagers were surprised to see anyone come to their aid in an official capacity. The lieutenant made his way to the inn after showing the village guard the King's written orders. They passed the makeshift checkpoint without incident.

"Hail, innkeeper, where be the band that held off the Red-Hand militia?" the young Human warrior asked with authority. He seemed to be a bit full of himself.

Kairoth sat up, to Sal'iabac's protests. He waved the mage off. "We are they. Who might you be, my lord?"

"I am Gregor, son of Thern, Lieutenant, Second Class, in His Majesty's army. I am the Commander of the Legion that has occupied this parcel of land until the order is fully restored. Why are you here?"

"Well, Sir,'" Kairoth said with disdain, "it is good of you to finally show up. We have done most of the dirty work already. There are probably scarcely twenty of the fools left by now. I will wager they have melted away, back to their farms while you were out practicing your technique in the yards."

"You will watch your tone with me, My Lord, or I will have you whipped," the Lieutenant snapped back. His face was red with irritation.

"Will you do it yourself? Or have some of your boys come over here and do it for you?" Kairoth stood up, his wounds now visible to the lieutenant, whose eyes widened for a second.

"You are the leader, I would presume," the officer said, removing his helmet and gloves and ordering a mead. "Make that eleven. One for each of these folks." The older woman complied, supplying the drinks, and then exited the main room to the back kitchen. Kairoth smiled, noticing she still had the cleaver with her wherever she went.

The Hodan warrior sipped his mead. "What can I do for you, fine fellows?" He looked unimpressed. The lieutenant was not impressed either.

"Who sent you here? What is your mission? Who do you work for?" the Commander asked in rapid succession.

"None of your business? None of your business! Ask your King!!" Kairoth replied smugly. The Hodan warrior reached into his shirt and pulled out a favor that he produced for his inquisitor. "We all have one. I do not answer to you."

The Lieutenant's immediate look of surprise betrayed him. "You hold the King's own favor? You must be ..." The officer looked around to verify who was in the room with them. "Special operations?"

"Yeah, that's a nice name for it." Kairoth walked over to the thief. "You about done lounging around, boy?"

"Yep, always itching for some action, oh fearless one," the thief quipped.

Kairoth shook his head and looked at the rangers who were finishing their breakfast. "You two fill this man in on what happened here. Specialist, give him your reconnaissance reports. We have other duties." The Hodan looked at the druid.

Reynir nodded. "That we do."

The rangers gave the army Commander the location, numbers, equipment status, and last known areas of operation of the militia. It had been mostly quiet since last week's major battle in the village. The villagers showed the military leadership where they had burned the bodies, sending all of the fallen off to the afterlife. The village leader stated that the number killed was counted at forty-nine, including one village boy.

The group stood outside in appropriate garb: three warriors, two rangers, two priests, two mages, and one specialist. The Lieutenant looked at the pyre mound and then back to the crew before them.

"They did this to them?" the Lieutenant asked a villager.

"Yes, My Lord. They did. The Hodan leader killed ten alone. He is a frightening soul, but on our side, so Haya blesses us." The old man bowed.

"It appears I have misjudged these people." The Lieutenant nodded to Kairoth, who saluted back irreverently and checked his blade.

"Where will you be off to, Kairoth, is it?" the Commander inquired.

"None of your business." The warrior smiled. The Lieutenant nodded, laughing. Kairoth replied, "We will leave the rest of them to you, but we will travel southeast through the Raven's Pass to the checkpoint before the Arondayre."

"Well, Gods be with you all, my brother in arms. Be safe and be well," the Lieutenant said seriously, saluting Kairoth. Kairoth stood and saluted back as a Hodan Elite Legionnaire would. "Your ancestors look upon you with favor, Hodan!" the Lieutenant shouted exiting the bar. He mounted his horse while quoting the Hodan blessing.

"May the mead be warm at your seat in Aeternum, Yslandeth!" Kairoth returned from the door. The Lieutenant galloped off, barking orders to his men who assembled to march North of the pass.

"The Red-Hand is about to be no more," remarked Kairoth to no one in particular.

"Good riddance!" Famlin declared, rubbing his itching leg wound.

"Agreed!" Kairoth laughed, scratching at a healed spear wound in his side. "Are we prepared my friends?" One by one, they affirmed that they were ready to depart.

"May the Holy Mother watch over you," the older half-Elfish innkeeper said to Valtyr as he mounted.

"And may it be with you always," the priest replied smiling. "Thank you for your hospitality!"

"It is we who owe you all. The threat fades, because you bled on this field for those who you do not know. You all are truly the heroes of the unwanted." She smiled, tearing up, and waved as the group trotted out of the damp courtyard. The entire village lined the entry path with flowers in their hands, throwing them in the way of the trotting horses.

Kairoth's eyes were reddened, but he hid them in the shade of his helmet. The rangers waved, smiling. Reynir was oddly quiet, and Valtyr observed him carefully, wondering what the matter was. The mages waved with embarrassed looks on their faces. They were not used to recognition. As they looked at all of the sad faces that lined their exit, they felt proud to have helped, if even in a small way.

Kairoth looked around. "All right, where in the Underworld is my specialist?"

Reynir burst into laughter. "Out being special again, I would suppose."

* * *

It had been a day and a half since the band had departed the village into the Raven's Pass. There had been no confirmed contact with anyone on their travels up to this point, but during the night prior, the rangers reported that they had detected movement just outside of the firelight.

"Kairoth, the day of the main battle, when you were knee-deep in militia, I was backing you up with my bow," Roland recalled. "There was an enemy specialist up on a roof."

"Well, apparently, you successfully dispatched him, and I am still here. Thank you," Kairoth responded, looking at the rising mountainous terrain on his left and right.

"One that I found was using poisons. He was most likely an assassin of some type, maybe Suden. He probably had skills the former leader of the Red-Hand desired. I am wondering how many more of these types they have employed." Roland looked around uncomfortably. "Usually, if an animal or a person mills about a location that I am scouting, I can find a trace of their movements. I can even track them to their destination, but last night there was no trace … but someone was out there. That concerns me."

Kairoth could see the look of worry on the ranger's face. It was a new look for him. Brynd had the same look of gravity. Kairoth looked carefully left and right, as if someone were about to jump out from behind a rock. He sighed, seriously considering their situation.

The Hodan leader said, in a subdued tone, "I don't know about either of you, but I am concerned about this choke point in the road ahead. If your ghosts are truly real and as skilled as you fear, they will probably ambush us there. We should stop and pretend to eat or take water while we prepare. Pass the word to the others."

Within a minute, all had stopped and pulled out their water skins. After taking a sip of water, they put them back in their places and subtly adjusted their armor and shields, and made ready their weapons. The rangers held their bows and an arrow at the ready in their left hand; the warriors pulled their swords halfway out of the hilt; and the mages set up their protective spells. Reynir could see the deforestation that Famlin had reported. It was visible from the valley and seemed to be centered on one prominent hill about one-thousand feet up the mountains on the northern side.

"I see it brother," Valtyr said with concern. "We shall get to the bottom of it."

Reynir nodded, but could not shake an unmistakable presence of evil that the nature around him echoed. A cold shiver ran down his spine. "Something is seriously amiss, brother."

As if on cue, the attack happened, just as Kairoth had predicted. The enemy started with a volley from the forest on the North and South of the pass. Thankfully, the team seemed to be out of range of the inferior bows of the enemy, or the enemy was just not that good of a shot. What concerned Roland and Brynd was that the attackers were extremely good at hiding.

"Over there, brother!" Brynd shouted, but by the time his partner looked, the archer was gone. "These are not a simple militia, brother."

"Agreed. We should attack in force to one side, then circle around to the other. We cannot stay in the center!" Roland looked at Kairoth, who nodded.

"On me! To the right! Shields to the front! Priests to the rear, mages center, and rangers on the flanks. Kill anything that you see. Run them over and let's end this now!"

Kairoth's orders were heeded, and the group formed a wedge, galloping up the hill toward the last location that they had received arrows from. A figure jumped up and began to run. He appeared to be a bush from a distance. Roland launched two bolts into the assailant, and he fell five steps from where he fled.

"They are in pits! They are camouflaged to appear as part of the forest. Be on your highest guard!" Roland barked out.

"Brynd, watch the left, brother," Roland ordered. Brynd nodded, smiling, as another figure lit out, dashing toward the road, in hopes of crossing to where reinforcements most likely waited. Brynd shot him with one arrow to the head, ending his retreat.

As the warriors thundered forward, weaving through the trees, another hail of arrows met them from the front. One stuck in Reynir's wooden shield. His eyes became as wide as goose eggs.

"Keep that thing in front of you!" Valtyr yelled at the druid.

"I did! I did! Why do you think that the arrow did not find me?" Reynir responded frantically.

As they closed with the suspected positions of the ambushers, the numbers of the assailants grew, but the enemy archers were no match for the armored riders, and some again fled to the other side of the road. Once Kairoth was reasonably sure that most, if not all, of the southern front of the pass was clear, he ordered the group to pursue the retreating ambushers. The wedge turned northward, closing quickly on those who left their positions late, killing everyone they encountered, but inevitably, a few escaped by running up the North side of the pass, as they headed for the thicker forest.

"Dismount and hobble the horses, quickly!" Kairoth ordered. The group made it so within a minute, but it was too late. The enemy melted into the forest.

"Now what?" Valtyr spat.

"We go in and root them out," Kairoth said plainly. "Rangers, go see if you can pick up a trail. Druid, is there anything that you can do?"

"Unfortunately, there are no birds here, or I would ask one to look for us. I cannot control the trees, as my Mistress does. All I can do is heal the wounded and use the plants in the area to our advantage, but I must see the enemy first."

"We can do this, Kairoth," Roland replied solemnly, looking at his partner. "Let's go, brother. They can't hide forever." The two grabbed forearms as always and departed immediately, disappearing into the forest.

"The rest of you form on me. Shields front, mages center; priests cover the mages as best you can. We need to make our way in there to aid them the best that we can. There have to be at least ten specialists on our two would-be Draj. Not a fair fight. Move out!"

Valtyr uttered a prayer as the group moved forward, and Reynir echoed his sentiment, asking for protection and for luck in battle. The group made their way toward the edge of the thick and could hear that combat had begun without them.

"No time for prayers, we must go!" Kairoth shouted, charging forward with the shields.

* * *

In the thicket, Roland took the lead, and Brynd followed immediately behind him. They walked together, back to back, as if they were one person, scarcely making a sound on the pine needle bed on which they tread.

"I don't like this, Roland," Brynd remarked, panning around with the end of an arrow to locate a target.

"I hear you brother, but we are here for this very purpose. Damn, these fools are good at what they do."

Roland shook his head as something moved, catching his eye. He let an arrow fly at the movement, and it appeared as a bush hopped up then took two steps and fell flat on its face. That is when the mayhem began.

Two hidden attackers popped up to the left behind Brynd. Before the ranger could react, Roland had pushed him out of the way of two incoming arrows, which both hit their marks. Roland returned the gesture taking the two down in the exchange. He now knelt, grimacing in pain and spitting blood from his mouth. There was a rancid flavor to his blood. He recognized it immediately.

"Poison, brother. I am done for. Get away from here and stalk them. You cannot save me!" Roland pleaded, nocking another arrow. He could see Kairoth and the group trying to enter the forest ring they had inhabited, but one of the warriors had fallen into a trap, and the others were trying with great effort to extract him from it. The mages were actively engaged in freelancing against attacking archers and making their prowess known, but Roland knew that help would not arrive in time to save his brother if he didn't leave immediately. "Go!"

"I will not," Brynd said calmly. "We have fought together since we were two whelps. I will not abandon you now, when you need me, you sorry bastard. Hang on. It is but a scratch. Help is coming." He launched two more arrows at charging assailants, but the enemy was regrouping and began swarming their position.

"I will go to Aeternum, right brother?" Roland asked coughing. "I should not want to see the Underworld." He was pale and had a concerned look on his face.

"Shut your mouth, we are not thinking about our retirement right now," Brynd joked, as six advanced on his position. He was now out of arrows. He handed the bow to Roland, drawing his sword. "You will hand this back to me when I am through with these Suden Toads."

Roland smiled, as his lips began to darken with the blackness of what he had coughed up.

Brynd stood and shouted. "I shall not retire. I will not yield this field. Kill me or die trying, Toads!"

Brynd attacked the first enemy with the speed of an Elf and the strength of a Human. The young attacker's eyes opened wide with the realization that Brynd had just dispatched him without a worry, and was onto his partner on the left. Brynd killed all six, when two more popped up from their lairs behind him.

"You cowards!" Roland gurgled as he sat up and fired one more time, killing one of the assailants. Then he received two more arrows from the other and fell silent.

Brynd charged, knowing that the archer would kill him enroute, but he had no other choice. The archer drew back, ready to release his arrow, when as if from thin air, a shadow raced from behind a tree and drove a blade squarely into the archer's spine. The projectile hit the ground several feet in front of Brynd as the ranger prepared for another foe, posturing up on the unknown attacker. In an instant, he realized that it was Famlin.

"Where in the catacombs of the Underworld did YOU come from?" Brynd snarled. "We might have used your help a few moments ago!"

"If you must know, I killed four, and I have two in poisoned traps. They are surely dead by now. I saw you and came as quickly as I could. I have been shadowing you all since we left, looking for the elusive enemy. Assassins no doubt," Famlin said, looking down at Roland with a look of horror. "Oh no."

Brynd knelt beside his brother who was breathing his last. "Burn me as we spoke of, brother. Send me home properly." Roland gripped Brynd's forearm tightly.

Brynd's tears fell freely on Roland's bloody chest piece. "I wouldn't have it any other way, my brother. I will send you off you as the hero you are. Your honor is intact. I owe you my life."

"You owe me nothing. I will warm you a mug of the finest mead," Roland sputtered quietly. "It's dark here, I feel cold … but I see a light. Do the Elves come for me, after all?"

Roland breathed sharply twice and then sighed his last breath, as Reynir finally broke into the clearing and rushed to the rangers' location. The two mages were finally able to clear a path to the spot where their teammates sat somberly. Famlin sat silently staring into Roland's lifeless eyes, and death now stared back vacantly at him. He put his head down eyes shut, shaking his head, trying to put it out of his mind. Brynd reached over and closed Roland's eyes.

"I'm too late," Reynir moaned as if in physical pain. "Damn it all to the Underworld!"

"It's no one's fault," Brynd remarked in a subdued tone. "The damn fool wanted to be a hero. We both did. He beat me to it." He lifted the body of his best friend over his shoulder and sadly carried him back to the edge of the clearing, where the group was standing. There, the trio saw another casualty of the battle.

In a six-foot-deep pit, on his back motionless, lay Medadel. Six two-foot-long spikes protruded through his chain mail. It looked as if he was killed instantly by a spike that severed his spine by entering the back of his neck. His eyes were already closed. Valtyr stood over the pit and wept. He was inconsolable.

"What good am I, Reynir, if I cannot call upon the Gods to save a friend." The priest sat dejected and looked to the heavens. "What purpose does this serve?!" he shouted.

"We are only men, brother," Reynir responded sadly. "Who are we to know the minds of the Gods, or to question their wisdom? It would be easier to count the sands of the canyon, than to know all that they do." Reynir hugged his surrogate brother around the shoulders and stood up. "We should get him out of there."

"Agreed," Kairoth said.

Brynd added numbly, "Be wary of the spikes. They are probably poisoned."

Kairoth only nodded and looped the ropes around his fellow warrior. The others worked to pull, and he lifted the body off of the stakes. It was done within a matter of moments, but no one felt any better.

Famlin spoke. "I know that no one wants to hear this, and we are not prepared to continue right at this moment, but I found a trail that leads northeast toward the peak that the druid was concerned about. I wonder if these bastards were trying to hide something? Maybe everything they've stolen over the past couple of years?"

Kairoth rebuked him sharply. "Treasure hunting is hardly the first order of business!"

Famlin responded. "I was not suggesting that. I was stating … forget it!" He spun around angrily and stormed away, beginning to leave the team.

"Where are you going now, thief?" Kairoth asked, mildly annoyed.

"I am going to scout out the path and make sure no more of these asses are lying in wait for us, if that is all right with you," Famlin leered at Kairoth indignantly.

"Fine, just be careful and report in periodically. We are going to make our way up that way within the next couple of hours. It would be good to know what the path has in store for us."

Famlin waved half-heartedly as he watched Brynd wrap both bodies in their bedrolls and drape them over one of the horses. He tethered the second horse to the first, placing the remaining gear of the fallen on the second. The young thief wiped away a tear or two, remembering Roland. He had shot him by accident on their first mission, but also came to his aid when he was later outnumbered in the village field and facing certain death. Famlin felt somewhat responsible for the loss of the men. "Sleep well, my friend, and enjoy your seat at the feast. You have earned it. I will miss your jokes."

Kairoth heard him. Wearing an angry scowl to hide the immense feeling of guilt and helplessness he now felt, the Hodan realized the cost and actual weight of leadership. Command was not for those with weak resolve.

Sal'iabac could feel his mood and crept up behind him, hugging him around the waist. "It is not your fault; it is their fault. The enemy did this, not you."

"I know," the warrior replied solemnly, "but it does not dull the sting of the loss of my men … of my friends."

After the remaining members gathered the horses, the thief returned with a report that the path was clear. The group mounted up and rode a couple of hours northeast, toward the peak of one of the mountains on the North ridge. Reynir noticed that the higher they got, the thinner the vegetation was. The remaining trees were dead, resembling husks of their former glory. Reynir quietly lamented their demise, frowning.

"What could cause the forest to leave or die this way?" the druid questioned.

As the group rounded a rocky curve, it was met by a sprinting thief who was signaling for all to stop. "There is a cave ahead. It looks like it was a natural cave at first, but something or someone has been working in there. We should go in tomorrow morning. It is too late to enter now." Famlin looked up and estimated that it was the twelfth hour of the day.

"Agreed," Kairoth said gravely. "This may the cause of the death of your trees, druid."

Reynir nodded. "Perhaps we should camp near those trees, there. They seem to be faring better than the rest. Maybe they will afford us some cover and protection?"

"No animals, so there's no worry there. I like this idea," Kairoth replied. "Cold camp in the trees. Secure the horses. Just to be sure, watches, keep a close eye on our 'passengers.' I do not want their bodies defiled by some hungry beast that wanders by in the night."

Brynd stated gravely, "I will sleep nearby them and protect their memory."

Kairoth nodded. "He would approve."

The camp was made. Indeed, it was a cold camp with no fire and a mood of loss and defeat. They had won the day, but at a steep cost. Sal'iabac made her way to Kairoth's side, attempting to comfort him as he brooded over his losses. Famlin brought wildflowers to Safiya, who held him close, appreciating that the next morning was never guaranteed. The two priests prayed late into the night, while one Hodan warrior stood the watch. It would be a long night.

Chapter 7

Valtyr opened his eyes with the rising of the sun. It was a crisp morning in the mountains, and he could see his breath as it puffed lazily from his mouth as he woke. Sitting up and rubbing his eyes, he looked around and did not recognize the terrain, nor the area surrounding the campsite. With a look of concern, he poked at Reynir, who was snoring quietly in his bedroll beside him.

"Get up," Valtyr whispered nervously. "Something strange is happening, and I cannot explain it."

Reynir rolled over, his nose barely poking over the edge of his blankets. He was not enthusiastic about leaving the warmth of his bedroll for the morning's misty cold. He looked at Valtyr with annoyance.

"What is the matter, brother?" the druid asked in a groggy voice, dozing back off.

"Wake up! I think the forest is different, or I am mad, which is entirely possible." The priest was now standing over the reluctant druid, kicking at his boot.

"Fine!" the druid said, wearily sitting up. As he opened his eyes, the same look of confusion was seen forming over his face.

"I told you that something was strange." Valtyr pointed all around the camp. A forest ring now stood where one was not standing the night before. "What does this mean, druid?"

"I think the Queen sent them. I wonder why. There is nothing up here," Reynir said, scratching the back of his head as he rolled up his bedding. He attached it to the bottom of his pack and walked out to the tree line.

The young druid bowed his head, speaking in an unknown language. Valtyr rolled his eyes and then sighed impatiently. Then the druid spoke, addressing the trees. "Hello. What brings you to this place, friends?"

The trees rustled, as if a wind blew where there was none. Reynir heard words in his mind. "Queen sends us."

"Why does Her Majesty send you?" the druid asked. "Is there a danger present?"

"Not know. Queen sends," the trees responded.

"Can you tell her that I thank her?" Reynir spoke softly, as if in reverence.

"We shall," the trees answered. The branches rustled and the conversation ended there.

"Apparently, the Queen has seen something that she does not like. Maybe she was able to witness our battle yesterday." Reynir looked at the bodies on the horses. "She treats me too well, I think." He smiled, touching the trunk of the nearest pine, and then returned to the fire, where the rest of the group was now up, eating and preparing to break camp.

"Your doing?" Kairoth asked Reynir, motioning in a circle toward the tree ring.

"No, this is far above my ability. I spoke with them. They said the Queen sends them to protect us from something. They would not elaborate." Reynir grabbed his pack.

"You 'spoke' to them?" Kairoth raised an eyebrow.

"I do that on occasion," Reynir stated, cracking a mischievous grin.

"Well, tell them to come with us and protect us. If they can move with us, they would be a great asset against whatever awaits. Too bad, they did not intervene yesterday." Kairoth shook his head with a frown, looking at the trees. "A lot of good they were then."

"I will ask them if they are willing to go," Reynir responded, looking at the trees apologetically. He turned to the nearest one and began speaking to it. As he did, there was a loud groan of wood creaking and a sharp snap. Then the trees started to go.

"Well, that didn't go as planned," Valtyr quipped.

"No, it did not. I fear that I may have overstepped. They do not respond well to anyone, but the Queen." Reynir looked up at Kairoth.

"Well, what did they say?" Kairoth asked curiously.

"They were indignant. I could feel it. Then the eldest pine yelled at me, 'You not Queen!' and then they left." Reynir shrugged. "I told you that they only work for her!"

"Oh well, it was worth a try," the Hodan leader lamented. "It's time to break camp and head to the cave mouth, the specialist ..." Kairoth looked around shaking his head. "Has anyone seen our specialist?"

There was only silence in the camp, and many people shook their heads. Kairoth rolled his eyes. "Let's go."

The camp was broken down. The King's band rode North up the path to a point where it ended by running directly into the cliff face. The road ended abruptly. Danzu's closer inspection of the road's dead-end revealed that someone had staged vegetation at the sheer stone wall, hiding a passage that was wide enough for two to pass at a time. From his vantage ahead of the group, the warrior dismounted and looked around cautiously, weapon drawn. The fellow Hodan warrior looked directly at Kairoth, communicating with hand signals.

Danzu gestured. "Hold. Trap. Enemy emplacement. Entrance detected."

Kairoth acknowledged Danzu and then held up his hand, giving the signal to stop and dismount. The party led their horses to the right side of the road and hobbled them as was the routine practice. Kairoth called for the remaining members to gather, as Danzu stood at the ready at the entrance to the underground passage.

"All right. This is some sort of passage. It may be close quarters. We must protect the mages and priests." Kairoth was serious.

The Hodan looked at Brynd, who nodded in agreement, but he was looking at the horses. The ranger missed his brother. They were most lethal when they were together. They always had each other's backs. This would be the first time he had ever gone into a situation like this without Roland. It didn't feel right, but here he was just the same.

The party moved forward quietly, forming behind where Danzu stood. The shields were put to the front, and Brynd brought up the rear. The priest was second from the back, then the mages in front of the priest, and then the druid.

Sal'iabac spoke to Kairoth. "Here, take this. It's dark in there." She handed the warrior a coin on a string.

"What do I do with this?" Kairoth asked with a perplexed look on his face.

"You say 'solus,' and there you go!" As the mage said the word, the coin illuminated like a bright lantern. Despite the bright morning sunlight, the coin blazed bright enough to be seen. "If you want to turn it off say, 'noctus.'" And the light went out. "Solus!" she repeated, and the coin again blazed with magic light. "Let's go!"

"One second," Reynir said, reaching into his pack gingerly, "Hello again, my little friend. We are on an adventure, and I may need your assistance yet!" He was talking to the small potted plant he was nursing in the camps at Empyr.

Valtyr rolled his eyes. "Why did you bring a houseplant? Are you mad?"

"You do your thing, I will do mine, brother. Do not worry about it." Then the druid tied the pot over his head like a hat, drawing a few chuckles from those who witnessed the act around him. "Laugh now."

Safiya pulled out a coin like the one Kairoth now wore and spoke the words. As they cleared the debris, a rectangular passage was detected, running off into the mountainside. The group entered two-by-two into the passageway that measured eight- or nine-feet wide with a roof of around twelve-feet. There were torch sconces on the wall at regular intervals. Some had torches in them, but none were lit.

Brynd went off to investigate. "Been a bit since these were lit, brother," he said looking at Kairoth, who nodded.

The group entered the passage cautiously, the light extending around the group in an oval, which gave them visibility of twenty-feet to the front and rear of the procession. About seventy-five-feet in, the passage took a sharp turn to the right, and the ranger signaled to Kairoth that he needed to take up the scout position. The leader agreed.

Brynd stopped and checked for footprints in the sand on the floor, noticing that those he found were not distorted or washed out by falling dust or breezes. He looked to Kairoth, making the hand signal for "Halt." He moved back to the party's position.

"Brother, the tracks ahead are either unnaturally preserved, or something is traveling these passages pretty regularly." Brynd looked around as he spoke.

"Militia or assassins?" the Hodan replied.

"Neither. They do not appear to be made by Humans, but they are most likely a bipedal creature." Brynd shrugged. "I have never seen these tracks before … but I have read stories …" Brynd looked at the floor, as if he was saying something stupid.

"What is it, man? What do you think that they are?" Valtyr interjected nervously.

"At the academy in Torith, we were shown casts of the scourge. They resemble Orc and Goblin tracks," Brynd said skeptically. "Or someone wants us to believe that they are."

"Maybe they are leftovers from the war?" Kairoth asked.

"Unlikely. That was around ten years or so ago. The rate of dust settling and general decay of the area would have obscured the tracks years ago." Brynd shook his head. "Do we risk this?" He looked to Kairoth, who had an eerie look of bloodlust on his face.

"Orcs and Goblins are potentially in the Kingdom? Of course, we risk it! It is our duty! We shall find them and kill them all, as Puryn and Orus did with their men when it was their turn." Kairoth drew his sword looking down the passageway.

"So be it," Brynd said nocking an arrow. "Let's go find out." Brynd lit one of the torches with his tinderbox and began lighting any others that he could find. "Might as well fight where we can see, eh?"

"Agreed," Kairoth said.

Sal'iabac looked at Safiya. "Here we go again," she muttered nervously, then said her words while holding onto her sister, enveloping them both in glowing blue light.

"I will be ready to do mass damage," Safiya stated calmly. "I am not toying with the idea of the scourge being down here. We are in their chosen environment. Nothing good comes from fighting them in their homes."

Safiya continued in a solemn tone. "If either of us tells you to withdraw, you had better heed our warning. We are going to rain the Underworld upon anyone who resides down here and wants to fight. It would be best that none of you were in the area of effect."

Sal'iabac chuckled. "You better listen to her, boys. She's got a special one lined up for this encounter."

The party moved as silently as possible down the passage and around a couple more turns, until Brynd called another hold. The party could plainly see a firelight up ahead and the entrance to an open room. Brynd looked into the darkness ahead of the light. He could make out several man-sized individuals, and several much larger enemies in the distance. Neither he, nor the party had not been detected yet.

The ranger crept as a Draj Scout up the passage, hugging the right wall, when he was halted by a voice that whispered to him, "Hold, brother." The voice quipped from the darkness, "Unless you wish to trigger that line, injure yourself in the process, and let those bastards know that we are here."

Brynd recognized Famlin's voice. "Would you please stop doing that!? You almost caught an arrow."

"It would not be the first time," Famlin remarked, revealing himself and moving toward the trap. "You should back up around that corner and take the rest with you … just in case I botch this. It will probably go badly for all in the vicinity. It looks like an explosive of some sort. Maybe even thunder powder." Famlin was examining the trip wire and motioning with his hand for the rest to get back. "Move!"

Feeling the wire, Famlin found another one, six-feet farther down the passageway. He traced both lines back to a spring-loaded lever attached that had an actuator, which appeared to release a flint that would strike on a steel receiver. The saboteur hoped to ignite an oily linen rag fuse, which was inserted into a small keg. Carefully, the thief wedged an iron piton into the device trigger, and then he removed the small cylindrical explosive device, moving it back toward where the party was.

"Why are you bringing that to us!?" Reynir asked nervously.

"Oh, don't worry, it's not able to blow up without fire. I removed the ignition source. The trap is disarmed now. It is safe to proceed, if you want to call proceeding to a room full of Orcs and Goblins ..." Famlin looked genuinely afraid.

"You saw them?" Brynd asked, moving a torch away from the keg.

Famlin nodded. "At least ten Goblins. Four or five Orcs. Then another chamber I could not get close enough to investigate."

"You were right, ranger," the leader nodded. "Mages, I hope that you are ready, for we are sorely outmatched on the shield wall. With two warriors down, the carnage will fall to both of you. Priests, keep them upright! Be mindful of your situation at all times, mages." Kairoth looked at Sal'iabac, who smiled back and winked at the Hodan. Safiya shook her head and smiled at Famlin. The thief bowed with his hand over his heart.

"Thief, give me that thing you disarmed. I have an idea," Brynd said with a mischievous grin. "Roland, my brother, you would tell me this was a bad idea, but to the Underworld with thinking this through, we need an edge."

Brynd removed the oil-soaked fuse from the small keg of black powder wrapping the fabric securely around an arrowhead. He tore a piece of cloth from his own tunic and sealed the fuse hole left in the keg.

"I go in first. Thief, come with me to detect any more traps." Brynd looked at Kairoth, awaiting a discussion. He got none.

"Do not take any unnecessary risks, Brynd. You have nothing to prove. We are right behind you," Kairoth remarked.

The ranger smiled widely. "I have nothing to prove? This coming from a descendant of Hodan? You never cease to amaze me, Kairoth! Are you now the group jester?" The ranger smiled.

Kairoth responded, deadpanned, "Do not blow yourself up, ass."

Brynd crept to where a sconce contained a lit torch, maybe twenty- or thirty-feet from the entrance to the room. There appeared to be some sort of a loud dispute occurring between several Goblins and one Orc within the chamber. The enemy did not see the thief and ranger approach.

"For Roland!" Brynd yelled, as he rolled the cask into the room. Immediately, the ranger lit the linen on his arrow tip with the torch on the wall. Letting the arrow fly with Elfish precision, it met its mark within two seconds of his battle cry. There was an Ert shattering explosion, as several screams filled the smoke-filled room. Then nothing. Brynd and Famlin moved forward and saw the decapitated body of one Orc and the remaining tatters of three Goblins. The room was cleared, but they were fully aware that this was far from over.

＊

Kairoth looked up the hallway in horror. The sound of the explosion left the entire party with a loud ringing in their ears. The Hodan leader could see the ranger motioning feverishly through the smoke for them to move forward. Off in the distance, the distinct growls and howls of a response team could be heard. Kairoth formed his troops.

"Move forward to the passageway on the other side of this room. We set two warriors and the priest in the front, druid and mages in the middle, and ranger, you cover the back side. Move!" Kairoth motioned for speed. The group moved as they were trained and plugged the hallway, where the enemy could be heard coming in a large group.

"I hear them coming, friend," Reynir said to his plant, taking it off of his head. Then, he pushed his way to the front. "Excuse me for a minute, warriors. I have something that I would like to try in a real battle," the druid remarked, as if he was in a laboratory at classes in Erynseere.

"Hurry up, druid! They close fast!" Danzu remarked.

Lowering his head, the druid chanted, placing his plant on the floor. Then he broke the pot and stated in a language that no one understood, "Grow strong my little friend and strangle the evil from our presence." The plant began to grow across the floor and up the walls on either side of the passageway. "Excellent!" Reynir clapped, smiling madly, as he took his position back in the center near the mages.

Sal'iabac knew the druid was up to something, but their magic was foreign to her. She watched the vines began to take hold and shrugged. "I hope they have time to take root, but in the meantime, we have something that we can use if that does not work." She looked at Safiya and grabbed a few reagents from her belt pouch.

"Here they come, sister. Luck in battle," Safiya said plainly. Sal'iabac just nodded. "Where is Famlin?" Safiya sighed shaking her head. "He's around here somewhere, and up to no good, I would imagine." She smiled.

The clamoring was interrupted by screaming. It was not Human screaming, but the screeches of an injured Goblin. Footsteps could be heard, and heavy breathing, rounding the corner toward the position of the team. Famlin appeared at a full run, and without missing a step, dropped to his side and slid under the shields and into the druid, who was knocked to the ground.

Getting up, the thief assisted the druid in standing. "Sorry!" he said to Reynir. "I got two, but then they saw me in the dark somehow. Here they come!"

"They can see in the dark! Stay in the light!" Kairoth ordered.

Then the remote clamoring became a nearby charging din of clanking armor. Swords and shields combined with growling and shrieking of the enemy. Fifteen Goblins and five Orcs charged the position where the party stood.

Kairoth shouted with command. "Stand! Lock! Repel!"

The shields were pushed backward six feet on the initial contact. Danzu lost his footing and fell over the druid, who was knocked off of his feet. Brynd and Kairoth held the front, but it would not be long before the Orcs pushed through.

Reynir rolled over and knelt. He held both hands out in front of him with his fingers open and motioned left and right, as if he were clawing at the enemy. Then he hugged the air in front of him, chanting wildly. The druid transformed into someone else, his eyes now contained a hint of red, and his little green potted friend began to respond to his call.

First, the plant grabbed at the feet of the attackers, ignoring Kairoth and Brynd, as if it knew who it was after. Next, as the enemy pushed against the two shield men, vines shot out and up the legs of the front line, tripping them and causing the next rank to be exposed. Kairoth and Brynd dispatched the three Goblins behind the two Orcs, who were now on the ground wrapped in vines, which had begun to squeeze the life out of them.

Kairoth looked down at them in horror. "You like this, don't you druid? The squeezing thing?"

"Oh yes. Nature is a devastating force if used correctly. I am nothing compared to my Mistress. She can destroy entire cities." Reynir said these words with a hint of pride and admiration. He smiled at the Hodan's discomfort. "I can stop if you wish!"

"No, no, excellent use of your skills." Kairoth looked at the now-dead Orcs, as he prepared to engage another twelve Goblins who had now formed a three-man front, four-deep. They had three archers and a couple of spears, and more shields than the group. Kairoth was concerned.

The Goblins advanced, stopping on the opposite side of the now-dead Orcs. The archers let loose with a volley of arrows, all of which hit their marks. Reynir was hit in the lower left side of his abdomen. Sal'iabac caught a bolt in her right thigh, and Kairoth was hit in his shield side shoulder. He was holding the shield up by sheer force of will, when the enemy attacked with spears. Danzu was hit in his left side, and then his right. He went down, bleeding profusely from both wounds.

"Mages! Do something now! If you do not, we perish!" Kairoth said, gritting his teeth and holding up his shield.

Sal'iabac rose gingerly, leaning on her sister. Then the two nodded and began their response. Chanting ancient words in the tongues of the mages, Sal'iabac held a fist before her. Her hair stood floating around her.

"Die," she said emphatically, as she opened her hand, looking down range at the hall full of Goblins.

Lightning streamed out of her hands with a loud arcing sound. A loud pop and then a zap sounded! Then half of the room fell to the floor in a smoking pile of clothes and leathery carcasses. Sal'iabac fell to the sitting position and tapped her sister on the backside.

"Your turn!" she said in an eerily buzzing voice.

Safiya grinned wickedly, and she held out a similar fist. The Goblins, seeing the scene unfold for the second time, decided this time to turn to run, but it was too late. The electric current left Safiya's fingertips and impacted another five Goblins. Two remained, and they were stumbling around, looking for a way to escape.

"Go!!!" Kairoth shouted angrily, as he charged, shoving one Goblin to the ground and shoving his blade into the vermin's throat. Kairoth sneered, twisting his sword as he withdrew it. The Goblin's lifeless body remained motionless beneath him.

Brynd released two arrows, dropping the last one, twenty feet down the hallway. Famlin quickly ran ahead.

"My turn," he whispered, disappearing into the darkness.

Kairoth panned around the room, looking for additional threats. There were none. He looked at the dead Goblins and Orcs before him. Then it set in that the Offlanders were still on the Ert. Maradwynne hadn't killed them all off as effectively as the legends had portrayed. Pondering the gravity of his discovery, he noticed the extent of the party's injuries.

"Priest, can you save him?" Kairoth asked, as he looked at the unconscious Danzu, who was pale and breathing shallow breaths.

"I think so, boss," Valtyr said, bandaging the wounds and stopping the bleeding. Then he prayed. The priest's rituals seemed to be working. Valtyr turned to Reynir's injuries. The druid waved him off and directed him to Sal'iabac. Valtyr attended to her, removing the arrow from her leg and healing her the best that he was able, outside of the temple. Sal'iabac thanked him and was able to walk on her own, but with some discomfort.

Reynir removed his own arrow, much to Kairoth's surprise. Then the druid said a prayer, chanting in a strange tongue, and his wounds closed immediately. "Let me look at that, Kairoth," Reynir said exhausted.

"Are you sure that you are up to it?" the Hodan leader remarked, looking at the state of his druid.

"I am just a bit tired from combat and injury. I can do this." Chanting again, the druid removed the Hodan leader's arrow from his shoulder and healed him the same way he had healed himself. "I think, with that, I am done for the day. I am able to serve as a warrior now. I have no energy left to cast."

"Understood," Kairoth responded. "Thank you … and you were most impressive with your plant. I apologize for insulting you earlier."

"It is nothing! I only wish to serve the Goddess in word and deed. So far, so good!" Reynir looked like his old self for a moment and then became a bit more serious. "I think that we should wait for the report of the specialist. We need to rest a bit before we do anything else."

"I agree. Everyone, find a place to sit and rest. We wait for the thief's return." Kairoth looked at the ranger. "Please take the watch, brother. I am in no condition at the moment."

"My honor to," Brynd responded. "Rest well."

* * *

It had been an hour since he had left the party. Famlin found himself spying on another room. This one was much larger than the one that the party occupied. Within this room were robed Humans, at least he thought that they resembled Humans. As one prepared to sacrifice a young half-Elfish woman, he dropped his hood, revealing a light-skinned individual with tattoos all over his skin. The others looked similar with slightly different patterns imprinted on them. They appeared to the untrained eye to be some sort of writing or runes.

Famlin had a problem. There were five of them and one of him, and they were preparing to kill a half-Elf woman. He was not sure of what to do. The only thing he could come up with was distracting them from their task, and then run back to where the party would be waiting. It was her only hope, and in his estimation, his also.

"Hey! Suden toad!" the thief cried out, stepping into plain sight while simultaneously delivering three throwing knives into the enemy priest, who was handing a sacrificial dagger to what Famlin assumed was some sort of head priest. The acolyte fell where he stood and the blade skittered across the floor, out of reach of the clergy for the moment. Famlin made several profane gestures as he turned to go, and then they came after him. He raced toward his friends, shouting loudly.

* * *

Brynd was the first to hear the commotion. Off just out of light's reach, he listened to a shout and then many voices shouting as one clarion call rang out from around the corner. It was undoubtedly the specialist. He had been discovered.

"What an idiot," Brynd muttered, hearing the cries for help getting closer and closer. "Kairoth. Idiot arriving in twenty seconds."

Kairoth sprang to his feet and grabbed his shield, scowling with a bit of pain, but the shoulder felt much better than it had. He drew his sword and prepared to receive the enemy. Danzu was still down, but breathing. Valtyr stood to help, but Kairoth dismissed the idea.

"Stay with him. He needs you more. There will be three of us on them. Sal'ia, do you have one more in you?" Kairoth looked over at the mage who nodded, but looked exhausted. She stood.

Reynir stood, grabbing his wooden shield and cudgel. He joined Brynd near the entrance. "What are you up to, druid? You are not suited for this type of combat!" Brynd shook his head and raised an eyebrow.

"You would not know what I've been trained to do, ranger. Worry about yourself." Reynir turned toward the oncoming sounds of running and shouting.

Brynd could see the thief as he nimbly rounded the corner with four assailants in tow. The robed figures were fast and strong, and they were gaining on him.

Brynd responded quickly, delivering two arrows, but the Human kept coming. He hit him two more times. Still, he came. Finally, with the sixth arrow, the enemy fell, but he still lived on the ground. He was muttering to himself.

"None of that! That will not do," Reynir replied in Elfish, smashing the enemy's mouth in with a blow from his cudgel. "He is a priest. He was trying to heal himself. I could feel his energy. It is not something I would like to feel again. He is of the Underlord. Todessen I believe they were called in my teachings. Bastards. Excellent in combat as warriors, but also known to be effective mages and clerics on occasion."

Kairoth was engaged with two of the enemy when a third arrived. Famlin stepped around to the third assailant's back, jamming a dagger in-between his ribs on the left side. The Todessen attacker remained upright and turned, cracking the thief across the jaw with a black, wooden staff. Famlin staggered and fought to regain his balance, when the Todessen struck again, this time knocking the thief unconscious.

Safiya, from her seat across the room, saw the exchange between the assailant and her love interest. She was not amused. Angrily, she uttered words unknown to anyone but her sister. The mage pointed at the attacker and unleashed several bolts of energy into his back, finishing him off. Safiya immediately fell to the ground and then passed out from exhaustion. Valtyr checked her for injuries, but determined that she had just spent all of her energy on the enemy and needed to rest. She had pushed herself to the limit, but was physically unhurt. The priest knew mages required sleep after using so much of their energy manipulating the elements and using magic. He made her comfortable and went back to watching over Danzu, who hadn't stirred in hours.

Kairoth let loose with a battle cry that made one of the Todessen look at the group and try to run. Brynd fixed that with two arrows to the Todessen's legs, crippling him. Then he drilled the enemy right between his eyes. Turning around, Brynd could see that Kairoth had overpowered his opponent, and was sitting on top of the wounded, but very much alive, new captive.

"Who are you? You're a toad, aren't you? A real one in the flesh! How is that possible?" Kairoth was not himself. No one knew exactly what his problem was, but he was thoroughly enraged, and no one dared to question him.

"I am a servant of the true God. We shall see his glory reign upon this Ert. You will all die in darkness and fire." The enemy spat blood from his mouth. "It has begun. It is too late for all of you now!"

Kairoth punched the enemy in the face with a gauntlet, opening up yet another wound under the tattooed man's eyes. "Of what do you speak, Toad? I will beat it out of you. Murdering scum!"

Kairoth began to mercilessly beat the Todessen man. When he was done, the warrior looked like a crazed berserker of old. His enemy's skull was crushed. Bone, blood, and brain matter, was spattered all over the Hodan warrior's hands and armor. Realizing what he looked like, Kairoth took a deep breath, stood and then began walking to where the thief had run from.

"Follow him!" shouted Sal'iabac. "Where is he going?"

Reynir, Valtyr, and Sal'iabac made their way to the large room at the end of the passageway. There, the four team members saw the horror of Haeldrun for what it was.

The room was a sacrificial chamber to the Underlord, who according to the books of lore, created the Todessen, Orc, and Goblin races on a distant world, called the Wargyrn. Haeldrun was Haya's betrothed, but when circumstances changed in the heavens, there was a rift created between the two Gods. Haya chose the light. Haeldrun left Aeternum and his family, descending into the Darkness, where he established the Underworld and all that dwells within it.

Valtyr looked around. He figured that the Todessen priests sought to appease their God and get back in his good graces. To do that, he determined that they had resorted to sacrificing people who they captured during night raids of the surrounding villages. Reynir heard weeping, and ran to the altar, where a young half-Elf woman laid half bare and crying.

She was wearing the standard of Yslandeth.

"Let me get that for you," the druid said quietly removing her restraints. To his surprise, she sprang up from the altar, sobbing, and hugged him around the neck. She could not stop shaking.

"Thank you for coming when you did! I was done for. Those bastards killed scores of people here." The half-Elf woman looked up at Sal'iabac with tears streaming down her face. Sal'iabac was getting ready to investigate a vat to the side of the worship area. "Don't look in … too late." The half-Elf recoiled.

Sal'iabac looked into the large container. It held the waste from the ritual murder of the victims. Within it, she found the carved up remains of an untold number of residents of the Ert. Some were Elfish, some were Human, and some were Dwarf. In the middle of all of that carnage were those of mixed races. Sal'iabac swooned, turning green, and then spun around quickly, throwing up violently.

"Who could do this?" The mage was shaken.

"The ultimate evil," the rescued half-Elf stated, as a matter of fact. "Come, let us release the rest."

"The rest?" Reynir asked in disbelief.

"My name is Draj Laerwen Mithraita. My unit was sent here by the King and Queen a couple of weeks ago. Those bastards had many more up here. We culled the herd nicely before we were surrounded and captured. They killed everyone I ever knew, right in front of my eyes. I am the last of my unit. I must return to the Queen and warn her of the evil here. It seeks to destroy the light. She must do something!"

"One thing at a time, Laerwen. We should release the captives, get you all some food and water, and get out of this pit of evil," Reynir replied.

"Agreed. This way." The half-Elf gestured to an iron-barred entrance.

"Kairoth, your assistance, please. Brynd?" Reynir asked, as he attempted to break the bars, which were locked in place by chains and a large lock.

Kairoth grabbed a bar and began working it until it spun, breaking loose. Brynd did similarly and was able to remove another bar. Soon, between the two of them, an opening big enough for a large person to pass through was created. The half-Elf called out in Elfish. That is when they came forward.

They were terrified, dirty, and malnourished. Some looked as if they had been in captivity for over a month. Others looked as if they had just arrived. All of them cried out, thanking the heroes for their rescue. Kairoth sat quietly, still covered in the remains of the enemy, trying to understand who he was up against. These were an enemy who had no regard for the life of man, woman or child. He would not abide them to live if he found them again.

"Can everyone walk? It will be a long journey back to Hero's Pass. Are any of you from there?" Most nodded yes. Kairoth counted ten head alive, but remembered the number of Hero's Pass missing to be near thirty. The warrior looked at the severed limbs in the vat that Sal'iabac has investigated. "Set this place on fire and let us leave this unholy pit."

Reynir and Valtyr desecrated the sanctuary to Haeldrun, by praying and consecrating the location as a holy place of Haya. The pair took the Todessen priest's oil and spread it on anything that would burn. As they left, Valtyr dropped a lit torch in the pit of body parts and walked out solemnly.

* * *

Kairoth picked up Danzu and carried him out of the underground lair. Brynd carried Famlin, and Valtyr carefully moved Safiya. When back on the surface, they realized that it was the dark. The captives cheered as they saw the stars above them. It was cold, and many did not have the proper clothing to be out in the weather, but no one appeared to care.

Kairoth planned quietly then asked, "Reynir, can you ASK the trees nicely if they wouldn't mind doing a perimeter like they did the other day? We can create a large fire in the center, and the captives sleep close by to it." The leader looked to the ranger. "Are the horses still there?"

Brynd gave Kairoth a thumbs-up, confirming that the equipment and all of the horses were still where they left them. Then the ranger herded all of the survivors over to the campsite and set a massive fire to keep their new charges warm throughout the night. The druid went about trying to contact the trees. He saw a large pine on the edge of the road.

Approaching the tree, the druid said his prayer and then spoke. "Friend, would you protect us this night? We have many who suffered due to the evil under the mountain. We have destroyed them, but now the innocent must survive the night's cold."

The tree groaned angrily. "You NOT Queen."

"I am not, but I am one of her students, Pine!" Reynir squinted angrily at the tree.

"I ask Queen," the tree responded.

"You do that," Reynir responded in an irritated tone. "Tell her that Reynir requires assistance. She will know me."

A few moments later, the tree responded. "She say yes. I tell others. She tell, 'Good job, Reynir.'"

Reynir turned to thank the tree, but it was gone. "How do they do that?" the druid muttered, returning to the camp. "Kairoth, after a bit of convincing, the trees agree to set a perimeter."

"Oh, thank the Gods. Good job, druid. Everyone, heal up, repair, and maintain your gear. Please, share your rations with the new folks if you have any. Some look as if they haven't seen food for several days. Everyone get some sleep. We ride out toward Hero's Pass early tomorrow morning."

* * *

Three days later, a village guard at Hero's Pass challenged an incoming crowd of people, as the mob, surrounded by several beaten warriors arrived at his checkpoint. He recognized his own daughter among the group, shouting with exuberance, a fist to the sky. Dropping his spear, he ran to her and hoisted her tiny frame up in a wild embrace. Both stood crying loudly with fierce emotion.

The Hodan leader glanced over to the two bedrolls on the second horse. This victory had not come without a price. He took some solace in the reunion he saw taking place in front of him. He waited for them to calm and then addressed the sentries on duty.

"Guard, tell the village elder that I bring ten back from the abyss. I fear the others perished before we could arrive. We too have lost friends in this battle and wish to send them off to Aeternum on their own pyre, as our ancestors dictated that we do. Will your village help us?" Kairoth looked at the bedrolls as fresh guilt in filled his heart.

"Of course, we will honor your fallen, heroes! We would not have it any other way!" The guard whistled, and the group was escorted by a few young spearmen into the village. When they arrived at the inn, the older half-Elf woman wept openly for the losses of the group. She welcomed her friends into her inn and gave them food and drink to their fill.

After a hot bath and washing their clothes, the travelers maintained their equipment. Later, the village gathered for the funeral of two who had bled so that others could live.

Brynd placed Roland on his pyre. With the ranger's body, he set his brother's Dwarfish blade, Elfish bow, a sack of gold coins and a mug filled with mead. Then the ranger doused the wood in oil and stepped back for a moment, before lighting the pyre of his best friend.

His voice cracking and a tear in his eye, Brynd declared, "Roland, my brother, you are a hero, and I send you to the Goddess as we promised each other that we would do. I will join you at the table in Aeternum. You once feared you were not good enough to enter, but you were mistaken. You are the best man whom I have ever known. May your soul be ever comforted within the light's rays, and may your cup be never emptied. Until we meet again, my dearest friend." Stepping back, Brynd threw his torch in the stack of wood, as silently his tears ran. No one had a word to say. All quietly bowed and paid their respects, preparing to do the same for Medadel, the fallen warrior.

Kairoth and Danzu placed Medadel upon his pyre in his armor, with a sword, shield, bag of gold coins, and a tankard of ale, which was the Yslan warrior's favorite. Kairoth spoke as the torch was lit. "No tears should be shed for the courageous. No wailing should be heard for one of honor, who saves innocents from those who would do them harm. Yslandeth goes before me unto Aeternum to join the heroes of old. Medadel will sit in his place of honor while we still seek to prove our worth. May we meet again, brother. May your soul be ever comforted within the light's rays and may your cup be never emptied. Until we meet again." Valtyr lit the second pyre and prayed for both of the departed souls.

That night, a strange celebration broke out at Hero's Pass. It was one of elation for those who regained their lost loved ones, but also a night of remembering lost friends and heroes. The King's specialists were emotionally and physically spent. One by one, they made their ways back to the inn.

"Sleep well, friends, for tomorrow we must ride toward Empyr and report our finding to Master Donick, or maybe directly to the King. Either way, it is imperative that we depart early. I am honored to serve with each and every one of you." The Hodan leader bowed solemnly.

Kairoth kissed Sal'iabac openly, and not to be outdone, Famlin kissed Safiya to her surprise. Neither couple cared about protocols or decorum. They were grateful to be alive and would enjoy the night with the person of their desire.

"Reynir, what is she here for?" Kairoth asked smiling at the druid.

Over in the corner, attempting to gain some privacy in the open room, was the druid and the half-Elf Draj, Laerwen. She looked up at the Hodan warrior, lifting one eyebrow.

"What is it to you, Hodan? I am an adult, and so is he. We do what we wish … as do you, do you not?" She smiled, laughing, and turned back to Reynir. Brushing away his long hair away from his face, "Now, where were we?"

Chapter 8

Puryn sat haggard, his head pounding from the excessive amount of mead that he had consumed the night before. Donick sat across the war room table and verified that the King was not mad. The returning specialist team had, in fact, reported living, breathing, and operating Offlander forces within the borders of Yslandeth.

The King did not take the news well. In public, he maintained his composure, but alone, when he sat by his hearth, it was a different story. Puryn downed several bottles of mead in succession, while his memory replayed the carnage of those dark days, and the hopelessness that he felt as he saw the black mass approaching his hill.

The King's mind meandered through the wreckage of his recollections. Puryn had purposely ignored the memories and the flashbacks to put forth an image of strength to his people, but at times, his dreams would get the best of him. Adasser would wake during those episodes and see the looks of anger and barbarity, as they flashed over her beloved's face. She noted that he never seemed to show fear, even in his dreams, only hatred and malice, as he shouted obscenities toward the enemy. These actions prompted the Queen, in these moments, to move beyond her beloved's reach, "just in case."

The Queen knew that something was not right with her husband. He was curt and distant. The elms who communicated between them, relayed a sense of worry about the King to their Queen. Puryn had told her to stay in Erynseere and not to worry about him, but she wasn't about to listen. Using the fact that Illari was at the Monastery, and that she had not seen him in some time, the Priestess departed for Empyr with a guard detachment, arriving two days after Kairoth and the party had given their report. The Queen knew that something was amiss. She headed for the war room, where she knew that her beloved would inevitably be.

"They were found in the Raven's Pass, in a cave?" Puryn asked again.

"Yes, Your Majesty. The scout team states there was a band of Offlanders in a cave complex. They had captured Yslan citizens and were sacrificing them to the Underlord to appease him, according to reports." Donick grimaced at the thought.

"This is a major problem. We cannot let the public know about this. It must be dealt with swiftly and silently, brother. So much fear is about already! Adding Offlander stragglers to the mix would cause chaos. Gods know that we have enough already." Puryn swallowed the last of his mead and called for more.

"Husband! It is but the third hour of the morning! How much have you had already?" Adasser remarked, entering the war room.

Donick rose immediately. "Good morning, Your Majesty. How are you this day?"

Puryn was surprised to see his lady standing there and shook his head at the porter, trying to shoo him away without Adasser's knowledge. The Queen sighed and then raised an eyebrow. The porter left quickly.

"My Love, why did you come? We are fine. We have got a handle on this situation." Puryn stood and pulled out the Queen's chair. She sat.

"Husband, there are only two instances when I see you drunk before noon. One involves brawling with your idiot friend Orus over your 'wager,' and the other is when something is troubling you. I do NOT see Orus anywhere. Where is he? You and he appear to be joined at the hip these days?"

"My Dearest, I have told you of the Offlander remnant that I have just been apprised of, but there was another development overnight." Puryn leaned over his board and reached toward Edenyag. There, he removed a Hodan unit marker and placed an Eden marker in its place.

Adasser squinted, her brow wrinkled in a question. "What are you saying, husband? What has happened?"

"King Cathir of Edenyag asked me to remove Hodan from its borders. I refused. He removed them himself. Orus asked me for Alliance troops to retaliate against the aggression. After much consideration, and with these reports, I declined to support him with Yslan troops." Puryn went to sip his mead, but frustrated by the empty cup, he set it down on the table and sighed.

The porter reappeared in the doorway. The servant looked at the Queen for approval before entering. Puryn shook his head. Adasser had a look of annoyance on her face, but called the porter in. He refilled the King's tankard and brought the Queen a cup of tea, then he departed the room once again.

"And? What happened?" Adasser pursed her lips, already knowing the answer.

"Well, Orus took it as a slight. The decision strained our friendship in a major way. He made excuses, but I know that he is angry with me. I feared that he may go after Edenyag on his own, so I warned him not to attack a Northern Alliance member. Cathir has agreed to pay reparations to Orus. This will allow Hodan to save face, but Orus will not forget Cathir's aggression, nor my betrayal. I fear our Alliance is a dying dream. He left 'to handle Hodan business' this morning. I am surprised that you did not encounter him on the road." Puryn downed another tankard. The porter appeared, as if from an Elfish spell of hiding, and poured more mead, scurrying away as quickly as he had appeared. Adasser glared at the servant.

"Orus will come to his senses," Adasser asserted.

Puryn chuckled. "You do know the man, my lady?"

Adasser smiled wryly. "Well, I can hope and pray to the Goddess for peace!"

"We may need those prayers yet. I have to form a team to journey to Cinnog. If I can at least gain control of one front of this mess, maybe we can gain a foothold and push the peace! At this point, Suden, Hodan, Cinnog, and Eden are nipping at my heels. I need to quell the unrest. If our team can reach the true heir in Cinnog and offer a pact and support from Yslandeth, maybe we can establish a friendly regime to the southwest." Puryn sipped his mead, under a judgmental stare from his wife.

"Your Majesties, I suggest that we use a veteran team for that mission. One with 'skills,' vice a green unit." Donick sipped his tea, looking at Puryn.

"Who do you suggest, my friend?" the King replied already knowing.

"That Kairoth lad, and his band. They are impressive. They dispatched the Red-Hand militia almost single-handedly, and they took on a band of Offlanders without support." The Master nodded. He was genuinely impressed that the scouts had survived.

"Donick, they lost two in the woods. Kairoth is Hodan, perhaps his allegiances will take him home? I am not against the suggestion, but will they recover from their losses? We could augment them with more warriors." The King finished his drink. "Yes, My Dear! Fine, I'm done!" Puryn looked at his wife's raised eyebrows and shrugged.

"I suggest that we leave them as they are, Your Majesty. To introduce new unknowns to their team may or may not cause them to be less effective. They have bonded as a unit. New people would not help their cohesion." The Master waited for the King's response, finishing his tea.

"You may be right, but damn it to the Underworld, Donick, I have stood where that boy stands now." The King angrily punched the table, scattering pieces around the war map. "I saw it in his eyes. It is never easy to hold your friends in your arms as the light leaves their eyes." The King was strangely distant as he spoke. "There is no comfort in lighting the pyres. Aeternum or not, these losses should never be taken lightly." Puryn's eyes had reddened. Adasser held his hand tightly.

"I understand, my old friend," Donick spoke. "I will inform them that they will be the choice, if that is your wish. If not, we will find another team."

"No, we shall deploy them again. They appear to be the best that we have. Were there any kin to the two who were killed?" The King stood up, kissing his lady's hand.

"No, Your Majesty, there were not. Both were war orphans. They were the last of their lines." Donick stood.

"Increase the wages of this team. Equip them with the finest armor and weapons available. I want them to come back, Donick … all of them." The King bowed slightly to his friend.

"I will make it so, my friend. Be well." Donick rose and left the room, leaving the King and Queen alone for the first time since Adasser had arrived.

"It is not your fault, husband," she stated, as a matter of fact, brushing the graying locks from his face and kissing him.

A distant tired look washed over the King, "But it is, My Love. Everything that happens in this Kingdom is my responsibility, down to the deaths of the individual soldier."

* * *

Kairoth was alone with his pay at a place known to the locals as the Red Horse Tavern and Inn. Sal'iabac had come with him, but she had decided to leave after looking around at the decorum and clientele. Kairoth was in a mood, and Sal'iabac did not like the tone or direction his behavior was headed in. She knew that something was about to give. The Hodan was not abusive toward her, but he was not enjoyable company either. She kissed him goodnight, as she warned an amorous barfly to keep his distance while she exited the tavern. Kairoth watched her go.

"Better leave that one alone, gentlemen." Kairoth laughed.

"What if I don't?" barked a young Human warrior, a year or two younger than he.

"You don't have to worry about me. Worry about her." Kairoth called for another bottle. He sat with his back to the wall and watched the crowd, as fight after fight broke out.

A couple of grizzled old men sat in the corner, watching the young peacocks, some in armor, others in cloth, posturing for dominance in an incessant circle of testosterone and alcohol. They both noticed the Hodan warrior, looking at Kairoth. One with several scars on his face saw the Hodan's expression and vacant stare. He watched as the boy drank his mead, sipping with purpose and glancing with a brooding glare toward anyone who fared too close to his table.

The old man nodded, then said to his friend, "That one has seen action."

"Which?" the other warrior asked, trying not to look directly in Kairoth's direction.

"The bigger one. I think he's Hodan. He's been through it. He has the 'look.'"

"Poor bastard. He's too young. Wonder what he's been up to?" He reached into his pocket and set a small gold coin on the table. A passerby looked at it with a covetous glance. The old man drew a sword six inches out of its scabbard. "Don't think about it." The admirer left quickly.

The other man pulled out a gold coin and added a second. "I'll give you two to one if anyone beats the Hodan."

The other man looked around the room. "Three to one."

"Fine, three to one. But the Hodan has to be carried out of here."

"Agreed."

The two men watched Kairoth with interest, as the Hodan slowly became more and more inebriated. Soon, the young Hodan warrior was on his way to a good hangover, and many of the crowd began to annoy him much. The Hodan scowled as he sipped his mead. He made eye contact with those who continued to work the room, in feeble attempts to assert some sort of dominance over the other patrons. Many were untested warriors from the regulars, with big mouths and little paychecks. Kairoth was not amused. He was starting to get angry.

"What are you looking at, dog?" one young soldier in mail taunted. "You better keep your gaze to yourself, Suden."

Kairoth did not identify himself as a King's man. He just smiled at the younger warrior, saying, "Big words from a warrior whose only triumph appears to be guarding the eating hall."

"What did you say?" The younger man approached.

The two older men sat up, their interest now peaked, exchanging coins and shaking hands.

"I said that I know women with more between their legs than you possess." Kairoth stood and sneered at the now quickly approaching band of four warriors.

"I'll stomp your mouth shut, toad," the warrior insulted.

Kairoth was now visibly agitated. He kicked his chair away from him, assuming a fighting stance, as he was surrounded.

"Five to one if he gets out of this one without being carried out," the bookmaker said to the other warrior.

"I will put five against the Hodan, but it's a fool's bet. He's going to kill these fools," the bettor responded confidently. "You had better have the twenty-five on you, Nyr, just in case they get lucky."

"Oh, I have it. Don't you worry," Nyr responded, showing the bettor his purse. He accepted the wager as the fight began.

One warrior grabbed Kairoth from behind. The Hodan warrior widened his stance, sliding down in the bear hug and putting the attacker off balance. Stepping backward, he grabbed low at the young warrior's belt and turned expertly, hip throwing the fool to the floor. Kairoth kicked him squarely in the mouth. The warrior's face burst into a crimson color, and the young man fell unconscious immediately. Three to go.

The mouthy one to the front of Kairoth, seeing his comrade fall so easily, swung at Kairoth, hitting him in the face with a gauntlet. This opened a small gash below the Hodan's left eye and staggered him for a second. The other two jumped on him immediately. That's when the Underworld was unleashed.

"Women. You fight four on one. You have no honor," Kairoth said, as he was kicked in the solar plexus by the one with the mouth. He let out a grunt and then went to work.

The Hodan kicked the man in front of him hard in the groin. The young man fell to his knees wheezing, and without hesitation, the Hodan kicked him again, this time in the face. The two holding Kairoth's arms attempted to take him to the ground and subdue him there, but that did not work out for them, as the Hodan warrior kicked out the knee of the man to the left, sending him crashing over a table, screaming in pain, grabbing his knee. One left. Kairoth turned to face his last attacker, who was backing away slowly with his hands up.

"Am I supposed to show you quarter now? Do you think that is fair?" Kairoth was now towering over the younger man, who was looking for a place to run.

"I was only helping my friends out. I don't want any trouble." The young warrior drew his sword.

Kairoth stepped inside of the blade arc, locking the arm of the attacker and turning his arm over in an arm-bar. From that position, he completed his execution of the move. The two bettors heard an audible pop, and the young attacker went to one knee. Kairoth had the attacker's sword leveled at the young Yslan warrior's throat.

"Please don't kill me!" the Yslan warrior pleaded.

"If you draw the blade, you had better be ready to use it, lad." Kairoth glared at the younger man.

The bar was silently watching the scene. Kairoth looked up, then stuck the sword into the wooden floorboards. He dropped the Yslan warrior. "You have that arm looked at by a good priest. Soon."

"Pay up," the bookmaker said. Grudgingly, the other man handed over the coins.

Kairoth sat back down at his table and continued drinking his mead. Very soon after the fight was over, a guard detachment arrived at the bar. The barkeep pointed at the Hodan warrior, and the guard approached Kairoth.

"Did you assault the King's men?" the guard asked.

"Only the ones who started it," responded the Hodan.

"You are under arrest," the guard asserted.

"I am? Think again." Kairoth produced the favor of the King.

"What in the … oh, you are one of 'those' people," the guard said and looked around carefully. "Put it away, and leave the establishment. The keeper wishes you to go. You are hurting business and injuring the patrons."

"The mead is watered down anyways," Kairoth lamented, knocking his half-empty tankard to the floor. He walked to the bar and slammed a gold coin down. "For your troubles, Sir."

The barkeep picked up the coin and nodded, stepping back warily. Kairoth smiled sarcastically at the man's sheepish expression and then walked away peacefully. He departed the tavern and headed back to the tent city where he would spend the rest of his night alone. He was sure that Sal'iabac would have nothing to do with him. He was covered in blood and smelled like a brewery. He would catch up with the rest of the party tomorrow morning after he slept it off.

* * *

The morning was gray, and it has drizzled overnight. Puryn had sent for the scout team. Heralds were sent out to the usual places that soldiers go to blow off steam. Within an hour or two, all of the group, except the druid, was assembled at the antechamber to the makeshift throne room adjacent to the war room, where Puryn spent so much of his time these days. All of the team was in their best attire, except for Kairoth, who arrived a bit disheveled and, in the clothing he had slept in. The heralds had not found him until the last minute, because no one in the team had suspected that Kairoth had taken a cot in the general troop quarters. They figured he may have staggered in there drunk by force of habit.

The team was called into the throne room. All of them bowed respectfully. All were surprised that the Queen was present, not knowing that she had arrived the day prior. Puryn addressed the group with a motivational tone. He looked better to her, but Adasser looked closer, trying to determine if he was indeed better, or just putting on his strong façade for the visiting troops.

The King addressed the team. "Good morning, heroes! I am glad to see that you still walk the Ert. I was saddened to hear of the passing of two of your number. They will be sorely missed, and I know that the loss of comrades is never easy." Puryn looked directly at Kairoth. The King recognized the look on his face. Adasser told Puryn when he wore it. Now, he could see what she was talking about. It was an angry, vacant look, intermingled with a lust for revenge. This man wanted payback.

"As you all know, the world is a dangerous place, as of late. I do not need to tell this to all of you. Because of your reports, we are forming elite teams to search out and destroy any Offlander remnants as we find them. Please, be seated." They all sat in chairs around the thrones.

Kairoth nodded with approval. Puryn smiled. He liked this boy.

Adasser whispered in Elfish. "Are you sure that you did not father any children who I do not know about, while in Hodan?" She smiled coyly at Puryn's look of shock. "He reminds me of someone who I used to know." Puryn relaxed and sighed, shaking his head at his wife's joke.

"Not funny, My Lady," the King responded in kind.

Sal'iabac snickered, hearing the remark, as did Safiya. Adasser's eyes widened, realizing that they understood her. Then the King changed the subject quickly.

"I called you all here to explain your importance. At this time, as you know, several hundred of your types are operating throughout the Ert. Through reconnaissance and scouting, we have determined that we have too many dynamic forces on our borders. Hodan has decided to focus on internal affairs for the moment. Edenyag has, for the first time in their history, successfully routed a Hodan Legion and liberated their lands." The King stopped to see Kairoth's reaction. There was none.

"Are the Hodan a threat to Yslandeth again, Your Majesty?" Famlin asked.

"I do not think so. King Orus is still my brother, and I will trust him to do the right thing." Danzu nodded in approval of the King's words. Kairoth stood stoically.

"Your Majesty, what would you have us do?" Kairoth asked calmly.

Puryn looked at the lad in wonder. Adasser smiled nodding. "Was she beautiful?" the Queen quipped in Elfish.

Sal'iabac and Safiya broke out in laughter, then cleared their throats and composed themselves. Kairoth looked at the women seriously, as they twittered a bit, whispering among themselves. The Queen smiled as she recognized Reynir as he entered the room, late as usual.

"Nice of you to join the party, apprentice!" the Queen said sarcastically.

Bowing, wide-eyed as a child whose hand was found in the cookie jar, Reynir sheepishly looked up at his Mistress. "Sorry, Your Majesty, I needed to find a new 'friend' for my journeys. Sadly, the other perished, but fought valiantly." The druid held up a newly potted plant.

"A wise choice, very viney!" The Queen smiled. "Come here, boy!" The Queen hugged her apprentice. She responded to him in a language only the two appeared to know. "You must be careful, young one. Do not imperil your life unnecessarily. I have come to like you!"

"I would never do anything without a purpose, My Queen. I will strive to live and return to our studies!" Reynir beamed at his teacher's kind words, and then bowed, returning to the group.

"I will have words with you afterward, druid," the Queen ordered. Reynir bowed in recognition.

"I am sorry, husband. What were you saying, My Love?" The Queen turned to Puryn.

"There is no offense, My Lady. Kairoth, you and your team have impressed Master Donick on every level. He and I have concluded that your team is the most qualified to lead a scout and diplomatic mission to Cinnog. I need your team to locate a Prince Basric and his militia, and deliver our peace proposal. We wish to back his bid for the Kingdom of Cinnog. If he finds this acceptable, we will need you to return with his mark on this Alliance treaty. It is imperative that you go in covertly. The militia are known to kill or deport foreigners, and several rival factions are operating in the northern region of Cinnog. We believe Basric to be in the North or northwest of Cinnog."

"We will find him and deliver your offer, My King," Kairoth replied bowing.

"I know that you will. I have the utmost confidence in your band. You are by far the best team we have produced to date. Be careful, teams like yours do not fall from the sky." The King smiled. "Donick."

Master Donick rose. "All of you will report here tomorrow morning for equipment issue and to receive the scroll for delivery. Your cover is that you are Cinnog residents from the South who are trying to escape the violence. You traveled North from the Citadel's ruins. We will give you specifics about the region so you can answer political questions without arousing suspicion. All rise!" The room stood.

Puryn looked directly at Kairoth, locking eyes with the young man.

"We will talk again tomorrow. Stay out of trouble tonight, Hodan, if you can! I heard that four of my warriors are in the healing tents for at least two weeks." The King looked at Kairoth, whose eyes widened. He was caught. Sal'iabac glared at the Hodan, who pretended not to notice. He knew he was in for it later.

"Yes, Your Majesty," Kairoth responded to the King.

Adasser addressed Reynir. "You will be approached by two new friends on the road. They are your responsibility. You had better treat them as if they were your own children. They are very dear to me."

Confused, the druid responded, "I will be on my lookout, Your Majesty. What do they look like? Do they have names?"

"You will know them when you meet them, my apprentice. Be well and stay safe!" Adasser smiled as she and Puryn left the chamber.

After the door closed behind the monarchs, Sal'iabac looked at Kairoth with judging eyes, shaking her head.

"What!?" Kairoth asked in frustration. "They started it!"

Sal'iabac rolled her eyes, grabbed him by the arm, leading him out of the chamber.

Chapter 9

Kairoth and his band had been on the road a week. They were on foot this time to give the appearance of weary travelers. They were not faking it. They were weary. The group traveled southwest on the King's road to the river mouth, and hired a barge to take them southward into northern Hodan. Quietly, they disembarked, and no one thought anything of a group of Yslan traveling to Hodan with two Hodan warriors.

It had been raining on and off for days. The group's appearance was perfect. They resembled the poor of every region. They were cold, wet, muddy and carrying everything that they owned on their backs. Very few who met them on their journey gave them a second look, but those who did think twice about the proposition of taking on four warriors, two of which were obviously Hodan. The team entered Cinnog's northeastern border with Hodan in seven days.

Walking over the dry, grassy plains of the Cinnog high desert, the team circumnavigated a small mountain range to their North, circling around until they found a small village to the West of the peaks. It was an impoverished region, war-torn, ragged, and exploited by the marauding militia, but the people still raised a wall for defense around the village, and their men stood the watch with crude spears and little else.

Kairoth nodded respectfully, acknowledging the courage of those who lived in the place. He called the group together to formulate a plan and get their stories straight.

"All right, this is the first Cinnog settlement that we have encountered.

We need to know what we are going to say." He looked around to see if there were any suggestions. There were none, just dirty, irritated faces. Kairoth chuckled at their glares. "Oh for the love of the Gods, you too, Danzu? May Gunnir turn from the sight of your belly-aching."

"I'm dirty, hungry, cold, and not in the mood, Kairoth. I will bathe in the horse trough if they have one." Danzu was frowning and shaking his head. Warrior or not, he did not like "long walks" as he put it.

"So, this is our story. We came from a small ruin near the Citadel. The area was too dangerous, so we grabbed everything we own and came North, looking for a new place to live. We came in search of a new King. Let them say the lord's name that they are supporting. No need to identify with the wrong faction." Kairoth paused for effect. Everyone nodded.

Danzu sighed. "Whatever, brother. Let's get on with it. Let Kairoth speak, and everyone else keeps their teeth together. Agreed?"

"Agreed," the rest responded.

"Then let's go, my friends. Time to do the King's will," Kairoth said in an eerily harsh tone.

"And to do the will of the Goddess!" Reynir added, smiling.

Valtyr nodded, but sighed at the never-ending optimism of his best friend. It was annoying at times, but no one could ever keep Reynir down. The group approached the ragged wooden-plank gate, where they were greeted by two local guardsmen and to their surprise, two uniformed crossbowmen. Kairoth turned and looked at his party one last time. They all acknowledged his concern.

"Halt, who goes there?" the middle-aged villager barked out in an authoritative tone. Kairoth got the impression this was not the first time this man had wielded a spear.

"Greetings, brother! We seek shelter for a few days and then we shall be on our way. Does this village have an inn?" Kairoth looked at the four guards with a hopeful expression. "We have been on the road for many days."

One of the uniformed men stepped forward. Kairoth could tell that this one had seen multiple battles. The evidence was not only seen in his eyes, but through the scars on his face and arms. The soldier looked the Hodan warrior up and down distrustfully.

"Who are you? Where do you come from? What lord do you serve?" the soldier questioned briskly.

Kairoth decided to take the chance. There was no way around the question. He had to declare his allegiance to this man, or risk a confrontation while on a diplomatic mission for Yslan. Looking around, the Hodan warrior noticed eight more uniformed soldiers and several ordinary villagers were forming in the center of the village behind them. Everyone was armed and had an impatient look on their faces. They were tired of war, but ready to fight.

"We are friends who lived outside of the Citadel. As I am sure that you are all aware, the capital is a mess right now! The pretenders to the throne attacked our camps, night and day, they stole everything but the possessions we carry. We scarcely left with our own skin." Kairoth looked at some of the faces. The villagers softened their stances, but the soldiers remained firm. Kairoth hoped that one might tip him off to what faction ran this region, but there were no tells to be had.

"Who do you serve, citizen?" the oldest looking soldier questioned.

Kairoth noticed that his group had assumed an excellent defensive formation. The mages were in the center with the priest and druid in the back. Kairoth stood forward with Danzu, and Brynd held on the left flank of the group. Kairoth made a subtle signal with his hand. Danzu pretended to sneeze and then slid over to the right, pretending to blow his nose. Kairoth was satisfied that if this went south, they were at least as ready for battle as they were going to be.

"We serve the only true heir to the Crown of Cinnog, Prince Basric!" As Kairoth finished his words, the entire party drew weapons.

The older man was impressed by their display and knew that there was more to this band of refugees that they were letting on. Still, they had answered correctly and were ready to fight, and he needed people.

"Stand down, young one. You are among friends. Enter freely. The inn is down our only road on the left. Marta is the innkeeper. It is not much, but you are welcome to stay if you have coin." The older man raised an open hand in a sign of truce. The party sheathed their weapons a bit too expertly to be everyday travelers, but the old man smiled. Maybe they could help.

"Where is Famlin, Safiya?" Kairoth asked loudly in a frustrated tone.

"How in the Underworld should I know. Perhaps he is using a tree somewhere?" Safiya responded, equally irritated.

"That is such a barbaric practice. Please, do not relieve yourselves on my friends. How would you feel if someone did that to you?" Reynir was disgusted.

"Oh, for Haya's sake, just shut it and get in the gate before they change their minds, you whining girl," Valtyr mocked.

"Oh, go ahead and piss on the wrong tree. I am not healing your wounds. You can suffer and remember that trees are not outhouses." Reynir was indignant.

Valtyr laughed and put his arm around the smaller Reynir. "Come on, tree lover, let's go."

When the party got to the inn and put their belongings away, they had a chance to look around the village that they had found. It was a standard agricultural community. Some meager crops could be seen growing in several private plots, and a large community field was charred and barren. There was a stable, which consisted of little more than a thatch roof and some branches tied into makeshift stalls. The corral was little more than old posts with more branches tied to the uprights. These people had very little, and it appeared whatever little that they had formerly possessed, was stolen from them. Kairoth was angry.

The Hodan approached the older soldier. "Excuse me. Who did this to these people?"

"Who do you think? Lord Palgur, the bastard, has his militia ride freely on these plains. He knows that the North is the key to his victory. The South is in disarray. If that pretender can muster enough consolidated troops and material support from the North and West, and then impress Yslan …" The old man trailed off in disgust.

"He is a despicable piece of filth who steals bread from children. I would love to see his corpse on a stake." Kairoth's eyes betrayed him to the older soldier. The Hodan quickly recovered, but it was too late, he had betrayed his secret to the observant old man.

"Who are you really?" the commander of the local occupation forces asked smiling. "Yslan? Hodan? Who comes to check up on us?"

"We are simply travelers, Sir. If we decide to stay here, we need to know what we are getting ourselves into," the Hodan warrior lied convincingly.

"So be it, young one. We want no problems from outsiders. Cinnog is a mess, but a proud mess." The old soldier smiled. "Get some rest. The bastards have not come this way in days, but they are due. You may get to see your fate, yet."

"I will inform my friends," the Hodan warrior nodded.

The soldier smiled wider.

"Damn it. You idiot," Kairoth thought silently. "He knows."

* * *

It was a chilly night. The temperature had dipped into the mid-forties, and it had begun to drizzle. Clouds covered the sky, and there were no stars or moon to light the evening. The guards were on alert throughout the village perimeter. Kairoth could see the civilian reserves gathered under a shed roof, talking about their duties.

Kairoth looked at his friends. The druid and the priest had finished their prayers and devotionals for the night. They were both lying near the raging hearth under their issued blankets. The two mages had studied and mixed their reagents, in preparation for what may or may not occur. Both had slipped off to a barn to do this in private. No one in the village was aware of who the women were or what they were capable of. Brynd attended to his equipment, drank a couple watered-down meads and sat up in a far corner with his back to the wall, facing the door. The fact that he had his bow in hand and an arrow nocked was not lost upon anyone in the room. Kairoth was worried about his specialist. He had not seen him since they had crossed the Cinnog border three or four days ago. He wondered if another one had been lost.

"Nah," Kairoth muttered. "He's probably out in a hole, cooking up all sorts of misadventures for those who would harm his team. He is good about that. Have faith in the thief." Kairoth laughed at the irony of having faith in someone who was supposedly of the lowest moral fiber, but he knew better. Famlin was different. He knew this thief and knew what he really stood for. Friends.

It was late when Kairoth finally sat up on the other far corner of the inn, sword draw six inches out of the scabbard, but covered by his cloak. He had slept peacefully, for the first time in days, when his bliss was interrupted by a clanging metal racket outside of the inn entrance.

"To arms! To arms! The enemy approaches! The enemy approaches!" a young boy was screaming while pounding a mallet into a large piece of metal.

Brynd stood immediately and drew his bow, surveying the crowd. Kairoth stood, drawing his sword and standing ready. Both men, realizing that there was no threat in the inn, relaxed. Kairoth nodded to Brynd, and they went about kicking at the rest of their party. The mages were up and preparing for battle, but the clergy were still out cold.

"Get up! Both of you! It's time to do the will of the Goddess. Apparently, she likes to work at night." Kairoth smiled and offered a hand to Valtyr, as Brynd assisted Reynir to his feet.

Brynd said to Kairoth, "Recon and report. Five minutes. Be back in a few, brother."

As Brynd ducked out the inn entrance and disappeared, Kairoth shouted, "Be safe, brother." The warrior called the remaining six over to where he stood, drawing a plan in the dust on a table. "You here, you here, priests support the ladies. Danzu, you and I will mingle with the regulars and make our presence known."

"Where is Famlin?" Safiya asked with a worried face.

"If I was to wager a bet, skulking around right under the enemy's noses and they don't even know that he's there. They will … soon." Kairoth's smile and confidence in Famlin brought a smile to Safiya's face.

"You're right, this is not the first dance," Safiya said words in an ancient tongue, touching her sister's shoulder. "We are ready." Sal'iabac nodded.

"Watch for arrows," Kairoth said with a concerned look, gazing at Sal'iabac for a moment too long.

"You watch for arrows. If anyone will catch one, it's you or Famlin! Why is that, sister?" Sal'iabac laughed.

The inn door opened and in slipped a wet ranger. He was down two arrows.

"Fifty militia on horseback. Moderately armed. Adequate armor. Standard is a black field with a white fist on it." Brynd nocked another arrow. "Anyone who you know?"

"According to the intelligence of His Majesty, this is the militia we are working against. Let's make them pay. Another day, another militia for this team." Kairoth picked up a shield that was leaning against the wall, not in use. "Let's get this done."

Brynd extinguished all lights within the inn and directed the elderly and infirm hiding there to get behind the bar and to barricade the door with the bit of furniture that could be found. The team slipped out of the door, dispersing toward the sound of battle. They could see the villagers and around twenty uniformed soldiers bracing the gate with poles and wagons, while the enemy attempted to breach the entrance. Upon two makeshift perches, archers were thinning the enemy numbers, but not with enough efficiency.

Kairoth found the Commander near the battle, yelling out to his men. They were outmatched, and the old man knew it, but he would not surrender. Kairoth was impressed by his bravery.

"Sir, is there another way out of this place?" Kairoth asked shouting.

"Leaving so soon?!" the old man joked sarcastically. "You don't want to stay and enjoy our visit with our unwanted company? I did not think that you would run."

"I will never run, Sir," Kairoth said with the stare on his face. The old man saw it plainly.

"I know." The old man pointed to a hole in the wall behind the stables. "It looks patched, but it's all for show. Tell the sentries to let you pass. Take the horses and do your worst, 'traveler.'" He smiled and nodded. Kairoth nodded back.

"We shall drink mead later, Sir," Kairoth stated. "I am buying."

"I will hold you to that, son," the old man replied, as Kairoth motioned to his team to gather and head for the stables.

* * *

The enemy was all around. It was cold and misty. The rain hung in the air, as if the water refused to hit the ground. The horses' hooves met the wet earth below them with a plodding, squishing sound. The thief watched as the horses slipped and fell here and there. This would be easier than he had anticipated. Famlin thanked the Goddess Aluia for her assistance, smiling and looking up into the misting rain. The specialist remained concealed in some brush to the side of the battle, working to make his plans a reality. He crept up to the edge of the light, where the enemy had staged his reserve cavalry. Famlin was a master tactician and had guessed correctly where he set his first trap.

Although he had left his cover and concealment, the thief wore a suit made of grass and had painted his face with charcoal and oil. The fools on horseback had no idea of what was coming. After crawling on his belly for one-hundred measures, the specialist grabbed a small explosive charge from his pouch. It was little more than a parlor trick he had learned as a child in Sudenyag, but it produced a flame and smoke, which was precisely what this situation called for.

Striking a small ignitor device, the specialist tossed the small cylindrical device into the middle of the undisciplined militia horsemen, who were milling around in a gaggle awaiting orders. Within seconds the device exploded with a loud bang and flash of light, spooking the horses and causing a massive stampede of frightened steeds. Horses ran, uncontrolled in all directions, crashing into each other. The thief threw another charge and then another. The mayhem Famlin created successfully injured a third of the mounts and killed a dozen riders in the crush. Then they saw him.

"There he is!" A rider pointed at Famlin who tried to hide, but it was now no use. "Get that son of a Suden whore!"

Famlin took that one personally. "We shall see who the son of a whore is, you piece of dung." He started to run toward a predetermined location where he knew that he had the advantage. The riders pursued.

Trip wires were activated by the lumbering pursuit of the undisciplined militia horsemen, setting off more explosive charges, which further spooked the horses, channeling them toward Famlin's main event. There in the killing pocket that the specialist had created over past four nights, the riders were thrown from crippled horses as they ran over caltrops or galloped over hidden ruts that the specialist had cut into the ground with his spade in order to break their legs. During the mayhem and death that he had created, Famlin spat toward the militia and then pulled his grass hood over his head, fading back into the shadows, his job now complete. Half of the cavalry was inoperative or dead. He moved toward the fires at the gates of the village. There, he knew Safiya needed him, and there, he would go.

* * *

Brynd found a high spot on top of a roof. He emptied his quiver, killing ten at the gates. Then he put his bow down on the roof and pulled his sword. He could see the rest of the party exiting and coming around on horseback, but knew that the warriors would not have a chance against the remaining numbers at the gate. There were at least another twenty-five to thirty heavily armed attackers. The defenders at the gate had lost several of their band from both the professional and citizen soldiers. Brynd quietly slid down and exited the village, creeping along the outside of the wall. He was hiding in plain sight, much like the Draj of Torith did, when a young archer turned and saw him, but it was too late for the attacker.

Brynd struck furiously, but in the din at the gate, the enemy never noticed the loss of several archers. The ranger collected the arrows, quivers, and bows of the dead, determining which was the most serviceable. He settled for a decent Yslan longbow, but missed his Elfish one. It would have to do. The good news was that the ranger had found twenty-five arrows along the way. As he saw the mages and priests dismounting to form their support entity, Brynd also witnessed the charge of his Hodan brothers. Smiling, he nocked another arrow.

"You ass," the ranger remarked, looking at Kairoth, as he laughed out loud. "This one is for Roland, toads. You will not claim another of my clan."

Then the ranger let loose, as only an Elfish Bowmaster can.

* * *

Sal'iabac and Safiya stood beside Reynir and Valtyr. The priests prayed for blessings and protection, as the mages readied to rain death down upon the enemy. Reynir had armed himself with a club and wooden shield and covered Sal'iabac, while Valtyr did similarly with a war hammer and small metal shield.

Behind them, Valtyr spied Sal'iabac readying a familiar spell. "Get out of the way, Reynir," the priest shouted, as the mage lifted her hand with her hair floating, as if in water. "Here it comes again!"

Reynir dove to the ground as Sal'iabac's hair began to float, as if she were in a pool. Her eyes displayed a small spark of electricity. The mage raised her hand in a particular manner, pointing toward several horsemen who had ridden toward the charging Hodan warriors. Five horsemen and their mounts fell where they stood, as the attackers, not noticing the small band to the side of the battle, looked to the skies thinking of the storm above them. Safiya responded in kind with a similar display, dispatching four more footmen, in an attempt to match her sister's five victims.

Reynir jumped to his feet waving his hands, yelling, "Hold your fire, sisters! Our men are too close to the impact area! Stop!"

Valtyr rolled over to see the Hodans' horses fall. Grabbing his hammer and shield, he stood and began to run to the scene. "Stay here and protect the ladies!"

"But …," Reynir protested.

"No arguments, brother! We may need more of 'that,' soon!" Valtyr said, motioning to the skies.

Reynir nodded muttering to himself as he watched his brother run toward the scene. "Don't go off and die, fool. We have much to do in the name of the Goddess!" Reynir frowned as he watched his brother run to battle alone.

Sal'iabac covered her mouth in horror. "I killed him, didn't I?" She began to cry.

Stoically, Reynir looked to the mage. "The battle is not over, sister. We have time to cry tomorrow. You must focus. Many still count on your skills."

Sal'iabac sniffled and cleared her throat, but tears ran freely. They were not noticed in the rain, as it began to come down harder.

Safiya put her hand on her sister's shoulder in reassurance. "Sister, if anyone could withstand that, those two are the ones. Keep hope. Valtyr is on it."

Sal'iabac nodded, looking toward the muddy ground. She was numb.

* * *

Danzu and Kairoth charged abreast toward the oncoming militia horsemen. No one on the field possessed a true warhorse, but the two Hodan were expert riders and horse soldiers. Hodan was known for its ability to use cavalry as well as Legions of foot soldiers. As they met the enemy, something strange occurred.

The air around the two Hodan tingled, as a bright light engulfed the entire area, and the whole scene was lit up momentarily like it was the day, then things went a bit fuzzy. As the horses fell dead below them, the militia riders were thrown to the mud. All of them were injured or killed during the event. Kairoth and Danzu, semi-conscious from whatever had happened, instinctively tucked and rolled out of the impact as they were taught as children. Both lay on the muddy ground, dazed and wondering what had just happened. Then the phenomenon occurred a second time, fifty feet away from their location, dropping four men where they stood.

"What in the Underworld was that Kairoth!?" Danzu exclaimed, regaining his footing and steadying himself. He picked up a random sword and shield from the carnage around him.

Kairoth did similarly. "I was going to say it was the Gods, but then it happened twice in a minute. The mages?"

"Oh, for the love of the Gods. We need to remind them that we are not immune to their trade!" Danzu said rubbing his neck.

"Agreed. Sal'ia and Safiya are probably fretting about us, as we stand here." The two laughed.

From the smoky mist, a man approached, carrying a hand weapon and a shield. Turning to engage, the two weakened warriors recognized their priest and relaxed their stance a bit, keeping an eye out for more militia who were within spitting distance. At the moment, the lightning attacks and the push toward the gate were occupying their attention. No one was paying attention to the three warriors collecting themselves on the edge of the battle.

"Are you two all right?" Valtyr asked.

"I have honestly felt better," Danzu said blinking.

"Agreed," Kairoth said rubbing his face.

"Both of you come here," Valtyr commanded, motioning and watching the area around him. The enemy had noticed them.

Valtyr laid his hands on both warriors, speaking in a tongue that neither understood. "Goddess, hear my prayers. May your light be upon these two souls who do your will and protect the oppressed. Heal them with your light."

As the priest finished his words, a light engulfed all three of them. A sense of peace of body and mind filled the three men, and then both fighters felt their vitality return.

Valtyr raised his shield. "Just in time. Here they come."

"Let them come," Danzu growled.

"Agreed. Kill them all," Kairoth said in a faraway voice.

The three formed a triangle in the center of the surrounding militia. There were at least twenty of them left, and the enemy sought to make a statement against this obstinate village and its heroes. They did not know what they were bargaining for.

* * *

The Commander was concerned that the focus of the attack had seemed to change. He had suffered considerable losses within the village walls to enemy archers, but that had ceased about an hour ago, with the arrival of a single Draj who he had detected on the field. The Commander did not know where the Elf had come from, but he was glad that he was on his side.

The melee attacks had turned to another point of focus. The old warrior climbed up into an archer's nest, lowering down the body of a fifteen-year-old villager who had been holding the position with a short bow. The Commander scowled and stood to look out over the field. There, in the middle of the carnage, he saw three individuals back to back, ready for overwhelming odds. The Elf had disappeared for the moment, but the three others to the left of the field, were preparing to do Gods knew what. He called to his men.

"Stand by to engage outside the wall!" the old soldier commanded.

Seven warriors of the original twenty formed up to go with him and eleven civilian militiamen. "You civilians, stay here and stop them at the gate if we are lost. Tell the Prince of our bravery, if you would." One soldier said solemnly.

The villagers opened the gate as the Cinnog regulars filed out in a column of twos toward where Kairoth, Danzu, and Valtyr prepared for the enemy. Cinnog was halfway to them when the enemy began their attack.

The Commander witnessed the brutality and carnage first hand, as Danzu and Kairoth waded through the rabble, killing everyone who came their way. Before the Cinnog forces were able to get on scene, five militia survivors turned and tried to run, but then the mysterious Elf appeared again, as if from nowhere, and dropped those retreating, one by one, as if he were shooting targets on the range. When the old warrior finally got a good look at the archer, he realized that the Elf was in fact, no Elf at all, but in actuality a Human ranger. When one of the enemies didn't die immediately, the archer pursued him like hunter tracks his prey, dispatching him by cutting his throat. Then the hunter disappeared again, into the murky night.

"Hold, hold, men!" the Commander called out. "It seems that we were not needed after all. We are too late." The older warrior approached the three warriors cautiously.

"Who goes there?" Kairoth asked, standing beside his priest and other Hodan warrior, while looking carefully into the darkness. "Who wishes to join these fools in the Underworld?"

"It is only I, boy," the Commander stated plainly. "Come, they are all dead. We will clean this field in the light."

Kairoth nodded. "Agreed. Let's go collect our people, Valtyr."

"Hey," a voice said quietly as if from nowhere. "Don't shoot. For the love of the Gods, do not shoot me with another arrow!"

"Depends upon who you are," the Commander said looking around, but not seeing anyone.

"Sir, I do believe that is my specialist," Kairoth stated plainly. "Why keep up the ruse? I know that you have suspected since the first moment, and what we did here has completely blown our story." The warrior looked out into the darkness and shouted, "Hold your fire, incoming specialist!"

The bowmen put down their weapons with the Commander's permission and were amazed as a section of grass stood up and began to run toward them. As the figure entered the dim light, they were able to make out that it was a man in a suit designed to blend in with the fields. They began looking around for more men in grass suits.

"I believe that I am the only one operating in the area, gentlemen. You may relax." As Famlin said this, he removed his hood and Brynd appeared from nowhere. "Oh yeah, and there's that one. I forgot about him." Famlin laughed and shook Brynd's hand. "Nice job, brother."

"Same to you. I saw a field full of dead and dying horses and men about a half mile South of here. Your doing I would suspect, or they were really clumsy horsemen?" Brynd laughed. "He took out around twenty horses, Kairoth. I think that deserves an ale!"

Famlin nodded, introducing himself to the local Commander. Reynir, Sal'iabac, and Safiya, seeing that the battle appeared to be over, ran to see the condition of their friends. Sal'iabac was relieved and overjoyed that Kairoth was still among the living. Safiya was equally happy to see her missing specialist.

"Oh, thank the Goddess! I thought I killed you, My Love! I am so sorry!" Sal'iabac declared loudly in relief. Then with a look of horror, she realized that she had finally announced her love publicly. Everyone looked at her sarcastically, as if telling her it was no secret, with the tone of the daily interactions between the two.

Kairoth smiled and let her off of the hook. "It was close, my love. Please don't send lightning from the skies to my location again any time soon." Kairoth, in an uncharacteristic display of affection, lowered Sal'iabac's hood, cradled her cheek in his right hand, and kissed her passionately.

Safiya grabbed Famlin and spun the thief around. "Would you, PLEASE, stop worrying me. For the love of all that is holy, I was worried sick! Why do you do that?!"

Famlin smiled at Safiya's dismay.

"Stop smiling at me like that. I am mad at you. If you keep mocking me, arrows will not be the only thing that you will be worried about." Safiya crossed arms and scowled at the thief.

"You don't want that. Trust me on this, brother," Kairoth said, while Danzu chuckled.

"I suppose not. Can I make it up to you, My Lady?" Famlin batted his eyes at the angry mage.

"Maybe. I don't know yet." She smiled reluctantly.

Famlin kissed her hard.

"All right, yes, I can think of several ways of recompense," Safiya said raising an eyebrow.

"Now we're talking," the thief said nose-to-nose with his lady.

"There is only one room in the inn. Behave." Valtyr rolled his eyes, then laughed loudly.

Chapter 10

The moon crept out from behind a cloud, as the rain began to let up. Kairoth and his band joined the Cinnog regulars as they trudged, exhausted but victorious, back to the waiting group of villagers, who had gathered near the front gate. The Commander frowned, hearing the wailing of several unseen women, who had undoubtedly found a loved one who had fallen during the battle for the defense of the town. The mood inside the walls was subdued. The somber congregation left Kairoth feeling as if this was a defeat vice a decisive win.

The Commander saw the look of dismay on the young Hodan warrior's face. He spoke quietly. "Do not be disappointed, young warrior. These folks have seen too much death, and they have lost too many children to night raids."

Kairoth looked over at the man with a face of disgust. "These dung attack children also?"

"It's unknown what they do with them. They have been disappearing for around a month. One or two, here and there, but no bodies found. We assume that Palgur's men are degenerates looking for entertainment or perhaps slaves," the Commander spat.

"Hold on. You say that they have begun disappearing about a month ago?" Reynir interjected, pushing his way into the conversation.

The older warrior craned his head around and looked at the druid. "Yes, so? People go missing in Cinnog every day. It is not an uncommon occurrence."

Kairoth wondered where the questions were going. Reynir was making him impatient. "Say what is on your mind, druid," the warrior said in an irritated tone.

"Well, one more question first, if you would not mind. Sir, have you noticed any trees dying in large numbers in the region? Perhaps, maybe on a mountain or near some foothills somewhere?" Reynir looked concerned.

Kairoth's eyes widened. "Are you suggesting ..."

"Let him answer, Kairoth, I need to know. It is what I do, after all." Reynir looked at the Commander patiently as they neared the gate.

"Well, now that you mention it, our local farmers and hunters report that the surrounding area is becoming less and less bountiful. Animals seem to be found dead, or ne'er found at all. I remember one who traveled up the mountain range East of here. He said there were great sections of the peaks that looked as if a blight had struck the forest. What does this mean?"

Kairoth looked at Reynir while nodding. Then he sighed. "Oh my Gods."

"What? What is it?" the Commander demanded.

"We have found the enemy in places as you have described, but we are not at liberty to discuss what we have found, by decree of His Majesty," Reynir said officially.

The Commander smirked at the words "His Majesty," looking over with a quizzical expression toward a now livid Kairoth.

Kairoth raised both eyebrows, shaking his head in disgust while looking at the druid. Then he sighed and replied, "You really have no clue of how to keep your mouth shut, do you, druid?"

"So, are we going to cut through all of the charades, Kairoth? It is Kairoth, is it not? Or is that a false name also?" The Commander looked at the Hodan squarely, demanding a straight answer.

"My name is Kairoth. That much is true. Let's get that ale or mead when we get to the inn. I will tell you our story once we are in the village. No use trying to pretend anymore. We were only hiding the truth to ensure that you were the people we were looking for. We are in the right place." Kairoth smiled and nodded.

Several men, young and old, pulled two larger wagons away from the gate with a couple of mules. Others unbarred the large doors and began pulling them inward. The doors were damaged, hanging at odd angles on their makeshift hinges, but the villagers were able to open the entrance wide enough to allow their warriors back into the village. Then they moved the barricades back into place and set the watch with the remaining men and boys. The elders bowed to the Commander. Several who had witnessed Kairoth, Danzu, and Valtyr stand against twenty nodded to them also. Valtyr was uncomfortable with the recognition. The Hodan looked as if they expected it.

"I must go fix what a large-mouthed tree lover has destroyed. Stay in the area, get any wounds looked at and get some sleep and food. We will most likely be seeing more action very shortly. Reynir may have stumbled onto something more serious than even the King knows." Kairoth held a finger to his lips. "Do not talk in mixed company. Keep this only among us for now."

The group acknowledged and watched as Kairoth and the Commander entered the inn. They had the room to themselves as they went to discuss the future of the village. Kairoth went to his belongings and brought out his satchel and the documents the King had entrusted to him.

"Marta, two ales, please. The real stuff. I will pay. Do not bring us the watered fare after what we've both been through." The Commander motioned to the innkeeper, who left the room and returned with two dusty bottles on a tray with two wooden tankards. Marta expertly broke both wax seals with her kitchen knife and pulled the corks, handing them to the Commander.

"Your money is no good here tonight, Sextus. Drink. It is on the house." Marta turned. "I will leave you two to your business. Two more are on the bar if you need them." She laughed, "If …"

When they were alone, the Commander began the conversation. The two sat across the table, both were covered in the filth of battle, but neither one cared.

"To your health, Hodan! What is your true mission here in this humble locale?" The Commander sipped from his mug.

"To your health, Cinnog!" Kairoth replied, eliciting a smile from the Commander. "As I have told you, I am Kairoth, but I am not from the Citadel."

"You don't say," the Commander said wryly. "Are you a Hodan expeditionary unit? I did not think that Orus used women in his armies."

"King Orus," Kairoth emphasized the word 'King,' "has nothing to do with this, and no we are not a Hodan invasion. You would know if Hodan invaded."

"I remember those days, vividly. I was not too much younger than you are now when Jabir brought Orus and his Legions to the Citadel. If it were not for the intervention of Swyk ..." The old man trailed off and grimaced.

"Those days are in the past, Sir," Kairoth reassured. "We seek to foster friendship with the true heir. King Puryn sends us with this offer of truce and treaty. If Prince Basric signs this scroll, Yslandeth will back him with logistics, and more."

The Commander picked up the scroll, opened it and read the offer. He set it down. "What we need is troops, son. Will Puryn send his men to die for Cinnog men and women who turned their backs on his call during the invasion? I think not. This offer looks good, but we need men, not platitudes."

"I have always considered myself Hodan, Sir. My father was Hodan and my mother Yslan, but in her heart, she died a Hodan warrior. I watched them both die during those days. Yslan took me in. Puryn's leadership brought me to this place. He gave me this honor. He is true to his word. I cannot promise you Yslan blades, but the King of Yslandeth does not tolerate aggression against his friends." Kairoth stared at his drinking partner.

"He turned on Orus," the old man stated flatly. "When Eden pushed the Hodan out. He did not come then. When Orus petitioned to annex Sudenyag, he only gave in to protect the southern borders from invasion and raids."

"You do realize that Orus asked for Cinnog also." Kairoth swallowed his last and stood to grab the other two bottles on the bar.

"Are you sure?" the old man replied in shock.

"I heard the conversation between Puryn and his Lady as I waited to be given these orders. Puryn stood against his brother to stem another injustice. Now there is a rift between them, and the King of Yslan seeks to repair one alliance and secure one piece of the puzzle. Cinnog is the obvious choice. Suden may be beyond fixing. Edenyag is becoming unstable. Torith and Dornat Al Ar sit on their hands and do nothing." Kairoth opened the two bottles and handed one to the man across from him.

"You are much wiser than a Hodan is allowed. You must take after your mother more than you let on!" The old man laughed out loud, and Kairoth smiled, looking at the floor.

"She was too beautiful for me to take after, Sir, but thank you for that compliment!" Kairoth's eyes were a bit misty, and that was not lost on Sextus.

"I am sure she was, son," the old man replied quietly. "So, you think that Puryn would send a couple of Legions of Draj South to help us quell the pretenders?"

"I would wager a month's pay. He will come to the aid of an ally." Kairoth swallowed another sip from his tankard.

"Then I will be true with you, now boy. You must keep this among you and your friends only, because I now trust you, seeing you bleed the fields for people who you have no bond with. You have established that bond Kairoth of Yslandeth." The old man stood and opened a small pouch from around his waist. He pulled a small ring from within it and set it on the table, grabbing a wax candle from the next table.

"Marta! A quill and ink please!" the old man bellowed.

"Hold onto your pants, your eminence," the almost toothless woman snickered, providing Sextus with a used quill and a small inkwell. She left the room immediately and went back to her kitchen. Kairoth looked at the old man in curiosity.

"I will accept this offer. King Puryn has chosen excellent diplomats." The old man dipped the feather in the ink.

"But Sir, respectfully, the Prince must sign this document to make it real, not even one of his Generals is a binding signature," Kairoth protested.

The old man smiled, showing Kairoth the ring. It was the High Seal Signet of Cinnog, worn by the King himself or the heir. The Hodan's eyes widened at the realization of who he was speaking to.

"But your name is Sextus. I heard the innkeeper call you that," Kairoth said confused.

"I am known as Sextus. It is my field name when I wish to remain anonymous, lad." The older man smiled. "I am Prince Basric, son of Sextus, brother of Lorus, the last King of Cinnog. It is nice to make your acquaintance, my friend, and brother-in-arms." The old man offered his hand to Kairoth, who shook hands with the future King of Cinnog. The Hodan warrior had a look of surprise on his face.

"I did not know, nor did I mean to be disrespectful to you in any way." Kairoth averted his eyes.

"Stop that right now, young man. I watched you defend my people against much superior odds. It is I who owe, YOU! You should not be so easily impressed by titles. Many work behind the pomp to make the system work. I will simply be the face. Men like you make the difference." The Prince sat and drank some more.

Kairoth watched as the Prince signed the treaty with Yslandeth. "You are not just a face, Prince Basric. You are a symbol of hope to your people, and a man of honor." Kairoth bowed.

The Prince stood and bowed back. "Like you, and all of your men and women are. Now that we have dispensed with the formalities and the introductions, what was your young druid going on about out on the battlefield?"

Kairoth's demeanor changed immediately. "I'm not supposed to talk of it, for fear of spreading terror among the nations." Kairoth took a big gulp of ale.

"Well, now you have me intrigued, young man. I must know what this new horror is!" The Prince stared impatiently.

"Fine, you will find out soon enough if we do not deal with the infestation immediately." Kairoth looked around. No one was present. "There are Offlanders in your mountains somewhere."

The Prince's face changed immediately to one of anger and malice, but not toward the warrior before him. "What do you mean, Offlanders breathe on the Ert? Maradwynne and her brood burned the filth to ash on the Arondayre. It is a fact."

"Well, some of the official reports and legends are not entirely accurate, Sir. My band found a nest of the bastards in the Raven's Pass. They were stealing women and children from a village known as the Hero's Pass." Kairoth stopped and looked away for a moment, collecting himself. "They were sacrificing them to Haeldrun. Blood sacrifice of man, woman, and child. None of the races and halflings were spared. We killed them all, losing two of my men in the process. Now they appear to be here. It was the same thing at Hero's Pass. Women and children disappearing and the trees dying up on the ridge-line."

The Prince slammed his almost empty mug down. "This cannot stand. We must purge our lands of this filth!"

"Agreed, but you should not go, Sir. You are the one true heir of Cinnog. We will go in." Kairoth swallowed his last and set his mug down.

"I will send soldiers to assist you."

"We are a trained team, Sir. Thank you, but they will be needed here, just in case the asses from the South raid again." Kairoth stood. "With your leave, I must go inform my team of our new objective. Also, would you send a messenger to Erynseere and ensure that the Alliance is officially formed? Please send a message to Their Majesties about what we have found here."

"I will do these things, Kairoth. Get some rest. If you change your mind about the men, just say the word, and they will be yours." The Prince stood and sealed the scrolls, securing them inside of the wax-sealed leather satchel. He called his most trusted man and handed it to him with instructions to take it to the court of Erynseere. The man mounted his horse and left immediately.

"We will leave at daybreak, Your Highness," Kairoth said, gathering his belonging and packing them up.

"Be blessed, Hodan. May Runnir and Gunnir strengthen your clan." The Prince opened the front door, leaving Kairoth to his thoughts.

* * *

The morning brought with it the horrors of war. Men and women cried out as they collected the bodies of their heroes and loved ones. The regular soldiers solemnly carried their fallen comrades to a place inside of the walls for preparation for the pyre. The order of the day appeared to be that everyone was to gather wood and oil. Many of both sides needed to be sent to Aeternum. Carrion birds were starting to feast on the enemy in the fields before the gates. The villagers strove to keep that scene from happening to their loved ones.

The band had gathered in front of the well near the inn. Kairoth was telling the tale of what had happened the night prior in the inn. Sal'iabac laughed and shook her head. Reynir sat with his mouth wide open, in shock that he had been fighting alongside a Prince the whole time.

"I let him know about the threat in the mountains," Kairoth admitted.

"Do you think that was wise, brother?" Valtyr asked.

"Well, priest, the man already had a good idea of everything else I was hiding. I guessed that he would figure it out sooner or later, and what if it was later and he realized that we knew of danger like that … and that we said nothing? What then? I did what I thought was right. He offered us help, but I think that they should stay here in case of a counterattack."

"Besides, we don't need unknown variables in our team right now. Shaky team members might get another one of us killed," Brynd added.

Kairoth nodded. "My thinking exactly. Is everyone fully healed and equipped for the job?" Kairoth looked at the mages, then shook his head at Reynir, who was watering his plant.

"What? You do remember what I can do with this little guy, right?" the druid asked, pointing at the potted plant.

Safiya looked at the plant sideways, as if it was about to grab her, and stepped closer to Famlin. "Yep. I remember. How could anyone forget."

"What?" Reynir asked looking around at the party.

"Well, then we should pack our gear and get going. It's a long walk up that mountain, and I'm sure if our luck holds true, the damned cave will be near the top of that range." Brynd was looking off at the mountain peak, which showed a hint of snow after the rains the night prior.

"Agreed. Prepare. We leave in an hour." Kairoth nodded, and the group dispersed to prepare.

* * *

The sun was rising in a bright blue sky, but the morale of the village was far from sunny. The Hodan warrior looked up at the mountain and remembered. He looked at Brynd, who turned and caught his demeanor. The ranger had the same look on his face. Brynd nodded to his Hodan friend.

"It doesn't get any easier, does it, brother?" Brynd asked solemnly.

"I don't suppose so, my friend. See you at the gate. Revenge awaits, my brother."

Brynd smiled. "That's what I wanted to hear."

Chapter 11

Prince Basric's rider was a professional scout. He swiftly navigated the familiar terrain, avoiding any enemy patrols, and eventually found himself a few hundred yards from the border of Yslandeth, a day's ride southeast of the Barony of Korin. Due to the Cinnog Civil War on the boundaries of the western kingdom and Yslandeth, Erynseere had deployed its Draj forces as border security against a potential spill-over of hostilities. Tensions were high, and the Commander of the Draj-Erynseere was restraining his men by the skin of his teeth. Truthfully, the old man was ready to intervene, but had other orders. Secretly, he wondered what his son was waiting for.

Palgur the Bastard, as he was known, had responded with several hundred, young, untested troops, who were encamped between Yslan's border and where the young scout had hidden. Maneuvering silently, the young man found himself in a situation where he had gotten as far as he was going to get without encountering his enemy. The young messenger tied a white banner to his bow and prepared to make a dash for it. Pulling out a favor that Kairoth had given him, he hung it around his neck and hoped the Draj would see it on him. Holding the white rag around his bow as if it were just a wrap, he brought his horse to a trot, then thought to tuck the favor inside his tunic for the time being.

Basric's man trotted up to the camp on his horse, bow in hand, wearing little more than ragged clothing and leather. The initial contact with the enemy went well, as they allowed him to pass, thinking that he was just a bowman or hunter from their own group. The enemy wore the pretender's favor, but there was no official uniform or tabard to be had. Slipping slowly and quietly through the camp, he estimated Palgur's men to be around one-thousand souls. Immediately, he felt fear grip him as he thought of a force this size marching on the Rordsburg, the village he had departed from.

As the messenger approached the enemy skirmisher lines, he noticed that the right flank was a bit less fortified and decided to try his luck slipping through those lines. Basric's man looked North toward Yslan. It was at least five-hundred measures to the border. Even in an all-out gallop, over open, semi-level terrain, he knew that he would be an open target for the enemy's archers for at least a minute or two. Then he had to worry about the Draj. Maybe they would not like him charging their position. He didn't like his chances, but he saw little in the way of alternatives.

"Halt! Who goes there?" a young Cinnog spearman barked. He was maybe fifteen years old by the messenger's estimation.

"Oh nobody, just me, a hunter, my friend." The messenger lied, quietly reaching under his cloak and drawing his short sword six inches out of its sheath.

"What is your name? I do not recognize you," the young man replied in the same tone.

"I have been here for at least a week. Traveled up from the Citadel. Not much in the way of work there, as you well know, soldier. I came up here to hunt and sell my kills to your unit for a profit. How do you think that you eat?" The messenger's right hand was out of sight and on the hilt of his blade as the young spearman moved his spearpoint closer to the man's chest.

"Get off of the horse," the spearman ordered.

"You will not take my horse, young one," the older rider responded. His sword was now palmed in his right hand under his cloak.

"You will dismount immediately," the young guard ordered again. Others were starting to notice the disturbance and make their way over to back up the sentry.

The messenger looked to the Draj fires over the border. He could smell their dinner, and this boy was standing in his way. Others were gathering. It was now or never. He looked at his opponent and felt pity for him, that was until the young soldier stabbed him in the left shoulder with his pike.

"What in the Underworld is wrong with you, boy!?" the messenger cried out, drawing his sword and rearing his horse. The horse knocked the spearman to the ground, but the boy stood and re-challenged the rider. "Fine, so be it."

Riding toward the spearman, the Cinnog scout anticipated the attack on his horse and expertly dodged to the left of the spear. There the Prince's messenger struck with his blade, severing the young soldier's head from his shoulders. The spearman's body was still standing, leaning up against his nine-foot spear, which was stuck into the ground. The head hit the wet dirt with a thud. Immediately, the call to arms was sounded, and men of the opposing faction began to rush to the scene. The messenger decided there was no option left. He goaded his horse and pointed it directly toward the Draj position.

"Go, girl, go!!!" the messenger shouted. "Yah! Run swiftly!" He had dropped his sword and was standing in his saddle with the bow and makeshift white flag held as high as he could manage with the wound to his shoulder.

* * *

Durn looked out at the open field between himself and the Cinnog militia. He seldom slept while deployed and was checking his lines for the tenth time, to the protest of his captains, who begged him to sleep. He waved his men off and told them to worry about the threat to the South and not him.

"I will sleep when they take me to my pyre, Captain!" the Draj Commander joked.

As the two men bantered and chuckled, a sentry ran shouting at the nearby camp. It was the duty runner. He had arrived to inform the Captain of changes in the posture on the border.

"Sir! There is a commotion on the enemy's left flank," the young man reported.

"What sort of commotion?" the Captain demanded.

Durn stood and stretched. He wondered if it was finally time to act.

"A man has broken through their ranks and rides at full gallop toward our lines. He appears to bear a white flag. The enemy is in pursuit of him. What are your orders?" The runner waited impatiently.

Durn interjected. "This is my decision, Captain. Send in a platoon of archers with full shield support." Durn grimaced. "The King can hang me later. I can sit by no longer."

"Yes, Sir!" The Captain saluted. "You heard the man. Sound the horns!"

Horns blew loudly as one-hundred archers and one-hundred shield men quickly formed. The runner informed the unit lieutenant of the Commander's order. It could be seen that the rider had been hit with a couple of arrows. He was one-hundred yards from the border, but his horse had fallen, and he was crawling, as best he could to the Yslan border. The enemy had dispatched two-hundred of its own to retrieve their prisoner.

"Go! Get him NOW! Kill anyone who engages you or tries to harm the refugee," the Draj Lieutenant barked out his orders, and his Draj immediately responded, moving as one toward their target, keenly aware of the militia that approached.

"Hunter teams, on me," the Lieutenant barked. "Sergeant you have the command. Kill them all for all I care, just cover us. Let's go get our man."

"Yes, Sir!" the Sergeant shouted. "Form skirmishers, archers to the rear. Engage anyone on the field or in support."

* * *

Basric's messenger could hear the clanking of metal from behind him. They were still a way off, but he knew that his death approached him and there was nothing left to do about it. He prayed to Haya for intercession and prepared for his end. His only regret was that he had failed to finish his mission, and with that failure, he feared for his Prince and the people who followed him. No one would know of the treaty in Yslandeth. No help would come. The pretender would win, because of his personal failure. He had failed his people. He set his head down. The arrows made it hard to breathe. Hopefully, the end would be swift. Maybe he would die before they could torture him. He prayed again.

As Basric's man laid his head down and prepared to die, another sound reached the wounded man's ears. It was coming from in front of him. He could not see well in the tall grass of the open field. The sun was going down slowly, but there was still light enough to see a contingent of Draj Erynseere entering the area.

"There was still hope," the messenger thought, "but they needed to hurry."

"Come on you, show ponies! Move your asses!" the messenger shouted, wincing in pain. He knew that they could not hear him and began to laugh sarcastically. "Hurry up, Yslandeth. Please."

A flurry of Elfish arrows filled the skies above him, as the messenger clutched the scroll case beneath him. He was starting to fade, but resolved to hold on as long as he could. The message needed to reach Empyr. That is when the Draj arrived on the scene. So did the militia from which he fled. The messenger sneered, thinking that his pursuers must have forgotten what had happened to the last army that stood against the Draj bows in an open field. The Battle of Torith was a significant defeat for the opposition then, and this skirmish looked to have begun in the same tone. The former defeated were hardened Hodan forces, not the rabble of Palgur the Bastard. This was not even a fair fight.

The Draj shield men engaged the shields and spears of the militia with fury and precision. From his vantage point, the messenger watched as the Draj cut the army down as if they were parchment. The enemy forces folded without barely a Draj casualty, running back for their encampment, but it was not over. Four Draj grabbed the scarcely conscious messenger and ran back toward the border. Basric's man could see the remainder of the militia forming for an advance against the Draj encampment. His saviors were tactically withdrawing, gathering their dead as they went. The Draj had lost less than ten men, while the militia appeared to have lost over fifty within minutes of the encounter.

"I must speak to your Commander," the scout pleaded, as the Yslan forces crossed the border back into Yslandeth.

"Funny you should say that, Sir," The Draj Lieutenant quipped. "He said the same thing. Healers! Now!" The Lieutenant motioned to the priest tent with fervor. "Move! Move! Now!" Priests and Elfish healers ran to the spot where the messenger sat on a hay bale.

"I must give my message. Please." Basric's man pled with the Lieutenant.

"Hold on. He is coming," The young officer said with concern. "You will be fine."

The messenger smiled, but knew that soldiers always said that sort of thing when the opposite was undoubtedly the case. The Lieutenant's face betrayed him.

Durn arrived on the scene. He saw the healers keeping the young man alive, but the eldest was sadly shaking her head out of sight of the messenger.

"What did you ride here for, boy?" Durn questioned sternly. "What had so much importance that you may have started a war."

The young man coughed and handed the scroll case to Durn. "It is all there, Sir. Your King, My King. The treaty is signed. We need you now. Our forces fail, and there are more I fear, than this rabble to contend with." The messenger weakly smiled. "Please give this message to King Puryn. Basric is his ally."

Durn hurriedly opened the case and cracked the wax seal on the scroll. He quickly read through the treaty legal jargon and looked at the signet at the bottom of the scroll. He noted that Puryn had already signed in the place of Yslandeth. It was real.

He rolled it back up and slid it back into the scroll case turning to one of his Draj runners. "Take this to Erynseere. Give it to Her Majesty. Tell her that Durn is invading Cinnog in the name of the Northern Alliance. The militia has engaged us." Durn paused. "Oh and ask Her Majesty to send us support. Trees, more Draj, whatever. There is a considerable force to deal with to the South by reports of the Prince's messenger."

"Yes, Sir!" the squire shouted and immediately departed toward Erynseere with haste.

"I know that Aeternum calls for me, Sir," the messenger said tasting his own blood in his mouth. "Please send me to Aeternum as a man."

"You will be known as the one who gave his life so that many in Cinnog would see freedom and hope. You will be sent to Aeternum a hero, son," Durn replied with a sad look on his face. There was always so much death to deal with. Durn was old, he would fight this war, then petition his son for retirement. He was done.

"Thank you, my friends," the messenger said quietly with a strange smile on his face. He had finished his mission and could rest well. The healers continued to try to save him, but it was no use. The young man succumbed to his injuries an hour later.

"He will not have died for an Alliance which bears no teeth. Form the men. Full attack on the enemy encampment to the South. We will aid our allies." Durn was deadly serious, and his Captains simply nodded and turned smartly, calling out orders and forming their units on the border.

The enemy seemed to be doing the same thing. They had formed a shield wall with spearmen behind it. Behind that was also a large contingent of archers, many of which wielded Elfish longbows. Durn was not concerned with the ground fighters. He knew that his Draj had, and would continue to decimate any forces that the militia put in front of them. The Commander was concerned with the unknown variable of how many Elfish bows were against him, and the accuracy of the archers wielding them.

"Gentlemen, beware of arrows. The enemy has the same weaponry as we do in that regard, but I doubt they possess the skill of our archers. Still, take no unnecessary risks with our men and women. I have no doubt of our warriors, but arrows do not discriminate. Even a fool can kill a hero from range." Durn turned and grabbed his sword and shield.

"Sir, we shall concentrate on the enemy archers first and maneuver as far from longbow range as possible, making the shots harder for them. Once we have bled them as much as possible, we will engage on the ground. If they come before we charge, we kill them where they advance." The Captain's face was like stone.

"As you say it, make it so." Durn shook the man's hand. "For Yslandeth! For the Alliance! For Honor and Glory! If our glaives and bows are not true, I shall see you all at the table in Aeternum. Let us give our enemy that honor, in advance of ourselves!" Durn raised his sword to the sky. "Haya be with you all!"

"Runnir and Gunnir would not hurt, Sir!" a random voice joked. There was a rolling laugh in the ranks.

"The brothers can help us if they also choose!" Durn laughed, responding, "Be careful my brothers and sisters. Let us all go home to our families when the war is won. If not, I will see you in Aeternum!"

The Draj lined up on the border in perfect rectangles. Sword and short glaive were sent to the front. Spearmen relocated behind the shield wall and the archers behind that. To the flanks were two-hundred cavalrymen on Korinian steeds. The units of Yslandeth stood out in white, and blue with banners flowing in the late afternoon breeze. The enemy formed similarly, but lacked the discipline and polish of the Draj. Durn did not care what they looked like. He knew that a dirty, disheveled man could kill a well-dressed one any day of the week.

The enemy was moving forward at a slow walk. They set up skirmisher units in a staggered formation and left their archers far out of range. Durn knew the Commander had a good grasp of Yslandeth's tactics. He was concerned.

"Advance at a walk, ladies and gentleman." Durn was on foot, despite the protests of his Captains. He walked behind the center platoon of his Draj, commanding from the ground. One-hundred yards in, the first Draj shield man fell to an arrow.

Durn motioned to a Draj nearby who fired a lit arrow up into the air. Suddenly, to the militia Commander's horror, the border behind the advancing Draj lit up. Hundreds of Draj bowmen had just lit their arrows on fire.

"Reeeaddddy! Loose!" the head archer barked out, and the sky was bright with streaking fire, and the enemy ranks fell in significant numbers. The dead began to burn, and the field appeared to be ablaze in several locations. The archers readied again. They repeated the action.

The militia began to adjust. The Commanders started to use their horsemen in an attempt to flank the Draj forward units. As they did this, the Draj cavalry met them. Due to better-than-expected militia horsemen, Durn lost half of his men to a force that was twice as large as first expected. Durn was becoming concerned, because the enemy seemed to be reinforcing and he had no indication from where.

"Where in the Underworld are they getting more warriors from? Send a scout to the nearest elevated position and report back immediately!" Durn ordered.

A Captain gave the orders, and a rider with a spyglass was dispatched. He rode up to a small hill and was able to make out a more substantial force joining the Cinnog rebels from the South. The Draj scout figured the number to be another one-thousand mixed forces. He rode back to the Commander.

"Sir, another unit approaches from the southwest. It appears to be of the same or similar size and composition as this one. We are currently outnumbered, two to one." The scout saluted and rejoined his unit.

"Wonderful," Durn said in a disgusted tone. "Time to get serious, ladies and gentlemen. They are coming, and I think they seek to invade Yslan proper. Not while I still breathe."

"We shall step up the fire, Sir. I will consolidate our remaining cavalry and send them wide around to the left flank. They were weaker there, from what I could see. If the cavalry can disrupt their archers, our foot soldiers will surely rout their militia." The Captain was very sure of himself.

"Do not underestimate the enemy, Captain," Durn warned. "Execute the orders. I want heavy archer fire. Wherever an enemy archer is, I want him to fear for his or her life. When the enemy archers are controlled, we will attack their lines. No quarter until I give the signal."

"Understood, Sir!" The captain turned and directed a messenger to ride to the archery lines. Shortly after that, the skies were filled with mixed volleys of fire and regular arrows.

"Nice touch," Durn chuckled, as he watched the enemy archers shifting to the left and right, to no avail. His corps was starting to see success.

The enemy could no longer get comfortable and aim. The other unit had arrived, but was little more than a ragged band of spearmen. This was routine for Palgur's men. He recruited with lies and promises of riches and glory, then sent unskilled men and boys off to do his dirty work with scarcely the tools of the trade. Durn shook his head in disgust. He almost felt guilty about engaging this rabble, but then he realized that he had lost nearly one-hundred men and women to this band of rebels, and that was more than enough to steel his resolve.

"Ladies and gentlemen, prepare to …" Durn's order was cut short. To his surprise, his order to charge was not necessary, as the enemy began to charge, en masse. "Stand by! REPEL! Kill them at will! Huzzah, Draj!!!"

A loud rolling cheer of, "Huzzah, Draj!" echoed off of the advancing enemy, as the crash of metal drown out the war-cry. The Draj cavalry, having dispatched most of the archers, began redirecting its focus to stragglers and the rear of the enemy, who had apparently forgotten about them. The horsemen rained death from the back of the militia shield wall, as the enemy crashed against an unmoving professional band of soldiers. The Draj were an unmovable force. They interlocked their shields and stuck their short glaives out from between the small gaps. The butts of their glaives were firmly on the ground with a foot behind them, providing what the Elves referred to in jest, as the porcupine. It was a uniquely Human invention, but even the Elves had adopted it.

The first wave of the militia was skewered, dying at the feet of the Draj forces, who now drew gladius swords as one. The enemy regrouped and set a static shield wall. The first charge had gone poorly, and they were taking damage from the remaining Erynseere cavalry. The enemy Commanders could be heard calling out commands to their forces. Their determination had not waned. Durn decided that it was time to force the issue. He had lost enough people to attrition. He needed to make sure the enemy knew that attacking the Draj was a lousy proposition.

"Captains, prepare for a charge. I need one-hundred on each flank to pincer around. I need two-hundred behind to be the hammer. I need five-hundred in the center to be the anvil. Send in the anvil, strike with the hammer, roll up the sides. Archers continue to shoot where it is safe to do so. Tell them not to shoot our own men and women." Durn looked out over his Commanders. Two were missing. He didn't have to ask. The faces of the remaining four said what he already knew. "Honor and glory, my brothers," Durn said saluting.

"Honor and glory," they responded in unison.

Durn looked out at the static enemy unit in front of him. This was the largest unit that he had seen on the field since the Offlanders attacked at Erynseere. He was tired of battle. This would be his last campaign. He was sure his son would understand. Durn just hoped that he would live to submit his retirement.

"Show this dung what it means to be Draj-Erynseere, my brothers, and sisters. Charge!"

The unit sprang into action as it had drilled a thousand times before. The anvil crashed against the super numbers, killing at will and opening a large hole in the center of the enemy lines. On cue, the hammer entered the breach, exploiting the gain. It split into two halves and pushed the opening even wider. The enemy unit was halved and the outside flanking Draj started picking off the disorganized warriors caught on the edges, as the group began a big push backward and to the exteriors. The Draj archers moved forward and supported from nearly point-blank range.

Durn had killed his fill. The old man had dispatched as many as twenty militia with his blade. Many of the faces would haunt his dreams for the rest of his life, as he saw his own son in many of them. Palgur recruited them young. He had no qualms with sending youth out to perish for his dreams. Durn hated the man with a passion. He wished it were his face he saw laying lifeless at his feet, but alas, it was some dumb farm boy who stood in the pretender's stead.

Within an hour, the Draj had subdued the threat, but not without a price. The enemy had taken the lives of two-hundred-fifty Draj before surrendering to Durn and his remaining captains. What had started as a militia of approximately twenty-five-hundred, was reduced to less than one-thousand. The Draj had killed at an average of four or five to one. Puryn would be pleased that the training and preparation were successful, but the King would be displeased with the loss of his men and women. Durn knew that his son was fully aware of the price of doing business when war was the occupation. Still, the King would take it hard, as usual.

"Set a good perimeter. Send specialists to scout the surrounding countryside. I want no surprises during the night," the Commander ordered.

Durn looked at the prisoners of war. His Draj had formed the camp around the enemy with their tents. All of the remaining militia were put in the center of the encampment. Fires burned around the containment area and no less than two-hundred Draj were on guard duty at a time. The remaining Draj were resting, patrolling, or healing.

"Captain. Send a messenger to Erynseere with this message." Durn wrote, "Your Majesty, tell Puryn that his father is within Cinnog. An enemy force of approximately twenty-five-hundred militia engaged and defeated. Eight-hundred or so prisoners of war. Seven-hundred-fifty Draj remains of one-thousand. Request immediate reinforcements and resupply. We are located approximately a quarter-mile South of the Yslandeth border. We will be the Elfish-looking encampment in the middle of the open field. Hurry up, please." Durn smiled and chuckled at his last two lines. "We need this in Erynseere, yesterday, boy," Durn remarked, handing the dispatch to the courier the Captain had requested.

"Understood, Sir. I will ride hard. I should be able to arrive by daybreak, if all goes well." The young man took the satchel.

Durn's mind wandered to the young man who'd brought him the treaty from Cinnog's Prince. "Be careful, son. Make haste."

The squire departed and rode hard toward the border with his satchel over his shoulder. Durn watched him go. "Protect that young one, Haya.

Too many have left the Ert, this day."

The Captain nudged his Commander, handing him a flask of whiskey. Durn took it from him smiling. Nodding, he replied, "Don't mind if I do, Captain. It's definitely been that sort of a day."

Durn looked at his captives. He didn't hate them. He saw the scared, young faces mixed in with the old, hopeless ones. He wondered what they had been promised to convince them to follow such a piece of dung as Palgur seemed to be.

The Commander turned to bid his Captains a quiet evening, and then retired to his pavilion for the night. It didn't really matter what they were promised. It seemed that a man didn't need much of a push to become a rabid dog these days. A charismatic leader, a scapegoat for all of his problems, or simple need was enough to corrupt all. Durn had seen too much of it in his years. He was ready to move on. He dreamed of a time of real peace, where he could make things grow, vice cut life asunder.

Durn laid down on his cot, closing his eyes then muttered a prayer quietly before falling asleep. "Goddess, please let me go home and be with my wife. Grant my son the peace he so desires. What does this constant strife serve, except death? Thank you for this victory, but I pray that I continue to honor only you, and if I don't, take me to Aeternum before my soul is beyond redemption."

Durn slept soundly that night, but many others kept the watch, as many sat fearfully in a cold, wet, circle wondering what the future would hold for them. They too prayed and wondered why Haya had not heard their cries.

Chapter 12

The Draj at Erynseere saw one of their own riding at breakneck speed up the muddy main road toward the castle. The sentry called for the bells, and the Officer on Duty formed the duty platoon in preparation for whatever was incoming. All stood ready at the gates. Adasser noticed the commotion as she looked out of her chamber window.

"What in the Underworld is that all about?" The Queen slipped on her dress and called to her handmaiden. "Find out what is going on. I will meet you in the throne room."

The Elfish girl bowed and exited quickly, running to where the Captain of the Guard had his men at the ready. Adasser slipped on her shoes and threw on a headscarf. "No time to preen today, Humans, something is afoot." The Elfish Priestess grabbed her staff as she exited the room and headed for her throne. She was apprehensive. War was brewing to the South, and her father-in-law insisted that he deploy with his men to the border. She had protested, but the old man was obstinate.

"It is no wonder where he gets it from!" the Queen huffed, as she sat down, thinking of her husband who was in Empyr, dealing with a plethora of pressing issues and political drama. She did not envy him. Adasser stood and reached out to a branch sticking into an open window. The Old Elm was by her side as usual.

"My dearest friend, please relay to His Majesty that I miss him and send love and encouragement for his day, for I know that he needs it badly. Also, please let him know that our soldiers stand at the ready for our castle, for some unknown reason. I will let him know more as I find out what is the matter. Tell him not to worry, I still have my Sylvan Family to stand with me. He knows you all, and what you can do. That should settle any worry in his mind. Thank you, friend."

The tree rustled as if a strong wind blew where there was none, and withdrew to the forest. The Queen turned to her throne and sat. The ladies-in-waiting noticed the Queen's hair and were horrified. Three of them insisted on fixing the issue, pouncing on Her Majesty with brushes, hairpins, and scarves. Within moments, Adasser was once again flawless, but very irritated. She hated when they did that, but knew that it was useless to argue. Human women could be such a pain.

* * *

The rider arrived in a hurry at the front gate. The sentry shouted down from his elevated position, as several Elfish longbows trained their arrows on the man at the door to the castle.

"Draj! Present your identification!" The sentry drew his bowstring.

The exhausted young courier reached into his satchel, producing a medallion signifying the favor of Erynseere, then presented a bag bearing the King's Draj insignia, the one that Commander Durn held.

The sentry commanded loudly, "Stand down! Stand down! Open the gate! Let this man pass!"

The gate was opened, and the young man was let into the courtyard of the Castle Erynseere. His horse was tired and hobbling a bit. The rider was not in much better shape. He looked at the sentry and motioned for him to come closer.

"This must reach Her Majesty immediately! It is from the Commander. Cinnog militia engaged on the southern front. Many of them were killed. We lost two-hundred-fifty of our own. Eight-hundred or more prisoners of war. The Commander is worried that they may have more reinforcements coming at any time. He requests reinforcements of our own." The young squire faltered, almost falling from his saddle.

"Relax, brother, we received the first messenger. We know that Basric is our ally and that we support his claim to the throne. We did not know that we would be called to action so quickly." The sentry turned to shout, "Captain!"

A man on a white warhorse trotted over to the young bowman who was yelling. "What is it, Draj?" the officer replied.

"This man says that Commander Durn is engaged with rebel forces in Cinnog, Sir. He needs us there now. He brings a message to the Queen." The sentry bowed.

"Excellent work, sentry." The Captain looked over at the haggard squire. "You! Come with me. Someone take his horse to the stables. Give the man some water."

After Durn's messenger had caught his breath and regained his footing, the Captain escorted the young man to the Castle throne room. There, waiting impatiently, was the Queen, who was receiving the report of her handmaiden. Food and drink were being brought into the room. The servants were lighting the lanterns and candles. This visit was much earlier than the Queen was used to, but she now knew, from her girl's report, that it was for a grave purpose.

"So, Palgur's forces have attacked Yslandeth?" the Queen asked in a severe tone.

"Well, not exactly, Your Majesty," the young squire remarked grimacing.

"Go on," the Queen dead-panned.

"We were on the border, observing several thousand militia gathering at a rally-point, Your Majesty, when a man burst out of their left flank on horseback. He was making a concerted effort to get to our lines while flying a white flag of truce." The squire waited for the Queen's acknowledgment.

"Understood, continue," Adasser said sipping her tea. "What else happened?"

"Well, Your Majesty, the enemy engaged the man and began shooting him with arrows. Then they advanced to take him, prisoner. The Commander watched until he could take the barbarity no longer. He held onto his patience as long as he could, My Queen." The young man was bowing, hoping to soften the news of an invasion against orders.

"Ah, Durn. Why? Why would you directly go against the orders you were given?" the Queen muttered. "How does one handle this? We cannot have Commanders just running amuck doing whatever they please." The young man heard her.

"Your Majesty, no disrespect intended, but we all know that your husband, the King, has long sought an alliance with Prince Basric to the South. Durn solidified it by getting that Alliance treaty back to you before my arrival. The man he saved, well sought to save, held it in his possession. He was Basric's man. He was on our side. Durn made the correct call."

"Commander Durn, squire! And watch your tone!" the Captain interjected angrily.

"It is fine, Captain. No insult is taken. This one is loyal to his Commander. No faulting the boy." The Queen smiled and looked at the squire. He was maybe sixteen years old and so full of idealism. She closed her eyes for a moment and remembered a young, blonde Draj who once saw her off when Torith was aflame. Then she opened her eyes and regained her composure. "That is between a father and a son. I am sure that it will be taken into account if anything comes of it. Regardless of orders and etiquette, what you all have done on the border is of extreme significance."

"Thank you, Your Majesty. The Commander did not take his decision lightly, My Queen, please know that." The squire bowed and stepped back as the Queen dismissed him.

Stepping forward, the Captain bowed. "Your Majesty, the Draj in-country call for aid. I ask for your permission to deploy two Legions and a supply train."

"Make it three, Captain. No use dancing around the issue. We are at war with Palgur and his militia. Basric is trapped in Rordsburg, and I have a sneaking suspicion that this Alliance treaty didn't just fall into his lap. My husband's scout teams are involved here. There may be need of one Legion traveling to Rordsburg to sort things out. Please make this so."

"So, Your Majesty calls for three Legions of Draj to deploy southward? Two to Durn and one to Basric, am I correct?" the Captain verified.

"Yes, Captain, that is correct," Adasser verified stoically.

"That will leave Erynseere with two Legions of Draj, and one Legion of reserves," the Captain stated.

"And a forest that will not suffer anyone to harm my people," the Queen reminded.

The Captain smiled, bowing and saluting Adasser. "Of course, Your Majesty. How could anyone who lives here ever forget! May Haya bless you, Holy Mother."

Adasser was not accustomed to a Human referring to her in this manner. With a smile, she replied, "And with you also, brother."

The Captain exited the throne room and began to call his fellow Captains to the war room for a planning session. Within an hour, they all left to their respective units to form up. Adasser watched from her window as three-thousand warriors, horsemen and supply train personnel formed within two hours. Within three hours, the First Legion stepped out of the castle gate toward the southern border. The last man was gone within four hours after the order was given. Adasser nodded in awe. Her man had created another Draj worthy of the original order.

The Queen bowed her head and prayed. "Oh great Goddess of all that lives, and of love and light, may these men find your protection and guidance in their duties and may their conflict be brief. I ask that as many as possible be allowed to return whole to their homeland and their families. Guide my leaders. Make them fight in righteousness and honor. Praised be your name."

When the Queen opened her eyes, several young girls stood holding refreshments. They had a look of awe as they beheld their Queen bathed in a white glow. The Goddess had visited her Priestess at that moment, and they were in her presence also. All in the room smiled peacefully at each other as the Queen sat upon her throne, still lamenting the new war that was coming to the South.

It was only the second hour of the morning, but it felt as if a whole day's tasks had been accomplished before the dawn had fully risen. Adasser sat quietly, then rose to speak to her friend. The Elm waited patiently for his Queen.

* * *

Durn woke to a clanging bell. One of his men was calling out for the morning meal. He looked around, cursing, wondering what time it was. The Commander sat up, shaking out his boots to make sure no little creatures had made them a home in the night. There was nothing to find, and he slipped the muddy leather onto his feet. Rising, he opened his tent flap to a bright, clear sky. It was at least the second hour of the morning.

"Good morning, Sir!" one Captain stated smartly, standing at attention.

"Morning it is, Captain! What time were you going to wake me up?" Durn asked smiling.

"Well, Sir, you looked like you needed your beauty rest," the Captain said chuckling, and then handing Durn a biscuit and some slightly undercooked bacon.

Sitting on a log, sipping a tankard of tea and eating, Durn looked out over the encampment. It had rained last night, and the temperature had dipped into the low forties. The prisoners were freezing, and some were becoming ill. They had no food to speak of, nor shelter. This would not do.

Durn cursed and set his food down. "Aluia, please hold back the rains for a week or so, please, Goddess," the old man muttered.

"What is the matter, Sir?" Durn's Captain asked sincerely, seeing the look of concern on Durn's face.

"Bandu, we cannot let these people perish out here in bad conditions. It is not only inhumane, but it is also dishonorable. We need to build fires for them immediately. Gather wood. DO NOT cut down trees in this area.

Anyone who does this does so at their own peril. You are Draj-Erynseere, you know who they serve." Durn looked at a pine warily. "Pick up the ground clutter. You will find it there, I am certain."

"At once, Sir," Bandu responded, grabbing a small contingent of workers to gather wood and others to set the fire pits. The men went to work without a complaint, which surprised both Bandu and the Commander.

Soon the enemy prisoners had warmth, but no cover from the elements. Durn had an idea. He had never done it before, but he'd seen Puryn do it many times. Walking up to the nearest pine, the Commander cleared his voice. "Hello, I am Durn, Commander of Their Majesties' Draj forces. I know that you do not usually listen to others, but if you could, would you please inform the Queen of the situation with the prisoners?" Durn looked at the tree. There was no reaction. "Well, I intend to ask her, to ask you all, to encircle and enshroud these Humans in a small copse of trees to protect them from the sun and wind. If that is acceptable, that is."

Durn waited. A moment later, the tree swayed as if a breeze blew through it where there was none. Durn backed away and bowed, not knowing if that was appropriate, but noticed the trees slowly thickening around the location of the prisoners. He had done it.

Bandu was in shock. "Are you too a druid, my Commander?"

"Far from it! I am just glad that the pine was patient and didn't squash me like an ant!" Durn laughed, but his laugh was cut short by screaming from the enemy. He looked over as he saw some trying to run and escape the trees, but everyone who ran was wrapped in vines and dragged back into the circle. Soon, all had stopped their attempts and sat in a huddled, terrified mass.

Durn shook his head and sighed. "Well, I should have seen that coming. I would have run for it also."

Bandu laughed.

"I must go talk to these people. Come on, boy, let's do this." The old man motioned to the Captain, who followed him to the tree line.

"Pardon me, trees, may I pass?" Durn asked seriously.

There was no response.

"Well, tell my wife I love her, boy," the old man quipped, entering the tree line with his eyes closed.

The trees opened up and allowed the Commander to pass unharmed. Inside the ring, the enemy captives were silent. They looked at the Draj Commander in awe. He was in command of not only the Draj, but now the trees also obeyed his commands. One young man stepped forward. He was agitated and obviously frightened, concerning what was going on around him.

"Who are you!?" the man in armor challenged. "What sort of magic is this?" He pointed to the tree ring. "Do you seek to crush us with these trees? Why? We have surrendered!" The man advanced on Durn, who immediately put his hand on his sword hilt, but before the Draj could draw it, several hundred tree branches shot out and surrounded the advancing man. He was surrounded by an iron maiden of sorts, as spears of wooden spikes pointed to within inches of every point on his body. Durn stood at ease looking on.

"Easy my wooded friends. He is afraid. He is not dangerous." Durn looked at his advancing adversary sarcastically. "You are not dangerous, are you, my lord?"

The advancing man shook his head vehemently, "No, Sir. No." The man was sweating profusely, and his eyes were wide.

"Please stand down, my friends," Durn asked politely to his tree defenders.

They complied by withdrawing their branches. The younger man dared not move. He sat on the muddy ground where he stood, frowning and shaking. He looked to the ground in defeat. He was filthy, injured, hungry, and cold.

"What is your name, my lord?" the Draj Commander asked.

"I am Broswyn, son of Rodren. I am the Commander of the forces you have captured, Sir." The young man looked up at Durn with a dejected stare. Durn could tell that he was a desperate soul and that he genuinely cared about the state of his people.

"Well, Commander," Durn said extending his hand and helping the younger man to his feet, "I am Durn, Commander of the first Legion of the Draj-Erynseere. Well met."

The younger man stood and tried to compose himself. Durn smiled and realized how young this man was. Then the Draj remembered how this man had fought on the field. He had taken two-hundred-fifty Draj Elites with the rabble. He knew tactics and was a decent General. He just didn't have the resources that Durn had.

"Rest assured that I do not wish to kill any more of your people, my adversary." Durn turned to the crowd and raised his voice. "These trees are sent by Queen Adasser, the High Priestess of Haya. She controls them, not I. They will defend anyone from Yslan and anyone allied with us. If you seek to harm a member of my forces, you will deal with them. It will not be pretty, let me assure you."

Durn turned and looked at the trees. They had set up covered canopies in locations. He nodded and smiled. "Also, if you want wood, ask! If one of you cuts down one of these trees, may Haya have mercy upon your soul … you will meet her quite quickly! Let me assure you all of that also."

There was a murmur in the crowd. Broswyn raised his voice. "Pray attend. Listen!" The militia Commander nodded to Durn, who bowed respectfully.

"I have asked that the trees shelter you and provide wood for your fires. We are not sure how long we will be here, or how long you will be captive. I hope to resolve this conflict quickly. Hopefully, my leadership and the leadership of Cinnog can hash things out at a table somewhere, and we won't have to revisit the discussion on the battlefield." Durn raised an eyebrow and saw many a toothless face nodding in agreement with his statements. The Draj smiled.

"So, we are safe to move into the pine-needled areas under the canopies?" Broswyn asked hopefully.

"Yes, that is our intention. To house all of you the best that we can," Durn responded. "I will see about food. We are short, but I have sent word to my Queen. I hope to hear something soon. Until then, we are rationing and will send in whatever we can come up with. If you have anything among you, sharing would be advisable. It may be a day or two."

The young man looked at Durn with curiosity. This man was a great General who waded through his forces as if they were made of parchment, but he was also a man of integrity and honor. Broswyn began to wonder if he was on the wrong side of this whole affair. He kept his thoughts to himself and resolved to continue watching the conduct of Yslandeth. Palgur had told the young man many things about Puryn, Orus, and the Northern Alliance. It was true that they were fierce warriors, but the ruthless and carelessness nature of the North's conduct, as stated by his ruler, seemed to Broswyn to be hugely overstated, if not, a blatant lie. He would watch and make his own determination.

After a long conversation with his remaining people, the militia Commander convinced many of the younger men and women to take shelter within the trees. Fires were made close enough to the perimeter of the shades to warm the people within, but not close enough to burn the trees. The circle provided wood without the need of cutting down any trees, and Durn ordered that every extra blanket was handed over to the prisoners. Many would have to share, but those who did, had no complaints after their frigid first night in captivity. The prisoners gathered their provisions into a small pile. Durn provided some hard biscuits and root vegetables. A few pots were rounded up, and several camp cooks set off to create whatever sustenance that could be had from the ingredients that they had on hand.

Durn returned to his encampment. The leadership had everything under control. A squire handed the Commander his dinner as the older man watched the sun begin to dip below the mountains to his northeast. He could already see his breath as the men stoked the field fires. It was going to be another cold night. He hoped that Yslandeth would not take too long in bringing supplies.

After a few hours had passed, Durn said goodnight to Bandu and the other Captains. He entered his tent and went to sleep, hoping for better news in the morning.

***

Horns were heard blowing to the North. Bandu snapped up with his spyglass to his eye. He smiled as he recognized the banners of his friends from the second and third Draj-Erynseere Legions.

"Huzzah! Sound the response!" Bandu ordered, and his own horns blared out in response.

Durn appeared at the flap, hopping as he fought to put on his right boot. "Trouble?" he asked.

"Quite the opposite, Sir! Our reinforcements have arrived!" Bandu said happily.

"Excellent! I hope they brought more bacon," Durn said looking northward. He was relieved that the next army he would meet would be one of his own. He was sure that he would get a "talking to" for his actions before the conflict, but he did not care. He had made the command decision. No one else was here to make it, and he would not apologize for doing his job.

He knew that his son would understand, even if his beautiful bride did not. He honestly did not care. He had things to deal with at the moment. He was the senior Commander on the field and had eight-hundred prisoners to deal with.

Courts-martial could wait.

Chapter 13

The morning was cold and dry, but the sky was overcast. Brynd sniffed the air apprehensively. He could see that the weather was bound to take a turn for the worse, and sometime soon. He looked up at the gray skies above him, noting that the tops of the mountains were obscured from view. The party had left before dawn at Basric's request. The prince did not want his people to know what the King's scouts were up to. Adding to the stress of an already exhausted populace served no one, especially a man who sought to rule the nation.

The band traveled up into the mountains, riding until it was afternoon. The temperature had begun to drop rapidly, dipping into the high thirties. Clouds were now much more menacing, and Brynd was growing concerned that the group may become trapped if a hard snow fell.

"Kairoth, the weather is starting to turn, brother. No telling what things will be like at a higher elevation." Brynd pointed ahead into the misty path as he spoke.

"Understood, my friend, but the enemy does not wait for fairer weather. It weaves its evil while we delay." Kairoth was anxious. He did not like the prospect of fighting the Scourge again and underground in their home, but he knew that he had no alternative. The enemy had the advantage. Why would they leave the cover of the darkness and the safety of their domain?

"It's cold, Kairoth," Safiya complained. "Can we pull to the side of the path and at least put on warmer clothing? The temperature gets colder the higher we go." Safiya was annoyed by the misting weather around her, and then the first flurries hit her nose. "Oh, wonderful," she snarled sarcastically.

"Pull over up there," Kairoth ordered, pointing to the right of the path. "Let's make sure that we are better clothed and ready for the enemy. Everyone, check your weapons and armor. Mages, er … Do whatever it is that you do."

Sal'iabac snickered and dismounted, walking over to Safiya. She helped her sister to put on the standard thick woolen cloak that they all had been issued in Yslandeth. Safiya sighed in relief.

"At least now I am not going to freeze to death. No guarantees about anything else killing me!" Safiya gave her sister a sarcastic smile. They both laughed. Kairoth was not laughing.

Out of the mist, there was a shout. Kairoth drew his sword while still in his saddle. He knew that the sound came from close by, but could not see very well in the fog. Brynd had an arrow nocked and was scanning the barely visible tree line.

"Druid! Was that you?" shouted Brynd.

"Yes!" responded a much calmer Reynir, walking toward them with his hands above his head. "Please do not shoot, friends!"

"What in the Underworld is your problem, druid?" Kairoth questioned in a subdued voice. He was agitated and was in no mood for foolishness from his band.

"Well, I was using the forest, if you know what I mean." Reynir gestured with his hands.

"Yes, yes! I understand." Kairoth shook his head in disbelief. "What startled you? I don't need to know the other details."

"Oh yes, well, while I was performing my necessary tasks in the woods, I was approached by two friends." Reynir smiled like a child at Winterfest who had just opened his favorite toy. "She sent them."

"Who sent who, druid?" Kairoth asked in wonder and annoyance.

"The Queen! My Mistress said that I would meet two friends on the road. Well, I met them." Reynir smiled broadly.

"Are they Elves? Dwarves? What?" Brynd stated abruptly. "Who are they?"

"Two saplings. Both pines. Scarcely ten, maybe fifteen years old, but already twenty-feet high and full!" Reynir sounded as if he were describing his calf at the farmer's fair.

"You have two trees now?" Kairoth asked raising his eyebrows.

"Yes, but they are still autonomous. They will come when I call and help me without having to check with, her." Reynir smiled. "I can't believe she trusts me this much." Reynir changed to a whisper, getting closer to Kairoth. "I do not think Prince Illari has trees, and he's the number one apprentice." Reynir's eyes widened at the thought.

Kairoth looked nodded. "Good show, druid. Maybe you can use them to scout ahead?"

"Good idea! Let me ask them to look up the path. One will stay back and relay whatever the other observes. This will be the most excellent thing that I've ever done as a druid. I'll be right back." Reynir trotted off into the mist from where he came.

"That boy is not completely right, Brynd, but he is deceptively useful and dangerous." Kairoth looked at Brynd, who nodded in response.

Reynir returned quickly. "One is on his, er, her … um, it's way up the mountain."

"Where is the other?" Kairoth questioned.

"Oh, right behind you, brother!" Reynir smiled, as Kairoth jumped, seeing a twenty-foot-tall pine within five feet of his position where none was standing moments before.

"My Gods, I will never get used to that," Kairoth said clutching his heart for a moment. "How are they so quiet?"

"Well, I think it has something to do with being connected to nature. They communicate by roots and by the breeze. I guess that one could say that they move like the wind … unseen and seldom heard on a fair day?"

"Oh, so now you are a bard also," quipped Brynd. "How far up the mountain is our scout?"

Reynir laughed. "He, oh whatever … they're going to be he's for ease of talking. HE is almost up the mountain already. He is unhappy with the deforestation and dead trees. Thankfully, no ancients perished due to whatever is going on. At least he doesn't think so."

"What else? What else?" Kairoth demanded.

"My scout says that there is evil in the area. Wait, I will try something." Reynir walked over to his other minion near Kairoth, placing his hand on the tree's trunk and saying a short prayer. His eyes were closed, and he began to shake. Tears fell from his eyes as he forced himself to break free. Reynir frantically addressed the remaining tree. "Call him back now, friend! Tell him to get out of there immediately!"

The druid stood up frowning, sniffled a bit, and wiped his eyes dry. Within a few moments, the other tree appeared next to its partner. Kairoth was concerned, but allowed the druid to collect himself. Reynir was talking to the tree that had gone scouting up the mountain. He was touching its trunk and speaking in an unintelligible tongue. Reynir was very contrite. The tree's branches waved, as if a breeze blew where there was none, and the druid stood upright, turning toward Kairoth.

"It is as we had feared, friends. The Offlanders are within these mountains. There is a cave five miles up this road. Same scenario." Reynir sat down and drank a bit of water.

"What did you see, Reynir?" Kairoth asked in an uncharacteristically sympathetic tone.

"I saw death. Hate. Murder. I saw the eyes of the Underlord looking at us. The Denir are here, I can feel them." Reynir was more grave than he had ever been.

"Denir? Like in the Underworld, Denir?" asked Valtyr, who overheard the conversation.

"The very same, my brother." Reynir took a piece of hardtack from Valtyr and began to munch on it to settle his stomach.

Kairoth drew a deep breath and stared up the mountain. He was unsure if his friends were up to this task, but they had little choice. They were the only trained forces in the area, and the threat of Offlanders taking villagers to raise the Underlord was too much to ignore. He closed his eyes and prayed to Haya for guidance.

"Everyone, gather around. All of you bring your rations with you. We must talk this out." Kairoth motioned for all to rally around him. He dismounted and grabbed his waterskin, taking a long pull off of it.

Sal'iabac and Safiya grabbed their reagents while stuffing some dried beef into their mouths. Brynd moved closer, but did not remove his arrow from his string, nor did he stop scanning the horizon. Danzu stood, his sword drawn, beside the ranger. Kairoth searched for the words.

"Reynir has seen things through his own personal tree scouts, provided by Her Majesty herself." The mages cocked their heads, and their eyes widened.

"The druid has trees?" Sal'iabac asked seriously.

"Yes, he does, but that is not what I called us together for." Kairoth looked around at the concerned faces that stared back at him. "The Offlander scourge is here and worse than the last site." The Hodan warrior wiped his mouth with his hand, continuing, "The druid felt the presence of evil. The Denir or Haeldrun himself."

There was a gasp from the group. "Surely, the Underlord is not here, in this tiny locale, Kairoth. I figured him more for a Sudenyag, man. Port of Valent, red district." Safiya laughed coarsely with her sister.

"Laugh, but you didn't see the druid's reaction." Kairoth looked at Reynir, who was still composing himself. "I could almost feel it by watching his face. It was despair and evil incarnate."

Reynir nodded. "He is not wrong."

The druid looked to the ground. Valtyr prayed silently to the Goddess for protection. Brynd smirked and shook his head in disgust at the news. The mages still thought this was some sort of a joke. Danzu gripped his sword tightly, worrying for the future.

"We need to be very careful when we enter this lair. Everyone must cover the other. No unnecessary risks. Where is Famlin? Why do I ask?" Kairoth looked at Sal'iabac, who snorted.

"Oh, you mean like someone riding off into an entire cavalry charge like a crazy maniac? Or maybe running into a sacrificial temple solo, while injured?" The group was looking intently at Kairoth.

"Exactly. Don't be foolhardy with your lives." Kairoth looked to the skies. It was darkening, and the flurries were coming down a bit harder. "We should camp here. We will need a fire, especially tonight. Reynir, are there enough trees to do a ring here?"

The druid asked his minions, and then replied, "No there are not. Only these two and a few stragglers. They will contact their forest and set up strategically around us. We will know if anyone attacks. The screams of the attackers will wake us." The druid's tone was strangely dark and angry.

Kairoth nodded. "Everyone set camp and get some rest. It looks as if it is warriors and trees on watch tonight. Mages, priests, and druids rest up. Tomorrow is going to be a busy day."

* * *

The fourth Legion made its way southward from Yslandeth and crossed the border with Cinnog at the second hour of the morning. There, they encountered minor militia resistance, quelling it without much ado.

The Commander was a younger man, name Furtim. He was a captain in Puryn's Draj forces, but hailed initially from Korin. His family moved to Erynseere after the War of the People left Korin in shambles. Unfortunately, his family sought to go away from one disaster, only to move to Puryn's land and see that a similar fate had also befallen the new barony. Still, his family was happy to rebuild with the first of Puryn's settlers, and they were granted lands toward the Hodan border.

Hodan was a worry in the beginning, but Furtim's father feared the rule of Athis, son of Verdin, much more than the threat of Jabir, for the new Baron of Korin was not yet known as one of virtue, but instead as one of greed and malice. Athis would later prove their fears wrong at the Battle of the Alabaster Sands, where the monk sacrificed himself and his unit, allowing Puryn and Jabir's replacement, King Orus of Hodan, to continue their fight against the scourge. Regardless of the redemption of Athis,

Furtim's inheritance had already been established in Erynseere by then, and there was nothing left for his family back in Korin.

Furtim was an active leader. He was fiercely loyal to Yslandeth and even more so to Erynseere and to Their Majesties. He was promoted to Commander of the fourth Draj Legion at the age of twenty-two, which up until then was unheard of. Puryn personally awarded him his commission, and Furtim never forgot that honor. Now the new leader sat on his horse in front of one-thousand Draj and support services, entering a hostile land for the first time in his life. In fact, he had never left Yslandeth before that moment.

"Gentlemen," Furtim called out to his Lieutenants. The four men rode to their Commander with a purpose.

One of them spoke. "Yes, Sir!" The others echoed the first.

"Send a scout to the village ahead. I believe it to be the location where we are to be deployed. It should be called Rordsburg, I believe."

One of the Lieutenants barked an order and off a squire rode at full speed toward the village. The rider had a lance raised with a white flag and the banner of Yslandeth flying in the breeze above him. He approached the ramshackle gate and wall of the village, where he was challenged by the guard.

"Halt! Who goes there!?" yelled an armored person from the inside of the barely standing gate. The sentry was accompanied by four archers and five older gentlemen with boar spears.

"Hail and well met, sentry, I am the messenger of Commander Furtim, of His Majesties' fourth Draj Legion. We travel from Erynseere by order of King Puryn to aid Prince Basric and those under his rule. Are you friend or foe, Sir? If you are a foe, I would suggest surrendering immediately, before my friends arrive. They will not come to talk it over." The Draj sat smugly on the horse, looking at the ragtag militia within the gate. The old man in armor was smiling, and then he began to laugh out loud. The Draj did not how to take the man's demeanor. He was not sure if he was mocking him and had a death wish, or happy to see him. The scout raised his shield, dropping the spear and pulling out his short glaive.

"Stand down, boy!" the older man replied walking to the gate. "Everyone, calm down! Let him in! We are friends, scout. I am Basric. I am he, whom your Commander seeks."

The scout relaxed. "Your Highness, I must return to my unit and tell them the good news. We will be here within the hour, Sir." The scout saluted.

"Of course! See you all in a bit!" The Prince was smiling for the first time in a week. He finally had an answer to Palgur. Basric knew that the coward would run.

* * *

The sun was up. It was a frigid morning. Nothing had stirred around the camp. The trees hadn't moved an inch since the group had set up their private shelters and laid down to rest for the night. Everything was covered in frost. It had snowed about an inch or two, but the snow was dry and powdery. The ground was in excellent condition, and the horses looked ready to get on the move. Sal'iabac walked up to the fire, throwing down some hay and shavings and then a couple of small logs. She said a short phrase, which caused the fuel that she had just set down to burst into flames. She coaxed the fire, fanning the embers and kindling. Soon, the flames were going well. The mage kept the fire small enough to be quickly extinguished, but large enough that two or three folks could break their chill from a night of sleeping on the frozen ground. Safiya promptly joined her, heating up some water and making some tea. The others wandered over, one by one.

"So, Reynir," Kairoth remarked while warming his hands, "your trees said three to five miles up the trail to the entrance of this place?"

"Yes. Probably closer to three, from the feeling that I got from our conversation." Reynir was having a hard time explaining talking to trees in words non-druids would understand. "It's kind of a combination of feeling and seeing what they experience, and broken Etah."

"Well, whatever it is, it's a handy trick, druid." Kairoth looked at the rest of the group. "We can be there within an hour or two if we take it slow. I think that we should. Not sure how icy it might be on the way up, or how steep, for that matter."

The group grunted in unison.

"I hate to say it, Salia, but we need to put the fire out and get moving," Kairoth frowned.

Sal'iabac laughed. "Yes, yes, I know. Time to freeze. Why did I come on this trip again?"

The group turned from the embers that were quickly extinguished by collected snow. Everyone broke camp and packed their belongings away. The horses were re-saddled, and the group was off within an hour. It was the third hour of the morning. The sun was bright and reflected off of the white of the snow on the ground.

"At least there is no fog, Brynd," Kairoth said quietly.

"Nor, warmth," Brynd laughed. "It's a nice day in the woods, brother. Hopefully, the day ends as peaceful as it began."

"Agreed," Kairoth responded, calling for the group to depart.

Within two hours, they reached their destination, high on a small plateau, in a dead forest where nothing dared to live. Even Reynir's trees were afraid to enter, and the druid ordered them to stay back.

"We wait here. You call, we come fast. Queen say so," Reynir's minions responded.

"Well, only come if it is necessary, my friends. Let Her Majesty know what we are up against."

"She know. She tell King. Men come." The trees retreated as they were ordered.

* * *

In Rordsburg, the militia had allowed Furtim and his Lieutenants into the village. The rest of the Draj Legion took up defensive positions around the township. Residents were seen poking their heads around their thatched awnings, and mud and waddle homes. They tried to get a glimpse of the pristine warrior unit that had just inhabited their immediate border. Some were frightened, but others were encouraged.

Inside the inn, Basric showed his credentials to the Draj Commander, and vice versa. Once the introductions and verifications were made, the Prince informed the Commander of the aggression of Palgur's units, and how a band of the King's men and women had come to Rordsburg and helped to defend his village against being overrun.

The Commander nodded, but was concerned. "Where are they now, Your Highness? Did they move on?"

"No, son, they went even farther to defend my people. Up in the mountains northeast of here, they detected an evil lurking underground. The druid with them discovered the trees were dying by the cord. All of the living creatures have left the area. I mentioned to Kairoth that we were losing women and children." The Prince paused. "I assumed that it was Palgur's militias, not demons."

"Demons, Your Highness?" The Commander was skeptical.

"Well, perhaps, perhaps not, but in the least, it's the work of some leftover Offlander priests to the Underlord, or some such evil. That is what the lad, Kairoth, told me before he took his people up the pass." The Prince shook his head. "And then it snows on them." He sighed.

"Offlanders? Sir, of what do you speak?" The Commander was alarmed now. His Lieutenants could hear it in his voice. "The Golden Queen vanquished them all with His Majesty and his men. There are no more Offlanders on the Ert!"

"One would think, but apparently the scribes were a bit hasty at writing the end to that tale. Kairoth, their leader, said that they had encountered them at Yslandeth's Raven's Pass. They, too, thought that a militia was stealing women and children there, only to find a smaller version of what they said they found here. I fear that our infestation may be even more dire."

"If this is true, I must assist these agents!" The commander called to his Lieutenants, "Form one-hundred Draj cavalry. Ensure that they have bows, as well as glaives and shield. Track a party of eight on horseback. It should not be hard to track them; they are not Elves."

"Yes, Sir!" they replied as one.

"Have them report to a man named Kairoth. A Hodan warrior. Support him in any fashion that he sees fit until I send reinforcements. He is leading a team of the King's Elites. Tell the men to be careful. The enemy is not militia this time. There are most likely Offlander remnants in the caves."

"Thank you, Commander," the Prince said solemnly. "They do not deserve to die that way."

"I will not suffer my own to die without doing my best to get them back alive." The Commander bowed and exited the inn to see the cavalry traveling rapidly toward the foothills of the mountains. He uttered a quick prayer and looked up toward Aeternum. He hoped that the Goddess was listening.

* * *

It was the same thing as Raven's Pass. Kairoth looked at the covered mouth of a natural cave that had been widened out by chisel and hammer. He recognized the work as the same design as the last time. He pulled out the coin that Sal'iabac had given him weeks ago.

"Oh, I had wondered where that had gotten off to!" Sal'iabac kissed Kairoth on the cheek. "For good luck and to remember that living wouldn't be a bad idea either, you oaf."

Kairoth stifled a smile. "Solus," he said, and the coin lit brightly.

Safiya clapped and sarcastically responded, "Oh! He is teachable! This one might be a mage in the making!" Safiya giggled at Kairoth's pretended anger.

"Enough! We must focus. We almost lost two last time we went up against this filth. Everyone be on their guard." Kairoth pointed at the mages and the druid. "What is that, Reynir?"

Reynir had a burlap sack with dirt and a small bush in it. "I wasn't only using the privy, I had to find a replacement for my friend who died valiantly crushing Orcs last go around!"

Kairoth remembered the incident. "Ah yes, definitely, bring it along."

Reynir smiled smugly. "Not so silly anymore is it?" he quipped to Valtyr.

"Listen you, quit fooling around and be serious. I want to sit around a nice fire, drink too much and pick on you in this life first. Aeternum can wait, brother!" Valtyr poked Reynir in the chest, eliciting a smile from his brother.

"Our days are numbered by the Gods. We will not live a moment longer. Better to go out on our feet than whimpering on our sick bed." Reynir smiled.

"Let's not get sacrificed to the Underlord. Can we avoid that please?" Valtyr rolled his eyes.

* * *

The cave stunk. The group had traveled long past the point of seeing the exit to the passage behind them. It was dark, except for the light that was emitted by the two coins worn by Kairoth and Safiya. There was some additional ambient light, because the ranger was lighting any torches that he found, and leaving them in sconces he encountered along the way. His efforts were helping, but they would not last very long.

Kairoth and Danzu took the lead, followed by Reynir, Sal'iabac, and Safiya. The priest and ranger watched for anything coming from behind. So far, there were no encounters with the enemy, but things began to change when Kairoth heard something coming toward their position. He called for a halt using hand signals. The party stopped and formed up defensively. A small, dark shape moved toward the group. It appeared humanoid and was moving swiftly and silently. It halted abruptly and seemed to be waving frantically.

Kairoth rolled his eyes. It had to be Famlin. The Hodan warrior whispered, "Hold your fire, Brynd, I think it's our specialist."

"He'll never learn, will he?" Brynd whispered back.

"Apparently not. He's not too bright, I fear." Kairoth motioned for the dark figure to move forward. It came slowly toward him.

"That's close enough," Kairoth whispered. "Who are you?"

"It's me, who else?" Famlin responded. "Big room of bad guys ahead. Not great odds right now, boss."

"How did I know that it was you?" Kairoth droned, rolling his eyes. "At least we didn't shoot you this time. How far to the enemy?"

"Two-hundred or three-hundred yards, at most. This is a guard post. There have to be twenty-five or thirty Goblins and five Ogres. I think that they're Ogres. Much too big to be Goblins."

"Oh, that's great. Ogres now. How big are those?" Kairoth asked, afraid to know.

"Nine feet tall, maybe ten," Famlin said reaching high with his right hand.

"Well, the first thing we have to do is draw them into close quarters. This hallway to be precise. Kill them two or three at a time. We might have a chance then. These adversaries do not seem to be too intellectual. We might be able to outsmart and outmaneuver them in tight spaces."

"I have set traps in the hallway, using small charges of Thunder Powder. I may be able to injure or kill some of them, but the group needs to stay back until all of the charges have blown. My traps will not discriminate as to who they maim or kill."

"Understood. Go make them bleed as best you can. We will form up at this corner. They will not see us and run right into us. The main force will not be able to stack up, because of the short length of the corridor. This is our best bet. Good luck."

Safiya pushed to the front, kneeling down and kissing the thief's coal covered face. "For luck."

Famlin smiled at her and then took off swiftly back the way he had come. Kairoth's band set up three feet from a ninety-degree turn, waiting in the blind spot. Shortly after the shield wall was set, the mages were in position. Shouting and growling could be heard coming from down the passageway. Twenty seconds later, there was a grand commotion, followed by a series of successive explosions and screams from the enemy. Within seconds, the sound of boots on stone could be heard distinctly, as someone ran down the hallway toward the shield wall.

"Here they come," Famlin said, dropping to the floor and sliding under the shield wall.

Reynir dodged the incoming thief and then set his plant on the floor, the second rank back. He prayed and watched as it began to take root within the cracks in the stone. Satisfied, he stepped back behind the plant line.

"Beware that my friend is ready. If you are pushed backward, come back to me, and I will send in the vines." Reynir's eyes glowed with a slight reddish tint.

"Understood!" Kairoth yelled. "Brace for impact!"

The faster Goblins got there first. The warriors in the front were thankful. As the rest of the enemy arrived, Kairoth counted seventeen Goblins and three Ogres. The specialist had made a significant dent in the enemy force, and not a soul was complaining from Kairoth's side. Shields crashed loudly in the enclosed space as the enemy charged with a vengeance, pushing the three-man front backward and behind Reynir's plant barrier.

"Druid!!! Now!!!" Brynd yelled, as Kairoth killed his first Goblin with his sword.

Reynir let out a throaty chuckle. Even the Goblins on the front ranks looked at the slightly built druid with confusion and fear, and some even contemplated turning to run, but it was too late. Five of the enemy attackers were tripped by vines and quickly enveloped by the plant's tendrils. The quintet died, gasping for air and wheezing, until all of them laid motionless. Reynir was invigorated.

"Yes, my little friend, excellent!" the druid commended. The plant released the dead and readied for the next wave. Reynir smiled, and his eyes glowed a brighter crimson.

The enemy stopped for the moment. They were not stupid. Many had fought against Puryn and Orus. They knew that the Humans were trying to draw numbers into a small space. They decided to use strength and power. Two Ogres charged next.

Kairoth did not have time to call for the ready. The enemy lifted the three shield men off of the ground, slamming Danzu against the right wall, Brynd against the left, while throwing Kairoth up against the ceiling and into the priest and druid. For a moment, everyone was in disarray.

Danzu was the slowest getting up. He was dazed. Staggering, he unable to recover before the Ogre in front of him hit the smaller warrior with a crushing blow of his mace. Danzu fell to the floor where several Goblins jumped on him and finished the job. Brynd was able to recover in time to see the Goblin advance and killed three, while they were busy with the defenseless warrior.

Kairoth stood. He saw Danzu and was enraged. Sal'iabac grabbed her sister, picking her up off of the floor, and refocused her attention on the front lines.

"Cover the ranger; I have my idiot." Sal'iabac limped over in front of the druid, who was collecting his senses. "Let's go, druid. Plants! Now! Please!"

The druid acknowledged and directed his minion to attack the two Ogres. "Valtyr, warrior down on the left, brother! I will try to grab the big one off of them. It's not looking good for my friend, though. They are really strong! Be careful, Valtyr!"

Kairoth was on the Ogre in seconds. He knew that he could not move him efficiently, but the Hodan was faster and more agile than his lumbering opponent. The Ogre lunged at the charging warrior, who dropped and slid beside its left leg. Kairoth cut the tendons out of the massive brute's leg, and then he kicked out its knee. The giant fell over on top of the motionless Danzu. Kairoth did the same maneuver to the Ogre's other leg and while it flailed around trying to stand, the Hodan maneuvered around to the back of his opponent, cleanly severing its head from its shoulders. Kairoth roared angrily, knowing Danzu had gone to Aeternum. He grabbed the

Ogre's head. Its face still moved as if it was trying to say something, but nothing was coming out of its mouth. Kairoth spat on its face and then turned to the Goblins, who were regrouping.

"A gift, Toads!" Kairoth said, throwing the twitching face into their crowd. There was shriek, and then they formed a shield wall of their own.

On the right side of the enemy's front, Brynd had made a veritable pincushion out of the other Ogre who was now on the party's front lines. Reynir's plant was barely holding on. The Ogre had absorbed at least ten arrows in every joint and body part imaginable, but the beast would not fall. Kairoth turned to the injured Ogre to his right, noticing that the Goblins had not come after him yet. He figured they were intimidated by the death of their Ogre savior. Kairoth wagered that they would indeed be unhappy if he could kill the other one. The Ogre fought Reynir's vines while Kairoth maneuvered quickly behind the lumbering enemy. The Hodan warrior could see the fear in the beast's eyes as it was unable to reach behind and grab him. Kairoth executed the Ogre in the same manner as the first. The warrior then turned and saw that the last Ogre had paused to consider its future.

The Goblins, seeing that the Ogres were of no effect, decided to attack as one. Before they could make it ten feet toward Kairoth, Sal'iabac chanted out her spell, and electricity shot out of her hands and into the crowd of vermin. Five died instantly, and four were incapacitated on the floor. Kairoth and Brynd dispatched the last four Goblins. The final Ogre had seen enough, turning to run down the passageway howling for help.

Kairoth closed his eyes and sighed. "Damn it all to the Underworld."

"I think we're already here, brother," Valtyr said checking Danzu's vital signs. The priest rolled the Ogre carcass off of his friend then sat by him, closed his eyes, and crossed his arms. Valtyr's voice cracked as he prayed for Danzu's soul.

"This is not over by a longshot. We must focus." Famlin was standing up and taking inventory of a stash of goods he had left in the corner of the room. "I can make some more noise, but those were just the soldiers. We have not seen their priests, nor their mages. It's only going to get worse, my friends."

"Agreed. I can only guess where that spawn of Haeldrun ran off to. How many more of these bastards can there be down here?" Kairoth didn't really want to know. He just wanted to get out of this place with everyone else intact.

"Set his body aside, brothers. We will come back for him," Brynd remarked. "We need to move. Specialist, I will track the Ogre. You set up some entertainment for anyone coming to visit our position."

"Agreed. Let's go, ranger. Don't shoot me, freaking half-wit." Famlin slapped Brynd on the shoulder.

The ranger shook his head and laughed. "Stop catching my arrows midflight, you arrow sponge!"

Kairoth looked at Danzu and was not in a laughing mood. He watched the duo leave as they crept silently down the passageway and out of sight.

Sal'iabac walked up to her man. "It is not your fault, you know this, don't you?"

"I am in command, Salia, it is no one's responsibility, but my own." Kairoth kissed her lips and then stood, composing himself. "I need you up front now, priest. Mail is stronger than the druid's leather. Besides, having you close as a field surgeon is never a bad idea."

"You be careful, Valtyr! I mean it." Reynir looked at his brother with a serious face, then frowned when he saw Danzu lying there motionless. "Damn it. How do men continue in this profession? If you don't die, you watch everyone you care about perish."

Valtyr hugged his friend briefly and then healed Kairoth's superficial wounds. "That charge could have been much worse, leader," the priest said, as a matter of fact.

"No doubt about that, priest. That druid brother of yours made the difference again, and Salia, too. We were just a rut in the road during the battle."

"Hardly. Two Ogres and seventeen Goblins. Two Ogres by your hand. Do not be modest." Valtyr finished bandaging the wounds.

"One was unable to move, priest. That hardly counts," the warrior said wearily.

"One saw what you did and ran. Effectively, you neutralized two and had assistance on the third. If those three had come at once …" Valtyr trailed off.

There was noise down the passageway. A clamoring and the sound of running. A distinct shout of "Make ready! Make ready!" Could be heard over the din. It was Brynd yelling and running.

"Everyone, quickly fill that passageway on the other side of the room. Do it now. Priest, up front with me. Druid, behind us. Mages, to the rear. Get ready, ladies. It's up to you now." Kairoth set his feet as lights danced in the distance off of the darkened walls of the passageway in front of him. The sound was getting closer. There were a few growls behind the two Humans who were running full-speed toward Kairoth and Valtyr.

"Make a hole and get down!" yelled Famlin as he tapped Brynd on the shoulder. The ranger dove to the side of the shield wall while Famlin ran on the wall to the left of Valtyr.

"Did you see that, Kairoth?" Valtyr asked lying flat on the ground beside the Hodan warrior.

"Nothing that you people do amazes me anymore." Kairoth looked up to see Brynd light an arrow and fire in one quick motion. Somewhere in the distance, there was a hiss and then sparks of a fuse burning toward the oncoming enemy. Brynd dove against the wall and hid his face, covering his ears.

Within seconds, the passageway was a cacophony of explosions and screaming enemy. The smoke of the charges filled the air, as did the smell of burning hair and flesh. The King's band stood up, one by one, some rubbing their eyes and ears vigorously, in an attempt to stop the ringing and clear the soot, but the gesture was futile. Famlin rejoined the party and called for it to form and stand ready.

"That's the last of it, Kairoth. No more powder, just good old-fashioned traps with pointy objects now. I think they're trying to figure out if they want to come down the passageway after that barrage." Famlin smiled. The thief looked tired.

"Well, now that we have them guessing, I say that we send you and Brynd forward to scout for the next brood that we need to deal with. We cannot afford to be surprised." Kairoth looked up the smoky hallway, half-expecting a charge at any minute, but he did not get one. He was grateful for the short reprieve. "Let's go, men, you are our eyes. Be careful."

Brynd and Famlin disappeared down the passageway. Any injured Offlanders that they found were summarily executed by the thief. Brynd was surprised by the cold efficiency with which the smaller thief carved up an adversary, many times ensuring that the victim was unable to cry out as it expired. The hair on Brynd's neck stood up when he saw Famlin's facial expression as he did the deed.

Famlin saw his displeasure. "What?"

"Nothing, brother. Forward, slow," Brynd replied nocking an arrow.

Another five-hundred yards down the twisting passages, the two came upon the room that they were looking for. A large circular chamber, hewn from the rock. It was several hundred feet across, and the ceiling was at least thirty feet high above. In the center was an altar with an unfortunate victim, upside down on a platform. There, the priests of Haeldrun had sliced the sacrifice's throat and collected the victim's blood in a stone trough that fed into a pool of blood below a statue of a hooded figure. Beneath the stone statue's hood, two eyes were glowing red from a fire that burned within the statue.

"This is definitely the place, brother," Famlin said in disgust.

"Yes, it is. Let's sneak back to the group and let ..." Brynd was caught short by the screams of a young boy and girl who were being led to the platform where a woman lay dead. "Oh, for the love of the Gods, really?" Brynd looked at Famlin. "Go get them. I will play tag with this scum until you return."

"To the Underworld with that idea. It's suicide. There are five priests in here." Famlin looked around. "How about this? I run out there while you think about it and you kill them while I distract them. Then we run like scalded dogs back to the group. Ready. Go!"

Famlin was off and running. He had backstabbed one priest and sliced his throat, when another grabbed him. The thief shrieked, slashing the priest, but the Todessen just healed himself. Brynd saw this happening and moved as the Elfish Draj do. Invisibly, he moved to a covered position and began loosing arrows on the priest, who was readying another go at Famlin. The ranger dropped the second priest before he took five steps, but it had used half of his quiver to do so.

"These priests are very durable," the ranger joked, picking up the injured thief, "and you are an ass."

"Well, it almost worked, and we killed two Todessen! I call that a win." The thief's legs buckled, and he fell.

Famlin was weakened and could not run too quickly, but that did not matter as the Todessen priests were preoccupied with something else. Brynd was not waiting to find out what they were up to. He ran back to the party, carrying the thief.

"What happened to you?" Kairoth questioned.

"Not sure, Toad priest grabbed me. Then I felt a horrible pain, and I'm very weak right now." Famlin sat down to catch his breath.

"Let me see," Valtyr offered. The priest of Haya prayed for his comrade. Immediately, the thief felt his strength return. He was back to normal.

"That is so much better, priest! Thank you!" Famlin bowed to Valtyr.

"It is nothing, specialist, but you must be more careful!" Valtyr responded.

* * *

In the sacrificial chamber, the priests of the Underlord sent prayers of intercession to their dark God. They pled for deliverance from the invaders of the Underlord's temple, and their prayers were answered. Haeldrun granted his priests their wish. He sent them an army suitable to fight back against the light. Standing around the sanctuary, were about one-hundred undead. They were the animated corpses of the victims who filled the sacrificial waste vats. The Head Priest of Haeldrun smiled and clapped as he witnessed the answer to his dark request. The bodies continued to animate and climb out of the vats until they were emptied.

"What is that sound, Kairoth?" Sal'iabac asked with curiosity. "Do the Todessen come?" She stood preparing.

"I don't think so. They're too slow," Kairoth responded looking down the passage with curiosity.

The first figure shambled into the room where they were resting. It was dressed in peasant attired and walking haphazardly around the room as if it was lost. Kairoth was watching it closely. It appeared to be a young woman who was disoriented. The Hodan warrior stood and grabbed his sword and shield, slowly approaching the meandering female.

"My Lady, are you injured?" Kairoth asked plainly.

The figured turned hissing at the warrior. By the light of Salia's coin, Kairoth could see the woman's lifeless eyes, twisted mouth and sliced open throat. His eyes widened as he noticed that many more were beginning to find their way into the room and they were now interested in his people, who were resting in the corner of the small room.

"Move! Get up! Get up! The dead are here in droves. Leave this place!" Kairoth bellowed. Then he noticed that Danzu was missing from his place. "Damn these Toad, bastards. I will kill them slowly. Where is Danzu?"

Kairoth and the others backed out of the room in defensive formation. Danzu was up and moving in the mass of undead. It appeared to Valtyr that whoever or whatever was managing to make this happen, had control over anyone who had died in the temple.

The undead began to seek out the party, following the living out of the underground temple. At the entrance, Kairoth had a realization. "We cannot suffer this evil to survive, my friends. Imagine this freely roaming the countryside!? Form at the entrance. We must kill them all."

The battle continued until the band was utterly exhausted. Kairoth knew that they had killed almost one-hundred undead, but they kept coming. The party could not keep fighting at this pace. The mages were spent, the druid was unable to hold his weapon, the priest was now a foot soldier.

Even Brynd had become a swordsman, having depleted his arrows hours earlier. The young leader looked at the sky and prayed. He knew the end was near if something did not change soon.

* * *

The one-hundred horsemen of the fourth Legion of the Draj heard a battle ahead of them. They pushed their horses, full gallop, toward the sounds of clashing steel. When they arrived, they saw seven holding the line against at least forty undead.

The Sergeant called out to his men. "Engage the enemy! Extract the King's team!"

The one-hundred broke into ten teams of ten. Each assault team knew their jobs. Instinctively, they formed into their groups. Soon, Draj archers were piercing undead skulls with Elfish longbows and cavalry were running down the undead and ensuring that this time, they remained dead. Three Todessen priests attempted to flee back into their cave, but unfortunately for them, Haeldrun had tired of them, and they had no power left to resist the newly arrived fresh troops. The Todessen were unable to respond with anything more than their blackened wood staves. They did not last five minutes against the one-hundred Draj.

"Burn this place," the Draj Sergeant commanded to his men.

"Wait, Draj," Brynd said in an exhausted voice, collapsing to one knee. "The last time, we encountered captives who were still alive within their temple somewhere. Look first, please."

"He speaks the truth, Sergeant," Kairoth verified, panting and leaning on his shield to remain upright.

"Fine, we shall look. Once we are sure that any innocents are all freed, we will burn their facilities." The Sergeant gave the orders, then told his men to hand food and water over to the remaining seven members of the King's Elites.

An hour later, thirty-seven men, women and children, all of Rordsburg, walked out of the Temple of Haeldrun, praising the Gods for their deliverance. All of them cried out to the Draj, praising their saviors. Kairoth looked at Sal'iabac. The mage rolled her eyes.

Valtyr blessed a water skin, praying to the Goddess. In response, the water skin glowed brightly for a moment. Smiling, the priest took the holy water to the sacrificial chamber and sprinkled it everywhere as he uttered prayers to his Goddess. The Draj toppled the statue of the hooded figure within the unholy sanctuary, utterly defiling the temple in the view of the Underlord. Then Valtyr, along with his fellow Draj defilers, burned the corpses of the victims, to include Danzu, who was lost in the carnage.

"Well, it wasn't the usual pyre, my brother, but wherever you are, I will burn another pyre to send your belongings to you, after the fact. I somehow doubt the Goddess will have a problem with that. Please take care of my friend, My Goddess." Valtyr wiped a tear from his eye as he looked at the gore in front of him. Kairoth had his head down in the nape on Sal'iabac's neck. He was spent. The mage sobbed quietly, holding the Hodan warrior. A similar scene occurred between Safiya and Famlin. Reynir was in no mood for bantering. For the first time in forever, he and Valtyr sat silently eating.

Brynd sat alone drinking a flask of Yslan whiskey. He put a shot in a small cup and set it on a stump by him. "That is for those who have gone before me. Honor and glory. Rest well, my brothers."

Brynd looked over at the thirty-seven souls who were spared from the altar. They all shed tears of joy and gratitude to the Gods. They celebrated their new chance, unaware of the pain that all of the warriors who stood around them had experienced. The ranger was angry for a split second, but then realized they were simple farmers and that all were in shock. None of them knew who had saved the day, or the names of those who had died in the effort.

"It is as it should be, I suppose. We fight for the King, not recognition. Honor and glory, brothers! I will see you when I get there." Brynd downed the last of his whiskey then looked for a place to sleep.

It would be a long ride back to Rordsburg, and he was out of arrows. He needed his energy if he was expected to make do and fight with a sword.

Chapter 14

Lieutenant Thad surveyed the carnage and noted that the sun was starting to dip below the mountain tops. He knew that the cold was coming. It had been a chilly week or two in the field, and the civilians he had just aided in rescuing were unprepared for the elements. There was no going back into the passage for the night. It was filled with the smoke and gore of the undead, as well as the remainder of the Offlander temple to Haeldrun. The young Commander looked about at his men. He wagered that the gambesons that his men were wearing would suffice for around a fire for the night. Those on patrol would retain their cloaks, thirty-seven lucky individuals in his ranks would give theirs up in service to the Goddess and the Crown.

"Sergeant," Thad called, motioning for the leader to come to his location.

His man rode with a purpose to his Commander, reporting in. "Yes, Sir, how may I be of service?"

"Choose thirty-seven Draj to give up their cloaks to the rescued victims. Those men will guard closer to the fires tonight. Anyone with a cloak will be fair game for roving patrols. Do you understand?" The Commander looked at his man seriously, waiting for a protest.

The Sergeant looked at the dirty, huddled faces and had no complaint. "Yes, Sir, right away. The watch will be formed within the hour. Shall I order the distribution of rations to the victims also?"

"Yes, excellent idea! Make it happen." Thad smiled and nodded to his man. The soldier rode off.

Off in the distance, Thad watched the Sergeant call his men to a formation. There, within an organized mob, were ninety-six remaining Draj warriors in full battle gear. It was an impressive sight. The Commander listened to the conversation to get a feel for the mood of the men. What occurred next surprised the young leader.

"Brothers and sisters, the Commander has ordered that thirty-seven Draj will give up their cloaks for the men, women, and children who we have recovered from the scourge. I would like to ask for volunteers before I have to order any of you to hand over your equipment. What say, you, Draj?"

The Lieutenant smiled proudly as he saw ninety-six Draj, including three Sergeants remove and offer their cloaks. Nodding, he knew that all was well with his unit. He dismounted, and a young squire took the reins of his warhorse, tending to it on the side of the road with the others that were not in use.

The people cheered the Draj, some wiping tears away as cloaks and food were distributed to the people who had successfully started a fire with wood collected from the area. The sun was almost entirely gone by the time all was accomplished. The Draj patrolled in the darkness and posted guards throughout the encampment. There was little chance of any hostile forces in the area, but no one was taking bets on this mountain. The memory of the living dead was far too fresh in everyone's mind.

Somewhere, someone played a recorder, and a woman sang a lively tune. The fire had begun to roar, and the thirty-seven survivors cheered their saviors and the Goddess as they ate and drank in warmth, beneath a clear, star-filled sky. The Draj pretended to be the stoic professionals of their reputation, but many could not help but smile at the display of the thankful happiness of these people. It was a peaceful night. Many prayed and thanked the Goddess for deliverance; many remembered the lost, but everyone was glad to be alive.

* * *

The party was downcast. Most sat talking in a subdued manner, looking over at the celebration that was forming around the fire. Reynir had set a small private fire for the group. Valtyr was finishing up with the last of Brynd's wounds. He sat down with a thud, exhausted from the day.

"Keep these wounds relatively clean, friends. I will rest, and tomorrow I will pray to heal the wounds. Right now, I can do no more." Valtyr looked as if he was about to collapse.

Reynir offered a bit of his ration and a water skin to his brother. "Cease talking and eat this, you have done enough. No use that you also fall, my brother."

Valtyr nodded tiredly and accepted the gesture. "Thank you."

Sal'iabac was concerned. She sat in the shadows and observed. Off by himself, Kairoth sat on a log watching the singing and dancing around the large fire. He was preparing for his own celebration. Hodan was known for sending their dead off to the afterlife with a party to honor their sacrifice. On top of a small homemade pyre, were a sword, shield, helmet, and a small bag of coins. They were Danzu's possessions. Kairoth had also seen fit to fill a small wooden tankard with the remains of a wineskin containing the rest of his stash of mead. He looked over at the mirth of the other fire and hoped his brother was in Aeternum experiencing so much more.

"Well, you get the last of it, brother. Enjoy it! You earned it. I will get more when I get back to that goat town below the mountains." Kairoth looked at the dancing women and children. "I know that you see this, you horse's ass." Kairoth frowned and stifled a tear. "You died a hero, be welcomed into the presence of your ancestors."
Kairoth did not realize that the entire party had quietly walked up behind him. Valtyr leaned on Reynir to stand. Everyone was silent and watched their leader.

Oblivious to anything around him, Kairoth stood with a lit torch. "I have said these words too many times in these past few months, but for you brother, I will repeat the blessing." Clearing his throat, the Hodan warrior sadly repeated the traditional Hodan send-off while lighting the pyre. "No tears should be shed for the courageous. No wailing should be heard for one of honor who saves innocents from those who would do them harm. A warrior of Hodan goes before me unto Aeternum to join our heroes of old. Danzu will sit in his place of honor while I still seek to prove my worth. May we meet again, brother. May your soul be ever comforted within the light's rays, and may your cup be never emptied. Until we meet again."

The small pyre lit up the night. Several of the rescued wandered over, wondering what was going on. A woman with a little boy stopped to see.

"What is going on, mother?" he asked in a much too loud voice.

"Be still, boy. A warrior has fallen, and this is his pyre," she scolded.

"I wish to give him my biscuit," the boy said defiantly approaching the fire, before his mother could get ahold of him. He ran up next to Kairoth who towered over the lad. "Are you a hero, Sir?" the boy asked in awe of the warrior before him.

Kairoth stared at the young face. He was speechless. Valtyr spoke on his behalf. "Yes, son. Yes, he most certainly is." Kairoth looked at the priest with misty eyes and then kneeled to the boy's eye level. The child held out a half-eaten biscuit.

"What is this, young one?" the warrior asked gently.

"I wish to add to this man's feast, Sir," the boy answered as a matter of fact. His mother stood in the shadows fearfully.

Kairoth smiled, taking the biscuit from his tiny hands. "Danzu is honored by your tribute, boy. Thank you." The warrior tossed the hardtack on top of the pyre. The smell of burning bread was immediately present.

"How did he die?" the boy asked innocently.

"Child, leave that man alone!" the boy's mother said nervously.

"It is fine, my lady," Kairoth answered. "Come forward. I do not bite, at least, not civilians."

Sal'iabac laughed. "That's not entirely true."

Kairoth shook his head and gave her a dirty look, then turned his attention back to the woman and child. "Danzu was a warrior of Hodan who came to Yslandeth at King Puryn's call. He died fighting the scourge. An Ogre ended his life. I returned the favor. His sacrifice allowed us to get to all of you."

The boy smiled. "See, momma! I am glad I gave my biscuit to this hero!"

Kairoth smiled messing the boy's hair up. "Get away from that fire, son, and mind your mother." The warrior walked over to the lady, handing her a small roll of hardtack and a piece of dry meat. "A boy with this heart should not go hungry. Teach him to be a priest or maybe a mage."

The lady was wide-eyed. Kairoth towered over her. He was at least a foot taller than she and still in armor. She could see the gore of battle all over him. The woman could tell from the looks of the party that the past day's combat had been a significant battle. She looked to the skies and thanked the Goddess again that her son was not present when the carnage occurred.

"Thank you, My Lord. I will feed him when he is done admiring the fire. I fear that he will someday wield a sword as his father once did. The militia took his life during one of many raids. When they took us from our homes in the middle of the night, I was sure we'd see him again, sooner rather than later. Thank you all for giving us another chance to live. I am sorry about your friend." She grabbed her son and turned to go. "Come. It is time to go."

"Farewell, heroes! I will not forget you!" the boy yelled in protest as his mother dragged him away.

Kairoth watched them go. "Forget us, boy. Do not seek after glory. It is hollow and stinks of death."

The warrior turned and finished a sip of mead in his own tankard and then headed off to his bedroll. Sal'iabac carefully approached him with a damp cloth, a small bucket of cold water and some soap. Kairoth nodded to her.

"I know that I have told you this, many times before, my love, but these events are not your doing. It is not your fault." Sal'iabac washed the warrior's face, kissing his forehead after she removed the gore of the undead from his face.

Kairoth had a faraway look on his face. "It's all my fault, Salia. I am in command. I didn't throw the blow that killed my brother, Danzu, but my orders led him to his death."

The mage hugged the warrior around his head. Kairoth buried his head in the nape of his lady's neck. She could feel the hot tears of a Hodan man on her bare skin, and he silently cried for his friend. The mage had no words. All she could do is gently rub her man's back, comforting him the best that she could. The rest of the party had retired to their own bedrolls and private shelters. There would be no mirth this evening. All were too exhausted and emotionally drained to send off the Hodan warrior with a party.

The pyre burned for a couple of hours, and then the embers slowly waned, until finally smoldering in the pit below the offering. Everything within the flames was consumed. Kairoth nodded, knowing that his brother had his belongings and a bit of coin to spare. Sal'iabac had fallen asleep holding her man. Within an hour or so, Kairoth joined her, pulling his filthy cloak over both of them. Tomorrow was another day.

* * *

Valtyr was up before the dawn. He prayed and then went about warming some tea and eating a bit of hardtack and meat. The party was waking, one by one. They limped over to the fire, where Valtyr intercepted them, praying for healing and mending many of their wounds.

Everyone seemed ready for the road and somewhat prepared for battle, except the Hodan leader. Kairoth was not seriously injured, but he was in a mood. Sal'iabac had learned to grant the warrior a wide berth during these times. She kept an eye on her brooding man as he ate alone in silence, just in the case that he may need her.

Valtyr approached his leader and gave the morning blessing. "Good morning, brother! May the Goddess's will be done today and may you receive her many blessings."

Kairoth stopped munching on his hardtack and glared at the priest, who was taken by surprise. "I would hope that she would bless us with one damned day where we could not wonder for our lives. Would that be too much to ask, priest? I wonder?"

Valtyr was stunned, "Broth …." As he started to respond, Reynir grabbed his arm and gave him a look.

"Remember when you say that I talk too much?" Reynir sneered. "My turn."

Valtyr turned from Kairoth, who had gone back to eating his breakfast in his sour mood. He answered the druid. "What do you mean by that? I can't have my own people and professed followers questioning the Goddess! I must counsel our brother and get him back on the correct path."

"Truly, a monster must have hit you on your head, Valtyr." The druid dropped his voice to a mumble, but Kairoth could still hear him. The warrior listened to the conversation in disgust, sipping his mug of hot tea. "You do realize that this man is Hodan and that he is in a foul mood. Remember the fate of the Ogres?" Reynir raised his eyebrows with a look of expectation on his face.

"Well, yes, but blasphemy is uncalled for." Valtyr looked genuinely offended.

"She's a Goddess, brother. Do you think she cares for the opinions of men? I seriously doubt it. Besides, she sees the heart, and his is always in the right place. His sword is always on the side of right."

Valtyr squinted, wondering how Reynir all of a sudden appeared to be the wise one. "Who are you, and what have you done with my brother, you fiend?"

Reynir laughed and handed Valtyr a piece of dried meat. "Leave him be. He will recover. He always does."

Kairoth heard the exchange between the brothers, but he was unsure of whether he was ready to continue down this path with his friends. He was becoming much too close to all of them, for him to watch them die off, one by one.

"What is the purpose of this suffering, Haya?" Kairoth asked quietly, packing his belongings and looking up at Danzu's mount. "Why have you put us here? Do we exist solely as entertainment for the Gods? What is the difference between the light and the darkness, if both paths lead to the grave? Please, if you could spare a moment, tell Danzu we miss him, and could you please clear a path home for your rescued followers? They did not deserve to live out this horror, but who am I to question you, right? I am only dirt, and you are the creator of all that lives. Regardless of my anger and doubts, I thank you for this day, and for the friends that you have graciously allowed me to keep."

* * *

In the more massive encampment, shouting could be heard, as the Draj unit was formed and role taken. After a minute or two of formalities, the unit Commander and his Sergeants organized a group of Draj, which would allow the rescued villagers to ride double on their horses. The thirty-seven warriors were placed in the center of the unit with the others dispersed in a protective perimeter. Lieutenant Thad could see a horseman light off ahead of them. He figured that it was one of the specialists, gone to scout out ahead. Thad watched with interest as a young Hodan warrior gathered his people and prepared to leave the mountaintop.

"Sergeant, what is that man's name?" the leader asked, pointing at Kairoth.

"Kairon? Kairol … Kairoth, Sir! Kairoth, the Hodan," the Sergeant responded by guessing.

"I should like to meet that man when we return to the village," the leader said to no one in particular.

"All formed and ready, Sir," the Sergeant said.

"Yes, of course, let us depart this place at once. It is a beautiful morning, at least. We need to get the civilians down this mountain. It is a frigid morning."

The Sergeant grunted in agreement, turning to bark out commands to the soldiers standing by for orders. Kairoth watched as the unit appeared to be moving off without them.

"Well, isn't that rude," Kairoth said sarcastically.

"What did you expect from those peacocks?" Brynd said chuckling. "I'm sure they saved those folks all by themselves. I can't wait to listen to the stories around the fire tonight. 'There I was! The undead all around me!'" Brynd laughed out loud.

Kairoth shook his head. "They better not do that around me, or I'm going to break one of the King's boy's faces. Not listening to that load of cow dung tonight."

Within a few minutes, the Draj unit had moved off with the rescued villagers on horseback. Famlin was up the road ahead of everyone, but Kairoth was just happy that he let the team know before he lit off alone; one less thing to wonder about.

"All right, let's go. They have a small head start, but they also have thirty-seven non-combatants with them. They'll be slowed." Kairoth mounted his horse and gave the hand signal for "form unit and move out."

Within five minutes, Kairoth and Brynd took the lead, with the mages in the center and Reynir and Valtyr pulling up the rear. It was the best that could be done. The group was down three warriors in a little less than six months. Brynd didn't like their odds.

"Well, brother, so much for retiring," he muttered, looking to the skies. "I guess either way, I will be at my leisure though."

The Draj, thirty-seven rescued villagers, and seven specialists all arrived by dinnertime at the worn gates of Rordsburg. The day had turned out to be a beautiful country ride. Upon arrival, the village erupted into a loud, raucous cheer.

"Huzzah Draj! Huzzah Draj! Huzzah Yslandeth!" the crowds bellowed out.

Off in the distance, by the inn entrance, Basric stood contemplating the day's events. He could see a ragged, exhausted team of seven, slide into the village gate without any fanfare. The people fawned over the pristine warrior saviors on horseback, but failed to see the real heroes who limped into the inn in search of food, drink, and maybe a bath. But Basric saw them.

"Innkeeper, everything is on me. The money of these people is not good in my Kingdom. Give them whatever they ask for if you have it, My Lady." Basric smiled and bowed to the party, who stood dejected in the inn. They were alone. They missed their fallen. No one sang their praises.

"Thank you, Your Highness," Kairoth responded with a smirk. "I hope the royal coffers have recovered, for you may have just bankrupted your nation!"

Basric laughed and turned to the innkeeper. "I'll take a flagon of ale, My Lady. I have much to talk to my friends about. I always enjoyed the company of heroes. I have known too many who no longer walk this Ert. Tonight, we will celebrate a few who still do."

The room raised their glass, and said as one, "To those who still walk upon the green."

Chapter 15

Durn looked out at the ring of trees containing his prisoners of war. In the darkness, he could make out the campfires within the forest. He knew that the enemy troops were questioning everything that they had been taught concerning the Northern Alliance and Yslandeth, but the Yslan Commander was unsure how many, if any, would cross over to Basric when the time came. Many were from clan territories and set in their beliefs and allegiances. The Draj Commander hoped that he could make a good impression on the leadership of the rebel militia. He was encouraged by the response of the enemy Commander, Broswyn, son of Rodren, who identified himself as the Commander of Palgur's fifth Militia out of the Citadel. He was undoubtedly a close man to the Pretender, and his faith in his leadership seemed to be fading with each passing moment. His support was the key to victory.

"Commander," Durn said respectfully, pointing toward the chair across the table from him. There were two other Draj-Erynseere Legion Commanders seated around the large oval table. The Cinnog Commander was impressed by the gathering and looked a bit worried, while he strained to maintain an air of defiance and resolve.

"Gentlemen, good day to you all. I would like to first thank you for the fair treatment and medical care that you have provided my men and I. I am truly indebted to your kindness and chivalry." Broswyn bowed to Durn, who stood and returned the gesture.

"Sergeant, remove the bindings from the prisoner, at once," Durn ordered, and it was made so immediately. "Commander, please sit." The

Draj motioned to a seat where food and drink were made available by porters who stood awaiting orders.

Broswyn sat frowning, his eyes teared up, and he swallowed hard. "I cannot accept this from you while my men eat what is left over, Sir. Thank you for your offer, though."

Durn smiled. "You are a peculiar one, my friend. Who exactly are you? You are not one of these farmhands who play at war. You commanded your limited resources with skill."

"I am Broswyn, son of Rodren. My father was a Knight of Cinnog who fell with Lorus at the gates when the black scourge came for our people. Da was a hero, as is your King and King Orus, though he was not as fortunate." The young Commander frowned and then sipped from a tankard of mead that was left at his seat. The other Commanders listened on as the two men spoke.

"Broswyn, do you recognize Palgur as the rightful heir to the throne of Cinnog? I get the impression that you may or may not still hold that belief?" Durn sipped his mead.

"Palgur is a lout. He holds our lands under his fist. We fight for him to preserve our families. Many here with me fear for our wives and children in the Citadel. Others were promised lands and seed or livestock. The man is a plague upon Cinnog. He dispatches us to kill the true heir, sending the old and infirm, or those too young to fight against Draj." Broswyn scowled and stared at the three Draj Commanders who looked back stoically betraying no emotion or inclination.

"Well, I would say that you have few options remaining, Commander. You can remain 'loyal' to the man who exploits you, or perhaps you switch sides and fight on the side of the truth." Durn raised an eyebrow. "Regardless of how you choose now, your families are in peril. Palgur will not tolerate the loss of this many men without retribution. Your best choice is to join the Alliance forces and fight to free your loved ones. Take what is yours. Establish the proper heir. Honor your father's legacy."

Durn's last four words hit Broswyn as if the Draj had stabbed him in the belly. "How will you trust us after we took up arms against you? I would not trust an enemy who had just surrendered. How do you know that we will not turn against you when the enemy arrives?" Broswyn noticed that one of the other Draj Commanders looked at Durn with a mild expression of surprise. The militia leader knew that the other Commanders were thinking exactly what he was thinking. Only this Durn fellow appeared to be open to joining forces. Broswyn looked at the older man squinting. Was the old man was smiling?

"I don't, but I feel as if I am a pretty good judge of character. You don't strike me as an unchivalrous person. I will allow anyone who wishes to remain loyal to Palgur to leave of their own free will, as long as they travel southward to the Citadel and do not return again to attack the northern territories. Anyone who goes back on their word will be summarily executed." Durn sipped more mead, then set the mug down and leaned forward on the table awaiting a response.

"You would do that?" Broswyn asked incredulously. "You would just let my men go if they pleased?"

"I would. Basric requires men. He needs experience and loyalty. Fodder can be found anywhere, unfortunately." Durn looked at the enemy Commander with a scowl. "I tire of war, but this one is necessary, only because of the man whom you serve."

"If you are willing to free those who wish to go and accept those who wish to change sides, what army will my men be joining? Yslan or Cinnog?" Broswyn wrinkled his brow.

"Your men will report to Basric's forces and Commanders. I will speak on your behalf to the Prince, asking for him to accept you as I do right now." Durn held out his hand.

Broswyn shook Durn's hand. "I will speak to my Lieutenants and the rest. I will have your answer in the morning." The young man stood and bowed. "It will be strange to finally be on the right side of anything, Sir."

The guard tied the bindings on the prisoner and led him out of the Command Tent. As he left, Durn held a finger to his lips to shush his friends around the table. He wished to wait until the young enemy Commander was out of earshot before the arguments began.

"Yes, yes, for the love of Runnir and Gunnir, I damn well know what you two are thinking." Durn was pacing.

"Durn, have you lost your damned mind, Sir!?" Onrius, the Commander of the second Legion exclaimed. "First, you disobey orders, lose a quarter of your men to this rabble, and now you seek to enlist them into Cinnog's army."

Durn shook his head and looked at Onrius. "Son, you would not see an opportunity if it bit you in the nether regions." The older Commander downed the rest of his tankard, slamming it on the table. "Besides, you were not here, and we were able to secure the documents that forged this Alliance in the first place." Durn had a defiant, angry stare. Onrius backed off and sat down. He sipped his mead and shook his head.

Ulric, the third Legion Commander, spoke in a softer tone. "Sir, it is unwise to trust these men. They would fight for filthy lucre over honor. They put their own welfare before the good of their own nation. How are we to be sure that they would not turn on the hand that feeds them for one who offers more?"

Durn raised his eyebrows and looked at the younger Commander as he finished. "Truly, do you believe that crock of horse dung that you just shoveled toward me, or are you quoting from some manual that you read about officer conduct or some such nonsense." Durn waved him off with disgust. "Please do not lecture me about 'the good of the nation,' while we turn a blind eye to the persecution of our own people. Many kill or maim in Yslandeth for a loaf of bread, and you pontificate to me about the morality of men of Cinnog who do the same? Hypocrite."

Ulric looked down shamed and tended to his flagon of mead. He had no response to Durn's scathing reply. Onrius looked as if he was ready to respond with another volley, but something in Durn's expression made the younger Commander bite his tongue.

"Gentlemen," Durn said sternly, "I may be court-martialed when I return to Erynseere, but until then, as Commander of the first, I am Supreme Commander when the King is not present, and this plan is the one that I choose. You will follow my command or step down and appoint a Captain to take your seat." Durn looked for any dissent, but found none.

"Good, then we will work on repairing ties with these people tomorrow and release the ones who wish to return to their homes on the other side of the field. One day, these people will have to live alongside the Alliance. Harshness and cruelty only lead to animosity and long-standing feuds. Kindness and respect mend fences. I expect your full support or resignations on my desk by tomorrow." Durn stood and left the tent.

"He speaks of following orders while he ignores his own and then calls me a hypocrite? Who is the hypocrite here? That horse's ass!" Ulric spat and then cleared his throat and angrily composed himself.

Durn heard the comment as he walked away, but let it go. He knew that Ulric spoke the truth, but Basric would need these men, especially Broswyn. Perhaps with a bit of help from the Goddess, and some decent treatment by his own men, this might be accomplished.

Durn walked a short way to his tent. Bandu stood up from his stool and offered him a flask. The Commander took the bottle absentmindedly staring out at the trees. After a long pull of whiskey, Durn handed it back to Bandu, nodding at his most trusted companion while entering his tent, never saying a word. Bandu sat watch.

* * *

The sun was up in a bright blue sky. Frost covered most things, but the temperature was rising, albeit slowly. Durn sighed and threw his cloak over his shoulders and walked to the Command Tent. There, he met Onrius and Ulric. They were already eating breakfast when he arrived. Both men stood as the Sergeant called attention in the shelter.

"Be seated, gentlemen," Durn stated, sitting down and eating a bit of egg and bacon with a cup of hot tea. The tension was palpable as Durn munched on the pork on his plate. He let the men sit and stew while he finished. Then he looked up as if he was unaware of what all the seriousness was about.

"Sir, if I may," Ulric stammered.

"You may, Ulric. What do you want?" Durn asked with half a mouthful of eggs, trying to ignore the gravity with which the Commander addressed him.

"Sir, after much contemplation, I would like to confirm my allegiance to your command and ask to be retained as a commander of the third Legion." Ulric stood tall.

"Well, as long as you don't mind the view from behind this horse's ass, from time to time … I accept your confirmation. You are third Legion Commander. Lead her well." Ulric's eyes were as big as goose eggs at the mention of 'horse's ass.' Durn acted as if he choked a bit on his eggs, stifling a chuckle. "What about you, Onrius, can you find it in your soul to follow a hypocritical old man into battle? It's not like it will be the first time we've dealt with mere mortals in command?"

Onrius smiled. "Of course, Sir. You always have my blade, even if I think you've lost your mind, from time to time. You are a good man, Sir. I just hope this plan works out as you envisioned it to."

"I hope so, too, son. I hope so, too," Durn replied.

* * *

The three Draj Commanders stood at the edge of the tree ring with a detachment of security. They entered the forest without incident and walked through the trees to a spot in the middle of the central clearing. Broswyn was present with several of his Lieutenants. Behind them, in a loose formation were the rest of the men, awaiting the arrival of their Draj captors.

"Hail, Commander Durn of the Draj-Erynseere!" Broswyn shouted bowing.

"Hail, Yslan!" the crowd behind him echoed. The Draj stood ready around their Commander.

"Stand down, Draj," Durn commanded calmly, wading through his own ranks and approaching Broswyn while extending his hand. The two shook hands and faced the crowd of militia, who were standing expectantly.

"My brothers in arms, please pay attend to the Commander of the Draj, Durn. He has a proposition for all of you to ponder carefully. I have spoken with many, but some have not heard this offer yet. Choose wisely."

"Thank you, Commander Broswyn." Durn nodded at the younger man, who stepped back toward his men. "As your Commander stated, I have an offer that is open for anyone who seeks to help their nation."

There was a murmur in the crowd, and then the militia settled down to hear what the Yslan warrior had to say.

"I know that Palgur the Pretender, holds many of your families hostage, or threatens your livelihood if you do not serve him. I submit to you, after this battle's outcome did not go his way, that he will mistreat your families, regardless of whether you return to be punished or resist. I offer an opportunity. A chance to switch sides without retribution. If you denounce Palgur and swear fealty to Basric, and you choose to serve in Cinnog's true army, you will be forgiven your treason and given a new chance to help establish the true King in your nation. If you still seek to support Palgur, you have the option to leave the North and return to the Citadel, never to return. If you return and violate this agreement, I will show you no quarter, and you will be summarily executed."

There was a gasp in the militia unit. Many voices spoke out of turn. Most were happy and upbeat, but some were angry and defiant. Durn looked on in dismay. He had hoped for a unanimous shift to Basric, but it looked as if a significant faction was forming to leave for Cinnog. Still, more stayed than went.

"All of you who have chosen to leave, may take one water skin, a large sack, and a week's provisions. You will not be given weapons to travel with. Remember, if I recognize you and you end up returning to do harm to the North, I will see your head on a pike." Durn motioned to the Legion quartermaster, who called to those who were leaving. The mob formed a line and was issued their equipment.

Durn looked at the almost three-hundred who set off to leave for the South. He shrugged. He had recruited five-hundred, including the prize he sought, Broswyn, who stood with those who asked to support the Prince.

Durn took out a scroll and scratched down a message. "Your Majesty, we require five-hundred suits of armor, hardened leather will suffice, because of the short notice. We also need two-hundred wooden shields and two-hundred short swords, one-hundred spears, and one-hundred Elfish bows. I have recruited five-hundred troops from the militia who wish to serve the true heir. They will need to be outfitted so that they are an effective unit. Thank you, Durn."

"Squire," the Commander shouted, sealing the scroll in a case. "Take this to Erynseere and give it to the Queen. Tell her it is urgent."

"Yes, Sir!" a younger armored lad shouted grabbing the scroll case, bowing and riding North as fast as he could.

"She's going to be thrilled, Bandu. I think a pine is looking at me crossly." Durn smiled, laughing at his own joke.

Bandu laughed.

* * *

One week later, horns were heard on the Yslandeth border, a little less than one-quarter mile from the encampment of the three Draj Legions. Durn looked up concerned, but then realized that the Fifth and Sixth Legions had arrived at the border. Durn knew that this meant that Adasser was relying on reserves and her trees to defend Erynseere. Durn was not worried about his Queen. He knew what she was capable of, but the old man knew that his son would be furious that she let all of her trained Elites march South and leave her "open to attack." Durn chuckled thinking of a time when one Legion and Adasser stood against several hundred thousand Offlanders … and the Offlanders decided to "go around them."

"Let's go meet them!" Durn cheered.

The Fifth and Sixth Legions were sent by Her Majesty to guard against the possibility of enemy retaliation. Durn saw that two Draj Legions stood between Yslandeth and Palgur's rabble. Durn was not concerned about Yslan's safety. He laughed considering a unit stupid enough to engage two-thousand angry Draj on the border of their Barony.

Five-hundred filthy Cinnog warriors and the remains of the First Legion moved to the border where the Fifth and Sixth received them warmly. Food and provisions were replenished, and Cinnog's men were given their equipment. The rabble began to look the part of a real unit, and Broswyn smiled broadly at the sight of a well-equipped Cinnog force. They were all trained. Some were past their prime, others hadn't reached theirs yet, but they were the best that Cinnog had to offer. They would march to meet their future King at Rordsburg with Durn's Legion.

The Second formed a base of operations ten miles South of the border, upon a plateau that stood about five-hundred feet above the open plains. They set up hasty pickets and began patrolling the countryside for brigands and wayward militia. The presence of the Second allowed Basric to regroup at Rordsburg as he prepared for war with the South. The presence of the Draj also re-established law and order. The people of northern Cinnog began to regain hope. No longer could Palgur send his troops North to pillage and murder with impunity.

The Third moved southward another twenty miles and set up another similar defense. They were a show of force that reminded Palgur that his days were numbered. The Third moved to hot spots within the area, engaging any troops that they came in contact with.

What the Draj Commanders had not realized from his silence was that the King of Yslandeth was on the move. He had a sizable force moving toward Erynseere. Puryn was concerned about how things were escalating, and as Durn had predicted, the young King was worried that his lady had left herself "open to attack" at Erynseere.

The King was marching to war, and Palgur had no idea what was coming as the Draj Legions to his North blinded his view of the northern borders with Yslandeth.

The Fourth Legion owned the northeast of Cinnog down the eastern river to the lands on the Suden border with the Citadel. Commander Furtim sent scouts to survey the situation, but awaited orders to assault the heavily fortified stone castle before him. Palgur knew that serious events were unfolding and that things were looking bad for him, but at this point, the Pretender had no other choice, but to fight. Either way, the traitor knew that his head would soon be placed on a block. He decided that it would not come to that without a fight.

Basric rejoiced at the thought of finally defeating the rebellion from the South. Every day, the Prince thanked Kairoth and the rest of the team for making all of these things possible. Puryn knew who was responsible for his successes in Cinnog and sent a messenger to Rordsburg. The squire delivered the notification that the King would arrive in the village within the week.

Kairoth acknowledged the warning and nodded to the messenger. He passed the word to his team. They spent the next week preparing for their King's visit and resting. It had been a long three months. They were ready to go home.

Chapter 16

Puryn arrived at the border with Cinnog. The King surveyed the scene before him and could see the telltale signs of battle and occupation. Durn's First Legion standard stood tall in the center of a large encampment of off-white tents. The entire camp was surrounded by pickets and obstacles, but Puryn knew that, by now, all of the threats that faced Yslandeth were far South of this locale. Off in an open field, a small detachment of Draj was working with a small unit of Cinnog militia. It looked as if they were working on shield wall drills and moving as a unit with cohesion. Lost in thought, the King sat on his white war horse, staring off as the Draj barked out orders to the less disciplined students. The Cinnog unit was having a bad day.

"What are you, a gaggle of Suden nursemaids, or Cinnog men?" the Draj mentor goaded. "Tighten it up! Shoulder to shoulder! When the enemy hits one shield, they should feel the brunt of them all!"

The sound of wooden shields clacking together and grunting could be heard. Puryn watched with amusement as a small unit of Draj formed, opposing the rabble on the Cinnog side. Twenty or so of Erynseere's finest were forming a wedge with the intent of breaching a unit five times their size. The King sat up in his saddle and awaiting the decimation of the student unit. A larger young man within the Cinnog group seemed to stand out and appeared to be commanding the unit. Puryn watched him with curiosity.

"Cinnog! Lock!" the young Commander barked, and his men responded without delay.

Puryn was mildly impressed.

"Prepare to repel!" the young man barked again as the Draj commenced their charge.

The Draj charged ferociously at their mock opponent. Several in the first rank Cinnog unit collapsed in the onslaught, but the young Commander called out to his group once again. "Form it up. Repel the attack. Push! Show them who Cinnog is!"

The Cinnog unit reformed on the move and began to show the cohesiveness that Puryn thought it had lacked a short time earlier. Within ten minutes, the vastly larger force has beaten back its Draj aggressor and claimed the field. The field instructor was not impressed and let his students know precisely what he thought of their small victory.

"Well, aren't you boys special! You routed a unit you outnumbered five to one! You should be proud!" The instructor's sarcasm burned as if acid dripped from his lips.

"Then make the field even, Sir," the young Cinnog Commander stated plainly. "Let's train for real this time. We have endured your abuse for how many weeks now? My men know their jobs. Enough marching around. Let us do war practice, or save your insults. Are the Draj frightened?" Broswyn removed his helmet. His dark hair fell to shoulder length. His face was determined and a bit angry. His men appeared to hold his same sentiments.

Looking up to the Draj Commander, the young Draj instructor waved a red signal flag, asking for permission to go full-on with the Cinnog unit.

Durn saw the flag and sighed. "Fine. They want to play hard, let us play hard. Wood and blunted edges only. Send the rider to the Lieutenant and tell him that no one is to die. This is training."

Puryn watched the Draj rider leave the command position and make a beeline toward the Draj instructor on the field. He arrived, saluted and then rode back to Durn's position. The King sat out of sight of the open area and watched with interest through his spyglass.

"Donick, do we know who this young Cinnog man is?" Puryn asked his minister.

"Your Majesty, he may be the Commander your father mentioned in his last message to Empyr." Donick watched the scene unfolding on the field. "This may be the man who directed the army that killed two-hundred-fifty of our finest."

"We shall see if he is worth his salt, or if it was just the result of superior numbers. How many does Cinnog have now?" Puryn asked.

"Approximately five-hundred remain of two-thousand. Three-hundred departed for the Citadel about a month ago. Twelve-hundred perished in battle against the First Legion." Donick had a look of concern on his face. "Do you think that the first will fight nicely? I fear this may be a bad day to be a Cinnog recruit."

"The Draj will come hard after the men who killed their brothers and sisters. I have no doubt of that. I just do not want to lose any more soldiers to foolishness. Let them fight it out for a bit, and then pull our troop up into view. Father has not seen us yet. He is concerned with the South." Puryn snickered. "The old goat has no idea that we're here yet."

"Be nice, brother, he's your father, for Haya's sake, and he is your best General!" Donick slapped Puryn on the shoulder, eliciting a laugh from the King.

"Still, brother, he disobeyed orders and brought us to war. I cannot let this pass without addressing it, or I will lose the control and respect of all of my Commanders. I will ask him to resign. If he will not, I will have to court-martial him." Puryn closed his eyes and frowned.

Donick looked ashen. "You would not shame your own father this way, Puryn, I mean, Your Majesty. Please reconsider."

"I will speak with him privately and plainly. We shall see what my da has to say for himself. He is a good man. I love him. I will protect him the best that I can, but I must protect the Kingdom first. I cannot let all things fall for one man, even if he is my own da." Puryn looked at the ground.

The King looked sadly at his oldest friend and then turned back to the battle evolving on the field. They were set on either side. Five-hundred slightly less pristine First Legion Draj against five-hundred leather-clad Cinnog militia. The shield walls stood ready with their wooden practice swords. Behind the shields, some held long wooden war hammers, blunted spears and various two-handed weapons. It looked like real war, but Puryn knew that this battle would result in many bruises to the body and ego, and little more.

A loud horn was blown, and the units were off. Cinnog stood their ground, forming a shield wall to the front and both flanks. In the center behind their wall, the roving mass weapons wielding troops prepared to pick off any Draj stupid enough to expose a body part. The rules were: beaten to the ground or submission. Once on the ground or submitted you were considered "dead."

The Draj Commander called out orders, and the Draj approached the Cinnog unit smartly and in perfect sync. The sharp contrast in styles was not lost on the King, but he had seen stranger things and knew that it was not over until the last man.

The Draj charged. The Cinnog unit repelled successfully, losing about ten-percent of their men, but rather than retreating, their Commander called for the men to shore up their lines. Then he did the unthinkable. The Cinnog Commander formed a column and sent them out in a flanking maneuver, surprising the overconfident Draj leader. As the Cinnog unit flanked left, the Draj responded, but did not expect the next Cinnog move, which was to press the middle and charge. This coordinated attack was much more precise than the Draj Commander, Durn, or Puryn has expected. The trio looked on from their various vantage points in disbelief, and Cinnog took down half of the First Legion in one maneuver.

After the dust settled, both Commanders reassembled their respective units. Puryn could see the Cinnog unit was no worse for wear, having whittled the Draj down enough to make the odds even on either side. Around two-hundred warriors remained on either side of the field.

Puryn smiled broadly at Donick. "Are those Cinnog dogs chanting? Are they letting loose a war cry? Call forward my armies, now! I will show them a war cry!"

"At once, Your Majesty!" Donick dispatched a rider who disappeared into the thick woods. The young squire called to the General of the Yslandeth Regulars. The army totaled somewhere near twenty-five-hundred horsemen on Korinian War Steeds, twenty-five-thousand warriors, and the required logistics personnel, all of whom were strategically concealed behind a thick forest, on top of a set of rolling hills leading up to where Durn's unit was encamped. No one from the First Legion was watching North, because Yslandeth had a unit stationed on the Yslandeth border and Durn knew that his rear was covered.

The sound of the troops moving from their hiding place was a thunderous combination of horse hooves, clattering armor, live steel, and horns blowing. As the two small units on the field clashed once more, they were startled by the way the ground shook as Yslandeth arrived on site. The two groups had stopped fighting each other and could see the massive army approaching. Both sides breathed a sigh of relief when they saw the standard of Yslan.

"Hold! Hold! Hold! Stop your fighting now!" the field instructor bellowed. "His Majesty approaches with Yslandeth in tow! All hail King Puryn! All hail!"

Everyone on the field knelt and faced the incoming entourage. The King, his guards, advisors, and ministers all rode up in front of an army, which stretched for as far as the eye could see. Within a few moments, they had arrived. The King and his men formed on the battlefield. The Lieutenant in charge of training ran to the King and presented himself.

"Good afternoon, Your Majesty!" the young man barked, officially bowing low, holding his bow for a second and then rising again.

"Good afternoon, indeed, Sir!" Puryn said smiling. "Where is your Commander?"

"Commander Durn is in the Command Tent, Your Majesty." The young man pointed to the most massive tent with many banners flying proudly in the light spring breeze.

"Excellent. We shall need this field to set up our encampment. I am sorry to interrupt your training. It appears that you have trained these Cinnog well, Lieutenant. They gave you a run for your gold!" The King smiled at the embarrassed Draj leader. "It is not anything to be ashamed of, Draj.

They were taught well. Be proud of yourself!"

"Yes, Your Majesty." The Lieutenant bowed and then began barking orders to clear the field, as the Yslan horde moved into the open area and started setting up shelters.

"Donick, it is time for me to confront da, about his escapades. As much as I loathe doing it." Puryn looked at Donick seriously. "I will talk to him alone."

* * *

When Basric's man failed to return to Rordsburg, the old Prince feared the worst. He decided to march toward the Cinnog border with Yslandeth, in hopes of locating and possibly rescuing his missing comrade. The Prince was not about to lose his messenger. That young man had been with him since he was a lad.

After conferring with Commander Furtim and Kairoth's group, it was decided that one-hundred Draj would remain in Rordsburg to defend against Palgur's minions. The rest of the Fourth Legion would accompany Prince Basric to his objective. To the Commander's dismay, the Prince appointed Kairoth's group as his personal security. They rode beside the heir, while the Draj surrounded them all in a vast square of security. No one between Rordsburg and the northern border with Yslan wanted anything to do with the unit as it moved westward, pushing twelve to fifteen hours a day. Even the Draj were feeling the grind of the push to the objective, but none complained, at least out loud.

Within five days, they arrived on the edge of the open high Cinnog plains near the border. Furtim's scouts returned at a gallop, reporting to their Commander. "Sir, over the next rise, there is a large number of troops gathered in an open field. They were just joined by an even larger unit that moved in from the North. They appear to be on the same side."

"What standard do they fly?" Furtim asked gravely.

"The smaller unit to the South is Draj. They are embattled and in a defensive posture. The North, I could not see well enough, Sir." The young squire waited for his Commander's response.

"Give me your spyglass, boy," the young Commander ordered, and the squire handed it over. Furtim rode off toward the rise with the squire in tow.

The Commander looked over the scene, and it was as the young man had reported. One Legion of Draj was encamped, but they did not appear alarmed by a massive unit moving in their direction. Furtim looked over at the lead entourage and recognized the heraldry of Empyr. He snapped and looked at his squire with an air of disgust.

"Really, boy? You didn't know what the seal of Empyr looked like on the other unit? That is the KING." Furtim slapped the squire on the back of his helmet. "Use your damn brain next time!"

"King Puryn? In the field, Sir?" the boy answered incredulously.

"Yes, apparently something big is going on, and we've been out of communications for some time. It looks serious. We must let Prince Basric know immediately."

"Know what?" Basric asked riding up quickly.

"Your Highness, King Puryn is on the field with Yslandeth Regulars and one Draj Legion. The reason is unknown. I shall send a rider ahead of us and inform him of your arrival." Furtim bowed slightly to the older man.

"Thank you, Sir," the Prince responded by nodding at Kairoth, who rallied his group and gave the marching order.

The rider rode toward Durn's position.

* * *

Durn was dressed in his finest uniform and ready for the arrival of his son. He was the King after all. Durn did not want to look like a slob for his court-martial. The Commander threw back another shot of whiskey and sat tall in his chair near his command table. He could hear the horses approaching. He didn't care. He knew he was in the right, regardless of how this meeting went.

Puryn lit off of his horse. A Draj took the reins and tended to the King's horse. Puryn motioned for everyone to disperse and then called Donick over to him.

"Donick, for the love of the Gods, tell these people to go eat something or brush the horses … whatever, just tell them if they come into that tent while I am speaking to my father, I will skin them alive. I want three bottles of mead and one bottle of whiskey on that table. Two glasses … and NO interruptions, is that understood, brother?" The King was deadly serious.

"Plainly." Donick motioned to a steward and then informed the King's servants and guards to back away from the tent or risk their own necks.

"Your Majesty, remember, he did what he thought was right at the time of the incident. Please. Remember that not everything must be equitable. You have a divine right to spare anyone who you choose. Surely, you can choose to spare your own da?" Donick pleaded.

"We shall see how this goes, my oldest friend. I do not want to punish the man I respect more than any on the Ert. I will not if I can avoid it." Puryn hugged his friend and turned to the tent flap. "Now get away from this tent, Master Donick!"

"Understood, Your Majesty." Donick bowed and left.

There was no one around when Puryn grabbed the tent flap. Upon opening the door, the King saw his father in the flickering oil lamp light. Several candelabras made the scene dire, casting a twisting shadows on the tent walls as the younger man entered the Command Tent.

Durn stood and bowed, then paused and stood straight at attention. "Good day, Your Majesty, may the Goddess watch over you and may she bless you with the wisdom and compassion necessary to lead our great nation in our time of discord."

"Thank you, Commander. May the Goddess bless you also." Puryn sighed. "Be seated, da. Please, let us just talk as men do."

"What do you wish to talk about, son?" Durn asked sarcastically.

"What were you thinking?" Puryn asked with an exasperated tone. "Why did you invade Cinnog against orders and put Yslandeth at war?"

"Well, son, I think that was inevitable, whether I went in first or waited for your blessing." Durn reached for a bottle of mead, pouring two tankards. "Cinnog was massing on our border for some damned reason. Then that messenger tried to reach us, and they attacked him. I had no choice. He ran under a flag of truce toward my position and was cut down by the cowards on the enemy's left flank."

"Cinnog's war is not our business, officially," Puryn said looking around. "I had operatives working the issues."

"And they found your man in Rordsburg, apparently. That is where the young man who I attempted to save was riding from with YOUR Alliance treaty in his possession. If I had not intervened, the enemy would know of your plans, AND we would not know that Basric accepted your offer. I think we did the right thing."

Puryn gulped mead. "But, da! How can I deal with your insubordination? I mean, if I allow it to go without being addressed, I will have men doing whatever they please, everywhere in the ranks!"

"Son, if you need my head on a block to save Yslandeth, then I will put it there myself, but know this, I tire of war and service. I was going to petition for retirement and head back to your mother and our farm. Well, that is, before I started another damned war." Durn poured two more drinks and looked at his son.

"I know, I know, da. I don't disagree with your decision. I just need to show that it has consequences, and NO, I do NOT want your head on a block. Far from it." Puryn threw back another tankard of mead. "I will accept your resignation and place Bandu in command of the First Legion if you agree to it. Do you think that he is ready?"

Durn smiled. "Bandu has been ready for three years, son, and you have turned into a fine King. I only wish to go on this last campaign beside you to the Citadel. May I retire after that?"

"Agreed. You will make the announcement tomorrow at morning formation, and we will prime Bandu for command. He will soon take your place, and you can return to Mother. Do not die on this campaign, old man!" Puryn smiled.

"I will endeavor to survive, My King." The older man smiled in return.

***

Donick stared out on the field as horns blared out a warning of an approaching rider. The Master knew that anyone riding toward Yslandeth with ill intent would have to be suicidal. There were nearly thirty-thousand Yslandeth regulars and Draj on the field.

"Who does he serve, sentry?" Donick asked.

"He appears to be Draj, Master," the sentry replied.

"Bring him to me. Do NOT disturb His Majesty and the Commander." Donick stood up and took a deep breath. "What in the Underworld, now?"

Within minutes, the rider was surrounded and the Draj patrol identified him as one of the scout recon riders of the Fourth Draj Legion out of Erynseere. As ordered, they brought the rider to Master Donick to receive his report.

"What news do you have, rider?" Donick asked.

"Master, Prince Basric of Cinnog, and the Fourth Legion approach from the East. I was sent ahead to alleviate any miscommunication and engagement." The young squire smiled. "Quite a gathering you have here, Master. Do you have any word for my Commander?"

"Tell your Commander that Donick says 'welcome!'" Donick laughed. "And warn the man that the King is here and NOT to be disturbed until further notice. Perhaps your unit can find room to camp to the southeast near the trees on the horizon? It's getting a bit cramped around here."

"I will tell my Commander, Sir. I will also advise about the location to set up camp. Thank you. Have a wonderful day, Master Donick."

The young squire nodded and then rode off quickly toward the rise to the East. There, he apprised Commander Furtim of the situation, and the

Prince was briefed. The Fourth Legion, Prince Basric, and his new security team entered the field to the southeast and set up an encampment. Within two hours, the Furtim's men were set up, and a watch posted.

* * *

Basric was getting a bit impatient with the delays. It had been three hours, and the sun was beginning to dip below the horizon. The Prince wished to speak with King Puryn as soon as possible, but whenever he asked to have an audience, he was told that the King was unavailable. Finally, four hours after arrival, the King appeared outside the tent. He was a bit drunk and accompanied by his father, Durn.

"Your Majesty, if I may," Basric bowed.

"Basric?" Puryn asked trying to maintain steady. "Is that you, Sir?"

"It is, Your Majesty. I wish to thank you for your support and ask if you intend to push southward with your armies toward the Citadel?" Basric looked hopeful.

"We shall talk about it in the morning, Your Highness. And yes, that is fully my intention. We must defeat this pretender and establish your Kingdom if we ever want to see peace on the Ert." Puryn took a deep breath. "Alas, I am not in any condition to discuss war at this moment, but tomorrow we shall revisit our conversation."

"Of course, Your Majesty. I will call on you at a decent hour tomorrow morning." Basric bowed and left.

"I am going to bed, da," Puryn whispered. "You should also go to bed!" The King giggled. "We are too drunk. I love you, da. I am sorry."

"Sorry for what, son? I made my decision, and I will live with it. I still say I did the right thing." Durn hugged his son. He was not a ten-year-old who wanted to learn to ride horses any longer. "You have done what you feel is right. I hold no animosity. I will fight this last war, then return to my Arla. We will grow beets and raise cows. It will be a nice change to see her face regularly." Durn had a tear in his eye. "I am so very proud of who you have become, son. Never change or compromise for anyone, except those you hold the dearest."

"Goodnight, da." Puryn waved and staggered off to his tent. Donick was there to steady his friend. "Ah, there you are, Donick! Good job keeping the busybodies out of that tent!"

Durn laughed and went back into his tent and passed out on his cot.

* * *

The morning was chilly, but not as crisp as it had been over the last five or six weeks in the field. Durn did his usual routine, then met Bandu for a quick bite to eat, before the morning muster and formation. The Commander could hear the changing of the guard going on in the courtyard in front of his Command Tent.

"Bandu, pay attention today. Important things will be passed. We go to war, but that is not all that is coming." Durn made an ominous face.

Bandu squinted. "Are you still drunk?"

"Maybe a little," Durn snorted. "That boy can drink."

The morning horns played the signal to form up. Thirty-thousand soldiers, minus those on duty, gathered into their respective units for the morning formation. Durn was only second to Puryn, in order of precedence in the command structure. He took his position to the left and behind the King. Donick was to the right.

The King spoke. "Good morning, heroes! Today is a glorious day under the sun. We are privileged to serve the Goddess! We are the saviors and protectors she has ordained to stand against the darkness and lawlessness to the South. We shall march to the Citadel, quelling any and all rebellion in our path. Upon arriving at the Citadel, I will petition Palgur, the Bastard, to surrender and hand over the castle to its rightful ruler, Prince Basric. I have a strong belief that he will not just give up." There was a chuckle in the ranks.

Puryn looked over at Basric and noted his security detail. The King of Yslan smiled, nodding. "It figures," he thought to himself. "All pray attend, to His Highness, Prince Basric of Cinnog!" Puryn gestured to the Prince who stepped forward.

"I would like to first thank His Majesty for his gracious offer of alliance. I commit my nation to this arrangement and promise that once Cinnog is restored, it will remain Yslan's staunch ally, at least as long as breath remains in my lungs!"

There was a raucous cheer from the Yslan armies. One small unit seemed to cower quietly in the center of the corps. This silence was not lost upon Basric, who looked at their Commander with a steely gaze.

"You there, come forward." The Prince pointed directly at Broswyn and his unit.

Broswyn turned smartly, calling his unit to attention. "Militia, FOR-ward, march!" The unit marched in perfect alignment to within ten feet of the Prince. "Militia, Halt! Parade rest! Your Highness! Unit prepared for inspection."

"You. Come here," the Prince bellowed.

"Yes, Sir!" Broswyn answered, running up to the Prince and bowing.

"Kneel!" The Prince was livid.

Broswyn knelt with a stoic face. He did not make eye contact with the Prince, but he knew that the old man was aware that he had fought for Palgur's side.

"Why are you here, traitor?" the Prince asked harshly. The old man could see the look of dejection on the faces of those behind Broswyn. The Prince drew his sword and held it by his right side.

"We wish to serve the true heir, Sir," Broswyn stated loudly and clearly.

Basric struck Broswyn with a backhand across his face. "You killed him. You killed two-hundred-fifty Draj. Now you wish to serve me?" Basric gripped his sword tightly.

"Who did I kill, Your Highness? I have killed many. Palgur keeps our loved ones hostage, and will kill them, if we do not serve him." Broswyn spat blood as it flowed freely from his lips. "I only wished to see my mother and sisters again. The Outlanders stole my father at the gates. I wish to see those gates rebuilt."

Basric was stunned by Broswyn's statement about his father. The Prince turned and looked at Puryn, who stood stoically beside his own father. "The one who you killed was a squire who I had by my side for ten years. I took him when he was ten years old. Your men shot him down, from what I am told. If you wish to serve me, there is only one way that it will happen. You stated that your father served as a Knight with Lorus at the gates? I will require the same oath of you. You will stand with me at our end, or I will cut you down where you kneel."

The unit was looking on at their Commander. Some had tears in their eyes. Others looked at the ground in shame. The Prince got the impression that they were serious about their remorse and decision to switch sides. He looked at Broswyn again, this time in a slightly softer tone. "Do you truly wish to serve me, or do you only serve yourself?"

"I would serve the true heir, as my father served the King, if I have the choice. I only served that traitor, because I had no choice. Neither did my men. I may as well fight to save my loved ones now. I have lost to the Draj. There will be no quarter once the Pretender knows that I am still alive." Broswyn looked at the Prince in the eye. "Accept me or strike me down, either way, it is a win. Perhaps if I am dead, he will spare my family."

"Fine, but know this, Commander, if you ever raise a hand against Cinnog, our allies, or me, I will see your head on a stick, along with every one of your unit who fought with you. Do you understand me? What was your father's name, boy?" Basric was now down in the younger man's face.

"I understand completely, Your Highness. My father was Rodren, the Brave," Broswyn answered stoically. Blood was drying on his upper lip and had run down his face into his beard.

Basric hadn't heard that name in many years. He looked a bit stunned and then yelled, "Scribes! Take this down in the record that Broswyn, son of Rodren, the Brave, swears fealty to the Prince of Cinnog. He will, from this day forward, be known as Sir Broswyn, son of Rodren. He will be

Commander of my first and only existing unit."

"Do you swear to uphold the laws of the land? Do you swear to protect the innocent, the women and children, and those unable to protect themselves from evil, harm, or aggression? Will you stand up against all injustice and remain faithful in the discharge of your duties as a protector of Cinnog, no matter the circumstances that you face, even it means your own death? So help you, in the name of the Goddess?" Basric laid his sword on the top of Broswyn's head. "Do you swear fealty by all that you hold holy? Do you swear that you and all who you command will remain faithful and loyal to Cinnog, no matter who the ruler may be?"

"I swear this and ask for the forgiveness of His Highness for all past transgressions. I am truly sorry for the death of your squire. I did not command the attack on him, but I was in command, so I take responsibility. I wish to redeem my soul through honorable service to the Crown. Thank you for this opportunity. We shall not squander our second chance, My Liege." Broswyn bowed deeper.

"Rise, Sir Broswyn!" the Prince bellowed. "Take heed, all who see these tidings and hear my voice, that by this oath, I do declare this man my own. I will rain down the fires of the Underworld upon anyone who smites him or his house. This I solemnly swear. You are forgiven, son. It is war. Remember your oath."

Broswyn stood. "Always, until my final breath, My King."

"Dismissed, Sir," the Prince said saluting his new Knight.

Broswyn saluted back, bowed, and turned about smartly. "Unit, about face! Forward, march!"

The Prince bowed to Puryn, who handed the formation over to Commander Durn. "I have an announcement concerning the command of the First Legion and the seat of Second Commander of the Draj-Erynseere. I am retiring."

Durn paused as the crowd of men began to murmur and some shook their head in disbelief. Sergeants called their units to order calling for silence.

"Now, I am not leaving immediately, ladies and gentlemen. I would not dream of doing such a thing, seeing that we have only just begun this campaign to free our Cinnog brothers from the oppression of the Pretender! I will continue command until the task is completed."

There was a hum of quiet commentary, but Durn and Puryn could tell that it was mostly positive and support seemed strong in the ranks for their Commander.

"Upon completion of this task and return to Yslandeth, Captain Bandu will assume command of the First Legion, per order of His Majesty, King Puryn. Bandu has been my right-hand man for many, many years now, and I fully expect him to carry this mantle with proficiency, tact, and honor. When the time comes, I will charge all of you with treating this man with the respect and honor that you would treat me. Thank you for your attention to this announcement. Stand by!"

There was a slight adjustment that rustled throughout the ranks, as each man stood a bit taller, awaiting dismissal. When the sound had ceased, Durn called out to his men.

"Fall out and carry out the plan of the day. That would be packing this encampment and readying to move South, ladies and gentlemen. Let us make ourselves known to Cinnog and the Pretender in this man's house!" Durn took a deep breath and bellowed, "Fall out!"

The unit leaders repeated the order to fall out all the way down to the smallest grouping. Soon, there was a great commotion as a small city-sized encampment began the arduous task of gathering all of their equipment and packing the wagons for the long walk South.

Puryn remembered his last long walk around the Ert. He wished he had Orus by his side.

Chapter 17

The logistics units, squires, Draj and Yslandeth Regulars efficiently broke down the entire encampment within a couple of hours. Teams packed all of the army's equipment within several hundred horse-drawn supply carts, then marked each with the number of the Legion and unit, so that each Commander could find their camp supplies when needed. Puryn figured that the encampment would be fully set up a few times on the road, but for expediency, the troops would mostly sleep under the stars in their own bedrolls that they carried under the packs on their backs. It was starting to warm in the evenings, but rain was still a concern. The King knew that this campaign would be a swift one, but he did not want to take anything for granted, warning his Commanders as much.

Yslandeth moved as a large unit southward toward their objective. The Citadel where they would face Lord Palgur's dug-in forces awaited the confident soldiers of Yslandeth, but Puryn knew that this could prove to be an ugly affair. Attacking a fortified castle was never an easy task.

Thinking of the task before him, his mind drifted to his recent visit to his barony. Puryn remembered how Adasser had laughed at him when he arrived in Erynseere, frantic that she was "unprotected" after she had sent the three Draj Legions South to reinforce Durn. The Holy Mother gently reminded him that she had an army of her own and that "in the not-so-distance past," it had held off thousands of Offlanders with only one of Puryn's Draj Legions present. The young King thought of the blackened field that she left in her wake and decided that she and their children were safe. He hoped not to see a reenactment of that scene with his own troops on the outside of the Citadel, as his own forces tried to get in.

The King, Commander Durn, Master Donick and the personal guard, led the large procession down the rough road. Yslandeth marched South. It was a thunderous, clanking and squeaking sound. The Cinnog residents looked in wonder, some in fear, not knowing why Yslandeth was in their lands. Regardless of the reason, many wept, wishing an end to the war and poverty.

* * *

It had been three months since the army had departed from the border of Yslandeth and begun its drive southward to liberate Cinnog. Palgur consolidated what forces he had within the walls of the Citadel, as expected. Puryn's officers advised him that there were approximately three-thousand to five-thousand militia within the walls. They estimated that the Pretender and his followers had at least three months of provisions, and were not exactly sure as to what types of siege weapons or archery the enemy possessed.

Puryn looked over the field maps. He was not feeling very confident, even though the troop morale was at an all-time high. The Draj and Cinnog Militia had lost very few in their long trudge southward. Many enemies who sought to resist, simply saw the numbers of the army and surrendered peacefully. Those who opposed were crushed without mercy. Yslandeth and Cinnog had routed every bit of resistance that they had encountered South of the Yslan border, but the Citadel promised to be different.

"Gentlemen, I do not need to remind you that so far, our victories have been against farmers and young boys." Puryn looked around at the room of tired warriors. "I am proud of how our forces have conducted themselves thus far, but I fear that we are getting too confident in our expectations of victory. The stronghold before us will prove to be a challenge, no matter the skill level of our enemy. They will have the protection of stone walls that are several measures thick, while we will be in the open. Remind your men and women of this tonight at your evening formations." The King took a long swallow of his mead and sighed.

Basric spoke. "Puryn, we have siege weapons of our own. We have the numbers and skills. I see this going a bit less painful than you imagine, but I understand your concerns, seeing that it is your men and women who fight my battles. Still, it is good to be cautious. Palgur will have something up his sleeve. I hear tales from my spies in Sudenyag that Cathir may be allied with that Pretender. He sends him aid in the way of food rations and barrels of some sort of powder. I have no idea what the kegs are used for, but it is probably magic that we may see soon."

Puryn shook his head, then finished his tankard, calling for more. A porter stepped forward and poured the drink. "Damn you, Cathir. Why do you not understand that I am on your side? Orus has not possessed your lands for some time, and I have damaged my bonds with my brother to back you! Still, you stick that dagger in my back. I will address that soon." Puryn was annoyed.

"My King, we should send a Draj scout team forward for reconnaissance," Durn offered.

"Yes, I agree. Send the Fourth's scouts. Notify Commander Furtim of the orders. He is in the field. I believe the Fourth is on watch tonight." Puryn could see Kairoth standing off in the shadows behind Basric. The King smiled that his agent took his tasks so seriously. He wondered where the rest of the team may be.

The King stood. "We shall revisit this plan in the morning. We are but one day's march to the Citadel. No doubt, our adversary will have his own Elites out here probing us or observing. Make sure that the watches understand the severity of punishment for being complacent tonight. I will make an example of anyone sleeping on post, especially tonight."

The Officers stood, acknowledging the King's orders as one. Then they departed for the evening formation, passing the orders. The Draj were especially watchful that night. No one wanted to be the King's example.

* * *

Durn woke to a call from his sentries. He stood in his undergarments, shaking the sleep from his tired eyes.

"What is it, squire?" the Commander moaned.

"I am sorry to wake you this early, Sir, but we have detained a small wagon train moving northward on our left flank." The young man stood at attention.

"Let Commander Furtim know that I am on my way to his tent. Do not wake His Majesty. I will wake him if this warrants his attention." Durn slipped on his tunic, then his boots, checking for anything that may have crawled into them in the night. He found nothing.

"Yes, Sir!" the young man yelled, causing Durn to scowl. The squire turned and ran to his duties.

"Damned squires. Always so damn noisy," the older man mumbled, putting on his belt and sword, then grabbing his shield. He muttered to himself, as he opened the canvas flap, "Let us go see what the matter is, Durn. There is always something afoot."

* * *

Durn arrived on scene within fifteen minutes and did not like what he saw. There, tied to a chair, was a middle-aged man in his late thirties. He was bloodied and beaten. One of his eyes was swollen shut and the other was barely open. The prisoner slumped in his chair, exhausted from the abuse. Commander Furtim stood over his captive, ready to attack again.

"Why are you here? Why do you watch us? Who sent you? Where is your army?" Furtim rattled off his questions without a breath, giving the man no time to answer.

In a tired, feeble, voice the bloodied man slurred, "I am a farmer taking my crops North for sale, my lord. This is my son. We have no interest in supporting either side of this conflict. We only wish to live."

Durn was appalled. After the man spoke, he noticed a young boy of about thirteen years, bound on the ground just inside the circle of onlookers. He could see the squire who called for him standing nearby, with a look of disgust on his face. His expression gave Durn the impression that the young warrior did not approve of the actions of his Commander. Durn wondered if he was woken by a squire who was jumping the chain of command.

Durn looked at the squire informant, squinting. The young warrior saw him, stood straight and then looked away, pretending he did not see anything. Durn knew it clearly then. Furtim had gone rogue, and his men were not a part of this atrocity.

"Commander! Cease immediately!" Durn barked out angrily.

The younger Furtim snapped to attention. The boy on the ground shouted out, pleading, "Sir! Please save us!"

Durn became angrier with the plea. "What in the Underworld are you doing, Furtim?"

"I am extracting information from an enemy spy, Sir," Furtim said without flinching.

"You are breaking the code of Chivalry and breaking the orders of His Majesty, himself." Durn glared at the younger, junior Commander.

"Really? You stand there in condemnation of me, when you started this war, old man?" Furtim answered forcefully. "We all know that you are 'retiring,' because if you do not, you will be court-martialed for disobeying your own set of orders."

Durn stepped forward angrily. "I came to aid a person who was being cut down, Draj. Who do you aid here, beating a father in front of his son? He is a farmer, you ass. Stand down, or I will put you down where you stand!" Durn unsheathed his sword and pulled his shield forward.

Furtim had miscalculated his own troop loyalty. He was considered a "golden child," having assumed command at such a young age, but his ego had grown much over the past year or so. The young commander had become a tyrant, and his own Draj did not respect him. As Durn challenged him, Furtim fully expected that his men would stand to protect him. He was shocked as the circle of Draj widened, as they backed away and let Supreme Commander Durn take the field. The squire who called Durn to the meeting dragged the boy out of the way. Several Draj picked up the captive man and then cut his ties. The Fourth Legion was having none of this. Furtim had made his choice.

"As you wish, My Lord," Furtim stated, pulling his sword. He knew that either way, he was dead. He figured that he may as well take the old man with him.

Durn assumed a defensive stance, then saluted the younger opponent. Furtim returned the salute and then assumed a similar stance. The Draj had formed a large circle of shields around the two warriors. There was plenty of room for both men to maneuver.

Furtim struck first and with a flurry of blows. Durn deflected them all, but the shield bash knocked the older fighter off of his footing and back a foot or two. Furtim pounced and pushed his advantage, swinging around the older man's shield in an attempt to strike him behind to the back of his neck. Instinctively, Durn crouched and threw a similar, but off-balanced, shot to Furtim's left thigh. It connected, penetrating the leather leg armor and chopping into the younger man's flesh. Furtim was hobbled a bit, but still on his feet. The wound bled freely.

The younger warrior backed off, allowing Durn to regain his composure. Not taking Furtim lightly, Durn covered himself. The elder warrior asked, "You are injured, Draj. Do you yield the field?"

"I do not yield!" Furtim asserted angrily, preparing for his opponent's assault.

"I do not wish to kill you, son," Durn stated somberly.

"Who says that you will, old man?" Furtim quipped. "The day is still young, and this fight is not over yet. I will leave with my honor intact … dead or alive."

"As you wish," Durn said calmly.

Durn approached cautiously. Furtim swung a vertical shot that skimmed

Durn's chest mail. Sparks rained for a moment as the elder warrior moved his shield quickly to cover. Furtim's shot had met its mark, but had done no damage. Durn moved rapidly forward, hooking the younger man's shield with his own shield edge. He pulled it toward him opening a gap in the younger opponent's defense. The old man swung horizontally across Furtim's eyes, blinding the younger man instantly, then followed with another horizontal slash to the throat in the opposite direction. The younger man reflexively attempted to get his sword in the way of the second attack, but he was too slow. Durn's cut met its mark and blood sprayed into his face from within Furtim's gorget. Durn shoved the younger man from him to ensure he was down. He was … permanently. Furtim sat on the ground, clutching his throat as he bled out within minutes.

The informant squire arrived at the victor's side. He held up a rag for his Supreme Commander. The old man took it from him, wiping the blood of his younger opponent from his eyes.

"What a damnable waste!" Durn shouted at the crowd of Draj looking on. "Do any of you feel the way that this man did, concerning my command? This is not Hodan. We do not fight for command or rule, but I swear on the beards of Runnir and Gunnir that I will defend my honor against any of you who feel it necessary to question my resolve."

The field was silent. Several older Draj picked up their former Commander and took him to a cart on the side of the Command Tent. Durn looked at the carnage that he had created in disgust.

"Who are you, boy?" Durn snarled to the squire beside him.

"I am Juhan, son of Porthus. I am squire to … I mean I WAS squire to Commander Furtim." The young man frowned and looked at the ground in shame.

"Boy, do not be ashamed. You obviously did not take this decision lightly, from what I see, by looking over at that farmer's face. How long did the interrogation go for, before I arrived?" Durn looked at the boy, who was swallowing hard and trying not to cry. He was maybe fourteen years old in the old man's estimation.

"Sir, the Commander captured him at the nineteenth hour of the day, right after midnight. He started by just verbally abusing the man, which I didn't think was an issue, but then the beatings began." The boy looked off toward the man, who formerly sat in the chair. "I am surprised that they both still live. I have never seen the Commander that way before."

Durn sighed. "It is good that you came to me. Pass to your Captain that I wish this Legion formed immediately."

"Yes, Sir." The boy walked over to an older Draj, who nodded and then began calling for the fourth Legion to form.

Within moments, eight-hundred-fifty men and women were formed. Many were in their night clothes. They wondered what the matter was. Durn marched out in front of the Captain and saluted, taking control of the formation.

"Listen up, Fourth Legion! In case you haven't met me, I am Supreme Commander Durn, second in command to His Majesty, himself. I command the First Legion."

Durn paused as if he was waiting for a question, but there was no sound.

Durn paced. "There seems to be some misunderstanding or malicious rumoring going on, concerning the tenure of my command at this time. Let me put your minds at ease. I am still in command of this army. I answer only to the King. I am retiring of my own free will after this campaign, but it is true that His Majesty requested my resignation, because of my judgment call, concerning the invasion of Cinnog." Durn paused again. "Be that as it may, the King requested that I remain in command for continuity, until our task is completed here within the Kingdom of Cinnog. I will not suffer any Draj to undermine authority or talk badly of a leader within the ranks. This is not only cowardly, but dishonorable. Talk to the man or woman who you have an issue with, not about them. If you are too cowardly to do so, then shut your lips and carry on with your mission." Durn surveyed the unit. He knew that it needed a Commander. "I will converse with His Majesty very soon concerning who will assume command of this unit. Unit further notice, you are directly under my command. Dismissed."

Durn turned around smartly and walked back to the Command Tent.

There, three sycophant Captains hovered around the Commander to his disgust. He shooed them away and instead went to a Sergeant who stood close by.

"Sergeant, collect wood and set the pyre for this man. He may have been flawed, but let us send him to Haya for her judgment, for I do not know his heart." Durn motioned toward the cart and walked away. The Sergeant acknowledged. Within a half-hour, the sun was starting to rise, and Durn could smell the distinct aroma of firewood and burning Human flesh. He wished that he would never experience it again.

* * *

Master Donick stood outside Puryn's tent and called out to his King. Puryn was half awake and half dressed. He unceremoniously swung the flap open, surprising Donick, who jumped back.

"Get in here," Puryn commanded.

Donick complied. "Your Majesty, something serious has occurred with the Fourth Legion."

"Oh, for the love of the Gods, now what?" Puryn asked with disgust.

"Brother, from reports that I have been given this morning, the Fourth captured a man and son traveling on the eastern road with a cartload of vegetables."

"So, what?" Puryn asked rubbing his eyes.

"So, Furtim decided that they were insurgents and arrested them," Donick replied.

"Again, I say, 'so what'?" Puryn looked up mildly annoyed. "Get to it, man."

"Fine. Well, Furtim began beating the older man and letting his son watch, trying to get them to admit to spying for Palgur. A squire, who had seen enough of his Commander's barbarity, snuck away and alerted your father." Donick paused as Puryn's eyes widened.

"Oh, for Haya's sake, are you kidding me?" Puryn stood, tying the waist to his pants. "So, what did da do now, brother?" Puryn slipped on his tunic and hauberk.

"He went to the camp and witnessed the 'interrogation' himself. Then he called Furtim on his actions, and Furtim called him on his invasion of Cinnog." Donick added, "… in front of the men."

"Oh, that must've gone well," Puryn said sarcastically as he finished dressing. "There is more, I assume. That is why you look at me with that long face, brother?"

"Durn challenged him to a duel," Donick said quickly grimacing.

"Is my da still alive, brother? I would kill that man if he killed my father." Puryn glared at Donick angrily.

"Your da is quite alive, and he has assumed command of the First and Fourth for the time being," Donick said plainly.

"That means I am down a Commander at this moment, doesn't it?" Puryn shook his head. "Really? Right before we attack a castle? What timing we have."

"The Commander had little choice, brother," Donick stated.

"I know. Hewould not be about killing his own men, unless it was inevitable." Puryn turned to Donick. "Assemble the council and bring me Kairoth."

"Kairoth, brother? The specialist?" Donick asked.

"Yes, that one. Bring me that man. I have an idea. Oh, and bring me the prisoners also." Puryn left the shelter for the Command Tent.

* * *

Kairoth sat in the shadows and quietly watched the scene as it unfolded before him. It seemed surreal to him to watch a Draj dare to duel his Supreme Commander, but after attempting to live as a Hodan for much of his life, he understood the concept of asserting and defending your honor by combat. Violence had been a large part of his life, and this scene just fell into the theme of things already in his memories. He walked back to his tent smirking. He didn't like Furtim that much anyways. Lately, the late Commander had presented himself as self-absorbed, mini-tyrant who had gotten too big for his britches. Kairoth sat and chewed on some hardtack and dried sausage, waiting for the day to begin. It was the second hour of the morning, and things were starting to move in the encampment.

"Reynir, do you have your plant yet?" Kairoth joked, half-serious.

"Why no, actually, brother. Do you know where I could find some nice viney ones?" Reynir smiled with an exaggerated psychotic look on his face. Then the druid laughed.

"Actually, off near that glen are plenty of viney things. The forest looks a bit aggravated. Do not get yourself killed." Kairoth smiled and waved as the druid left eagerly to find the plant he needed.

Valtyr yawned, and exited his tent with a hot cup of tea. "Where's he off to, Kairoth?"

"He's going to find a new viney friend," Kairoth quipped.

"Ah, good idea," Valtyr said, moving off to a more secluded area to say his morning prayers.

Sal'iabac and Safiya left their tent together. They were talking about ingredients and exchanging reagents as they approached the fire where Kairoth was seated. Sal'iabac winked at Kairoth who smiled back at her in return. Both women then went to a wash basin to groom themselves. The mages both yearned for a hot bath. Baths were very scarce in the field, and they were ready to finish with this adventure and head back to civilization.

Brynd appeared as if from thin air while eating his breakfast and checking his bow over. He looked over at Kairoth. "Hey boss, have you seen Famlin this morning?"

Kairoth raised an eyebrow. "What do you think?" The two laughed.

"Damn it! I was hoping that he had some bowstring wax. I will check with the quartermaster. See you later on, brother." Then the ranger left toward the supply tents.

Kairoth watched as his team went about their morning routines and preparations. "I have been blessed," the young warrior thought to himself as he finished his breakfast and stood.

"Kairoth?" a young squire asked. "Are you Kairoth?"

The larger and slightly older warrior turned and looked at the young squire, furrowing his brow. "Yes, I am. Who is asking?"

"His Majesty requests your presence, Sir," the younger boy declared officially.

"Well, I guess I should get moving then, and no, I am not a 'Sir,' so do not call me that," Kairoth asserted.

"Yes, Sir, I mean, mi'lord," the young man replied.

Kairoth changed clothes and went to the Command Tent on the hill. He wondered what this was all about.

* * *

When Kairoth arrived, he announced himself and requested permission to enter the High Command Tent. A squire opened the flap and led him to the table where the King of Yslan, the Prince of Cinnog, and all of the Commanders were gathered in a large circle around a table. A large animal skin map was unrolled, and there were figurines placed around a diagram of the fortress city, known as the Citadel. Kairoth stood silently, waiting to be addressed. The young Hodan warrior watched intently, to Durn's amusement.

"So, gentlemen, I see a frontal assault as a major issue. If we go in full bore on the front door, we give Palgur the advantage. I have two witnesses to what is happening within the walls." Durn gestured for a beaten, middle-aged farmer and his son to come. They were led to the table by several squires. "Tell us your tale, Sir," Durn said to the man.

"We live in the Citadel. Palgur gives refuge to the half-bloods within our Kingdom. It is the only kind gesture that he has shown, but it is for his own benefit. There are several science advisors to Lord Palgur who are

Dwarves. They have devised a weapon that they call a Thunder-ballista." The old man paused and looked at Durn.

Some of the officers present raised eyebrows and sighed, thinking the old man would say anything to save his own skin.

"Continue your report," Durn said calmly.

The farmer continued. "The new weapon is exceedingly loud and can throw a twenty-five-pound stone several hundred measures. The Dwarves have also devised a multiple projectile shot that is meant to shred a shield wall at close range. I was nearby when they tested it within the walls on hay bales and wooden planks. All that was left was shredded kindling."

"What do they use to cause the rocks to fly?" an officer jeered. "Fairies?"

The tent all chuckled, except for Puryn, Durn, and Donick. Even Basric was smiling.

"No, Sir. They use something that I overheard a guard talking about, called 'thunder powder.' They are getting it in shipments from Edenyag, disguised as wagon trains trading with Sudenyag's tribes. I hear several shipments have come up short or missing. Palgur was very angry and executed a minister who told him of the shortage."

Kairoth listened to the old man intently. Famlin had been using something very similar for some time. He had never asked the specialist what it was. Kairoth naturally assumed it was a new weapon, issued to that class of warrior. Now he was concerned. Puryn looked surprised. Kairoth did not think that the King was faking. Famlin was not a scribe, so he was most likely not of Edenyag. Where did he come by that powder, if not by Sudenyag? Kairoth sighed. His specialist had to be an agent playing both sides, but that was not surprising, considering his profession.

When the laughing had stopped, Kairoth stepped forward and spoke. "Excuse me, Your Majesty, and all other esteemed men in this tent."

Puryn smirked. He liked this young man and wondered what he was up to.

"Yes, what is it, Kairoth?" The King acknowledged. "Continue."

"I have a specialist under my command. He has used a similar substance. I never asked him where he got the powder that he used on our excursions.

I think, perhaps my man is a Sudenyag citizen who has connections. We have been using this thunder powder to devastating effect for almost nine months now. Do not discount what this man is saying. If Palgur possesses a large quantity of this substance, he can do us grave damage." Kairoth bowed and stepped back.

Puryn pursed his lips. "You have heard the testimony of one who lives within these walls, and another who has seen what this new weapon is capable of. Do any of you wish to chuckle more?"

The room had regained silence. There was a murmur in the crowd of leaders when the old farmer stood and spoke again. "Your Majesty, I must confess more."

Puryn looked at the old man with interest. "Continue."

"Palgur holds my wife and daughters. He has commanded the rape and execution of the families of those who stand against him." The old man swallowed hard.

The farmer's son shouted. "No, da! Do not tell him!"

"Hush, boy, there is no choice, but to reveal all now." The old man looked back at Puryn, who was now very interested in the farmer.

"What is it, mi'lord?" Puryn demanded.

"I was sent on a suicide mission last night by Palgur's Elites. They sent my son and me with a wagonload of grain and a cask of thunder powder hidden in the sacks. Enough to kill a hundred men or a full Command Tent." The old man swallowed hard.

Puryn stood. "Why do you tell me this, knowing that your head will be removed from your shoulders?"

"They hold my wife and daughters. Let my son go home to them. Let him live. He is young and has done no wrong. I only came this way, because I had no choice." The old man hung his head. The murmur in the tent became louder.

"Pray attend!" Donick shouted in his characteristic tone. The order was restored.

"So, you wish me to spare this whelp and simply take your head?" Puryn asked plainly.

"I would willingly give my life for my family's," the farmer replied.

"Show me this thunder powder keg and explain how you were to use it. We shall see what we are up against. Since you have given us the advantage, we will take it. I will spare your life and the life of your son."

The room protested. Donick rose. Without a word being said, order was restored again. The farmer looked to the floor, speechless.

"This is my idea. You say that this is an incredibly powerful weapon?" Puryn questioned.

"Yes, Your Majesty," the farmer affirmed. Kairoth nodded in agreement.

"Would they hear it from where they sit?" Puryn smiled.

The old man perked up. "Yes, Your Majesty! There is an observation unit about a half mile South of this camp. I am sure that they are listening for the telltale 'boom' of this powder. They don't dare come too close. Palgur sends children to do his dirty work. I guess that maybe a squire or two run the rabble observing us."

"Excellent. Commander Durn, will escort you to your belongings. We will set the cask far from our camp to the South." Puryn looked at Kairoth. "How did your man use the powder?"

"Fire, My King. Burning arrows or some incendiary device each time." Kairoth bowed.

"So, my new friend," the King said to the farmer, "we will keep you here, as our 'guest,' after we detonate this cask. This will make it seem as if you died on your mission, satisfying Palgur's expectations. It will also alleviate any suspicion and chance for capture and interrogation, although you have proven yourself to be a tough adversary, Sir. I do apologize for the actions of my man."

The farmer was silent and looking at the floor.

Puryn continued. "We will send the boy back to the unit. Do you think that you can lie and tell them that you killed my Command Tent, boy?"

The boy was smiling, "Oh yes! Yes, Sir! Will you come to save us from the Pretender!?"

"He won't see me coming if he thinks me dead. Just tell them that you 'think' that I was in the tent, but that your father died in the attack. You barely escaped." Puryn chuckled.

Durn interjected. "Still, Your Majesty, they have the weapon inside the walls, probably at the ready. How do we defeat their advantage?"

Puryn smiled. "Farmer, is there drainage or an exposed block wall near the base fortress where I can send a specialist team in to infiltrate the castle?"

Kairoth was nodding and smiling. Puryn grinned looking at his man.

"Yes, Sir! I know of one," another voice called out. It was Sir Broswyn of Cinnog. "I know exactly the best avenue of approach. We should return with a wagon and in rags. Hide the team in the wagon and approach in the darkness while the army harasses the guard and keeps their attention. If we can get close enough, do you have a team with the skills necessary to create an entrance?"

"I have a team in mind," Puryn remarked looking over at Kairoth. The Hodan warrior had his arms crossed and nodded confidently at his King. "Lead us to the cask. Our scientists need to examine a bit of the substance, so save a small quantity. Let us set our ruse in play."

The farmer led Durn to his cart. Under several large sacks of grain was a small wine-cask-sized container. The farmer backed away from it slowly.

"Be careful with that cask, gentlemen," the farmer said as the Draj removed it from the cart.

The Draj pried the top of the container open. It was filled with a black, gritty substance. The farmer backed away as the Yslan scientists removed a tankard's worth of the material. Then the Draj affixed the lid, and one of them slung the cask over his saddle roughly, making the old man cringe. Then the soldier rode several hundred measures from the edge of the camp. Criers were warning the camp not to venture anywhere near the cask. A crowd had gathered in curiosity.

Kairoth stood near the King. "Your Majesty, my thief had about a tankard's worth of this material and was able to do a lot of damage with it. That much is a bit worrying."

"Then we shall shoot it from here." Puryn looked around. "Draj! Bring me the Archery Champion."

"Yes, Sire!" a man responded, and he ran off into the camp calling out.

Within a few minutes, the Draj returned with a young lady, which surprised the King, then she removed her hood, and he saw her pointed ears. "It figures," the King thought to himself, smiling at the young half-Elf Draj before him.

"Good morning, Your Majesty. What is it that you require of me?" The young Draj bowed, paused, then stood tall.

"Take a flaming arrow and hit that cask in the field that is marked with the flag. Do you see it?"

"Plainly, Sire," she responded.

"Scouts, where is the Cinnog reconnaissance team?" Puryn asked.

A young squire responded. "They are still in the same location that the farmer stated this morning, Sire. They look to be young boys."

The King looked at the fourteen-year-old in front of him, raising an eyebrow. "Boys. Afraid of us, I'm sure. Perfect. Sound the warning."

Horns blared, and the crowd stood by wondering what all of the fuss was about. Commanders had relayed the message about a new weapon that Cinnog possessed, but no one believed that a cask of the size in that field could be much of anything. Still, they watched in interest from over one-hundred-fifty measures away.

"Stand by!" Durn shouted. "Loose!"

The archer lit her arrow, aimed and let loose. The arrow flew straight and true, striking the small barrel in the side. Nothing initially happened, and the crowd began to laugh and joke, but after a short time, the fire reached its mark.

There was an Ert-shattering boom. Small rocks and debris hit the first rank of observers, and the crowd hurried quickly from the lines to cover. No one was laughing now. Puryn had an immediate look of concern on his face. Sudenyag had several shipments of this powder, if the farmer was correct. Orus was there with his armies. The King closed his eyes and sighed. Sudenyag had just become twice as dangerous.

"Send the boy back to the recon team," Puryn said to his father.

"At once," Durn replied.

"Tell him to make it a good story. I died gruesomely." Puryn laughed, as did Durn.

Durn turned to the boy, thinking, "Thankfully, it is only a story, my son."

The boy ran South toward the hidden rebel team.

* * *

Palgur received his reconnaissance team report. It was everything that he had hoped for. The head of the snake was removed, and now the Draj would be in disarray. Yslandeth regulars were a concern, because of their numbers, but if the command was compromised, perhaps the embattlements would hold, giving him a chance to repel the invaders. The Pretender felt emboldened.

"You say, Puryn died in tattered rags?" Palgur nodded with a sinister look on his face. "Excellent work. Free that boy's whore mother and sisters. Give him a bag of silver for his father and tell him 'well done.'"

A Dwarf stepped forward, bowing to Palgur. "My Lord, the weapons are placed in their parapets. We have the standard and 'special' rounds available at each station. There is sufficient powder for several volleys per day over the next two or three days. After that, we have conventional weapons only."

"Excellent work. Be sure to conserve the new weapon and to only use our charges when maximum damage is ensured. Otherwise, send in the fodder to shoot arrows. They are cheap, and we have many arrows … and fodder." Palgur snickered and drank from his wine glass.

"As you command, My Liege," the Dwarf stated bowing.

Palgur's minions did as they were told. Most only complied with coercion. The young boy and his family were released back to their farm outside of the wall. Secretly, the boy waited eagerly for Yslandeth and Basric to arrive. He hadn't even let his mother know that his report was a lie. His mother hugged him in sorrow, crying for her lost husband. His two sisters did similarly, hugging each other. As badly as he felt for his lies, he knew that their ignorance ensured their safety if anything went wrong. He would go to his grave without admitting the ruse to Palgur or his men. The boy did not care. He prayed for a day when he saw the Pretender's body on a stake, with birds picking at his flesh. He hated the man with all of his being. His family would forgive his lies when they found out what he was up to.

The boy watched a covered cart being led by a familiar face to the castle. The untrained guards gave it little attention. Slowly, as the sun began to set, the team emerged from under the tarp and made their way to the edge, where Broswyn promised a way in. The boy sat and smiled quietly, losing sight of the specialists.

Palgur's day had finally come.

Chapter 18

The trees relayed the scene to their Queen. Adasser walked around her garden and spoke to the Elms that gave their spy report. Puryn was gearing up for the final blow. Adasser sat and pondered the possibility that the Citadel might hold its ground. She shook her head in irritation.

"What is wrong with these damned men?" the Queen asked no one in particular. She turned to an Elm and thought for a moment, then gave her orders. "My friend, we are called to action once again." Adasser frowned. "I do not wish to send you into harm's way, but my beloved seeks for peace, and it is a worthy cause. I should like to see his face again in this life."

The tree swayed as if a stiff breeze blew. Its leaves ruffled as if the feathers of some great bird of prey.

Adasser stood and bowed to her friend. "You are my greatest ally, Elm. Contact my apprentice and his two minions. We must organize support and cover for the Draj as they assault a stone fortress." Adasser sighed nervously. "Please conceal my love and his soldiers from the enemy's view and give them aid as is possible. Thank you."

Adasser closed her eyes. When she opened them again, the Elm was gone.

"Be safe as well, my friends." The Queen returned to her throne room, thinking of the violence that was to come. She was saddened.

* * *

It was several hours before sunrise. Kairoth and his band crouched behind a berm created to aid in defense of the castle. The berm was about five feet in height and hid the party from prying eyes. As Reynir approached the drainage grate before him, Kairoth signaled for silence and to take cover.

"Someone comes," Kairoth mouthed whispering ever so slightly.

Sal'iabac turned to face the direction of the intruder, her hands dug furiously in her pouches, then she found what she was looking for, and nodded to her sister, who nodded back. The ranger had his bow drawn and was aiming down the trench toward the incoming sound. Kairoth grabbed his arm, giving the signal to stand down while shaking his head in dismay.

"It's Broswyn and his boys," Kairoth whispered. Glaring at the militia leader, the Hodan gave the hand signal for "hurry up" and "quiet." Broswyn looked at Kairoth with a bit of annoyance, but then nodded and passed the signals back to the fifty or so warriors who followed behind him, single file. Broswyn arrived at the specialist team's location within a minute or two and gave his report.

"Kairoth, I have fifty of my best here for support at the King's order. I know my way around this place. We will need this at some point, I am sure." The Cinnog leader handed a small container to Kairoth. He took it gingerly, realizing that it was the sample of the thunder powder that was extracted before the charge was detonated the night prior.

"I thought that they needed a sample?" Kairoth questioned.

"I also, but the King said that they have plenty more inside. So, we use this bit, and we get more later." Broswyn shrugged.

"That's fair. Now we just need to get into this wall, quietly." Kairoth looked at his druid.

"I believe that I can do this, but I might need to bring in reinforcements." Reynir looked off toward to nondescript saplings about one-hundred feet from his location. Peering over the berm, he could make out his two minions clearly. "Good, they are there."

"But they are all of the ways over there," Broswyn protested. "How will they help from there?"

"Give him a moment. He has an interesting skill set," Kairoth stated sarcastically. Sal'iabac and Safiya both snickered.

"I'll say," Brynd muttered, watching the druid close his eyes and whisper something unintelligible, while setting his viney friend down on the top of the berm.

The plant took root immediately and seemed as if it grew larger by the second. Reynir smiled widely. "Hello, my new friend. Please tell those two stragglers out there to come to us."

The plant responded by shooting roots deeper into the soil and reaching its tendrils farther outward. The two trees returned within seconds, appearing as if from nowhere on top of the berm.

Reynir smiled. "Thank you, my little friend."

"Where did they come from?" Broswyn gasped.

"Oh, just wait until you see the rest," Brynd dead-panned.

"They are my friends, provided by the Holy Mother in Erynseere. She blesses me, because I am her student," Reynir said as a matter of fact. "My friends, can you work the bars on this grate and open us a hole large enough for the biggest of us to pass through?"

The trees swayed and then began their work. Roots worked their way under the mud, spooking Broswyn and a couple of his men. The trees started to wrap around the bars and to push into the crevices between the stones where the bars were set. Soon, there was a creaking and squeaking sound that concerned Kairoth and Broswyn. It was pretty loud.

"Kairoth, we shall skirmish with the guard and set a diversion for this noise. I will leave you twenty of my men. Good luck." Broswyn nodded and left with thirty men before Kairoth could object. The Hodan motioned for those remaining to get close up to their position and to stay as hidden as possible. Shortly after that, a fight broke out East of the party. Kairoth knew it was Broswyn. He hoped that the King was watching closely. Things were getting messy and fast.

* * *

Puryn awoke to the sound of fighting in the distance. He quickly threw on his cloak, and rushed to the observation point on a hill about a quarter of a mile from the Castle. He was pleasantly surprised to find his army hiding in a newly formed forest that was not on the hill when he had gone to sleep. Durn was waiting.

"Well, son, it seems the Queen has arrived." Durn smiled.

"It was only a matter of time, and I'm sure she's been spying the whole time. She is quite stealthy that one." Puryn looked at the Elm near him. "You do not have to tell her that I said that, but you are going to anyways." The King laughed as the tree swayed. "Tattletale!"

"We have a small unit … looks like Broswyn engaging small units on the outskirts." Durn looked puzzled for a second and then told Puryn what the King already knew. "A diversion?"

"Most likely, father. We need to bolster his assault." Puryn looked around. "Which Legion is on duty?"

"First is on duty, Your Majesty," Durn said, becoming the Commander he was, once again, vice the father he wished to be.

"Send Bandu and the boys to the front," Puryn ordered. "Have them make a lot of noise. While they are there, have them soften the defenses for the main assault."

"I respectfully request to lead my troops into this battle, Sire!" Durn objected. "What is this?"

"Commander," Puryn said with a look of concern on his face, "I need you to run the whole show, not just that one Legion. Bandu can handle that, father. Come, let us set the plan in motion."

Durn stood tall. "As you wish, son, but I am not pleased with this order. I follow it under protest."

"Understood, da. We will talk about it later!" Puryn turned and smiled weakly at his father, leaving to call the army to arms.

It was an hour before sunrise when the First Legion left the wood and marched down the road to meet the enemy. The Draj met weak resistance at first, but the intensity of combat increased as they neared what was left of Broswyn's militia.

"Hail! Cinnog! We reinforce you!" Bandu declared.

"Thank the Gods," Broswyn shouted back. "Watch the towers for the weapon!"

"Gentlemen, execute the battle plan," the young Commander said to his Lieutenants. The men acknowledged, and the unit split into platoons, attacking at various emplacements, drawing a lot of attention to their positions. So far, the enemy seemed in disarray, and all seemed to be going well.

A bell began ringing in the towers. The sounds of activity could be heard within the castle. Bandu wondered how much luck they had left, muttering a prayer to the Goddess.

* * *

The Pretender was wakened by the bells. It was still dark outside his window, but he knew that the Draj had no problem with fighting in the darkness. As he left his bedchamber, his Generals followed him down the hallway in tow. Two Dwarves awaited him in the war room.

"So, what of the enemy?" Palgur demanded.

"They have sent one Legion to harass and weaken the outer defenses, My Lord," a Dwarf answered gravely.

"Only one Legion? Perhaps the army is not as vast as once reported … or perhaps they seek to lure us out into the open? Fools, ready the weapons and wait for a chance to deploy them!" Palgur smiled with an evil grin. "We will make them think twice about storming our walls."

"As you wish, My Lord," the Dwarf responded relating specific tasks to his engineers. They departed for their duties.

"What of our army? What do we have within the walls?" Palgur was animated.

He seemed nervous, and this was not lost on his Generals. Secretly, four of the five men in front of the Pretender had plotted to overthrow him and clear the way for Basric to assume the throne without a bloody battle. The only concern of the Generals was, that although the people seemed ready to rebel, few seemed capable. The few who did, waffled when push came to shove, worrying about family and loved ones who may be caught in the fray. The men played along.

"My Lord, we have three-thousand men at arms, five-hundred archers of varying skill, mostly farmers. We have five thunder-ballista, four on the corners of the castle and one behind the portcullis. We also have four trebuchets and one conventional ballista." The man bowed.

"Employ them in the most tactical way possible, gentlemen, and be sure to cover the front door sufficiently. They shall not just walk in and take this place from us." Palgur retired to a tower in the center of the yard that allowed for an elevated view all of the ways around the battlefield.

The Generals went about their business, but much was done half-heartedly. The vast majority of Cinnog was ready for this charade to be over, but the battle was still underway.

*　*　*

The sun had just risen when Bandu's platoon reached the drawbridge. It was down. The Draj moved in a tight formation. The three other platoons were finishing up their mop up the area and were running to rejoin with their Commander on the bridge. Within another thirty minutes, they had arrived and reformed.

"Shields to the front, archers to the rear!" Bandu ordered. The men shuffled and reformed. "Forward at a walk!"

The remains of the first Legion reached the portcullis. It was down, but was constructed of bars of iron, which one could see clearly through. There were about six inches of room between the bars, and for some reason, the thing was moving upward. Bandu became concerned.

"Unit halt! Prepare to repel!" the Commander ordered. He could see a large gathering of armored rabble on the other side of the gateway. He figured that this would be a spear battle; a battle of attrition. He liked his odds. The Draj covered down in the ranks and set to receive the enemy charge.

When the portcullis was raised almost three quarters, a loud shout of commands came from the back of the Cinnog rebel unit. Bandu called his men to lock shields, expecting that this would be the charge he had been waiting for, but instead, the army ran in either direction, revealing a large silver tube and several Dwarves who were lighting one end. It was too late to react.

"Everyone, down!" Bandu screamed, knowing what was about to happen. He had been fooled, and the enemy thunder ballista was about to fire. There was no time to retreat, and they were caught in a tunnel in front of the portcullis.

There was an ear-splitting explosion. Smoke was everywhere. Bandu found himself several ranks behind where he had begun. Strangely, he felt nothing. He was dazed as he looked at his tattered arm. He could see holes in his armor, and he was bleeding profusely. Looking around, he could see several hundred Draj, torn to tatters, lying in uneven heaps all around him.

"Haya helpus," Bandu muttered as the calls to retreat filled the air. It was the last thing that he heard.

* * *

Puryn looked on in horror through the spyglass. "What in the Underworld is Bandu doing!?"

Durn ripped the glass out of his son's hands, looking at the portcullis of the Citadel, as a thunderclap met his ears. "Oh no! You damned young fool!"

The Commander could see the remaining five-hundred or so Draj

250

retreating in formation, shields up and returning fire by bow, but there was another explosion from an adjacent tower, then a third from the tower on the other flank of the entryway. Durn dropped the spyglass, falling to his knees.

"I trained those boys myself, Puryn. They are all gone now." Durn was distant, and tears fell freely from his eyes.

Puryn closed his eyes swallowing hard. "That might have been you, da," Puryn said sadly.

Durn sprung to his feet angrily, getting in his son's face. "It SHOULD have been me, you damned fool, not some boy who signed on as a constable!"

Several of Puryn's guards drew close to the King. "It is fine, men, stand down. Leave him be." Puryn's tears now fell freely. "I am sorry that it was Bandu, father, but I am not ashamed to say that I am glad that you are still here with me."

Durn turned and hugged his son, sobbing. "Damn that man. I will be the one to remove his head. Promise me this, son. I owe him much more." Durn's voice was strangely dark.

"It is done. You will execute that piece of dung. His corpse will hang in Empyr for the crows to eat." Puryn patted his father on his back. "It is not over. We cannot advance on THAT." Puryn pointed to the castle.

"I hope that Broswyn fared better than the Draj. Kairoth and his team need to get into that castle and give us some advantage." Durn sniffled, wiping his eyes. "Enough tears for now. I have killing to do. I will make them bleed dearly for the First. They will all die in flames." Durn pored over his maps and diagrams.

Puryn looked at his father. He had never seen him in this foul a mood, but he understood completely. The King looked over at a squire. "Come here, boy. Ride to Hodan and deliver this to King Orus. Tell him if he will assist me in this, I will owe him dearly."

"Yes, Sire!" the young boy said as he stood by. The King wrote a note on a parchment, sealed it with his signet ring, and handed it to the messenger. The squire left on a Korinian steed, making a beeline for Warrior's Crossing in Hodan.

The note simply said:

"Greetings, brother,

"We have not spoken in some time, and I do not know if you will be willing to aid me or not. Edenyag allies with my enemy. The first Draj Legion was destroyed by their treachery, through the providing of aid and weapons to Palgur. Beware of this new siege weapon known as a thunder-ballista. It can be used against an entire Legion with effect. Three killed eight-hundred without effort. They are most likely deployed inside of a castle, perhaps even within the Great Library complex itself.

"Invade them, conquer them, burn them to the ground … I care not. Do as you please. Just bring me Cathir's head. I will send you support in Sudenyag to help quell the syndicate and the tribes, as repayment of this debt. Long live Hodan. Long live Yslan.

"Your brother,

Puryn."

"Father, those responsible will pay dearly. Orus will burn their villages to the ground in retaliation, if I know my brother well enough." Puryn was angry and growing angrier by the moment, as the loss of another eight-hundred souls began to sink in.

"Good, I hope that pompous politician and his sycophants suffer a worse fate than Bandu and the First. Hodan knows how to kill, that is for certain." Durn stood, saluted his son and called out to his Legion Commanders. They would find a way to bring down this fortress.

* * *

Reynir's trees had done as much as they possibly could. The stone was too strong. The bars were bent, but not enough. Even the viney plant tried to pull at the rocks to no avail. Then there was a loud thunderous explosion to the East of their position. Kairoth was concerned.

"I would guess that was a thunder ballista. We need to get in there, druid! What is taking so long?"

"Take it easy, Kairoth!" Valtyr answered. "Castles are built to be hard to breach. I am sure that they are doing all that they can."

Brynd could see a mass of people running toward their position. He quickly recognized Broswyn and ten of his thirty men, as they hurdled into the large ditch beside the berm and ran through the smoke and the confusion toward the team's position. "Incoming, boss," Brynd said, pointing toward the group.

"What in the Underworld is going on out there!?" Kairoth yelled as the second explosion shook the hole he stood in.

"Thunder-ballista hit the Draj on the drawbridge in front of the portcullis. It is not a pretty sight." Broswyn grimaced and looked to the ground.

"Are you all ready to fight?" Kairoth asked seriously.

There was a third explosion, and then the sound of a rushing army, as the Cinnog rebels cleared the bridge of any survivors. Kairoth was disgusted and angry.

"Brynd. Here. Druid, get your trees out of here and grab your plant friend if possible. Move to a safe distance and take cover." The Hodan leader handed the thunder powder cask over to the ranger. "Blow this thing to smithereens. Enough diddling the milkmaid here."

Broswyn motioned. "Move back."

Everyone backed off. Brynd set the cask in a spot he figured would do the most damage and backed up and took cover as best that he could. Brynd lit his arrow with a flint and steel.

"Aim true, Draj. Aim for your brothers," Kairoth said.

"Huzzah Draj! May their mothers be forever blessed!" the ranger said releasing his arrow. It was a direct hit.

* * *

A smaller explosion was heard off in the distance. Puryn walked over to an Elm. It swayed expectantly.

"Thank My Lady for your presence and ask her to advance you to surround the Citadel at two-hundred measures. We will need to use you all as cover. We will advance behind your lines. I know that she must give you that direction." Puryn turned to go and then remarked. "Thank you, Elm."

The tree swayed. Puryn turned back, and it was gone. In fact, over the next two hours, the forest thinned to nothing on the hill, reappearing at a ring around the Citadel.

Puryn called to his father. "Da, we have cover. My lady and her children provide it. Let us move forth."

"Agreed." Durn left his son and began barking orders to his Commanders.

Approximately twenty-eight-thousand-five-hundred Draj and Yslan Regulars formed and marched forward to the new tree line. Puryn smiled, knowing that Palgur would soon realize that Erynseere had arrived. "I should ask Adasser to tear that place to the ground," the King said offhandedly.

Basric answered. "It is not the building or the people who commit these acts. It is the one who sits falsely in the seat of power. We will have justice, my friend. It comes."

"Just the same, Basric," Puryn replied. "I will not let down my guard again. The first time it cost me dearly."

Basric nodded and wondered how his own Champion was faring.

* * *

Kairoth waved his hand furiously, trying to clear the dust and smoke. Brynd approached cautiously, bow in hand, the string drawn at the ready. Upon arrival, both men quietly cheered when they saw the hole created by the explosion of the thunder powder.

"Excellent!" Kairoth stated calling everyone forward. "My team in front, mages, and druid in the center. That lightning trick would be a great asset today, My Lady." The Hodan smiled at Sal'iabac.

"Oh, you know it, My Lord. We are both ready. Priests, standby to aid the wounded!" Sal'iabac grinned evilly. "They will pay."

"Where is Famlin!?" Safiya remarked. "I have not seen him in a week. I hope he is all right."

"Wherever that man is, if he's not full of arrows, I will wager he is fine," Brynd quipped.

"Enough chatter, let us do the King's bidding," Kairoth said drawing his sword.

The hole was big enough for one to enter at a time. Brynd went in first, followed by Kairoth, then Valtyr, Reynir, Sal'iabac, and finally Safiya. Broswyn and his thirty remaining men entered behind the party. Brynd looked down the drainage pipe, finding a grated cover about one-hundred measures up the passage. It was located under what appeared to be a kitchen. The ranger called the Hodan forward, and Kairoth eased the grate up and off of the massive drain.

The Hodan pulled himself up into a food preparation room and scullery. Several young boys and girls were cowering in the corners of the rooms, as the towering warrior stood and looked around. The children were even more terrified as the rest of the party made their way up out of the sewer and into the room.

"Which way to the throne room, children?" Brynd asked coldly.

One boy stood. "Do you come to free us all?"

"We do," the ranger answered. "Where do we find Palgur the Bastard?"

"Left out of the door. Follow the hallway until it goes left and right. Take a right. You can't miss the large throne room at the end." The boy looked at Brynd. "There will be guards, no doubt."

"We will manage, young one." Brynd motioned for his group to come forward and follow.

As the team left, the boy's eyes widened as Broswyn, and his thirty men came forward from the drain. He smiled at the warrior who nodded back somberly. Broswyn figured that the boy hadn't laughed in some time. The child was gaunt, dirty and appeared to have been beaten recently. The warrior was beginning to enjoy his job. Time for Palgur to pay.

The unit made its way down the hallways through screaming servants and advisors, all of which surrendered immediately and without a fight. Upon entering the throne room, Kairoth noticed one Dwarf was intently looking at a drawing on a finely carved war room table. The engineer turned in horror to see the Alliance Unit filing into the room. He ran.

"Oh, it is too late for that, my short friend," Brynd smiled and released an arrow that pierced the Dwarf's right knee. The runner fell flat on his face, howling in pain.

"Please, I am only a servant. Do not kill me!" the Dwarf pleaded.

A lady-in-waiting spoke up. "That is false! He is one of Palgur's engineers, My Lord."

Brynd smiled and nodded. "Thank you, My Lady." He approached the Dwarf with a second arrow drawn. "All right, scum, where are these devices located and how many of them are there?"

The Dwarf stood silent and feigned ignorance of what Brynd spoke of. Brynd released the arrow into the Dwarf's other knee, seemingly without looking, grabbing a third. The Dwarf's eyes widened as he squealed in pain.

"Oh, so that is how you want to play this?" Brynd asked grimly as he drew the bowstring.

"Brynd," Valtyr roared.

"What?" Brynd asked looking over at Valtyr. "Show him mercy after he murdered eight-hundred of my Draj brothers? Not likely, priest."

"Never mind. Carry on, then," Valtyr said with a sickened look on his face.

"Oh, excellent! You are learning the ways of neutrality and balance!" Reynir said in a much too jubilant tone for the moment.

"You shut it," Valtyr barked at his brother.

Kairoth waited impatiently. "Where are they, Dwarf?" The Hodan turned the arrow in the Dwarf's right knee. He sang out loudly in pain. "One more Alliance life dies, because of your treachery, and I will make you suffer much more than this."

Kairoth's eyes were the darkest Sal'iabac had ever seen. She shuddered to look into them. "Please stop," she begged.

"Not yet, My Lady. He must tell us what we need to know," Kairoth deadpanned, never looking up from his captive.

The Dwarf looked genuinely afraid. "If you let me live, I will tell you whatever you need to know."

"I can only guarantee that you will not be killed by my people. The King may have different ideas." Kairoth stroked the arrow fletching, and leaned toward the Dwarf menacingly.

The Dwarf closed his eyes and winced, awaiting the pain that did not come. "Five. Four in the towers. One in front of the portcullis."

"Where is Palgur?" Kairoth demanded.

"The center observation tower with his guard. Please …," the Dwarf begged, sobbing.

"Enough," Kairoth stated coldly. "Valtyr, fix this Dwarf the best that you can, then bind him until this is over."

"Thank you, brother," Valtyr said in relief.

Reynir shrugged. "He chose his side. I am not sorry for him."

* * *

Puryn ordered the trebuchets set up twenty-five measures behind the tree line. It had been long enough. He had no idea of the status of his specialist unit or Broswyn's militia. He wanted Palgur to know that he was here.

"Send in rocks for the first hour. Slow volleys. Concentrate on the towers and the front portcullis. Let him know that we are thinking about him." Puryn retired to his Command Tent. Durn was present. He was in a foul mood. The sound of machinery hurling rocks filled the morning air.

"Good. I hope you drop one right on his head," Durn said, swallowing a pull off of his flask. "I am sorry for earlier, my son. I was in shock."

"I understand the guilt of surviving, da. Believe me when I tell you I live every moment in it. I loved Bandu also." Puryn took the flask from his father.

"I will switch to fire pots at night. We will bombard them until morning. Maybe we can set their powder on fire," Durn suggested.

"A sound plan, father. Remember that you must live to see retirement. Mother needs you." Puryn shook his father's hand, but Durn pulled him close, kissing his son on the forehead.

"You will always be that ten-year-old to me, boy. I cannot wait to raise cows." Durn left to inform the artillery of the new orders.

* * *

Broswyn led his small unit to the courtyard and sought to reach the closest tower. There, in the yard, was a unit of rebel militia and one of the enemy weapons. The first one that had been used on the First Legion. Kairoth called out to him to retreat, but the young warrior had other plans.

"I have this, Hodan. Take the towers down, then we all go for Palgur. We must open the front door and let your friends inside!" the Cinnog Commander hollered.

There was a loud roar, and then a splintering crash as an eighty-pound stone impacted the tower closest to where the group stood. The tower absorbed the hit, but it was evident that it could not sustain many more direct impacts without collapsing. It was already damaged from centuries of war, and Yslandeth's trebuchets were nothing to toy with.

"I think the King is tired of waiting for us," Kairoth laughed. "Stay out of the blast area of that weapon! Luck in battle!"

"Luck in battle!" Broswyn responded.

The Cinnog unit charged toward the rebel militia, who were now in disarray after several more shot hit the castle tower and walls, sending large chunks of debris down upon the ranks. Several men were crushed as parts of the tower began to fall on their position. Many men broke ranks and started to run. Three Dwarves worked furiously to load and reposition the gun toward Broswyn's advance. Another volley from Puryn's artillery ceased their efforts as they were buried in rock and castle wall. The weapon stuck out from beneath the rubble. Broswyn's unit approached carefully, weapons drawn, as the barrage continued.

"Help me dig. Let us get this thing free. Point it toward the center tower. We light it somewhere in the back, I do believe from what I'm told. We will figure it out! Hurry men!"

Broswyn's men dug furiously as the barrage changed from stone to fire pots. After about an hour or two, they had freed the weapon and with twenty men, repositioned it upward toward the central tower. Broswyn looked at the tube and found a small chamber with an oil-soaked rag inserted into it.

"Looks like the spot to light this thing. If I'm wrong, all I will do is blow us up!" Broswyn chuckled loudly, but no one else was laughing.

As they readied to fire on the observation tower, the farthest West tower erupted in an explosion that rocked the entire courtyard. Broswyn and his men were knocked from their feet by the concussion, rising with their ears ringing.

"I hope the specialists were not in that tower. On second thought, I have a better idea for this weapon. All right men, position it toward the other front wall tower that still stands. We shall see what it does to towers from the inside." Broswyn directed the aim and then lit the fuse.

* * *

Kairoth looked to the exploding tower with a look of terror. "Move!"

The specialists dove beside the center tower, covering against debris from the falling structure, as it collapsed in the fire, soot, and thick dust.

There were not any screams, because no one could have lived through an explosion that great.

"My Gods, that magic is powerful!" Sal'iabac stated clinging to the wall.

"It is amazing that man and Dwarf created such a thing! Haeldrun must be rejoicing," Valtyr said in disgust.

"Let's move. The King is raining the Underworld on these fools, and we are in the impact area!"

The team slid carefully around the perimeter of the center tower. Smoke covered their movement, and Palgur's Elite personal detachment saw nothing. As they approached the door, several guards advanced on Kairoth, but Brynd evened the odds quickly, leaving Kairoth only two, which he dispatched without breaking much of a sweat. Once inside the tower, they made their way up a very narrow and steep spiral staircase. About half of the way up, Palgur could be heard fretting about the assault and cursing at his Generals. A scuffle had begun.

"You will pay for your treachery, Generals. All of you!" the Pretender screeched.

When the team reached the doorway, several guards were dead, and several were protecting four out of five of Palgur's Generals. The fifth, who was a loyalist to the Pretender, lay dead on the floor in a pool of his own blood.

Kairoth stepped forward. "Hold your blade, Sir!"

"Who in the Underworld are you, boy?" one old soldier asked.

"I am a forward team for King Puryn of Yslandeth. We stand outside of this castle and bombard it. My King wants this man alive, I would wager. Please allow us to take him to His Majesty." Kairoth looked at the man like he was not giving him a choice, but was merely being polite asking. The attitude was not lost on the old man.

"How will I know that you will not just set him free?" the General asked.

"He killed my King's Draj. He will pay with his life after my King ensures justice is served," Kairoth said firmly.

"Fine. Take this piece of dung before I change my mind. Tell your King we seek to surrender to him. It appears that the vast majority of his loyalist militia have perished at the portcullis in a rain of stone. Most who remain were bound in service by debt or coercion. Your King must spare these people. They had no will to fight, and no reason to oppose Basric. They simply could not stand up to this filthy swine," the General spat on the Pretender.

"We will need a large white flag," Kairoth suggested.

"Take some the white linen off of this table. This tablecloth will do," a servant suggested, tying it to a spear shaft.

As they were preparing to go, another loud explosion filled the air, shaking the room. This time the blast was from the courtyard and the far northeastern corner of the castle fractured from the impact of a weapon within the castle.

The General snorted. "Your friends have apparently captured a weapon and redirected it. It appears the front door is now open and the dogs are no longer there to guard it." He smiled at Kairoth, then leered at Palgur. "King Puryn comes, as does the true heir, you pig. You will rot on a stick."

Kairoth looked down at the courtyard. The General was correct. Broswyn and his entourage were cheering as they pulled their fingers from their ears. The front of the Citadel was rubble. Yslandeth would ride on this immediately if the King were paying attention.

Kairoth knew he was. There was no doubt.

* * *

Puryn cheered the direct hit on the western tower. He laughed as it exploded and fell into the courtyard. Later, another direct hit by his artillery sent the opposing tower crashing down in a cascade of debris and flame. There was still a tower to go, and it was barely out of range. Puryn was devising a plan to advance on the portcullis and deal with the other fortified tower, when a third explosion occurred, this time from within the compound. To his surprise, the other tower fell without his intervention.

"The team lives." Puryn smiled. "I shall have to promote those people."

Durn ran to Puryn winded. "The towers are all down, but the one in the center and the northwest. I think that we can advance safely, My King."

"Agreed, let us depart and take this objective, once and for all." Puryn hugged his father, and the two formed the army for an advance.

Within two hours, a ring of trees had surrounded the Citadel, strictly around its outer wall. Nothing could enter or leave that was not a friend of King Puryn. The Citadel residents cowered in fear, knowing that not only had the Champion of the Golden Queen arrived, but so too had the Holy Mother of the Forest. No one wished to fight. The armies of the North walked into the Citadel unopposed.

In the courtyard, Palgur was bound hand and foot and laid before four Generals. Behind them were fifteen-hundred remaining Cinnog rebel militia, and behind them were one-thousand terrified slaves. The armies of Yslandeth and Cinnog quickly filled the broken courtyard. Aside from the four Generals, who stoically awaited their fates, the mob looked terrified.

Puryn rode out in front with his father and the elite guard. Basric rode up behind them with Broswyn by his side. The army cleared an area for their King and their Commanders.

All eyes were on the King as he stepped forward. "I am King Puryn, the Champion of the Golden Queen! I bring Cinnog its true heir. Let all of you bear witness that anyone who opposes or rebels against this man or his rule will incur the wrath of Yslandeth and the Northern Alliance. This I do swear from this day forward. Yslandeth recognizes Basric as the true heir to Lorus. May any who seek to undermine him do so at their own peril."

Puryn turned his horse and joined his father to the side as Basric rode forward to speak. "People of Cinnog, this war has been a costly one, as all wars are. Men of ambition drew all into this petty conflict, which cost us our most precious resource, your sons and daughters. I weep daily for the loss of their many lives and seek to redeem their sacrifices by rebuilding our nation as a just and fair Kingdom."

The crowd murmured quietly. Some wept, while others could be heard pleading for mercy. Many just stood and wondered what new abuse this man would bring. Basric could read the hopelessness in their faces. He sighed.

"So much despair in this courtyard." He looked to a young boy's face, as the child waited with bated breath. "I will free all in slavery this day. All who owe debts are free, all who were sold are no longer the property of another, and if you opposed me, I would forgive your transgressions if you swear fealty this day and promise me your loyalty from this moment forward."

There was an outburst of enthusiasm with this declaration, which prompted another statement from Master Donick, who sat up in the saddle. "You can start by closing your filthy mouths and listening to what His Highness has to say! Shut up, all of you!"

Basric nodded, smiling at his friend Donick. He had only known him a short while, but he liked his straightforward demeanor. Puryn just chuckled, shaking his head. The crowd quieted down.

"Grab ahold of the man, woman, or child near you. Make a chain to this man in front." The King of Cinnog pointed to the General in front of the gagged Palgur, who sat in abject horror as the swearing in began. "General, touch my sword."

The General touched Basric's sword. "Repeat this oath. This day, I do swear my loyalty and my fealty to the Kingdom of Cinnog and to its rightful heir, King Basric of the line of Lorus the Bold! I swear to remain loyal and faithful to my land and to the King, as long as breath remains in my lungs."

The people repeated as one, and then Basric continued. "For my part, I will protect you and your families. I will provide justice and freedom to all who walk in righteousness and loyalty. This I do swear as Basric, King of Cinnog."

One man who had been freed, began rejoicing loudly, and several others followed suit. Before long, the entire mob was chanting Basric's name. Unity had been achieved in Cinnog. Peace was finally real. Basric looked at Palgur, who was bound at his feet.

"Ah, yes, there is one more thing to do. We shall deal with you in the morning, Pretender. I do not think that I will forgive or forget your disloyalty, lies, and deceit. You will pay for your murderous reign of terror. Enjoy this, your last day, before you enter the Underworld." Basric rose from Palgur's face.

"My father would like to do the honors, King Basric," Puryn stated without emotion.

"Of course. Of course,he would. So, shall it be done, my friend." Basric looked at Durn.

The Commander stood up. "My last action as the Commander of the First Legion will be to avenge it. A fitting end to a long and eventful career." Durn stood and bowed to Basric. "Thank you for this honor, Your Majesty."

"Without your sacrifices and the sacrifices of that crew over there, I may not be here to see this day." Basric gestured to Kairoth and the band who were sitting off by themselves, eating their rations and drinking from a keg of ale that they had found in the pantry.

Puryn replied, "Underestimate that bunch at your own peril, Basric. They are a formidable asset."

Basric nodded and commanded that Palgur be locked in a room within the last remaining tower. The guards left him bound within his cell, standing outside to ensure that he stayed there.

The sun had long since set, but the fires of the battle still lit the night, as the new King surveyed the rubble he had inherited. Basric did not care.

They would rebuild.

Chapter 19

A humid, cool spring breeze blew softly, causing the flames of the campfire to gently wave in the darkness of the early morning. The temperatures were finally rising with the first growing season approaching. It was a welcome return and change from the raw, damp cold of the port in winter. Famlin was awake and sitting up alone beside the light of the fire. He was no longer tied up by his captors. Once the Suden syndicate patrol, which captured him, realized that he was the apprentice of their Master, Irshad Il Nadur, they released the thief, but held him under orders, until the Master arrived to sort things out.

Famlin looked westward and wondered for Safiya and the others; he was not sure of how the battle had gone for them. He only managed to see the power of the new weapons from afar as he sought to pilfer more thunder powder from Irshad's syndicate stash house near the Cinnog border. Unfortunately, the sentry on guard was better at his job than Famlin had guessed and he woke near the port, a prisoner. There was no explaining this one to Kairoth. His cover was blown, thanks to an overzealous guardsman. Famlin remembered his sister, Inua, who Irshad held as insurance, guaranteeing his loyalty and compliance. Famlin had not seen her in years. At this point, he wondered if the bastard had not killed her, or sold her off as a slave without telling him. Famlin hated Irshad Il Nadur with a burning passion, but he also feared his organization and their fanatical loyalty to the man.

"You there," Famlin said softly, "is there anything to eat or drink here?"

"Not for you, traitor," the younger boy said munching on a flatbread of some sort and sipping water.

"For your information, you dullard …"

Famlin sat up, and the boy readied his hand on his blade.

"You are wise to reach for your weapon, young one. Regardless, you would be dead if I wished it so. As I was saying, for your information, I am an apprentice to Master Irshad, and I was on assignment, spying on the operations of Yslan and Hodan. I was taking the powder so I could remain useful to my team leader and continue to collect information. Your fools at the stash house have ruined that now. I cannot explain this absence for so long, and my team will smell my lies when I make excuses for missing the battle at the Citadel. Fools. All of that time and effort lost for a cask of powder?" Famlin feigned disgust, but in reality, did not really care that he was caught. He had resolved to tell these brigands nothing that they didn't already know.

"Save it for the Master, traitor. I have no reason to believe anything that you say." The younger thief relaxed his hand on the dagger and went back to eating.

Soon, several others joined the two by the fire as reinforcements. They had been listening in the shadows. Famlin made sure to brag loudly. He was not sure how many remained obscured, but these followers were young and foolish. The specialist figured that most had left their hidden cover to create some sort of a show of strength in numbers. Famlin assessed his foes. He knew that he could decimate this band in short order and that concerned him. Why, if he was so important, would the regional leader assign such rabble to guard him. The specialist decided to stay his hand for the moment, because there was something wrong with this scenario. He was armed, in a camp full of novices who were guarding him, and his Master was supposed to be inbound. Something smelled fishy to him.

Famlin faked a look of defeat when the ten or so younglings surrounded him around the fire with daggers drawn. "Are you sure that I cannot at least have a piece of bread?"

The boy, satisfied that Famlin had been subdued by their show of force, gave in. "Fine, here." He handed Famlin a small round flatbread and a piece of the local cheese.

The specialist smiled for a moment, remembering his mother and eating bread and cheese with her in the mornings as his father left to work the docks every day. "Thank you," is all he said, eating quietly, wondering what was actually going on here.

* * *

Orus was wroth. Faylea looked at her father with concern. He seemed angrier and more worried than ever, concerning the status of his reign and his nation.

"What is wrong, father?" the Hodan Princess asked, already knowing the answer.

"Daughter, my reign will not last if Hodan thinks me weak. I have failed in Edenyag, and now Cinnog regroups on our western border. Surely, Basric is no threat in the state that their army is in, but their King is seen as defeating the foes of its people, and that solidifies their loyalty. To the North, my brother is as strong as ever and his people, for the most part, love him. To the East Edenyag laughs at us and Dornat Al Ar and Torith keep to themselves. We have no true alliances. The only pact that truly matters is with Yslan, and that one is on shaky ground. Soon, someone will come for my head and try to assume this crown if I do not do something to turn the tide in the eyes of the Hodan."

"You worry for nothing, father." Faylea's lies were not convincing Orus. "The people remember what you did on the Arondayre. They have not forgotten, My King."

"They have lived through utter annihilation and destruction, only to be cobbled back together as a shadow of what they once were. It weighs on the morale of the warriors. Their stares are not lost on me. I see their questioning eyes. They ask me, 'when is it our turn for glory?'" Orus sipped a tankard of mead.

"I think you see too much into their demeanor. The people are simply tired of struggling, father. The people support you. I support you." Faylea hugged her much larger father, who kissed her gently on her forehead.

"Hodan must redefine itself if we are to survive and flourish in this new world we have created. Our people will not sit idly by and become a vassal state to Yslandeth's grand Northern Alliance. Our culture has bred us to stand on top, not be buried beneath." Orus looked out of his window. The fields were beginning to green again.

A guard knocked at the door to the King's living quarters, reporting in. "Good morning, Your Majesty. A rider from Yslan has approached our city gates. He says King Puryn has sent a missive for your eyes only. We have escorted him to the palace." The man saluted.

Orus stood looking at Faylea with a questioning glance. She shrugged.

"Bring him to me, immediately," Orus commanded, pouring another mead and offering one to his daughter. She refused.

Within moments, the rider, a young squire, presented himself to King Orus of Hodan, handing him a handwritten scroll from King Puryn of Yslandeth. It was sealed. Orus read the message and smiled.

"Boy, inform your King that I will comply with his request immediately. Tell him that it will be my pleasure." Orus stood. The boy saluted, the King returned his salute, and the messenger was escorted to his horse, leaving immediately toward Cinnog.

"Father, what was that all about?" Faylea had a look of mild concern on her face.

"The chance we have been waiting for to mend fences and strengthen our position on the throne. Oh yes, and a chance for a bit of retribution."

He handed the scroll to Faylea, who smiled reading it. "The 'Grand Man of the North' still needs your help, after all, father. I told you that you were still his brother. Excellent development!"

"Guard! Call my Generals," Orus commanded sternly.

"As you command, Sire." The guard ran off toward the Military High Command.

"We shall ready for battle. Cathir will pay for his treachery. I have been vindicated. Now Puryn sees who he is dealing with." Orus smiled, as if he were a man on death row who was exonerated by last-minute evidence.

"Edenyag will remember who Hodan is," Faylea said in a grave tone. "They will pay for their actions."

* * *

The Citadel was quiet. The morning light shined over the toppled towers and the rubble of the fortress walls. Groups of men were gathering with trees, tackle lines, and levers. They were collecting as much good stone as they could, and an old man with a long beard stood out as he directed the orderly rebuild of a serviceable outer wall.

Basric knew that it would be months before the perimeter was completed to a height of six feet. At this time, the repair teams looked to patch the walls that remained standing, and the more skilled masons began the process of fitting and stacking the salvaged stone where no wall remained.

"Puryn, what will you do with the Pretender?" Basric asked the young man seated across the table from him.

Puryn looked up from a plate of eggs and pork. "I will beat him in every town and locale on my way back up to Yslandeth, to show the locals that he is indeed defeated and you are the true King of Cinnog." He went back to chewing for a moment. "Then, I will hang him from the gates of Empyr with a sign on him, for all to see what happens to those who stand against the Northern Alliance and its friends."

Basric nodded and smiled nervously. He had not seen this side of the King of Yslandeth. Puryn's demeanor was subdued, but the Cinnog King could feel burning anger just below the calmness the young man displayed. Puryn was still stinging over his Legion. It was apparent to Basric.

"That will do, nicely, my new ally. It will reassure the Kingdom that change and stability have come." Basric nodded and smiled politely, turning his view back toward the rebuilding. He hid his look of concern from Puryn's gaze.

"I must return to my men, Basric. I will leave five-thousand here until you are rebuilt, if you do not object." Puryn waited.

"Of course not, my new ally. I will welcome your peace-keepers. It will be some time before we are completely back on our feet." Basric shook Puryn's hand.

"Of course, we will also send aid to your people to help in the rebuilding of your nation. From time to time, I will move a rotation of troops down to allow my warriors to return home to their families." Puryn stood and turned back to Basric. "Of course, I realize your autonomy, and I will send a rider requesting permission to do these things before moving large armies within your borders, my friend. I only wish to help you, after all. I do not wish to rule Cinnog, as I have enough to worry about with Yslandeth! Peace is my goal ... with Cinnog, Hodan, and eventually with Edenyag, after I deal with Cathir."

Basric smirked; the boy had read him after all. "You are a wise leader, Yslan. We will be your friends again, and peace will be our pact."

Puryn smiled and bowed, exiting the chamber and returning to the Draj units, which were still camped outside of what was once the Citadel. Commander Durn was alerted to the King's arrival by the horns of the watch.

"Ah, it is time," Durn remarked, noting that Palgur was being led in a cage on a cart behind the King's guard. "Good."

Within minutes, Puryn arrived at the Command Tent, and the guard snapped to attention. Durn stood tall and addressed his son. "Good morning, Your Majesty, do we prepare to return to our beloved homeland soon?"

"You are very perceptive, da. Yes, gather your Commanders. Choose one Draj Legion to remain here and four-thousand Yslan Regulars. I would like to rotate our forces every three months, if that is possible."

"Very possible, Sire. May I suggest that we also set strongholds along the main towns and locales? For 'rapid response,' and such things." Durn smiled.

"Yes, excellent idea, da. A hundred per small village? Five-hundred per established town?" Puryn suggested.

"As you wish, Sire. I will pass the orders." Durn looked over at the prisoner. "What of this dung?"

Puryn sneered at the captive. "He will be paraded in every locale so the people know that the right heir is now on the throne in the Citadel. He will also be scourged for his crimes in the larger towns to drive the point home of what happens to resistance to the Northern Alliance." Puryn looked around for dissent, but no one dared to blink. "Then, you shall put the rope around his neck and pull the lever on the gallows at his execution at the courtyard in Empyr. His corpse will be hung at the gates with a sign denoting his offenses, as a warning to those who would oppose peace."

Durn swallowed hard; he hated Palgur, but the grim tone in his son's voice concerned him. He had never heard him speak so cruelly, and the lack of emotion in his demeanor worried the Commander. He answered the King. "It shall be done as you say, son. Huzzah!"

The guards cheered once and returned to their duties. Puryn nodded and called for his mead. Durn turned smartly and executed his son's orders. Unbeknownst to Puryn, Durn stood a way off and observed his son with concern. The King's heart was troubled, and he was changing. Durn was concerned that it was not for the better. He uttered a prayer to Haya, and continued planning the troop movement home with his Commanders.

* * *

As the sun cracked over the horizon, Famlin recognized the familiar terrain of his home city of the Port of Valent. He quickly scanned the locale and knew precisely where he was. This group of captors was either extremely stupid or ill-informed. Carefully, using his peripheral vision, the thief looked around at his surroundings, getting the lay of the land and ascertaining his real situation.

Off in the distance, the morning routine had begun. The ladies of the evening were making their ways back to their hovels to rest and preen for the next night's customers. Several bread vendors were crying out to the public in efforts to advertise their wares. It was a quiet morning, but something felt wrong. That is when the specialist started to notice them.

Here and there, Famlin noted men working, but accomplishing nothing. Some wore leather, and on occasion, their weapons glinted in the morning light, alerting the specialist to what he had felt all along. There were more out there. He counted ten older, and more experienced agents pretending to work in the immediate area.

Famlin snorted and stood.

"What are you doing, traitor?" the young guard asked forcefully.

"I need to piss, whelp," the specialist sarcastically replied, "and soon, or I'll be doing it on you."

The younger guard was not amused. "That would be unwise." The boy grabbed the handle of his dagger.

Famlin laughed. "Will you call over your older brothers over to aid you? Or are they your fathers?" The specialist waved to the men milling about, feigning occupation. They all looked away as if they didn't see him. "You people are ridiculous. Where is the Master? I must speak with him. I do not have time to waste sitting here around a fire. I have work to do."

"That you do." A familiar voice came from a figure huddled under a blanket beside a nearby cart. He removed the cover to reveal an older, much better-equipped man. It was Master Irshad.

Famlin bowed, averting his eyes. "Master, I had no idea that you were this close by." It was a lie, and the Master knew it.

"I feel that you tell me a half-truth, apprentice. You have known that something was amiss, ever since this boy first threatened you." Irshad slapped the boy on the back of the head, and he bowed awkwardly, then ran toward the group of waiting young-ones, who immediately melted into the debris that was once the Port of Valent.

"Master, I was trying to continue my mission. I had not forgotten you or my orders. I was delayed, because of the conflict. These fools interrupted my mission, and now I fear I am discovered if I return." Famlin told half-truths and admitted nothing.

"Why do you steal powder when all you needed to do is ask?" Irshad questioned.

"Master, I was in the field. I did not have time to formally request everything that I needed." Famlin lied.

"What of the sabotage of several covert storehouses?" Irshad approached Famlin and stood up close, almost nose to nose.

Famlin did not flinch. He knew the discovery of his actions would threaten his sister. "Perhaps, the Shadow has been keeping tabs on us, My Master. I have no idea what happened to those locations."

"I have trained you too well, apprentice. I cannot tell if you lie to me or not." Irshad turned and began to walk away. "You will remain in Sudenyag. We are in the middle of a major offensive against Hassim and his resistance. I will need your services to kill this pest."

"As you command, Master," Famlin answered. "What of my sister? How does she fare? I have not seen nor heard from her in some time, Sir."

"She is well. You should worry about your own health, and of the tasks you have been assigned." Irshad muttered something to a bodyguard nearby.

"What do you need from me? How will I know what I am to do and when?" Famlin cried out.

Irshad turned and replied, "Hassim will be here to speak about peace and reconciliation, because he is a weakling and has figured that he will take the place of power when I sign on to his plan. What he does not realize, is that you will be his undoing. I will require your life in exchange for the life of your sister. That is how you will redeem yourself for failing with the Yslan."

"But Master, what do you mean, I will be his undoing? How will I take down the Shadow?" Famlin was appalled by the statement.

Irshad rushed to Famlin angrily. He grabbed the specialist by his throat, slightly choking the younger man. "Hassim, the Shadow, will show up for a parlay. He thinks he has the upper hand, but you will deliver the blow that kills the Shadow, even if it means your death. You will end him. If you do not succeed, I will send your sister to meet you in the afterlife. I am sure that you can hold her hand while you both rot in the Underworld."

The Master released Famlin from his grasp. The specialist sat down on a log, dejected. There were few options left for him. He was trapped, and an innocent life hung in the balance.

He had no idea how he would kill a man who his Master had not been able to touch.

* * *

Yslandeth was packed by midday. The supply carts were laden with the large pavilions and the rest of the logistics. Each soldier carried a small personal shelter and bedroll on their backpacks. The army was excited to return to Yslandeth and to their loved ones. Chatter in the ranks was mostly of planned recreation mixed with a long-needed rest.

Kairoth was not interested. His love was with him in the field. He had no one to return to and would only end up in a bar, fighting some mess tent guard who spouted off at him, as in the past. Sal'iabac sensed his apprehension.

"What is your trouble, My Love? We go home!" The mage looked at him with a smile.

"I have no true home, My Lady. It was burned when I was a child. It is a ruin and my family no longer lives. I have nothing to return to in Yslandeth or in Hodan." Kairoth's looked at the ground.

Sal'iabac kissed his cheek, grabbing his hand. "You have me, you ox! We can be a family if you wish it."

"Everyone I love dies, Salia. I don't wish to mourn you also." Kairoth turned and grabbed his pack, securing it to his riding horse. He went about checking the straps and saddle bags. The others were doing the same.

"Well, fine then. I will take a nice, long, hot bath ... alone." Sal'iabac walked by Kairoth and slapped him on the backside as she passed.

The Hodan laughed. "Maybe I could use some soap and water." He smiled at the mage.

Safiya looked at the bantering couple. "I wonder what became of Famlin."

"He is fine, sister. That one is good at survival." The older sister hugged Safiya around her shoulders. "He will turn up at the most opportune moment. You watch!"

"I hope you are right, sister. I worry for him." Safiya mounted her horse.

Valtyr prayed in an open space where no one was milling around and packing. The noise was distracting, but he felt that he needed to ask the Goddess for protection and guidance on the long trek homeward.

Reynir did similarly, then waited patiently for his brother to finish his devotions. "Here," the druid said, handing his best friend a small loaf of fresh bread and a wedge of cheese. "Eat, you will need your strength to heal that one." The druid gestured over to Palgur, who sat in his cage. He was resolved to his fate and sadly awaited his demise.

"Agreed," the priest said thanking his brother for the food. "Something feels wrong about this, Reynir. It seems cruel and unnecessary."

"I don't feel bad for him. He chose his path. This is the logical end to his treachery. I know you don't want to be a part of this, but it is the King's decree." Reynir mounted his horse.

"I know, brother, but somehow, I feel Haya will not be pleased by our actions, and I do not want to incur her wrath." Valtyr was concerned.

"Agreed, my brother, but Puryn is her chosen. We must trust that he knows what is best for the moment." Reynir trotted toward the party.

Valtyr was unsure.

* * *

In little more than a week, Orus arrived at the Edenyag border with five Legions of Hodan Elites. He was greeted by a sight he did not expect.

The border was manned by a combined force of Elfish Draj and Dwarfish Commandos. Orus held his position within the Hodan border and sent diplomats to his allied army lines. He did not wish to give the wrong impression and spark a conflict with the elder races. They had been quiet, but now they stood between Hodan, Yslan and Cathir's head. This was an unexpected aggravation.

"Why in the Underworld would the elder races decide to back Edenyag?" Orus was angry and impatient. He awaited his heralds to return with word from the front.

Within a half an hour, the riders returned with word from the border.

"What is this?" Orus asked impatiently.

"Your Majesty, the Elves and Dwarves have been watching the developments over the past few months. They discovered that Edenyag was supplying the Suden syndicate and Cinnog with thunder powder. The very same scouts report that Dwarfish defectors joined Palgur in Cinnog and crafted several thunder ballistae that were used against King Puryn and Yslandeth, as the Northern Alliance sought to liberate Cinnog from the Pretender."

"Tell me things that I don't already know, soldier." The King shifted in his saddle.

"King Bogrol and King Glorin send their greetings and hold Hodan in the highest regard. They sent their forces into Edenyag and were able to capture the Great Library Complex and the castle without much harm to the civilian population. The two Kings state that they were concerned that Hodan may seek to avenge its forceful expulsion from the buffer zone by Cathir's forces. They only sought to preserve life and the remaining artifacts and knowledge within the walls of the Library." The scout paused for input.

"So, they have stolen my glory once again? Are they going to hand over Cathir, or do I need to get Puryn to ask for him personally? I am tired of being treated as if I am second fiddle to the other nations. Hodan will not be treated as the illegitimate offspring who needs to be hushed in a corner. We are Hodan. I will not stand for interference. This is insulting already."

Orus scowled. "Tell them to hand over Cathir, by Orus's order."

The riders returned to the border and relayed the message. Glorin and Bogrol sat around a table in a Command Tent and pondered their options. There were five Hodan Legions outside of the border and only two Legions between Torith and Dornat Al Ar. They knew that they were outmatched by Hodan, even if Edenyag brought forward a few thousand spears. An angry and insulted Hodan King and five-thousand motivated Hodan Elites was enough to conquer any locale on the Ert at the time being.

"Glorin, we must hand over Cathir," Bogrol said solemnly. "Unless we choose to fight Hodan and our chances are slim."

"Agreed, Bogrol, but Cathir is a King. Will we just kill the monarch of a nation, because we disagree with his politics or alliances?"

"If Cathir had only allied with Suden and Palgur it would have been one thing, my brother, but to kill the Draj in Cinnog? I can only imagine your son-in-law's rage! Especially, after turning his back on Orus's request for retribution when Cathir recklessly attacked Hodan peace-keepers? I know that Orus is working at Puryn's request. I think we tell the Hodan we accept his offer, hand over Cathir, and do not mention Puryn in the equation." Bogrol sipped some tea.

"So, we make it seem as if we are capitulating to Hodan's demands, not Yslandeth's?" Glorin smiled. "I see. Hodan looks as if it exerted its will and we let Orus retain his honor without shedding blood! You are an excellent diplomat, my brother!" Glorin raised his glass.

"So, we are agreed? Turn over Cathir, then slowly withdraw to our own homelands, allowing Edenyag to patrol their own lands again." Bogrol sipped more tea.

"An excellent plan, my ally. The new Eden King may be young, but his advisors will keep him out of trouble. If not, we are only a few days' march away. We can maintain the order in our little part of the Ert." Glorin finished his tea and sent the messenger to the border with their response.

When Orus's heralds returned and related the victory of Hodan to their King, the Commanders cheered. Quickly, the tales of how the Elves and Dwarves cowered in fear at the mere sight of the Hodan spread among the Legions. Orus did nothing to stop the stories. Hodan national pride was invigorated. Orus was revered again, and his crown secured for the moment.

Now the King awaited the delivery of his prisoner.

* * *

Two men prepared for the gallows in Empyr, as two Kings readied to see the sentences carried out. Several days before this moment, Puryn and his remaining ten-thousand Draj and Yslan Regulars had returned to Empyr with their prisoner, Palgur, the Pretender (or Bastard, depending upon who you asked.) Puryn's forces, led by his father, Durn, marched proudly into each hamlet, village, and town within Cinnog with King Basric's approval, spreading the news of the Pretender's defeat and the coronation of the true heir to their Kingdom. Basric had his hands full with the rebuilding of his nation, but Puryn made sure to leave a significant military deterrent to any aspiring foes, both internal to Cinnog and external. No one entertained any new ideas against the new crown.

In addition to the forces of Yslan, Queen Adasser reinforced the eastern and southern borders of the rebuilding western nation. She sent glens and small forested hills to keep watch over potential invaders, but the Holy Mother doubted anyone would test her husband's resolve, whether they be of Hodan, Sudenyag, or Edenyag, after seeing the fall of the Citadel to Yslandeth's might. Cinnog roads were open and passable, and Yslan's aid and goods began flowing southward, immediately after the return of the heroes to the northern capital.

While Yslan toured war-torn Cinnog for several weeks, King Orus of Hodan and four of his Hodan Legions marched northward through Edenyag, past the Plains of the Arondayre, and through the Raven's Pass. The Hodan Army bore the tabard of the Northern Alliance and traveled unimpeded to Empyr, except for the occasional throng of curious onlookers. Anyone in an official capacity who asked what the Hodan were doing in Yslandeth, was met with the scroll from Puryn to Orus. They were shown the prisoner and accused war criminal, Cathir, former King of Edenyag, who was in chains and on a mule-drawn cart. No one challenged Orus's claims.

Two weeks before Puryn finally arrived in Empyr, Master Donick's apprentice, Norwyn, met Orus at the gates and accepted Puryn's scroll, as if it were the King's own orders. The minister took custody of the prisoner from the Hodan King and granted Orus permission to set up his Hodan war camp outside of the city gates. The Hodan were allies, so they were given leave to traverse Yslan without impedance. Orus waited for the return of the King of Yslan, while Cathir rotted securely in one of the newly rebuilt tower prison cells.

* * *

Puryn stood and finished adjusting his crown. Adasser was not in a good mood. Something was bothering the Elfish druid, and Puryn felt it plainly.

"What is the matter, My Love?" Puryn asked genuinely.

"Nothing, My Dearest." Adasser averted her eyes and avoided the conversation.

"It is not 'nothing' if you cannot bear to look at me," Puryn said, meeting her downward gaze.

Adasser sighed, and her brow wore a concerned wrinkle. "When will the death stop, My King?"

"When? I suppose when the enemies of the light cease their treachery and allow peace to flourish," Puryn said tenderly to his wife's saddened face.

"Cathir was a friend once, husband. He only sought to retain power, much as Orus does. Now we condemn him to death for doing what he thought would secure his throne?" Adasser replied plainly. Her eyes were red.

Puryn was annoyed at the suggestion and retorted. "My Love, Cathir stood against us! Against Yslandeth. He cost me the lives of eight-hundred Draj, who perished before my eyes. That is not a betrayal that I can take lightly, nor ignore. If he would kill us there, and oppose our alliance while pretending to be a friend, what else is he capable of?"

"I understand, My King, but I know his family, as do you. You would sacrifice anything for us, no? Why would you expect any less from him? I fear that we execute too many with impunity, citing glory, honor, and justice, when all things degrade over time to a simple need for power." Adasser kissed him on the cheek. "I love you and support you, My King, but we must be careful to stay on the side of the light. We tread dangerously close to the shadow these days."

Puryn was cut to his heart by her words. He watched her walk out of the small living quarters in the rebuilding castle complex. He knew that she was right, to some degree, but he also knew that he needed to ensure that a statement was heard, loud and clear, upon the Ert. "Yslandeth will suffer no treachery against itself or any of its allies."

* * *

Orus sat outside on a provided chair. Beside him was his daughter, Faylea. They were both dressed in their best regal garb and in armor, as was the tradition for Hodan executions. Orus saw Adasser look in his direction as she exited the stone building nearby. She quickly looked away and hurried up the road to the Towers Monastery with two ladies-in-waiting in tow.

"His Queen is not happy with these proceedings," Orus said to Faylea.

"She's an Elf, father. They hate death unless it suits them." Faylea looked at her King reassuringly. "This is what is necessary, father. Remember, 'a son for a son,' that is our law. So, shall it be done, My King."

Orus smiled at his daughter. "Your heart is of stone these days, my girl.

You will rule well someday."

Faylea laughed. "That will be the day, father."

Horns played loudly as King Puryn entered the courtyard. Several thousand Yslan Regulars and Hodan Elites came to attention as Orus joined Puryn on the large stone platform above the yard. Durn stood on the gallows where two men awaited their sentences to be carried out. The old Commander showed a strangely dark mood as he stared at Palgur. Palgur stood silently, frowning. He knew that his time was up. The other bound man stood more proudly. Cathir defiantly stared up at Puryn and Orus. He looked as proud as ever.

Durn spoke. "Palgur the Pretender! You have been tried and found guilty of subversive activity, treason, and murder, for your actions against the Crown of Cinnog. By the wishes of King Basric of Cinnog and in adherence to the agreements made between the allies of the North, you are sentenced to die by hanging, by my hand, at the stroke of noon."

Palgur looked downward and sighed. There was nothing left to do, but wait now. Strangely, he closed his eyes and prayed. This was not lost on Puryn, who watched intently, remembering Athis. Puryn closed his eyes and composed himself.

The King frowned. "Brother," Puryn said to Orus, "I just want to get this whole thing over with and quickly."

"Agreed. This is not my favorite activity. I would rather kill them in battle, than hang them with a rope. This seems cowardly in some way." Orus glared at Faylea, who slapped his arm.

On the platform, Durn continued his announcement. "Cathir, of Edenyag, by your admission of guilt to the charges of supplying arms to revolutionary forces within Cinnog, you are condemned to death. You aided the very man who stands convicted beside you, in his efforts to deny the rightful heir of Cinnog his crown. Your contributions to his cause also resulted in great harm to the forces of the Northern Alliance, which are in direct violation of treaties that you signed by your own hand between our nations. For this, you are convicted of treason and murder. You are sentenced to hang by a rope until death at the stroke of noon."

Puryn watched the spectacle. He thought about what he would have done in Cathir's place. He could not rule out that he would have done similarly if pushed, but knew that he could not let his adversary go free. Yslandeth and Hodan needed to send a strong message to those who opposed peace. Puryn also had calculated that Orus grasped to solidify his hold on the crown of Hodan. Order with Hodan was paramount, and his brother's security was Puryn's utmost concern. At that moment, he realized that in effect, he was no better than Cathir. He prayed to Haya for forgiveness.

At noon, the bells tolled, and the horns blared. Durn turned to the platform above him, facing both Kings, who stood proudly upon it. The Commander saluted and awaited the call. As one, both Kings raised their right hands.

"Call it, brother," Puryn said to Orus.

"One … two … three," Orus said quietly, and both dropped their hands.

Durn pulled both levers. Both men dropped through the floor as the hatch opened. A grotesque snap was heard, and many in civilians in attendance gasped at the grisly scene. Durn watched until both men stopped twitching and thrashing, and then the Commander cut them down from their ropes. The bodies were set above the gate to Empyr, at the King's order, each with a sign declaring their crimes against the Alliance. Adasser quickly left the capital, and did not return until the bodies were taken down thirty days later.

Quietly, Puryn sent both men to the afterlife on their own pyres, each with provisions. He again asked the Goddess for forgiveness.

Orus returned to Hodan a hero. His crown was securely upon his head. Faylea smiled, knowing her father was safe and that his honor in Hodan was once again beyond reproach. One Legion of Hodan Elites remained on the Eden border, on the Hodan side, as a reminder that Hodan would not tolerate any more of Eden's duplicity. The new King of Edenyag, Philip, son of Cathir, heard the message loud and clear: "Honor your agreements. Be trustworthy, or else."

The boy was fifteen years old when he assumed the throne of Edenyag. He never forgot the day that his father died at the hands of his allies.

He turned his focus inward, and Edenyag became very isolated and self-concerned. Their nation paid lip-service to the Northern Alliance, instead choosing to focus on rebuilding its own infrastructure and economy. This ushered in a new age of learning and prosperity for the Eden populace, as no other nation was concerned with the affairs of a country of quiet scribes and poets.

Yslandeth rested for a bit on its accomplishments. King Puryn knew that Sudenyag still festered below the surface and that it would need to be dealt with in the future, but not just yet. Still, Puryn was worried, because he knew that Hodan looked southward and that Yslandeth had given Orus unofficial backing.

Yslandeth was peaceful for the moment, but Puryn knew that events could change that very soon.

He left Empyr for Erynseere.

Chapter 20

Famlin sat quietly across the circle from the Underground's delegation. Hassim, the Shadow, was a well-respected and feared leader from northern Suden nomads. It was said that Hassim was a ghost, a spirit which would gather within the dark spots in your home, lying in wait. He was Irshad's boogeyman, and all of his boys and girls were terrified that the Shadow of Death would visit them in the night and exact his revenge. The Syndicate leader used this fear to solidify his hold on power. A people in constant terror were easily controlled and tended to join the flock, much like sheep did when seeking protection. Irshad banked on the legends to cement his hold on masses, and so far, it was working.

It had been several weeks since Famlin was captured by Irshad's outpost guards. The young specialist looked for clues as to where his Master could be holding his sister hostage, but no clues were to be found. As the days progressed, Famlin listened, eavesdropping on conversations between members of the community who had a tendency to brag about their personal exploits, while giving commentary on what they thought was going on to the North of the Port of Valent. From what the young captive specialist gathered, Irshad was covering up the facts of significant losses to the Bedouin Underground. Hassim's tactics were taking their toll, and Irshad kept up appearances to maintain the status quo.

The air was cold, but humid. The breeze off of the bay was misting, and the Port of Valent stood covered in a foggy haze. The sun was setting and giving way to a cloudy, starless night. The sky was the color of blood as the sun sunk slowly into the sea. In its crimson hue, Irshad appeared confident, but Famlin knew his master much too well. The old assassin was far from composed. His body language implied impatience and a hint of apprehension. Famlin saw the leader's expression change to one of dire seriousness. It was a gravity that the specialist only saw when Irshad was struggling to control a situation that had gotten away from him. Famlin hoped this one would be his Master's undoing.

"Greetings, Shadow," Irshad said in a low tone from his seat.

Famlin could see snipers in the shadows. They were better than average at concealment, but he doubted that Hassim had missed them. After a while, Famlin looked again for the archers, but strangely, none were to be found. The young thief smiled wryly, wondering if the Shadow had other plans in mind, rather than talking.

"Good evening, Irshad. I see you have brought an army to discuss, peace?" Hassim was sarcastic as he openly glanced about at the now empty sniper locations.

Famlin was seated to Irshad's left hand. The young man snickered. For the slight, he received a backhand from his Master. The lightning-quick blow brought the taste of iron to the specialist's lips. He composed himself and dared not look at the Master with any belligerence.

Hassim looked at the young specialist, sizing him up. Feeling as if the Shadow was reading his thoughts, the younger man glanced away, hoping that the man beneath the hood could not see what his mission indeed was, by sizing up what was in his heart.

"What is your reason for calling this negotiation, Irshad?" Hassim sat with several large, confident, and heavily armed warriors surrounding him.

Famlin wondered how many more were in the shadows. He pondered how many arrows were aimed at his head.

"I call you here today to seek an alliance of our two clans." Irshad was lying. Famlin already knew his intentions.

"You would call for our capitulation to your demands. You wish us to surrender the northern territories and my people. Is that not what you truly wish, Irshad? But we shall not bend to your will. Who do you think that you trifle with, assassin?" The Shadow sat picking at his nails with a silver dagger. His hood obscured his face. Famlin tried without success to see the eyes of the man he was ordered to kill.

"Who do you presume to be, Hassim? Are you now King? I seek peace, and you seek to insult me!?" Irshad feigned anger.

Famlin pursed his lips in disgust. The facial expression was not lost on Hassim. The Shadow stifled a chuckle and replied, "The North has no need of you. From the looks of the faces of those you lord your power over, the South would be better off without your influence. It only needs to realize it and rise up."

The hair on Famlin's neck stood up. The Shadow's eyes were now visible from under the hood. He was looking directly at the young specialist, as if the words were meant for only his ears. Famlin looked at the man across from him, then to his Master, who was oblivious to the side conversation the Shadow had started with his apprentice. The young man looked away, then peered back cautiously. The Shadow squinted, sizing up the younger apprentice, then continued with the parlay.

"Do you seek to spread your message to my people, or to join us in strengthening Suden's borders against Hodan and the North!?" Irshad shook his head and carried on, as if he was surprised by Hassim's speech.

Famlin rolled his eyes silently. No one noticed, except the Shadow, who now openly smiled in the direction of the young apprentice. Famlin was unnerved by the man's overt show of derision.

Irshad was livid at how Hassim made light of the meeting. The Master now stood and was angry at the open mocking of his rival. He was animated and was becoming more unstable with each moment. Famlin wondered what was going on. "How dare you mock me in my own house, you goat-herder!"

"A goat-herder who crushed your forces in and around the great temple to the North, and who has liberated the villages from the borders of Cinnog and Hodan, to the borders of this capital. If I am a herder, you must be the goat?"

Hassim stood, removing the hood that he was wearing. He had long, dark hair with streaks of silver. His face was bearded and scarred, as if he had seen many battles. He had burns on one of his hands, and his left was missing its ring finger and pinky. The Shadow stood with dignity and pride. His stature seemed to dwarf Irshad's petulant display.

Famlin was impressed. This man was inspirational and imposing. One thought kept pestering the young specialist, between bouts of worry over how he would kill this man and save his sister and himself. Famlin muttered under his breath, "Is he the one, is he truly 'the Captain?'"

"Irshad, Il Nadur, your father was an honorable merchant. A man of wealth and influence under King Yanat il Arnar. It pains me that his penchant for wisdom and diplomacy did not somehow find its way into your thick skull." Hassim was no longer hiding his disgust. "Who in the Underworld do you think that you are, pig!? How many brave Suden bled the fields red under Offlander boots, only to have their descendants trod upon by yours? I have put down one tyrant in my days and lived to tell the tale. You are not even a fly to be swatted away in comparison. Who are you to challenge me? I have stood with the chosen, upon the Fields of the Arondayre while you skulked in these ruins to rape and steal what was left by the hordes. You are not worthy of governing our remnant. You will die for your treachery and abuses."

"KILL HIM! NOW!" Irshad screeched at Famlin, who was startled and snapped up to his feet in fear. He looked at the Shadow, unsure of what he could do. Looking at Irshad, Famlin frowned and grit his teeth.

"Stay your hand, young one, for I know you act not without coercion!" Hassim smiled knowingly as he whistled.

Several men led a person to the fire circle. There was a captive with a burlap sack over his top. Famlin watched intently, dagger now drawn. He was on the defense, but did not quite know from whom yet. He looked with questions at the person who was led out in plain view.

"What is this?" Irshad spat angrily. "Who is this? Famlin, do as you are ordered, or your sister will pay the price for your treachery!"

Hassim ordered the sack lifted and the gag removed. Famlin stood and looked at the dirty young lady before him. Her back was to him as they removed her restraints and the gag.

"Last week, West of this locale, my forces liberated a small village. Many women were being held captive by the forces of the Syndicate. My scouts returned to me after searching that location, and we then realized it to be one of the many internment camps that this coward uses to hold men in his service. My Elites tell me that you are called Famlin. We sought to enlist you as a spy, son. You are, after all, this swine's apprentice and right-hand man, even if it was by coercion. Worry no more for the life of your sister, my boy. For here is Inua, and she is free."

The young lady turned, and Famlin saw her plainly. It was indeed his sister. "Famlin?"

Irshad was enraged. "If you do not do your duty, you traitorous scum, I will follow through with my threat, if it is the last thing that I do!"

Irshad rushed forward toward Inua, but the large warriors surrounding Hassim grabbed the girl, dragging her back out of harm's way, but not before Irshad cut two of them down in the process. Hassim whisked Inua back to his waiting scouts, who appeared from thin air in the mist and then disappeared into the night with the girl.

Famlin looked up at the brawl that had erupted in the campfire area. Men from both sides were killing each other. Some around the fire, some from within the flames. Famlin crept silently up beside one of Irshad's bodyguards, stabbing him deftly under his ribs, through the kidney and up into his lower lungs. The man fell, gurgling. The specialist made his way down the line with intent.

"Kill my traitorous, scum of an apprentice, and get the Shadow!" the Syndicate leader bellowed.

More and more young men poured into the streets and the carnage intensified, but after thirty minutes of devastation, Irshad's forces stopped coming. They knew it was a losing battle and none were too fond of Irshad, or in the least bit loyal to his cause. They just wanted to live. The populace sat and watched as events unfolded, most figuring that they would live to see the next day, no matter what tyrant owned Suden. They just wanted to survive this night.

From the darkness, arrows pierced Famlin's side. He felt the familiar sting that he knew only came from poison. The young specialist resolved to make his death count. After dispatching the last of the guard, he limped toward his Master with a short sword in one hand and a dagger in the other.

"Master!" the specialist cried out in bitter anger. "Here I am, you cowardly lout! Turn and face me like a man! Or will you continue to send your children to defend you? Look and see how many I have sent to Haeldrun. I will set up your reunion with the children of the dead of your creation." Famlin stood ready, smiling at the reaper who he knew positioned in front of him. His sister was safe, there was nothing left to worry about. His life was ebbing, and he would make his last moments count.

"After I kill you, whelp, I will deal with this Pretender," Irshad snarled angrily.

Irshad roared and swung in a wide arc. Famlin dodged expertly as he was taught by Puryn's Draj. After his feint, the weakened young man slid in, expertly, and sliced his Master at the waist, drawing blood, as an Elfish warrior would. The younger man stumbled and then fell, rolling out of the reach of his Master, as he swung again and nicked the apprentice across the left cheek.

Famlin spat black blood from his mouth. "If today is my day to join my ancestors, I will bring you to meet mother, you swine!" The young apprentice smiled, remembering Kairoth as he badly misquoted a Hodan proverb. "He would slap me for that one," the specialist thought, as his thoughts returned to the situation at hand.

The specialist lunged forward again, ducking, as his Master swung in a tight short chop designed to remove the younger man's head from his shoulders. The thief dropped the angle of the sword blade using a Hodan parry, partially blocking it, but still catching another slash across his face. These cuts were bleeding freely, but that last sacrifice had been a great trade-off, as the specialist positioned himself inside his Master's guard, burying his blade just below his Master's ribcage on the right side.

Irshad bellowed for his men, but none came. He knew that he was mortally wounded. Famlin's blades burned with poison, and the Master knew he was defeated. Irshad looked for an escape route, but every avenue was covered by an agent of the Shadow. In his final moments, he resolved to take his traitor with him to the Underworld.

"We will have plenty of time to revisit this fight, my son." Irshad chuckled, wiping the blood from his lips. "I will kill you for eternity in the Underworld for your treachery."

The older man staggered over to Famlin. The younger thief was now retching from the poison as it went to work. After he had finished emptying his stomach, he turned, smiling to greet the final blow. "You cannot hurt her anymore, coward. Come and get me." Famlin staggered to his feet and held his sword out, preparing to die.

"I do not think so, Irshad. I have need of this one. Archers!" Hassim called out sharply. The Shadow was answered by a thousand whistles in return. Famlin hit the ground instinctively, as he heard the swish of distant bowstrings.

The arrows entered Irshad from every angle. So much so, that the body was unable to hit the ground until the volley was completed. The thud of Irshad's lifeless corpse beside the place where Famlin lay, and his Master's blank stare of horror that met Famlin's gaze, were the last things that the specialist remembered, as he succumbed to his injuries and the poison.

"Grab that one, and administer the antidotes and herbs. Clean this mess up and let us call for the people to assemble at the docks. We must pass our message of hope and dignity." Hassim looked at his men. They all nodded and ran to the streets, calling out the news that Irshad was dead and that they were free.

"Sir, this one is bad off, but he is strong. The antidote appears to be doing its job, but we will not know until the morning." The apothecary stood and bowed. "I will leave my apprentice to watch over him, if this pleases the Shadow."

"It does, My Lady," Hassim replied, smiling. "We must do all that we can for that one. I have plans for him. He will come in handy when the time is right."

* * *

Orus sat on his throne. The Hodan capital was beginning to recover, looking more and more like the cities of old. The King looked out over the countryside at the homes and farms that had started to spring up as far as his eyes could see. Orus was satisfied that the nation was rebuilding, but he feared for the military morale, as always. He was justified in his concern. Hodan had not conquered any new territory after an extended time of hostilities. Many of the rank and file resented the perceived interference from Yslandeth, and in quiet circles, Orus could hear his officers muttering about their King's suspected subservience to Puryn.

Orus sighed and sipped from his mug of mead. Faylea sat in the corner of the room, looking with concern at the tired face of her father. Yslandeth was inbound to meet with Hodan, but the young Princess feared that it would be more of dictation from Yslan than a discussion. She did not like the established pecking order and had repeatedly told her father so. She and many Hodan felt slighted by the new line of power. Her father had stood the line with Puryn on the Arondayre. Hodan had been there at the end. Why were they now considered little more than a vassal state to Yslandeth?

"Father, if he respects you, you must press our rights!" Faylea stood, speaking emphatically. "He cannot demand that you sit on your hands. He has gained the world, and you have gained nothing, but more demands of Hodan."

Orus sighed again, this time with irritation. She was right, but he did not want to hear it right now. "Daughter, please, sit. Give your tongue a rest! My brother and I will talk, and we will decide the best course of action for the Alliance."

"The Alliance, the Alliance … what of Hodan, father?" Faylea walked to her father and put her hand on his shoulder. He was looking out over the fields once again. "Our honor is overdue."

"Please, leave me. I wish to be alone for the time being, Faylea. I understand your points, and they are quite valid, but I must play the hand that I am dealt. We shall see what the morning brings." Orus sat up, noticing the standard of Yslandeth processing down the main road from the North. He knew it was Puryn. "See, he comes, my girl. Now go. Leave me. I will call for you later."

"Yes, da. Be well. I love you." Faylea kissed her father's face, frowning, as she saw the worry lines on his brow. He had worked so hard to save Hodan from Jabir, then he defended the Ert from Offlanders, and now, in peacetime, he was faced with the expectations of his own people. She felt sorry for the man. "Call for me when he is gone. Please. I must know what is to come."

Faylea left the room, closing the heavy oak door behind her. Orus could hear horns blowing outside on the guard towers, as the caravan from the North entered his city gates. It would be another hour before all of the ceremony and pomp allowed his brother-in-arms to make it to the throne room. The old Hodan warrior sat back in his chair and took a nap.

* * *

Puryn walked up the stone stairs to the Hodan throne room. He was alone. His guard had complained, but the King of Yslan ordered them to wait outside. Puryn was going to talk candidly with his brother. He wanted brutal honesty, and the best way to do that was to keep the prying eyes and listening ears out of the room. This angered many of the advisors from both camps, but Puryn did not care.

The young King worked the knocker on the large oak door. "Brother, are you in there?"

292

There was a click and then a quiet creak, as the door opened inward and a slightly disheveled Orus appeared yawning. "What brings you to my humble abode, great King?" Orus snickered.

Puryn laughed. "It surely is not the whiskey, you old goat!" Puryn hugged his brother, and Orus smiled widely.

"Come in and let us warm ourselves by the fire a bit. You arrived late, Puryn. What took you so long?" Orus questioned.

"Brigands as usual. We stopped to clean up a small matter South of Erynseere." Puryn scowled. "Apparently, some do not understand that the halflings are our brothers and sisters. They refuse to behave until they force my hand. It is unfortunate."

Puryn sat in a padded wooden chair beside a nicely made table where two tankards and a large pitcher of mead sat ready for the taking. Orus nodded. "Drink away, my friend! I have mine right here." Orus raised his mug and laughed, sitting down in a chair across from his friend.

The Yslan king sipped from his tankard. "Brother, I hear rumors of unrest in your ranks. Is this true?"

"Yes. Peace is fine, but Hodan warriors want glory. They think of me as a knitting old maid, I fear." Orus raised an eyebrow.

"That is foolish. The people know who you are, or at least they should. It has not been that many years. A little more than ten years ago, we fought that evil as one. Now we fight the avarice of our own people." Puryn looked at his cup.

"Be that as it may, brother, the Alliance holds true. Your forces have secured Cinnog, and over the past few years they have healed their wartime scars and have returned to the path of prosperity. Yslandeth and Hodan are inseparable now. Edenyag has toed the line since Cathir was executed for treason. The elder races still keep to themselves, but come when asked." Orus finished his cup. "But ..."

Puryn finished his thought. "But Sudenyag remains a disaster."

"Aye, and they now attack our southern borders at will," Orus replied. "I wish to invade and restore order. Truthfully, I wish to annex Sudenyag, if possible, but the Syndicate and the Bedouin are deeply entrenched there.

I cannot do it alone. I am up to fifteen Legions now, but that is scarcely twenty-thousand men with support elements." Orus poured another drink.

"I have thought that you would request this, brother. I hear you clearly, and I agree that the South is a serious issue that we must deal with. How extensive are the raids to your South?" Puryn picked at a piece of bread from a tray near the drinks.

"Truthfully, little more than a nuisance, but with the calls for action, the stories become much bigger than the actual events. My people want blood for blood. They say that in some attacks, the Suden are kidnapping women and children. I cannot confirm this, nor deny it with any certainty. If they do steal our women and whelps, it is presumably because they are too cowardly to attack a Hodan man directly." Orus had a look of pride on his face as he visualized the prospect of engaging a gaggle of ruffians from the Suden ruins with a Legion of his own men.

"Propaganda can be a help or a burden. I understand this clearly." Puryn set down his mug and sat forward. "What if I sent three Legions of Draj and twenty-five-thousand Regulars for combined operations to the South of Hodan … for peacekeeping. Hodan gets to rout the rabble and clear the enemy from the lands South of its borders. Then, you send in a contingent of solely Hodan forces as 'buffer zone' enforcement. Over time, we just move the borders on the maps southward, and Hodan keeps the land it wins. I doubt that any other nation on the Ert would object if Hodan could quell the unrest to the South, even if it were just to a dull roar."

Orus wore a look of surprise. "Who are you, and what have you done with my brother?" The older man laughed. "I like this idea. How far southward will we invade? Ten miles? Twenty?"

"I'll let you decide, brother, but I do not have to remind you of the logistical nightmare of a large area of operations. You already know these things. The more you take, the more resources it will require to maintain, but once you quell the resistance and make the Suden see that Hodan is the best option, they will truly be your lands."

"How quickly can you be ready to deploy your forces, Puryn?" Orus asked seriously.

"Two weeks, maybe three?" the younger King replied, sipping from his cup.

"I accept this idea and will claim it as my own publicly. I had sought to ask a similar request of you, but you have beaten me to the punch, as always!" Orus smiled and extended his hand.

Puryn shook his hand and then pulled the Hodan close, hugging him. "You are my brother. No one shall oppose you. We shall ensure that."

Orus pulled back, nodding. "I should inform my officers of the coming storm. As always, you are welcome in my house at any time. Stay the night and depart in the morning, if you wish."

"I will take you up on that offer, brother. Goodnight." Puryn turned and left the room.

With the exit of Yslandeth, several attendants entered, clearing away the dishes and going to work, cleaning the throne room. Orus called over one of his servant boys, ordering, "Go and fetch the Princess. Tell her that her father has good tidings to share!"

"At once, Your Majesty!" the young man said bowing and then jogging quickly down the hallway and out of sight.

Orus again looked out of his window. The sun was set, and the hearths were now visible through windows, far and wide. The older man lit up a pipe and sat back, smoking, enjoying the view from his vantage.

"I will see the glory of Hodan reclaimed. I will secure the southern borders. Thank you, Runnir and Gunnir, for your favor. Thank you for true allies." Orus sat back and exhaled smoke out of his open window.

The weight upon the King's shoulders was greatly diminished. He sat at ease for the first time in many months.

Chapter 21

Illari had been within the walls of the monastery for close to ten years. Over that time, he visited many times with his family, but much like his father in days gone by, he formed relationships with the clergy and students, which were forged in his heart, as close as those of blood. After graduating the course of study, the young Prince declined the priesthood and an offer from the Order of Haya's Dawn to become a full-fledged monk. He did this not out of disrespect for the Order, but rather out of respect for his mother and the line she led. He chose to follow the ways of nature, as an Elf, but now, he also knew the ways of man and the monk.

After academics were officially complete and Illari had mastered all that he was presented, the young half-Elven druid stayed on in Empyr for a while longer. The now grown man had learned the ways of politics and public opinion. He sought to aid Master Donick in the rebuilding of the castle at Empyr. The city walls were now fully restored, the markets were bustling, and the temple completed. Even the two towers were restored to their former glory. Illari barely remembered the times before the Offlanders, but he imagined that his father, Puryn, rebuilt the city exactly as it had been when Swyk had ruled, almost fifteen years prior.

The young Prince mingled with his father's ministers and Generals. Puryn was not seen in Empyr much these days, with most of his time spent dealing with Erynseere, the Queen, and a myriad of new problems that had been simmering to the South for many years now. Sudenyag was occupied by Hodan with Yslan reinforcements, and the Bedouin, led by the Shadow, were having none of it.

Illari sat in the square, sipping a hot tea, when he saw her walking his way. Standing, he bowed, smiling. It was his mother. As usual, she was shooing her ladies-in-waiting away and glaring at her guard whenever he scowled at a traveler-by. She would never change, and that is why he loved her so.

"Good morning, my son!" The Queen hugged her boy openly. These days, Illari did not shy away from her embraces and was not the embarrassed adolescent who he had once been.

"Good morning, Your Majesty," he replied, winking. The Queen shook her head, rolling her eyes, and then sat.

"I have come to visit, but also to talk to you about a strange thing that a friend has told me ... about you." The Queen raised an eyebrow.

Illari's forehead furrowed as he sat, sipping his tea. "About me?"

"Yes, you, my son. Something that puzzles me, but does not surprise me, in the least." The Queen took a cup of tea from a servant, blowing gently on the hot mixture and then taking a sip.

"What have I allegedly done?" the Prince asked, raising an eyebrow, much like his mother. The Queen smirked at the expression, recognizing her reflection.

"One of my children says that there is another who calls to them from the stones." The Queen leaned forward, down to eye level with Illari, who now gulped hard.

"Mother, I can explain ...," the Prince stammered with his hand up.

Adasser sat back laughing loudly. "Please do."

"Mother, I did not call to them, I swear." Illari looked around and saw saplings everywhere that were not around the square when they initially sat down at tea. He sipped his tea, wishing he had a flask instead. "They approached, ME."

"Mmmhmm," the Queen stated, sipping her tea with a look of expectation on her face. "Go on."

"What did they tell you?" Illari asked, scowling at a nearby tree. The trees rustled, as if the wind was present, but there was no breeze. Illari looked away for a moment, and it was gone. He noticed that his mother was deep in thought at the moment. She had drifted off from the conversation and was staring into her tea, as if she remembered something important. The young Prince shifted nervously in his seat.

* * *

Adasser quietly thought back to a day in Erynseere when her oaks were strangely quiet and distant. Many of the pines avoided her presence, as if they were afraid of her. She felt as if she were standing in front of one of her mortal children and that they were hiding some misdeed from her. Puzzled by this behavior, the Queen asked her oak what the matter was. After a time of deflection and avoidance of the question, Adasser finally coaxed the story from the oak. She was floored by the news it told. Once she had calmed and was reassured by her children that Illari was, in fact, safe, she poured herself a glass of Elfish wine.

She sat on her throne in Erynseere, contemplating the report of her trees and what it all meant for the future. "How could her male child be a Talker?" This had never occurred in all of the histories of the Elves. Several times in the years that followed, she would notice a delay in response to her call, as if her trees and animals were preoccupied elsewhere. She suspected Illari's direct interaction with her forests, or that they were, by some compulsion, running to his aid by their own free will. At that moment, the Queen began to realize that something bigger was happening with her son, but she decided to wait and see how things played out. When it became more commonplace, she chose to travel to Empyr and ask him plainly what was going on.

"Goddess," the druid Queen remembered asking in the silence of her throne room, "I know not what your plan is, but I know that you are greater than I. Your will be done."

* * *

Adasser shook her head, as if awakening from a trance. She looked up at her son before her. He had a look of worry on his face. She pitied him. He had no idea what was coming his way.

The Queen replied to Illari's half-hearted demand for information. "Oh, just that once upon a time, in the monastery, a young Prince was attacked by several students over his heritage. They said that the young victim fought valiantly, but that there were simply too many to defeat. So, recognizing the blood of a Talker, they intervened. No one died … at your, I mean, the victim's request. Make no mistake, they were preparing to kill the attackers, every last one of them."

The Queen was deadly serious. Illari looked down, swallowing hard. It was a hard memory that had turned to a nightmare on occasion; a dream where the trees did not stop, and the eagles picked at the lifeless eyes of his foes. He shuddered and remember the day.

Adasser awaited his response with concern. Illari was red-eyed, and veins now protruded from his forehead as he collected his thoughts. She waited for him to compose himself. "It is all right, my son. Be not distressed."

She could see that her words were falling on deaf ears.

* * *

Illari looked as if he was far away for a moment, as he remembered begging Haya for assistance on that night. Five older, more substantial, boys were cat-calling him a half-breed, while they encircled him, kicking him in the face and body. He was the son of Puryn and showed his prowess, having seriously injured two of the gang, but there were just too many to face. Then, much like in a time long before that night, when a wolf instead stalked the life of this same small half-Elf boy at a family picnic with his mother, they once again came to his defense.

In the courtyard, the trees surrounded the attackers before they knew what was occurring. Within seconds of the arrival of the trees, the ruffians were whisked away, one by one, as they screamed. Illari remembered pulling himself up to his knees to see several pines and an oak tree beating the attackers with branches and bouncing a couple of them off of the ground for good measure. The Prince begged them to stop. He asked for their lives to be spared. Staggering to the nearest oak, the young Prince reached out, touching its proud trunk.

"Thank you for saving me, my friends. Please do not kill these fools," Illari asked emphatically. "Haya does not wish for death, only life and light. Did my mother know and send you?" he asked in embarrassment.

The old oak creaked and responded in a language that Illari had learned from watching his mother. "You are the son of the Queen. Your blood is her blood. We are your servants. No one will harm the Queen or her loves. We came on our own."

Illari smiled with tears in his eyes, but then the hair on his neck raised, as he noticed that several eagles had perched in the branches of the trees. They were looking intently at the now suspended and beaten attackers.

One eagle screeched loudly, and Illari heard it as if it spoke Etah plainly. "Kill!"

Illari pointed at the eagle. "No you will not! Stay there, bird."

The tree spoke again. "You are a friend of the forest; you are of our Queen. We will honor and serve you. We are your servants and protectors."

"You must not, Oak! My mother will be furious! She will think me stealing her children. Please, put them down and go your way. I thank you for intervening, but I am not the Queen, I am only half an Elf, and yet a boy, I am less than an animal to these people … a half-breed." Illari looked at the terrified faces of the now conscious attackers. Some pleaded for mercy. "Set them down, Oak. Please."

"As you wish," Oak said, and then all of the trees complied.

Disappointed, the eagles cocked their heads and lit off into the sky. Illari watched them go. The five attackers were now huddled back-to-back, in a circle. The trees were still behind him as Illari surveyed the bruised and bloodied faces of his foes. They were still pleading for their lives.

"I will spare all of you this night, on one condition," Illari angrily bluffed. "You must agree to never again attack anyone weaker than you, or below your station. If at any time you do so, know that 'they' will see you. You will pay, trust me. These are but a few of my friends." Illari looked at the oak, nodding. The tree's leaves rustled as if a strong wind blew where there was none.

"We swear, My Lord," the five responded in unison.

"Then go, and we shall not speak of this incident again," Illari stated, turning to the oak. "Thank you, again, my friend. Be well. Please do not tell the Queen of this event. She will only worry."

"I shall try, Prince," the oak responded and then it was gone.

Illari stood in the courtyard after his assailants had departed, praying and wondering for the future. There had never been a male Tree-Talker in the history of the elder races. The tired Prince looked to the sky and saw the full moon, bright in the starry sky.

"What does this mean, My Goddess?" he asked the twinkling stars above.

There was no immediate reply.

* * *

"Illari, what is your relationship with my trees?" the Queen asked smiling. She pursued her lips, trying not to laugh at the pale, sweaty face of her son, sitting across from her.

"I do not know what their problem is, mother." Illari was glaring at an eavesdropping branch as it poked around the corner of the courtyard in which he sat.

Adasser laughed. "They are worried, my son. They feel that they are in trouble, but for what?" Adasser asked, guessing the answer from her son's demeanor.

"Mother, I did not want to worry you. I was attacked years ago by several older boys. They were beating me pretty badly when I prayed to the Goddess for intervention. They showed up." Illari pointed at the branch that was trying to get closer to hear. "Them!" The branch recoiled and disappeared out of sight.

"They just came to you?" the Queen smiled. "I am jealous!"

Illari looked at his mother with a puzzled expression. "Jealous?"

"It took me almost a year of coaxing to get them to trust and love me, boy." She pointed at a branch that was once again sneaking around the corner, and it pulled back out of sight once again. "It seems that they like you more than I, perhaps? Do they speak to you plainly, son?"

Illari's face was one of surprise. "Yes, mother, they speak to me, but I do not think that they like me better. They told me something to the effect that I am of you, so, therefore, they will follow me, because of my blood. If anything, they still follow you, just by proxy through me. Oh, and eagles also."

The Queen's head snapped to look at her son's worried gaze. "Animals came to you also?"

"Yes?" Illari said, as a question.

"Hmm. Trees, animals, I'm sure insects will follow," Adasser said, as a matter of fact.

"There is more, mother." Illari winced while saying the words, as if they hurt him physically.

"More?" Adasser perked up with interest. "What do you mean 'more'?"

"I have visions. Some days they are dreams, other times they are in the day." Illari wrung his hands as he spoke.

"Visions of what, son?" the Queen questioned with concern.

"Some days of you and father. Other days and nights they are dark scenes." Illari drew a deep breath, "In some of these visions, I see and speak to the dragons, mother. I have spoken to Maradwynne on one occasion."

Adasser's eyes were the size of large silver coins. "Dragons? They speak to you also? What do they say to you, son? When were you going to tell me of these things!?"

"I hid it, because I did not want to worry you, but since you already know of the half, I figured you should know it all." Illari looked over his shoulders. Small branches were all around him. He shook his head.

Adasser giggled at the persistence of the trees. "Get used to it, my son. Tell me what the dragons say to you."

"There is one reoccurring theme. I am the anomaly. I am a Tree-Talker where no man should be. They tell me that it is a sign of the evil to come, mother. The dragons warn me of their brothers and sisters from beyond the Ert. The evil perverts the young of the protectors, creating a destroyer. Maradwynne has warned that the protectors are fading and the destroyers are gaining strength. I know not the time of their invasion. It may not even occur within our lives, mother, but the Black Dragons come to avenge the Offlanders. They come to honor their Lord, the ruler of the Underworld. Somehow, I am involved in Haya's response to this. I know not how. It terrifies me, mother. I am not my father." Illari frowned at this realization.

"You are only half your father, boy. Half of you is me. I think the Goddess has bonded the strengths of both of us in you. Your father spoke to the dragon and continues to do so on occasion when he thinks that I am not looking. You do the same, and now the trees and nature come to you. We did well sending you to this place to learn, as your father did as a child. Now, I must take you back to Erynseere to teach you our ways, the ways of the forest and of the elder races." Adasser took her son's trembling hand. "You will be a great man, your importance cannot be overlooked, but remember to remain humble so that the Goddess may use your heart."

"Always, mother. I will go with you today. What of Elpis in Edenyag? She has been training for six years with their mages. Will she too come home to be with us?" Illari smiled, remembering the evil redheaded little sister who tormented him as a child. "Altwidus will never leave his horses!" Illari laughed, eliciting a chuckle from his mother.

"I do not know, son, but you are correct in the case of Altwidus! It will be easier to travel to his barony in Korin than to get him to visit Erynseere! He has bred such lovely steeds. He will never leave his stables! Even the

Elves are jealous! Elpis, well, she is living her life as a mage now. She is not only learning at The Great Library, but she now teaches the young there also. She has her own life and seeks to marry. Many have their eyes on her. I have many eyes on them." The Queen smirked.

"I would not wish to be her suitor!" Illari laughed. It was the first real smile that the Queen had seen all day.

"You are not in trouble, my son. You are gifted, and I must teach you the ways of the priesthood." Adasser stood. "Come, let us gather your things and you may travel with my caravan back to Erynseere. Will you travel home?"

"Yes, mother. I am eager to return to our studies." Illari smiled again.

* * *

Puryn was South of his borders again, to his wife's chagrin. She was tired of these trips, but they were necessary for morale and to prove his resolve to those on the Ert who doubted it. He was all-in, backing Hodan and its peace-keeping mission in Sudenyag. Truthfully, both he and Orus agreed that it was a sanctioned invasion of the southern lands, but neither man saw an issue in taking the lawless, unruled lands, and turning it into one of peace and prosperity. The brothers-in-arms were not considering that many remained in the much-maligned lands of Sudenyag, who held allegiance to the same.

Men still lived who would fight to the death to expel the invaders and restore the rightful rulers to their own throne. Neither northern King took the threats from the Syndicate or Bedouin seriously, that is, until their men started to die. When the resistance became a reality, Orus and Puryn doubled their resolve and their troop commitments. Sudenyag was officially a war zone, and this time, it seemed, that Orus and Puryn were now the aggressors, although they played the public roles of liberators.

Against Puryn's advice, Orus pushed his initial advantage when he invaded Sudenyag. There was little or no resistance at first, and this emboldened the Hodan King. Hodan expanded its lands almost two-fold. Orus directed his armies on the field, invading southeast over the river border between the two nations. He proceeded to move southward to five miles North of the Great Temple of Haya. After securing the northwestern region of Suden, the Hodan screamed from the streets for more, and Orus complied with their cries, pushing eastward. Hodan captured all of the lands until the border of Edenyag with little more than a skirmish. Hodan had effectively cut Sudenyag in half, North and South.

With the significant increase in landmass, came the logistical nightmare of defending it against raiders, brigands, and the Underground, led by Hassim, the Shadow. Orus successfully petitioned Puryn for an increase in aid. Before long, both men had over thirty-five-thousand men committed on the ground in Sudenyag. The situation was not dire to either northern Kingdom, but their losses and expenses were starting to add up. Orus had the full support of his nation. He sat securely upon his throne.

Yslandeth was focused on rebuilding its own infrastructure. Food had become a non-issue over the few years, and the hatred of the Elder Races and half-bloods was on the decrease. The new settlements of halflings were now prospering, as were everyone else, and no one seemed to pay them any mind. Suffering was at a minimum at the moment. The Ert did not need a scapegoat to blame for suffering when very little existed.

In Sudenyag, it was a different story.

Hassim was busy. His troops, many times, were little more than boys. The leader had many sleepless nights as he lay awake, thinking of those who would not return to their mothers. His people were sick of war. They were sick of death. The former King Yanat Il Arnar sold their souls to the Underlord for his throne, and although he was long gone, the curse remained.

Hassim sipped a hot cup of tea and looked at Famlin, who was pretending to be asleep. "Oh quit with your faking and just get up."

Famlin scowled. "There is no fooling you. Why is that? How do you always know?"

"It's a sixth sense now, boy. I should have been dead so many times before this day. Haya, Haeldrun? I know not who still has need of me." Hassim held out his hand, pulling the specialist up.

Famlin smiled. "I am glad to finally be making a difference, Master. For once, I feel like I'm on the side of right."

"Puryn is not a bad man, Famlin," Hassim said in deep thought. "Orus can be a bastard, at times, but he is not evil either."

"But still, both invade our home, to claim it as their own," Famlin spat.

The Shadow chuckled. "Are we truly a Kingdom any longer without a King? Without a government?" Hassim raised his hand, as if pointing out the sunrise. "All these lands and one-hundred different tribes squabbling over patches of dust and despair."

"I can think of a man who would lead. The people would follow." Famlin looked intently at Hassim.

The Shadow stepped back and recoiled. "Still a fool, I see. Why would anyone want to rule this place!?"

Famlin laughed out loud. "Whatever you say, boss. What are we up to today?"

Hassim looked North. "Same thing as we were up to yesterday. Bleed them until they leave."

Famlin looked North and wondered about Safiya. He hoped his actions would not cause her any harm. Looking down, he betrayed his feelings to Hassim, who watched him intently.

"You do not seek after death. Your soul is still on the side of the light, young one," Hassim remarked.

"You defend the defenseless, Master. You are my example. If I am a hero in your eyes, you are one tenfold in mine," Famlin said looking down.

"Perhaps more fire and smoke today, and less death, my apprentice?" Hassim winked at his student.

"Maybe we can scare them off?" Famlin smiled deviously.

Both men turned to their preparations, laughing at the joke, but with heavy hearts. It seemed, at that moment, that Sudenyag would never see a peaceful sunrise and no one could figure out the cause or a viable remedy.

The dream of freedom and the mission were all that they had to hold onto.

Chapter 22

Puryn looked over the fields South of the alliance position. All was quiet. The King could see several caravans of tradesmen were moving their wares to the East. Off out of direct sight, smoke rose from known tribal camps. Sitting in his saddle, the Elfish-mailed warrior felt uneasy. It was too quiet. Riding to the heavily guarded Command Tent, he dismounted and entered a briefing that was underway. A young lieutenant was pointing to suspected enemy locations on a map. The reconnaissance teams had returned undetected.

Orus was listening intently. Faylea had insisted upon accompanying him on his trip to visit the deployed armies. The young Princess scowled, as the officer briefing the Hodan King described what he thought to be a rebel stronghold directly South of their encampment. A major force was suspected of operating near the now-razed Grand Temple of Haya. They were less than five miles from direct contact. Faylea grinned maliciously. She had wanted to see the Shadow's head on a spike for some time. That would solidify Hodan's hold on Sudenyag and her father's grasp of the Hodan throne.

"Your Majesties," the young man continued. "Reports of major activity continue to pour in from all patrols South of our location. Many report unexplained deaths of our warriors, and some units have failed to report in altogether." He took a deep breath and continued. "We can only surmise from our intelligence that the enemy has a large underground contingent near the temple."

Orus saw Puryn enter the tent and addressed him, asking, "So did you hear what he said, brother?"

"I did." Puryn sighed. "We must push farther South to quell this aggression, I fear." Yslandeth looked at Hodan with a tired face.

"I agree," the Hodan King replied in a subdued tone, catching a smile on his daughter's face. Orus shook his head.

"Yslan, support King Orus with whatever he needs. We will see this war through and establish peace where none has existed in almost two decades. Maybe this will be the action that breaks the back of the rebellion." Puryn turned to Orus and Faylea. "One can only hope and pray."

Orus nodded wearily. "Agreed. Let us finish with this insanity."

Puryn looked toward the corner of the tent. Kairoth sat quietly, listening to the battle plan. He was no longer a whelp, but a full-grown warrior. Nodding, the young man stood and left the tent. Puryn knew that wherever the man went, it seemed mayhem was sure to follow. The Yslandeth King asked Haya to watch over his covert teams. Over the years, they had served Yslan well.

* * *

Kairoth returned to the pavilion where his team was camped. The two mages had long ago sectioned off a corner with blankets, creating makeshift walls for privacy. Everyone was quietly going about their morning routines, preparing for orders. Seeing the professionalism of his team, Kairoth quietly smiled and nodded, satisfied with what he saw. Pushing the tent flap open, he entered and sat on a stool near the entrance. The tent stopped and looked up expectantly.

Sal'iabac spoke. "So, what now?"

The team sat silently, as if they asked the question as one.

"Well, since a bunch of regulars went South and got themselves killed or taken prisoner, both Kings have decided that our armies will push southward toward the old temple." Kairoth looked sarcastically around the group. All of them looked at him in apathy. "Yes, I know." The Hodan warrior sighed.

"Why don't WE go down South and see if there is something that we can do to alleviate the need for our Kingdoms to walk right into another ambush." Brynd was visibly upset. "Are these fools paying attention? How many times do we need to repeat the same mistakes, before they stop giving the enemy the advantage?"

"What do you suggest, ranger?" Kairoth deadpanned. "If it is a large force, a team such as ours will not be able to quell it. If it is a small force, we may not be able to locate it. If Their Majesties set the woods on fire, the vermin will run out of the trees into plain sight."

"Or the vermin will simply move to the next glen and wait for us there, attacking us while we sleep, as they always do, Kairoth." Reynir yawned as he replied. He was tending to another plant in a pot.

"There is little else that we can do, but follow the orders we are given, brother. Who are we to question both Kings?" Valtyr asked with annoyance.

"Well, quite frankly, my brother," Reynir said, covering his mouth as he yawned again, "I can question whatever I want to. I don't have to like the orders I am given. I simply have to carry them out. I can complain if I wish." The druid smirked and pushed his brother playfully.

"Be serious!" Valtyr protested.

"I am always serious. I am always at play. I find a balance where it can be found." The druid stood and patted Kairoth on the shoulder. "I will be ready." Reynir left the tent to use the privy.

"I will go where my sister goes," Safiya stated plainly as she packed her reagents into her belt pouch.

"This could be the push that is needed, my friends. Perhaps we can retire from our adventures and go back to leading our normal lives!" Kairoth said emphatically, in an attempt to lift group morale.

Sal'iabac growled. "I've heard that a few times before." She snorted, rolling her eyes.

Kairoth bit his lower lip and silently shook his head. Once again, they would be going into harm's way. They had been together for over five years now. Sal'iabac had seemingly tired of the Hodan's temperament and moved on. Safiya still stung from the loss of Famlin, holding out hope of seeing him again. Brynd was ready to retire, and the holy men of the group were as cynical or sarcastic as ever. Even Reynir's youthful outlook and playful banter had disappeared. The band was war-weary and tired of service. They were ready to be released. So far, there was no sign of it coming anytime soon.

* * *

Famlin looked with fear at his Master. The field was full of them. They seemed to be coming from within the razed temple, and there seemed to be no end to them in sight.

"I have seen this before, Hassim," Famlin said with apprehension.

"You have? Where?" The Shadow asked with concern.

"In Cinnog. My team … the one I once served in Yslandeth while spying … we entered a cave. It turned out to be a Todessen shrine of some sort to the Underlord. We were told by one of the occupants that they sought to raise their God upon the Ert with the blood of innocents." Famlin looked over the field with concern.

"So, the dead were alive there also?" the Master asked with dismay. "When were you going to let me in on this information, apprentice?" Hassim was grinning now.

"We thought that group was the last of them. I figured telling you was a moot point, My Master. I have told you of everything else, but did not think that this horror would revisit me. I was wrong." Famlin frowned.

"You obviously miscalculated their resolve." Hassim chuckled softly. "These Toad vermin are very persistent, let me tell you. At least the appearance of the undead has forced the rival tribes to unite. I can see their encampments encircling the area. We will try to thin the dead and engage whatever is causing them to come to our lands."

"Master, we may need help to extinguish this evil." Famlin looked at his Master. The tension was evident on the specialist's face.

"What are you proposing, my student?" the Shadow asked.

"Let me travel North covertly, with a small team of Elites. I will seek to contact my old team. I know that they operate in this locale. I had come across them several times, and withdrew before I was detected. Kairoth lives, and he will bring Yslandeth and Hodan to our aid." Famlin sighed nervously.

"You are not turning tail and running, are you?" Hassim asked seriously.

Offended, the thief replied, "Never! I am trying to be of use to my Master!"

Hassim eyed the young man closely. He sensed he was telling the truth, but was still skeptical. "Why should I believe you, when you fooled Irshad for so many years?"

"You did not hold my sister hostage to coerce me to service. Master, I came of my own free will. I have told you everything about the military tactics of Yslan, Hodan, and Cinnog. I have shown you the training that I have received while in Yslan. I fear that this evil may be too great for a few Elites and a gaggle of untrained pickpockets. We need help, and I think that I can get it. My sister still lives in this land. I have much to lose if it is taken from us." Famlin stood, looking at his Master in the eye.

"Famlin, I will hold you to your word. Many say that we have no honor, but we know better. Go and take a team of four with you. Do not engage the enemy directly. Contact your friends, if you are able. If they are unwilling, you know what you must do." Hassim looked at his student intently. Famlin knew.

"Yes, Master. I will leave at once. The teams are located in the great war camp to the North. I will seek to make contact, when they inevitably come South to scout at the behest of Puryn or Orus. It is what they do."

"Good luck and may the Gods favor you, son," the Master replied, standing.

Famlin stood and bowed, grabbed his team and headed North as his

Master watched him go.

* * *

Kairoth and the team had left the northern encampment and were a couple of miles into enemy territory. Before he left, he informed Puryn of his intentions and the King of Yslan agreed immediately. The team left within hours. It was now dark, and the sky was clear. The moon shone brightly and was high in the sky. It was a warm spring evening and the group, although traveling behind enemy lines, seemed a bit at ease as it made its way silently southward. After a few more hours, they stopped, set up a small camp, and tried to appear as if they were Suden travelers. Most paid them no mind, thinking them to be Bedouin, but for some time, Brynd had the feeling that they were being watched. He told Kairoth as much.

The team sat around a small fire they had started. They ate their rations and drank water from their skins.

"Someone tracks us, but I cannot detect them plainly," Brynd said very quietly, covering his mouth with a scarf while scanning the area.

Kairoth looked up at the party. All had heard the statement. "Prepare yourselves discreetly."

The party went about preparing for bed. Kairoth stood the watch with Brynd, but the ranger disappeared quickly, as the Draj often do, making it appear as if the warrior stood alone. The Hodan had his sword drawn and was oiling the blade.

The night seemed to be progressing slowly and peacefully, when the stalkers showed their hand. From the shadows, a dart found its mark, hitting Kairoth in the back of the neck.

Kairoth shouted. "Get up! Get up! I have been poisoned! To arms!"

The party scurried to come to his aid, watching their leader fall to the ground with a loud thud. As each member exited the small group tent, a similar dart found each of them. Famlin and one of his team entered the encampment and began binding the party members tightly.

Brynd appeared as if from nowhere, his bow drawn. "Put them down, or I will sink an arrow into each of your hearts, Toads."

Famlin removed his face covering. "Stand down, my friend. We only come to talk."

"Famlin? You fight against us? You, traitorous son of a whore! You are truly a Suden piece of dung. Toad! I will kill you first, turncoat!" Brynd aimed.

"Not advisable, brother." Famlin pointed behind the ranger.

Turning quickly, Brynd saw another specialist readied with a bow. Again, the ranger postured to shoot.

"Think again, you oaf," Famlin said calmly, pointing off on the edge of the darkness as another of his team emerged, bow in hand.

"You are a coward and a piece of filth. You will die for this," Brynd angrily sneered. The ranger put his bow down in front of him and then he was also bound.

"Be careful with that one, gentlemen. He's a damn Elf-trained scout, that one is a Hodan Elite, the two women are capable wizards, and those two misfits are clergy, but not the praying type, the killing type." Famlin looked to his men. They nodded. "Do not take your eyes off of them for any period of time. Wake me when they wake. Two of you on watch, two sleep. Do not trifle with these people. They will kill you without effort if they get free."

The specialists set the watch and slept in shifts.

* * *

Safiya woke first. Her head pounded, as if she had drunk too many tankards of mead the night prior. She was bound hand and foot and laying on her side. She could see that her reagents were nowhere in sight. Someone had put a small pillow under her head. She was puzzled, but not complaining.

As he walked around the tent with a cup of warm tea, she saw him for the first time. It was Famlin.

"What in the Underworld are you doing here!?" Safiya shrieked. "I thought you were dead." She began choking on her words as tears welled up in her eyes. "Are you my enemy now? You bound me like a criminal?"

"My Lady, you forget that I know who you are. I know what you are capable of. I know what all of you can do." Famlin knelt beside her and helped her sit up on a blanket that he had provided. He held the tankard of tea up and allowed the mage to sip the warm mixture. "That should aid in the headache. I am sorry, Safiya. Truly, I am," Famlin frowned.

"You are Suden, aren't you?" the mage asked sadly. "You were a spy?" she asked. "You lied to us. Did you lie even about you and me?"

"I am Suden, Safiya. I served as a spy to Irshad, my former Master, who captured my sister and made me do it. I had to lie to save her life. Now, he is dead, but I have joined my people in defense of our lands. I am the apprentice to Hassim, the Shadow. He is a hero. Yslan and Hodan need only pull out of our territory, and all will be well." Famlin looked into Safiya's eyes as a knot formed in his throat. "And no, I did not lie about us. That was real."

"I don't believe you," Safiya said with tears rolling from her eyes. "I cried for months after we lost you. How dare you come back now ... but it appears you did not come back for me. You have a mission, and this is just an unintended reunion, I'm sure."

"I have seen your team when you venture in our lands. I have encountered your patrols five times in the past year. I never once attacked your party, knowing full well, who you are and what your mission is. Know that I did this to protect YOU." Famlin whispered as he stood, looking at Safiya's saddened face.

While the two spoke, one by one, the rest of the team woke from their drug-induced slumber. Each one had a serious headache and was given some of the tea to alleviate the after-effects of the sedative.

Kairoth was concerned. He did not know why he was alive, but he was happy to note that the rest of his group had also survived the encounter.

"What is going on, Brynd?" Kairoth asked and irate ranger who was tied up next to him.

"Oh, nothing much, boss," Brynd quipped. "We've been captured by a Suden specialist patrol led by none other than, Famlin, our missing specialist. Oh, here he comes now, the piece of filth that he is."

Kairoth looked at Brynd like he was mad. "What?" Then the warrior looked toward where the ranger gestured with a nod. "What in the Underworld!?"

"Greetings, Kairoth," Famlin said sitting down.

"If I get my hands on you, I'll …" Kairoth grit his teeth.

"Precisely why you were drugged and bound," Famlin said, as a matter of fact.

"What do you want, Toad?" Kairoth squinted angrily.

"I want to set up a meeting between Puryn, Orus, and my Master," Famlin offered.

"Really? To surrender, or so that you can capture them for a ransom, you thieving bucket of piss." Kairoth struggled against the bindings, but the more he pulled, the tighter the bindings became.

"Keep that up, and I fear that your fingers will soon appear to be sausages. They may even pop off, Hodan," Famlin stated plainly.

"If I could set up a meeting, why should KING Puryn or KING Orus meet with anyone from this Gods-forsaken pile of dung?" Kairoth was livid.

"Well, I don't know," Famlin replied in an irate tone. "Maybe because just South of here, the fields are full of undead? Maybe because the razed Great Temple seems to be where they are coming from, but we are unsure and incapable of dealing with the threat? Maybe because you know of what that means, and all petty grievances and illegal invasions aside, nothing will matter if the Underlord comes here and squashes all of us like insects!"

"Undead? Fields?" Kairoth looked at the thief in disbelief. "You mean like in Cinnog? You mean like when we lost Danzu?"

"Yes. Exactly. Except for this time, it is on a grander scale." Famlin took in a deep breath and sighed. "Bigger than anything, we've seen as a group."

All of them were listening now.

"So, what happened to you, traitor?" Valtyr interjected.

"I snuck down to the border of Suden and Cinnog to steal thunder powder from a cache that Irshad Il Nadur's forces had stolen from an Edenyag shipment to Palgur." Famlin's face twisted. "I was captured and could not return. Eventually, through a failed coup attempt, Irshad ended up dead and Hassim, the Shadow, took over as our uncontested leader. Just recently, with the rise of the undead and possible Todessen activity, we have solidified the support of the Bedouin and Syndicate. Suden is united, but we are not strong enough to stand toe-to-toe with the nations of the Ert."

"So, you speak as if you are fully on the side of Suden?" Reynir stated plainly.

"I am, but I still love each of you like my family and wish you no harm. I have purposely avoided all contact with your group, so as to avoid fighting against you directly. I know that you are all decent people. I need to make this meeting happen for the whole Ert, not just Sudenyag. I hope that our cooperation may lead to an understanding and maybe to peace. Regardless, if we do not do something soon, I fear that our fates will be decided by the Underlord and his minions." Famlin looked southward and shivered when remembering the walking corpses.

"A nice story, liar," Kairoth responded. "Why should I believe you now?"

"I will release you all if you promise not to attack us. I will lead you South to where the problems lie. See for yourself! It is not a lie. It is the end if we do not act, brother. Do you agree on your honor to a truce, for the time being?" Famlin's eyebrows raised expectantly.

Kairoth pursed his lips, scowling. He saw no other option. "Only if we are free to go after witnessing your concerns. We will be freed to return to our armies."

"I agree. I hope that when you witness this for yourself, you will honor my request and deliver this scroll to your Kings. They need to know. The Ert must know." Famlin placed the scroll by Kairoth. "So, we have a deal, on your word?"

"Yes. Cut these damned bindings already!" Kairoth demanded.

"Cut them loose and give them their equipment back," Famlin ordered.

The party was loosed immediately.

* * *

The parties headed South for two miles. About one-half mile from the area that Famlin wished to show Kairoth the party encountered several undead shambling zombies. They were dispatched by Famlin's men without incident, and the group moved as silently as possible to their vantage point.

Up, on a small hill, North of the former Great Temple of Haya, Kairoth and the rest of the party members could see a great open field surrounding a large razed building. To the East was an enormous area that appeared to be nothing more than a graveyard full of headstones and tombs.

Kairoth pointed. "What is that, Famlin? Is it a burial ground?"

"It is, Kairoth," the thief replied. "When the war was over, we dug mass graves for the commoners and buried their remains under the Ert. Do you think that is where they are coming from?"

"That would be my guess," Kairoth responded looking through his spyglass. "I would wager the undead are a byproduct of whatever the Toads are doing under the old temple. This IS bad. You weren't lying."

Famlin nodded. "I was not lying about many things. I hope to prove that to you someday, if you do not kill me first." Famlin smiled mischievously, and Kairoth squinted at him menacingly. The Hodan had a feeling that his former thief was being truthful, but could not tell when the specialist was speaking truth or lies.

"Let's get out of this place. I will tell King Puryn and King Orus of this evil. I am sure that both men will want to come here personally." Kairoth grabbed the thief's tunic, drawing him near. "I will only warn you one time, traitor. If you threaten either man's life while they visit, I will wear your ears on a chain around my neck and see your corpse on a post for the birds to eat. Do we have an understanding?"

Famlin nodded knowingly. "I know that is not an idle threat, my brother. I promise you, no one will harm them during this meeting or while they travel, under the protection of Hassim, the Shadow. Anyone who lifts a hand against them will not see another breath after doing so."

Kairoth released the thief and nodded. "Let's go, quickly. There is no time to dawdle."

"Agreed," the thief said, motioning to his men to pull back. "I will notify my Master that the meeting will take place in two days at this location."

Kairoth nodded and turned to go. The party headed northward to the occupied territories.

Chapter 23

Kairoth handed over a scroll to Puryn, who was reading it while listening to the younger man's report. The King of Yslan nodded with a concerned look on his face, turning his gaze to Orus, who sat across the table from him. Orus stared back blankly. Puryn rubbed his temples as Faylea gave her unsolicited input.

"Father, we must act now! We must destroy these Toad invaders, before they wreak havoc upon our homeland! Perhaps we save the Suden in the process, but it is of the utmost importance to keep these evil bastards out of our borders!" Faylea was wildly gesturing with her hands while pacing madly.

Orus looked up with annoyance. "Leave us. Allow us to confer privately. We will come up with a suitable response."

"But father, what is there to think about? What is there to debate? The end brews South of us, and you wish to speak as if this is just another battle? This is 'the one!' This is the most important crisis of your reign!" Faylea was emphatic.

"I am King, you are not. You will do as you are told, girl. Leave us, now!" Orus bellowed angrily.

Puryn said nothing. He sat pondering his options.

"Your Majesties, if I may …," Kairoth continued.

Puryn sighed and sipped from his tankard. Orus glowered at the younger Hodan warrior. Faylea had a look of exasperation and defeat on her face as she stood to go.

"What do you wish to add?" Orus asked.

"I know that I am a common warrior, Your Majesties. I know my opinion doesn't count, but I agree with Princess Faylea, King Orus. To do nothing or to address this with less than a full commitment will result in certain doom for all of us. Your Majesties, they seek to raise the Underlord on the Ert!" Kairoth stood stoically at attention.

Faylea smiled, sizing up the slightly younger man. He was handsome and an excellent physical specimen. Most of all, he was on her side, and he had the backbone to stand in front of two Kings and to tell them their business. Her interest was piqued.

The vein in the center of Orus's forehead was throbbing and appeared ready to burst. Faylea saw that it was time to retreat and regroup. The Princess knew her new interest was about to be reprimanded for his input. Smiling, Faylea blurted out, "Father, we will go now. Please take our words into account when you make your final decision."

Faylea grabbed Kairoth's arm, saying quietly, "Let's go. NOW." Kairoth nodded, bowed, and exited the tent quickly.

Once outside, the two could hear the conversation clearly. Orus was livid. Puryn was trying to calm him down. They were drinking a few meads while contemplating the future. A short time later, Orus eventually relaxed and cleared his head. The real planning then began.

Faylea was smiling at Kairoth. He was a bit uncomfortable with her attention. Looking over at the young lady, who was clad in tight-fitted black leather armor, the young man swallowed hard. The ramifications of any contact with this woman would be catastrophic, but who was he to say no to a Princess. Amused, but worried, the young warrior waited for her to make the first move. He was not disappointed.

"Kairoth, is it?" Faylea asked.

"Yes, Your Highness," the warrior said stoically looking forward.

"Hodan?" Faylea inquired.

"Half on my father's side of the family. Born and raised in a small village North of Warrior's Crossing." Kairoth answered like a machine.

Faylea moved directly into his view. His eyes betrayed his interest. She smiled slyly. "Am I that hideous that you will not look upon me while speaking to me?"

Kairoth closed his eyes to compose himself and to formulate his answer, as a minister burst from the tent, running to one of the officers on duty. Faylea knew her opportunity to toy with him had been derailed. Just as well, he was a commoner and father would have a fit if she pursued him openly.

"I would like to speak with you again if the opportunity arises, warrior," Faylea said with authority.

"As you wish, Your Highness," Kairoth responded, bowing. Glancing at her face, the young man could see that she was smiling. "I must return to my unit and scout forward of the main body. It appears that they may have heard our ... I mean ... your appeal."

"Make no mistake, Kairoth. I saw you take my side in the argument. I saw you stand up before two Kings and stand your ground. I know of your prowess on the battlefield. Why have you no wife?" Faylea asked grinning mischievously. "Hodan women would fight to take that place." She raised an eyebrow, as if stating an obvious fact.

"I have not yet found a suitable match, Your Highness," Kairoth said modestly. He was now blushing, and that made Faylea's grin wider.

"Humility is also a desirable, trait," she replied. "We shall speak again. Do not get yourself killed, warrior."

"I will do my best to survive," Kairoth replied, smirking.

Faylea walked away. She knew he watched her go. She smiled, thinking of the concern on his face when she addressed him. "He's interested ... good!" she thought.

* * *

The army deployed by the two Kings was much too large to send in covertly, under cover of night. Fifteen-thousand combined forces of Yslan and Hodan marched openly into Suden territory. They were immediately monitored by covert Suden operatives posing as Bedouin tribesmen. One tribe lit a large bonfire to notify the surrounding families of the incoming units. They disguised the overt signal as a religious ceremony and celebration, but every tribe heightened their defensive posture, just in case.

Three miles into Suden territory, the army stopped for water and rest at a well-known oasis and watering hole. There, four or five caravans, mostly composed of poor families, pitched their large, flowing tents. They ate under cover of their canvas and played drums to pass the time. Puryn and Orus looked around at their surroundings with concern.

"You can never tell where the dart comes from in this place, Orus," Puryn said, looking around intently.

"That is for sure, brother. Be wary of your surroundings." Orus looked over at his daughter, who handed him a skin full of mead. He nodded to Faylea. "Thank you, daughter."

The army set up their tents away from the local groups who inhabited one side of the watering hole. Kairoth could see the Northern Alliance encampment from the cover of the trees surrounding the area. He could also see enemy operatives in the area, as Brynd pointed them out clearly.

"That little turd had better keep his promises," Kairoth scowled, "or I will pull his arms from his sides and use them to beat him to death."

Brynd snickered. "I want to watch that."

"Let's approach the watch. Famlin's people are here and waiting for our signal," Kairoth ordered.

The ranger made hand signals down the line. The party responded by moving silently toward the posted guard. They caught the young man by surprise.

"Hail, Northern Alliance, specialist team Erynseere reporting in," Kairoth said plainly from cover.

"Halt! Guards!" He paused for effect. "Advance and show yourself!" ordered the young warrior while covering in a defensive stance. His eyes darted from tree to tree.

Removing his favor from his pouch, Kairoth advanced on the guard who had two more sentries backing him up and several more on the way. The Hodan warrior kept his hands above his head and walked slowly toward them, the King's favor in hand.

"Halt! That is close enough," the first guard said. "Kneel!"

Kairoth knelt, noticing that two heavy crossbows were now trained on his person. "My team is undercover in the wood. I wish to establish who we are before accidentally causing an incident." Kairoth looked up at the young man, as the guard advanced and looked at the favor.

Nodding, the younger man ordered, "Stand down! Please rise, Sir. My apologies, we are in enemy territory and on high alert."

"No apologies necessary. Fine job, son. I will call my team now."

"Please continue, Sir," the young sentry responded.

"Come on out with your hands up and don't do anything sudden, please!" Kairoth ordered toward the woods. One by one, the team joined him with their favors in hand, and they were immediately recognized by their credentials.

"Please pass through the checkpoint and have a wonderful evening, My Lords and Ladies," the sentry stated bowing.

"Be safe, brother," Kairoth said, departing toward the Command Tent with his team in tow.

* * *

Orus, Faylea, and Puryn sat around a campfire drinking. Puryn was getting impatient, and Orus was becoming more concerned with the passing hour. Where was the contact that the Hodan fighter promised? Both began to wonder if this was a setup.

Puryn looked at his Draj General. "It's been several hours since we arrived. Surely, they know that we are here and surely, they observe us closely. Double the guard as a precaution."

"Yes, Sire," the General said, departing and making the adjustments.

Kairoth bowed to the departing General, approaching the fire from the darkness. A guard challenged him loudly, garnering the attention of both Kings and the Princess, who looked to see what the matter was. Puryn saw who it was plainly.

"Guard, he is my man. Let him pass," the King ordered.

"Yes, Sire." The guard relaxed, allowing Kairoth to approach the fire.

The Hodan warrior could see Faylea, who had now leaned back a bit more provocatively than was necessary. She seemed a bit tipsy and smiled at him in an overtly amorous manner. This caused the warrior to swallow hard, clear his throat, and speak. The eyes of King Orus darted back and forth between the pair. His face showed no emotion.

"Your Majesties. Your Highness." Kairoth bowed. "The Shadow and his apprentice, Famlin, are here. We have observed their men in the forest." Kairoth glanced around the perimeter. He was unable to detect anyone from his vantage point.

"Why have they not made contact yet?" Puryn asked plainly.

"I am not certain, Your Majesty," Kairoth replied. "Perhaps they were waiting to see if I would show up. Famlin and I have a history." Kairoth looked angry. This fanned the flames of Faylea even further. She smiled at Kairoth without taking her eyes off of him for an instant. This was not lost on Orus, who was becoming visibly irritated with her.

"Is there a signal that you can use to let them know that we are ready to meet?" Puryn sighed. "I do not like this feeling of being a sitting duck, Kairoth."

"Agreed, but I have no signal to give, Sire," Kairoth replied.

As the warrior finished his sentence, he noticed that something was amiss. The guards did not appear to be at their posts, and the usual industrious individuals were not present, doing the busy little things that they did during the evenings in camp. In fact, there was no one in the direct vicinity of the Royals. Kairoth drew his sword.

"What is it, boy?" Orus demanded.

"They are here," the Hodan replied. "Our guards are missing, as are the stewards."

Orus sat up abruptly, drawing his sword. He could see that the lad was right. "Where?"

"I do not know, Sire," Kairoth replied. "Most likely, they surround us."

Puryn stood with his glaive and shield in hand beside Orus. Both men were an inch taller that Kairoth, who had a sword in his hand also. Together, in the flicker of the firelight, the three towered over the sitting Faylea. Her eyes were wide as she saw them through a fog of the evening mead. She had never seen both Kings, side by side, as they joined as brothers for battle. They looked as if Runnir and Gunnir stood ready to challenge the world. This is what the enemy saw, and she now understood clearly where their fear came from. These men appeared as Gods and Kairoth was another giant—their instrument of destruction. She wondered if someday all would be legendary heroes of old. She grabbed her fighting knife and wondered how history would remember her.

They appeared out of the evening mist. Walking into the fire's light, two hooded figures approached the fire. Kairoth recognized the first as he removed his hood. It was Famlin. The young Hodan warrior stepped in front of both Kings.

"Is he here, traitor?" Kairoth demanded.

"Perhaps, but he will not show himself unless he is assured of his safety. Do you blame him?" Famlin smiled, looking at the posture of the three men. He caught a glimpse of a fourth individual in the darkness with a dagger. She moved with stealth, but he was tracking her. Famlin uttered something in a strange tongue to the man beside him who whistled. Seconds later, Kairoth and the two Kings heard a scream, and a shout, as a scuffle broke out.

"Faylea!" Orus yelled stepping forward. "You swine had better hope you have not harmed a hair on her head ... or I will drink from your skull and wear your teeth as an adornment on my armor!"

Famlin said something in the same strange tongue. This time, Kairoth could tell that he said his peace with a bit of anger and concern. The man next to the thief whistled and a man dragged the Princess back to the circle, dropping her roughly on the ground.

"Pig!" Kairoth bellowed, as he leaped on the man who threw the Princess down. "How dare you!"

Famlin held his hand up, and his men stayed out of it. Kairoth was on the offender in a flash. The knuckles of his left gauntlet opened the young Suden warrior's face just below the right eye. He fell to one knee. Kairoth pummeled the specialist to bloody rags within a minute. Enraged, covered in blood and brain matter, he released the husk of the Suden attacker. It hit the ground like a wet sack of sand. Turning, the warrior scowled at Famlin and his partner, gingerly picking up the slender Princess and bringing her to her father.

Orus looked intently at the young warrior. Scowling, the King nodded as the Princess began to stir in the warrior's arms.

"My hero," the Princess muttered as a medic took her from Kairoth, who wore a concerned look.

"You did not poison her, did you, traitor?" Kairoth demanded of Famlin. "If so, you have seen your last day."

"It is only a drug, brother, relax," Famlin replied.

"I am not your brother," Kairoth deadpanned.

"As you wish." Famlin nodded. "We allowed that recompense, because I assured you that no harm would come to the royal family in our borders during this parlay. That fool went beyond his orders, injuring a Princess. I would have killed him myself, but I figured that the Hodan in you would rather do it personally."

"Much appreciated, Toad. Where is your Master?" Kairoth growled. Orus was watching. He was becoming impressed with this Hodan-born specialist.

"Know this, all who are present here. You may possess the numbers, but we have a sizable force in readiness. We use poison, traps, drugs, and animals to fight our war. We also use stealth. You will not easily win, if you win this battle at all. Stand down," Famlin ordered.

"You are bluffing. I saw maybe one-hundred in the trees," Kairoth replied. "Where is your Master? Stop stalling."

Famlin looked toward the trees. His partner was now concealed.

Shouting out another order in the strange tongue, a loud whistle was heard coming from within the tree line. "Listen," Famlin responded calmly. The countryside was immediately filled with whistling. They came from all directions, as if an echo from the first call. "Do you believe me now?"

Kairoth looked around, shaking his head. "Your Majesties, it appears that we are surrounded."

Puryn looked at him, responding sarcastically, "You think so?"

Orus called his Generals. "Tell the men to allow the emissaries to enter. Stand down. Do not attack unless attacked. Assume a defensive perimeter." The Hodan military made it so.

Smiling, Kairoth looked at Famlin. "I hope you Toads brought a lot of darts. Pathetic cowards."

"I get what I want. The objective is achieved. The meeting occurs. Your opinion of me or of my tactics is none of my concern. You are still an oaf." Famlin turned and walked into the wood. He shouted, "We will be right back, you oversized child."

* * *

Orus and Puryn sat around the fire. Puryn was saying something as they sipped their mead, but Orus was not really listening. Kairoth now stood at the ready beside the healers who attended to the Princess. He was a gory mess from battle, but Orus could not help but be impressed. He shook his head remembering when he and Puryn wiped the innards of goblins from their eyes with filthy rags as they retreated across southern Yslan toward the open fields of the Arondayre. A chill ran down the Hodan King's spine with the memories and emotions of that day.

The emissaries appeared from the darkness, including two hooded figures and seven men wrapped all in black. The seven had their faces covered. They were armed with bows and short swords. They formed a circle around the two in the center.

Famlin spoke to Kairoth, who still stood at the ready. "We are here, brother. Is she all right?"

"She will manage. She is Hodan," Kairoth deadpanned. "Your Majesties, the traitor returns with his owner." His disdain was palpable as the warrior made the announcement. Orus smiled, chuckling.

"Allow them to enter, son," Orus replied.

Puryn nodded. "Bring mead," the Yslan King ordered a servant. Several bottles were brought to the fire with tankards.

"Come," Kairoth commanded. The second person did not remove his hood. Kairoth kept a close eye on him.

"I would not try anything with him, brother. If you do, you will meet your comrades in Aeternum quite soon," Famlin cautioned. The hooded figure said nothing.

Kairoth backed up to within sword range, never removing his eyes from the man. "Sit, I will back away from the fire and allow the rulers to speak without common ears listening. Famlin, you should come also."

"I do not leave my Master's side. You are not my Master." Famlin spoke plainly. Kairoth scowled, then spat, moving just outside the light of the fire. He eavesdropped despite his posturing.

"I am Puryn, son of Durn, King of Yslan," Puryn stated raising his tankard.

"I am Orus, King of Hodan," Orus stated doing the same.

The hooded figure raised his mug with one hand, tugging his hood down with the other. The jaws of both Kings dropped as he replied, "I am Harun il Arnat, Captain of the Suden remnant, also known as, the Shadow."

"Harun! You weasel! I knew not to trust you!" Orus slammed his cup down.

"Wait! Wait! Orus! Please wait!" Puryn begged. "Hear this man out." Puryn looked at Harun as if he had seen a ghost. "Is it truly you? Have YOU organized all of this?"

Famlin was indignant. "Yes HE organized all of this. He fought injustice within our lands, freed slaves and captives, and now he battles invaders." Famlin stared at both the Kings intently.

Orus drew breath to retort, but was cut off by Harun. "Please, gentlemen, we can catch up in a bit, but we need to discuss peace and how we are going to deal with the evil South of here."

Orus settled back and poured himself another mead. Puryn's eyes had not left Harun's face. Famlin was very agitated and nervous.

"Orus. You have invaded us without provocation. You have essentially split our lands in two. Of a truth, most of the northlands are unsettled and frankly, useless to us. We cannot govern them, and their agricultural value is very low. I am prepared to sign a treaty with Hodan that allows your Kingdom to retain possession of the lands of the northwest of Suden, twenty-five miles South and twenty-five miles East of the southern Hodan border. You must relinquish and return all lands East of that new border. In exchange, we establish peace and diplomatic relations with the Northern Alliance. I wish to reestablish trade immediately. Suden is in dire straits financially, but we are still a people. We are still a nation."

"Why should I give you the lands that I have conquered?" Orus ridiculed. "Come take them … oh, that is right, you cannot."

"You know that if Yslan withdrew today, we would bleed the fields red with Hodan blood. We can project power by subterfuge and trickery. We have done this for years now, and continue to kill your people with impunity. How many towns have you razed since we stepped up our attacks? None. Because YOU cannot hold them." Harun was irritated.

"Still, I see no reason to capitulate," Orus retorted.

"During the invasion, all those years ago, I ran to your people in search of a savior. You protected our remnant, and we, in turn, fought beside you, all of the way to that hill on the Arondayre … and beyond! Scarcely fifty men remain from that day, and many are my Generals now." As Harun spoke, he could see Puryn's demeanor change.

The Yslan King spoke. "Quite frankly, Harun, the Hodan would not take too warmly to giving back half of the land their men died to take. That would not bode well for the King who allowed such a thing."

"What of honor, Puryn? We were your brothers in the end, and now you are our oppressors? What grand new world did you bring for us, Champion?" Harun sarcastically stressed the final word. "My people fight amongst themselves, but I am slowly uniting them under a common banner. Yet, you would force yours above ours, as if you possess some right to invade any sovereign nation at will? Are you a God or a man?"

"Assuredly, I am but a man, Harun. A flawed one. I sought to assist my brother in quelling the outspoken in his restless warrior nation. This conquest would sate their need to show their prowess." Puryn looked at Orus. "No offense intended, brother."

"None taken, you speak the truth," Orus replied.

Puryn continued. "We also sought to quell the lawlessness of the South. First, we re-established Cinnog's rightful ruler, replaced the treacherous leadership in Edenyag, and again united the Elves and Dwarves. Suden remains a cauldron of danger and violence that raids our borders from the South. We sought to assist. Truthfully, when we invaded the barren northern plains, I did not think that anyone would care, but here we are."

Harun replied. "Imagine if Suden claimed Erynseere after the war. 'Because it was a dead and wretched place,' citing that we only sought to rebuild and establish peace. How would Yslan and history view us?"

Puryn looked at the fire and nodded. He looked at Orus. "Brother, we cannot continue here for eternity. How long before we push South and attempt to quell it all or cut our losses and make a compromise?"

Orus knew that both men were right. He hadn't really wanted to invade in the first place. Unfortunately, politics had forced his hand, and the morale of his Legion was as low as it had ever been before. "We have taken much of Sudenyag. I will accept lands fifteen miles South of Yslandeth, from the western river to the eastern river border with Edenyag. This will set a straight-lined border from West to East between our nations. This action would return more than half of the lands we have acquired, but to our advantage, provide more access to the Great Lake and to Edenyag."

Kairoth, from his listening post, could tell that Orus had contemplated this conversation many times in the past. The description of the offer was too perfect to be spontaneous. The Hodan warrior was encouraged by the fact that Orus was considering the prospect of peace long before this meeting. Then he remembered the undead and knew that no peace would be established until this crisis was dealt with. He sat silently at the ready, but it was more for a show as he continued to listen in on the negotiations. He could see Faylea was now sleeping peacefully on a mat, under a blanket, with her head on a pillow. He grimaced as he remembered pulverizing her attacker. "To the Underworld with that Suden dog," he muttered.

Harun looked at the map. He would receive almost twenty-percent more land with Orus's proposal, and Hodan got what it needed from the deal. There was nothing to lose. The North was uninhabited by Suden since the before the war. The South was where the infrastructure used to lay, and where the wealth and prosperity would once again spring from.

Harun extended his hand, nodding. "Agreed. I will accept this. No one will oppose me. If they do, then you will be contacted by my replacement." The old thief smiled. "Our political system has much that is in need of repair."

Orus shook his hand. "We shall draw up the treaties. What of the evil to the South?"

Puryn perked up, setting down his mug. "What are we dealing with? Our man says thousands of undead are coming from an old Temple?"

"Yes, we believe that events within the Temple are raising the dead. They aren't really alive anymore, though. More a walking, mindless corpse, than a living thing. It is an evil I cannot describe. They are very aggressive, but very stupid. If a small contingent of men is smart and sets up a choke point, many can be destroyed by very few. However, if they overtake you in the open, the sheer numbers ..." He trailed off. "They will tear you apart, and you will join their numbers when you die."

Puryn looked to Orus. "I think My Lady should be here. She may be able to bring the Goddess to our side directly. She has been known to converse with Haya in her meditations."

Orus agreed. "Aye, brother, if you think that she would be safe, I would welcome the light in this dark, wretched, place ... especially when dealing with evil such as this."

Puryn looked around for a moment and then saw who he was looking for. "Kairoth, please come here for a moment."

Kairoth jogged over to his King. "Yes, Sire, what do you need?"

"Tell, your druid friend—you know, the one who My Lady trained for a time—to contact her directly with the trees and inform her to join us here, in Sudenyag. Tell her everything. She will not be opposed." Puryn looked for affirmation from the warrior.

"Immediately, Sire." Kairoth departed.

* * *

Kairoth found the party around their own fire, eating and drinking. Valtyr met him at the edge of the firelight.

"How did it go?" he asked.

"It's not over yet. It looks as if a peace treaty has finally been signed, though." Kairoth smiled.

"Peace? Really!? Excellent!" Valtyr was elated, then he came back to Ert. "What is the catch?"

Kairoth laughed. "Well, Hodan keeps a chunk of Sudenyag, and we're going South to deal with the Toads again."

Brynd rolled his eyes. "Just 'us'?"

"No, the armies, the Suden and 'us' …," Kairoth said seriously. "In fact, Reynir, the King orders you to contact the Queen via the trees. Tell her of our predicament, and tell her the King requests that she travels to our location. I am sure the trees will show her exactly where we are."

"Yes, that they will," Reynir replied. "Why would the High Priestess of Haya be required to deal with a den of Todessen devout. We have routed them every time we have met them."

"Routed? Really? You think losing half of our men in three battles is a rout? I think of it as a costly engagement." Kairoth looked at the druid with annoyance.

"Well, we are doing the will of the Goddess. We are making a difference, my leader. I will contact Her Majesty and report back." Reynir left to the tree line.

"Check over your equipment. Tend to your weapons. Ladies, please restock your supplies. I have a bad feeling about this one. We are walking into the dragon's maw this time, I fear." Kairoth nodded and left.

* * *

Kairoth returned to witness the signing of the peace treaty and the handshake. Faylea was awake now and looking intently and seriously at the young warrior, who was still covered in the innards of the man who had attacked her. She wore a somber look and smiled modestly. Kairoth dared to smile back, then turned to face his King.

"Your Majesties, the druid is contacting the Queen. I have ordered my team to prepare to break camp and depart South to go ahead of the main body. Do you have any specific orders, King Puryn? If not, I ask my leave immediately to scout forward and watch for possible problem areas."

"Do as you have spoken, Kairoth. Excellent job, as usual." Puryn stood and shook the warrior's hand, surprising him.

Bowing, the warrior stepped back and left to rejoin his team. He was intercepted out of the fire circle by Faylea, who grabbed his hand as he passed.

"I was told what you did, my hero. You avenged me and protected me, knowing that thousands hid in the shadows, ready to shoot you down as you did. Why? You do not know me. You are not my subject. I flirted momentarily with you. We are nothing." Faylea looked into the Hodan warrior's eyes. He was six inches taller than she.

"First, Your Highness, you are a Princess. Second, you are a lady. Third, it is my duty. Aside from all of that, honestly, I wanted to. How dare they treat you with such disrespect. Suden dogs!" Kairoth's demeanor soured, thinking of the event.

Faylea's palm stroked the crusted blood on the rough three-day-bearded

Hodan warrior's face, freezing him in his tracks. The Princess stood on her tip toes and kissed him gently on the lips. "We are something now, if you wish it, my protector."

"She is the Princess of Hodan, you idiot," Kairoth reasoned in his head. The ground seemed to spin beneath his feet. All that came out of his mouth as he replied to her lovely face was, "I wish it."

Faylea squeezed his hand and smiled. "Do not die, warrior!" She ran off grinning, periodically looking over her shoulder to see if he watched her go. He did.

"What am I doing?" Kairoth thought. Then, gathering his senses, the leader headed back to his group. "Sal'iabac wants nothing more to do with me. There is nothing for me to feel guilty about," he muttered.

Chapter 24

Adasser paced. She was concerned. The trees had just relayed the unexpected news of Haeldrun's minions to the South, in Sudenyag. The Queen could not understand how such evil could exist on the Ert without her knowledge. "Surely, her trees had noticed something? The birds flew over, but were unaware? How did nothing that she was in communion with find this pestilence before now?" She was puzzled.

Realizing her folly, she knelt before the representation of the Goddess. She prayed and reasoned that if Haya was all-powerful and could hide things from the Underlord, surely, he, being her equal and opposite in all ways, could do the same to her. Adasser worried. The Underlord had been found out, and the King and his forces moved on the position of the Todessen followers, but Puryn had thought it necessary to request his lady's assistance with this event … something that had never occurred in their history together. "What could be so dire for him to call for her in the field?"

The Queen called to her Commanders. "Gentlemen, our King has need of us. I will travel with you to his location."

One man asked, "Where would that be, Your Majesty?"

"Apparently, Sudenyag, Sir," the Queen replied gravely.

"But, Your Majesty, your safety is paramount. We cannot guarantee you safe passage in Suden. It is a free-for-all down there! Anarchy is the rule."

Another voice protested loudly. "I will venture with you to secure your safety, My Queen."

His voice was deep and familiar. Adasser smiled without looking. "Lord Durn, you are retired. You are a farmer. Arla will be livid if you arm-up once again."

"She has the cows to keep her company until I return," the old man bantered. "I am still quite capable of wielding a sword, if that is your worry, My Queen."

The Commander present was offended. "I am in command, Sir, not you. My unit will accompany Her Majesty, and therefore, so shall I."

Adasser thought for a moment, then responded gently. "Hold for a moment, Commander. I would not want to pull more forces from our barony … so many are already present in Sudenyag and the occupied territories. I will require you to remain with the people, in case the enemy somehow makes it here. Without the Draj to protect us, the people are little more than fodder for the Todessen."

The Commander's face blanched at the statement. "Toads, Your Majesty?"

"Yes, Todessen, Sir. It would be wiser for you to strengthen Yslan's defenses and allow Sir Durn to form an Elite Draj unit to accompany me. He will provide for my personal security, while you provide for our common defense."

Relief spread across the worried Commander's face. Adasser saw it plainly. She played as if she hadn't. He replied, "Yes, Your Majesty."

"Durn, I accept your offer. Please draw your equipment and tell Arla that I am sorry. I trust your judgment, my protector." The Queen stood. Everyone in the room stood and bowed as Adasser exited the sanctuary and called out to her girls. Packing would begin now.

* * *

Adasser rode an armored, black Korinian steed. Durn ensured his Queen was armored also. She was clad in leather, per the compromise she made with her protector. The Queen would have nothing to do with chain. She complained to Durn that it was too heavy and encumbering for her to perform her magic.

Durn assembled fifty Draj men and women. All were experienced war veterans who were able foot soldiers, archers, and cavalrymen. The unit rode in a perimeter around the Queen. Every Elite wore Elfish chain and carried the standard Draj glaive and shield. Their bows hung at the ready on their saddle horns. Erynseere was a day's ride into Sudenyag when the Bedouin began tracking the Queen and her forces.

* * *

Tinan ran silently back to his encampment. There, the boy found an elder and began reporting what he saw.

"An Elfish noble of some sort comes toward us, uncle. She is on horseback and clad in leather. Is she an assassin? If so, why does she also bring fifty or so warriors to back her?" Tinan's eyes were wide.

"She is no doubt someone of interest, boy. Assemble the men and track them, but do not be detected." He grabbed the Tinan's arm as he turned to leave. "Do you understand me?"

"Yes, uncle, I understand." Tinan ran.

Speaking in a low tone to those he found, the messenger found a young man who nodded, calling others around him. A short time later, the young leader, called Dalat, and a party of twenty-five armed men left the encampment toward the location reported by the messenger. They moved stealthily toward their objective for several hours. It was only the first hour of the morning when they finally arrived at their destination. Locating the reported cavalry encampment, the band laid in wait, observing, as ordered.

Dalat saw a beautiful, black-haired Elfish woman, who sat close to a fire in the middle of the camp. All around her, men clad in bright, shining Elfish chain stood watch. They wore tabards that showed the heraldry of

Yslandeth. Half of the men slept or tended to their equipment, while the other half guarded with roving patrols. They were obviously professional warriors.

"It is an Yslandeth invasion force," Dalat said to his friend, Zalin.

"Perhaps, cousin, but there are too many of them to capture this group." Zalin felt unsure of their position. The young man's eyes darted around warily, as if something moved within the trees. "There is an uneasiness in the trees tonight. I do not know why I feel this way."

"Yes, I know. I felt that way earlier," Dalat responded. "But we cannot leave our observation post. Send Ilar back to camp. Tell him to let the Chieftain know that something is not right about this group."

Zalin nodded and silently made hand signals to a boy about his age. The boy responded affirmatively and left silently through the underbrush.

* * *

"Durn, do not be alarmed, but apparently we are being watched from the trees," Adasser said quietly while poking at the fire with a stick. "My trees tell me that there are twenty-five and that one has left to get others."

"Suden Bedouin, most likely, Your Majesty," Durn responded. "They would have detected us as soon as we entered Sudenyag. If they wished to fight, we'd be in a battle already." Durn stared off into the woods, but could see no one there.

A tree had positioned itself behind the Queen. Adasser turned and smiled at the elm. "I am in your debt, my family," Adasser said to the tree, as she glanced back over her shoulder.

Adasser looked out over the wood, sipping tea, in her armor beside the fire. She smiled and leaned back against the trunk of her large protector. Durn looked up and shook his head.

"They don't know what they are in for, Elm, do they?"

* * *

"Ilar has not returned, cousin," Zalin said nervously. "Why have they not moved their forces? It is almost midday!"

Dalat replied, "Control yourself, Zalin. It is several hours roundtrip, from our position to the camp, and back. Do you think that Ilar can fly? I do not know why they do not move. Perhaps someone is injured. Perhaps they have figured out that we are here."

"Figured out we are here!?" Zalin stammered. "Then we should attack them immediately, cousin. The camp is in danger! Our families are in peril."

Before Dalat could respond, Zalin let out a sharp cry and he was gone into the underbrush. Dalat could not determine where his cousin had gone, because the foliage was too thick.

"Zalin, you fool, where are you?" Dalat whispered with concern on his face.

There was no reply. Soon, there were other screams from the trees surrounding the clearing that Dalat observed, and then he knew that they were under attack.

"Assassins! I knew it!" Dalat said to no one, drawing a short sword. "I will not be taken."

With that, a vine shot out and grabbed both of Dalat's legs, binding them together. He thrashed violently, attempting to break free, but to no avail. Soon, the vines began pulling him backward, and others wrapped more securely around his feet. Expertly, the young man severed the vines and began running toward the clearing in terror.

"What is happening!?" the young man cried as he entered the clearing to escape the forest.

Durn and his men heard the commotion and immediately surrounded the Queen, who was still leaning confidently against her elm.

Yawning, she smiled. "Greetings, young one. Why do you stalk us as if we were your prey?" Adasser stood, and her guard moved forward with her as she walked toward the terrified younger thief. "Do you not recognize me, young one?"

Dalat was now shaking. "No, My Lady, I do not know who you are, but I know that Yslandeth's banner does not belong South of the Great White Wall. Why do you invade us? What would we possess that someone as wealthy as yourself would need?"

Durn stood silently, looking for additional threats. "My Queen, it is not safe here. We should move into the forest for cover."

Dalat's eyes widened, and then a look of abject terror crossed his face. "You are Adasser? You are King Puryn's Queen? You are the Elfish Holy Mother?"

Adasser's gaze softened as she watched the now trembling Suden warrior. He stood and looked her in the eye, proudly, expecting his death was near. She would not let him off of the hook just yet.

"I am Queen Adasser, Holy Mother of the Forest. You are correct, My Lord."

"Are my friends dead?" Dalat asked plainly.

Adasser looked at the elm that swayed. "Not yet, young one, but their fates rest in your hands."

"What am I to do, so that they may live?" Dalat responded, dropping his sword and looking down in a defeated manner.

"Nothing, but sit and be at peace with us. Can we do that?" Adasser responded smiling.

"Truly? You would let us go?" Dalat looked up with reddened eyes.

"I do not seek after death, young one. I seek to aid my husband in finding out what is wrong with the ruined Temple southeast of here. I have no desire to conquer. That folly is the pursuit of men, not Elves."

Adasser said something in an ancient tongue to the elm. It swayed as if a strong wind blew, but the air was still. "Gently, my children," the Queen said plainly. "They come, let us sit and drink tea. Are you hungry?"

Dalat tentatively moved forward, surrounded by rough-looking Draj warriors. He could hear an occasional "Oof!" and then a shout, accompanied by running toward the clearing. The young thief smiled as he counted all twenty-four of his band enter the clearing unharmed. They were met by the Draj and corralled to the side of the clearing. None dared to resist the Queen's guards. They sat on the ground and awaited death, but instead, were given water skins and bread. Worried, they looked at Dalat, who sat by the fire with the leather-clad Elfish Lady.

"We come to join Puryn, Orus, and Hassim. There is an evil South of here that consumes Sudenyag. It will soon make it's way North, East, and West, if it is not addressed. My husband thinks that since it concerns the dead and the darkness, that I may have better luck quelling this abomination by bringing Haya and her light and life to the battle. I am not sure if he is correct, but I have decided that I would entertain his request and journey here to help."

"It is true, Your Majesty. The dead walk around the temple to the South. They will consume any living thing, if given a chance. They seem to have no end." Dalat shuddered, thinking of the times that others had been surrounded by the shambling masses. There was little left of them in most cases, and those who had anything that remained of them, inevitably rose and stood on the side of the darkness, joining the mobs of shambling attackers.

"Release them!" a voice shouted from the cover of the trees. "We have spread oil within these woods, and we will encircle your encampment in fire if you do not return our family immediately!"

Dalat recognized the voice immediately. It was his uncle and Chieftain, Armash. The reinforcements had arrived, but they were unaware of the peril that stood around them.

Dalat looked at Adasser in fear. "Please, they do not know who you are or why you are here! They only know that we are captives! They only seek to free us."

"Regardless, if they burn my trees, I will see them dead personally." Adasser's eyes were red coals.

Dalat swallowed hard. He shouted, "Uncle stop! She is the Queen of Yslan! The Elf Priestess! Do not do this, I beg you. You cannot win."

Adasser stood and walked to the center of the clearing. She could see several young men, covered in oil with torches in their own hands, preparing to immolate themselves to ensure that the job was done. She shook her head, but was impressed by their devotion to their tribe.

The Queen's voice unnerved the nervous Bedouin in the wood. In a strangely Godlike tone, Adasser warned, "Burn my trees to the ground, fools, and they will regrow two-fold. Kill me, and you still do not win, for they are eternal, as is the mother of all life. They will avenge me and protect those who I love. Know this, my adversary, that I commune with all that lives upon the Ert. You will find no safe place to rest your head if you proceed with this action. Every blade of grass will betray your position; every bird will sing songs to me of where you are hiding. Nothing that you love will ever be secure again."

The hair on Durn's neck stood up at his Queen's statements as his men encircled her.

"Uncle, please, she does not bluff. We were captured by the same trees that you stand within right now! Do not do this!" Dalat was frantic.

Armash looked at the one-hundred souls he had under his command and thought about the consequences of this attack. Then he responded, "I will refrain, only if you agree to return our sons. If not, my life is not worth the breath I draw. You will die in fire and misery, but for your information, Priestess, my people have survived your reign thus far! If a power such as yours could destroy a nation—remove a people from the Ert—then it is far darker than what waits for us to the South! Should we not gather to oppose you also, just as we do them? For who is better in the end—one of the light, who would kill us, or one of the dark? Both results are the same in the end, no matter the side that does the killing."

Adasser heard his words, and they stung in her heart. He was right, and she knew it. Her eyes returned to normal, and the trees relaxed their posture. "Will you come in and talk, Chieftain? Or shall we kill each other today?"

The Draj looked fiercely toward the trees. The boys now looked to their Chieftain with worry. Armash replied, "I shall come forward to talk." He looked at the boys with torches. "If anything happens to me, burn it all to the ground." There were grunts of affirmation, and the older man walked into plain sight.

Armash stood a bit taller than Adasser. He was slightly built, but Adasser figured what he did not have in the way of physical prowess, he would assuredly make up for in skill and intellect. She could work with that.

"Please sit around my fire with your nephew, Chieftain. We have been talking about the problems to the South." Adasser motioned to her Draj to relax. They responded by backing away, but staying at the ready.

Armash sat. "We do not want war. We only wish to be left in peace, Your Majesty. Why do Hodan and Yslan invade our nation? We will not be your dogs."

"Puryn," she paused, "I mean, the King, wishes to quell the unrest and get things back to normal on the Ert. So far, he has quelled rebellion to your West and cut off the head of a snake to your East. He has brought prosperity to both Hodan and Yslan, while promoting peace and unity with the elder races. Sudenyag is the only place left that needs assistance." The Queen sipped a cup of tea, brought by her sole lady-in-waiting.

"Yslan rules all. Cinnog is a puppet, as is Eden. Hodan is his dog on a leash—for the moment. The Suden are reviled throughout the Ert, although we fought the scourge, just as all of you. We suffered the most of any people and continue to suffer now. Now, the Underlord threatens to revisit the curse of King Yanat upon us! Our King was a greedy fool." Armash sipped his tea, nodding in thanks to Adasser. "Still, I would rather die a man on my feet, than a dog under the foot of any master."

Adasser smirked, envisioning Puryn saying the same thing, if he was in the same predicament. "Know this, Suden, my King is a just man. He will return your lands to your people. Hodan is our friend. Orus is also a good man, but under pressure from those who forget what war is like. We seek to change the culture of the Hodan by showing them a new way, but that will difficult. They are Hodan, after all."

Armash chuckled. "Easier to teach a camel to dance, I would wager," the older man said dismissively.

Adasser smiled and giggled. "Perhaps we can start again? I am not your enemy, Sir. Tell them to come out and eat some bread."

Armash was a good judge of character and an expert at reading a person's face and body language. He could tell plainly that Adasser spoke the truth, or at least, she believed in what she had told him. He nodded to the Queen.

"Extinguish the flame! Drop your weapons and come forth into the clearing. Do not engage the Draj in any way. We are under a truce at this time!" Armash looked intently at Adasser, who smiled and nodded.

"Draj, stand down! These men are our guests," the Queen commanded. "Perhaps you can show us the quickest way to circumnavigate the temple and find Hassim to the South of it?"

"That will be no problem, Your Majesty. Hassim is no longer hiding. Our armies amass to the South of the temple to contain the expanding darkness. Your King and Hodan stand with another ten-thousand or more of their own. It is quite impressive to see, but we do not know if it will be enough."

"Puryn has many more men, as does Orus, my new friend. Unfortunately, if the Underlord is present on the Ert, as some fear, there are not enough men in the world to defeat him. I know that the Goddess is watching, Sir. She will have a plan." Adasser looked skyward as if questioning Haya.

"What is she waiting for?" Armash said sarcastically.

* * *

Several days passed without incident. Armash and his band led the Queen to their camp and introduced Adasser to the people of the tribe. After a bit of wariness, the people warmed up to her. The peace was greatly aided with stories of Adasser's restraint and willingness to treat the Suden as equals. After a day of getting acquainted and celebrating their new friendship, the entire caravan packed up and moved as a unit southwest to avoid the Temple area. About a week later, they had circled far enough around to see the Northern Alliance and Suden forces encamped about a half-mile South of the affected area. From their vantage point, both Adasser and Durn could see that the fields were filled with aimlessly shambling creatures.

Even from their elevated position, several miles away, Adasser felt ill from the evil emanating from the Temple. She sipped a healing potion to stem the sickness.

"It is bad, Durn," she said, looking at the warrior with concern. "I have never felt a blackness like it. We must reach my beloved and aid him in any way that we can. Everything depends upon it. If this evil fully manifests itself and is left to thrive unchecked, it will make the Offlander invasion look like a spring picnic in comparison." Adasser took a deep breath and composed herself. She looked a bit green to Durn.

"Are you all right, Your Majesty?" Durn asked with concern.

"As well as a Priestess of the Light can be in the presence of ultimate darkness." She wiped her mouth with a handkerchief. "We should go to them immediately."

"As you command, My Queen." Durn bowed with concern on his face. "Move out! We make way for the Yslan encampment on the horizon. Be wary of the undead. There may be stragglers to contend with."

"My trees have pulled back, my protector. I am glad that you are beside me now," Adasser said plainly.

"As am I," Durn replied.

Chapter 25

The Bedouin caravanserai arrived before the evening that day. Adasser's team dismounted, remaining around their Queen as she rested for a bit. Durn left to find his son. The King must know that they had arrived. Looking around, the old Commander recognized his former command pavilion. Many new banners were flying beside Yslandeth's and Hodan's, including that of the Syndicate and the new Bedouin Alliance. Durn smiled. His son had finally united the Ert. As he walked with purpose toward the entrance of the pavilion, he noticed two smaller encampments off on the horizon. To the East, the elder races had brought two Legions of their own. The Elves and Dwarves seemed to be holding the line against the evil that was trying to move further East, toward Edenyag.

The guard challenged Durn. "Halt! Who seeks to enter?"

"I am Commander Durn, of the First Draj Legion–retired, that is." Durn removed his helmet. "I must see the King immediately."

"Please stand by, Sir." One of the guards entered the tent.

There was a bit of commotion, and the flap of the tent opened widely. "Da!? What in the Underworld are you doing here?" Puryn was beside himself.

"Escorting your Queen, by her request, son. She is here and will be by to visit, shortly. In the meantime, I bring fifty Draj Elite specialists with me as her guard. May I enter to get a briefing on the current situation?" Durn stood at attention.

"Da, please, there is no time for this, please come!" Puryn responded.

Durn entered the tent. Orus, Faylea, Hassim, and a gaggle of junior Officers and Commanders all crowded around a table. They were civilly discussing battle tactics. Durn smiled again. "He *has* done it!" he thought. "Now to defeat this evil, once and for all, and see peace a reality."

* * *

Famlin cautiously approached the encampment of his former team. He paused for a moment, expecting that someone would challenge him, but much to his surprise, no one came out to greet his intrusion. He walked to the edge of the encampment and stood in open view.

"Hail camp. Permission to enter," Famlin declared loudly to alleviate any possibility that someone did not know the thief was there. He knew he was still very unpopular with his former friends.

Reynir was near the small cooking fire, boiling something in a small pot. He replied, "Oh Famlin, it is you. Come in."

"Why are you so receptive, druid?" Famlin asked with surprise.

"I simply do not get the feeling from your aura, that you are truly evil or that you tell us lies. I believe you were under duress. The rest of these people do not have the intuition that one of my training possesses." Then he rethought his response. "Except for that bear of a brother of mine, and he chooses to ignore what his heart tells him, and instead harbors a grudge."

"I heard that!" a muffled cry came from within the tent.

"Oh, of course, he hears that." Reynir rolled his eyes.

Famlin snorted. "You two never change. That is refreshing. I always know what I'm going to get from both of you."

"What is it that you need?" Valtyr asked with an annoyed look on his face, as he opened the tent flap with a loaf of bread in his hand.

"I just wanted to inform Kairoth—and Reynir—that Queen Adasser has entered the war camp and will be up at the Command Tent soon, if she is not already there." Famlin looked up at Valtyr with a serious, no-nonsense face. "This is not a regular battle, my friends, when the King of Yslan calls for his Priestess to back him—something is definitely wrong. Puryn and Orus have Yslan, Hodan, Torith, Dornat Al-Ar, and Suden to do battle on this one field. I think that there are some twenty-five thousand souls here, or more. Even Eden sends pike men. From what I am told, two-thousand arrived in the camp of the elder races at sunrise."

"That is KING Puryn, and KING Orus, you Toad," a voice said entering the camp. It was Kairoth.

"My apologies, My Lord, for my lack of etiquette," Famlin said sarcastically. "I will take my leave. I just wanted to let you know that your Mistress has arrived, Reynir." Famlin bumped shoulders with Kairoth while walking by the Hodan, receiving the worst of his attempt at intimidation.

This made Kairoth smirk and chuckle. "Ass," the Hodan said as the thief walked away and didn't look back.

Famlin silently smiled. The Hodan might forgive him yet, but not today.

* * *

Sudenyag camped together. The Bedouin made a blood pact with Irshad's former faction, sealing the peace between the former adversaries. The Syndicate collective of misfits became its own tribe under the law. There was little opposition to the merger, or to the fact that Hassim had seen fit to place his apprentice, Famlin, of the Syndicate as their new Chieftain. The new tribesmen were called Basq Il Famlis, or "Camp of Famlin." The people took to their new identity with pride and supported the hero who defeated Irshad Il Nadur and brought peace with Hassim the Shadow. Soon, the Suden nation looked to appoint a new high ruler. Someone had to become their King. A great council was called.

After much arguing and drinking—and a duel or two—the names came down to a handful of finalists. Two were old, wise men and one was the hero, known to all as Hassim. After the names were read from a scroll, declaring the candidates, the twenty-one tribes of Suden awaited their turn to be heard. As the two wise men were presented, one-by-one, to the anxious crowds of onlookers, cheers from their affiliated tribes could be heard roaring from the fringes of the large gathering, but still, there was no consensus.

Finally, Hassim the Shadow, also known as Captain Harun Il Arnat, the hero of the Battle of Arondayre, reluctantly stood before the crowds of his countrymen. After watching the reception of the other well-known and well-loved elders, Hassim doubted that there would be any consensus among the tribes, and seriously had his doubts he would fare better in the court of public opinion. He was led to the elevated podium under the hanging lanterns and in front of the bonfire that lit the circle as if it were the day. Harun's face was illuminated upon the elevated make-shift podium.

It started with the wail of a toothless old woman speaking in the Suden tribal language. She called out loudly to the gathering. Hassim understood her clearly. He bowed his head in embarrassment at her words. He was not a hero in his own eyes. He was simply a patriot who sought to heal his Kingdom.

"Behold, Suden, your savior stands before you! From the brink of extinction, he has delivered you!" Her voice fluctuated wildly, as her voice cried out to the tribes, tears now streaming from her face. "He, who saved the remnant! He, who stormed the stronghold of the Offlanders with his band! He, who slew the Commanders of the Orcs and brought their heads to the Hodan! He, who joined with the Northern Allies to defend the weak against the scourge. He, who brought the remnant he had saved safely to Empyr! This man who aided Haya's chosen on the hill, when the dragon came to save us all from the end of all things! Here is your King, my people! Look upon his face! He is our champion! In him, lies the honor and glory of Sudenyag!" She wailed, tears of joy streaming from her eyes, as her kin tended to her with a water skin. A young Suden grandson held her, as her gaze never left Harun. Her stare haunted the

Captain as his head swam.

Hassim was speechless, as forty-two men in ragged armor approached the podium on which he stood. He recognized every face. They were his heroes. The ones who stood with him upon the Arondayre. They surrounded him. They were from all of the twenty-one tribes and had, themselves, become the Chieftains and leaders of their people wherever they had returned to.

The heroes of the Arondayre spoke eloquently for their Captain, each one kneeling and rising, swearing fealty to the man who had led them in the battle against the scourge, and then in later years, helped to rebuild and heal the people of Suden. No one surrounding the podium opposed him. When the warriors were done speaking, the two wise men, who were the only opponents of Hassim, smiled and gave their endorsement of the Captain, hugging him and kissing him on each cheek.

The vote of the people was a moot point. Famlin cheered loudly with the remnant as they cried out to Hassim as one. "Rei, Rei, Rei, REI!" The sound was deafening as the remnant chose their King, fists pumping into the night sky.

* * *

Puryn sat off in his own encampment with a spyglass and several bottles of mead. He did not drink alone. Adasser, Durn, Orus, Faylea, and Kairoth were there together in the balmy evening air, drinking around the fire, as they awaited what everyone expected out of Sudenyag.

Puryn smiled. "He did it, Orus!"

"That weasel united Sudenyag, Gods help us," Orus droned.

"Oh, for Haya's sake, you old goat, give the man a break." Puryn turned, closing the spyglass and putting it in its case. "We did invade them, after all."

"Yeah, yeah, whatever, brother," Orus said to a sympathetic face on Faylea.

The girl giggled, and her father cracked a smile. "At least we keep some land, and this damned place has a chance of reconstruction with that fool at the helm. He has his uses from time to time."

Kairoth was looking at Faylea intently. She was smiling and happy. The Hodan people seemed happiest on the battlefield, around a fire, or getting drunk when there was nothing else to do. He liked this proposition more and more.

Faylea caught the warrior looking. "What? Am I growing another, head, My Lord?" she bantered quietly, snuggling closer to the warrior.

"No, My Lady," Kairoth responded a little uncomfortable that she was showing her affection overtly in front of Orus. "I simply enjoy seeing you happy."

Although the young man had tried to say his words privately, the old King heard him plainly and smiled momentarily. "He will see her smile. I can work with this."

Adasser chimed in. "Apparently, we have a new King in the neighborhood, husband?"

"Yes, My Love, it appears so. At least he is an honorable and formidable man," Puryn responded.

Orus snorted. "I have to admit, he has been a thorn in my heel, for some time. I will welcome having them killing someone else's men for a time."

Faylea scowled. "They are nothing but peasants and common thieves, father. They are not to be counted as warriors and men."

Kairoth smirked at her words. She saw him and cocked her head to the side, as if looking for an argument, but Kairoth said nothing, chuckling and sipping from his tankard. "I didn't think so," the Princess chided and then scooted up under his free arm.

Durn stood. "Your Majesties, I will depart and prepare our unit for action. My Queen, I will leave four men to guard you. Is that sufficient?"

"More than adequate, father," the Queen responded smiling. "Rest and be well. What is coming will require all of our efforts and strength. Good night."

The party in the Sudenyag encampment raged. Adasser smiled at their pure joy. They were finally a people again under one banner. Her face turned somber as she looked a half day's ride North, at the barren fields she knew contained the living dead. Closing her eyes, the Queen prayed.

* * *

The sky resembled gold in a Dwarven foundry, its burning golds and oranges illuminated by the cold white orb that slowly made its way into the sky above the horizon. The edge of the skyline appeared in dark contrast below the fiery display above. The Altyr was visible and looked to Adasser as if they were jagged teeth set against the heavens. In her mind's eye, she almost expected that upper fangs awaited their time to descend from the ethereal and bite down upon the world. Frowning, she looked to the North and could see the field full of death beginning to become lit. Shivering, she closed her cloak around her.

Puryn exited their tent with two cups of hot tea and a small tray with biscuits on it. He saw his wife's concerned looked. Smiling, he said, "They are all that I could find, My Love; we have no pastries here." Puryn smiled, knowing Adasser was not concerned about the pastries.

"It is fine, My Love," the Queen responded, taking the tankard and the hard biscuit. She sat beside her husband as they both looked northward. Startled, she felt her husband grasp her hand tightly. "What is wrong, husband?"

"I do not wish you in harm's way, My Love, but I cannot defeat the Underlord. Haya must come to meet him, or we are doomed. Even Maradwynne cannot help us now." Puryn was deadly serious.

"Do not lose faith, husband. Once, not too long ago, hundreds of thousands stood against you and your cohort. I remember that it did not go as well as they had planned. Now they skulk underground, stealing our women and children as sacrifices. Haya will not stand for this, My Love." Adasser looked up at his weathered face.

The man was entering the middle years of his life. She frowned. She knew that he could not live forever, nor could she. Even with the assurance of Aeternum, she knew that it would seem an eternity before they were reunited, once he had passed. She shook her head and put the thought to the back of her mind. Reaching up, she brushed his cheek with her hand.

"We are as ready as can be, My Love. Please pray for us," Puryn said, grabbing her hand that touched his face. He kissed it then rose and kissed her lips. "No matter the outcome, whether I live another day, you will always be my Princess, and me, your pauper."

"You were never a pauper, Chosen One," the Queen responded. "We will face the end again, and defeat it as we did the last time. Illari once told me he had no doubts the first time around! The boy is intolerable. He steals my trees now!" Adasser laughed.

"He what?" Puryn asked surprised.

"He is somehow a Tree-Talker, husband. The only male Elf to ever be such a thing. Oddities never cease with our family, it seems." She looked around carefully. "Do not tell anyone yet. He is a bit overwhelmed, but he does have command of the ring at Erynseere while I'm away."

Puryn's jaw dropped. "Well, that is an interesting turn of events. What does it mean, My Love?"

"I do not know," is all that Adasser responded.

* * *

It was the second hour of the morning. The armies were formed in perfect rectangles, readying to march northward to face the undead. There was an intangible air of dread within the ranks, but no one said anything. All stood looking forward, ready to step off at the command of their leadership. Puryn, Orus, and Durn saw a horse riding up toward their position. It was Harun, the newly crowned King of the Suden.

"Well, Your MAJESTY," Orus bellowed, "nice of you to join us!" The

Hodan King laughed. The Suden King looked at Hodan with a bit of annoyance, until Orus stuck out his hand and shook Harun's. "We are brothers, once again, Suden. All past misdeeds and rivalries are behind us. I must know who stands beside me. Are you a friend or foe?"

"I have sworn the allegiance of Sudenyag to the Northern Alliance. I have signed a peace treaty with Hodan. You have no more to fear from Suden, as long as Hodan honors its agreements," Harun replied.

Puryn's eyes widened at the Suden King's bold declaration. He coughed loudly, looking at Adasser with concern.

Orus's face twisted. "Know this Suden, we fear no one and our honor is held with the same weight that we hold for our families and those we love. We will honor the pact. Do not be concerned about the future. We must focus on today."

"Agreed, Orus," Harun replied smiling. "I just had to poke you in the eye this morning. A little payback for all of your ribbing!"

"Horse's ass, Suden!" Orus said stifling a laugh.

"Excellent, we are friends again," Puryn interjected. "Commander, send a rider to the elder races and request that they set an eastern flank. Ask them to kill anything trying to escape toward Edenyag. We shall form a square and kill them as they advance on four combined shield walls. Are we all ready, gentlemen … My Queen?"

All responded affirmatively. Puryn called out in the voice of Runnir. "FOR-WARD!"

The Commanders parroted to the formations. "FOR-WARD!"

"MARCH!" Puryn barked.

"MARCH!" the leadership echoed.

The thunderous sound of thousands of boots crunched northward on the sand and rock of the high desert terrain. Somewhere a bugler played and the cavalry formed behind the main body, at the ready.

"Here we go, gentlemen … and lady," Durn said enthusiastically.

"Did you miss this, da?" Puryn asked sarcastically.

"Oh no … not at all," Durn said setting his jaw. "I am a just farmer these days."

* * *

Glorin and Bogrol sat on the East side of the field, controlling the hordes of undead as they milled about mindlessly. Neither King had lost many men, because of the apparent mindlessness of their opponent. As they discussed battle plans, a young Elfish squire ran to their position. It was a very early morning.

"My King, My King, I must report!" the squire shouted.

"What is it, lad!?" Glorin asked with concern.

"Commander Feli has ridden off on his steed toward the graveyard." The boy's face paled as he thought of the foul place.

"Go on, boy, spit it out!" the Elfish King demanded.

"He saw a dark-clothed individual with some sort of orb, calling forth these creatures we see on the field. He went after the mage, and I fear that he may be outmatched."

The boy's sad gaze caught the King by surprise. After the Battle of the People, when Feli froze, and Puryn took command of the Draj, the people publicly forgave the loss of nerve, but in silence, many gazed upon the young disgraced Commander as if they looked on him with pity. Many still thought of him as a coward within their hearts, but since the King had forgiven him, they kept their lips sealed. Glorin knew that this was not lost on his young Commander. The weight of failure weighed heavy on his heart, and the young man waited for an opportunity to rise and show his people a hero, vice the coward they felt he was.

The King saw the young messenger's favor was Feli's. He was his squire. "Boy, your Knight is a good man. A fool, but a good man, nonetheless. Where did he go?"

"There, Your Majesty." The boy pointed to a crypt in the center of the huge graveyard. "He is there somewhere, My King. I can barely see his horse. It is still alive. I know not if Commander Feli lives."

⁎⁎

Feli hid in plain sight. He could see the necromancer and his black, but glowing orb. The Todessen was chanting and unaware that he was being observed. Undead broke through the ground near the Elf's position. He held perfectly still and avoided detection.

The orb appeared to be made of crystal or glass. It was definitely the instrument that controlled these undead minions. Feli wondered how many of these things existed, and how many mages had the power to wield them. Silently, he nocked an arrow from behind a large gravestone.

Closing his eyes, Feli visualized the position of the mage until it was clear in his mind. In one motion, the Draj opened his eyes, drawing the bowstring, standing, and releasing. Then, as the arrow left the string, he dropped again behind the stone, taking cover and avoiding detection. There was a loud yell and what appeared to be muffled attempts at cursing. Feli nocked another arrow, trying to find shadows to move into and hide within.

The Todessen priest had been hit in the neck, piercing his larynx. He was unable to speak, because he could barely breathe, with the arrow in his throat, and the arrowhead had damaged his vocal cords. Feebly, he tried to pray for healing, but there were no words. The bleeding was profuse, but the devoted priest continued to perform his mission of raising the dark army. Grabbing the orb, he used his will to direct the undead in a search for his assassin. They began to look in an organized manner.

Feli was concerned. The undead were getting closer to his location, and the Draj could not determine if his enemy had anyone assisting him who might, at any minute, come by to render aid. He decided that the time for action had arrived. He would prove his worth now or die in the attempt. Live or die, the people would know of his bravery.

Firing his second arrow in the same manner as the first, he caught the Todessen priest off-guard again, striking the opponent in the face. The arrow grotesquely passed through the left side of the man's face lodging in his upper right jaw.

"That will silence your vile tongue," Feli said with satisfaction, dropping his bow and swinging his shield around to the front of his person. He drew a Dwarven mace from a rig that held it over his right shoulder. The undead were closing to answer Feli's attacks. There were many. "Haya, bless me as I deal with these abominations. Grant me the strength to destroy this evil and to take care of its Master, who lies over there!"

Feli fought through the gaggle of corpses that shambled his way. They were not fast or dexterous enough to effectively deal with a motivated Draj. He began making his way toward the maker of the undead, who was looking worse for wear by the moment.

The Draj Commander ran leading the undead through a large crack in the wall of an old elaborate tomb. It was a large room with only one entrance and exit, not counting the damaged wall. This corralled many of his pursuers inside a confined space, leaving the undead only one avenue to approach him. The Draj warrior dispatched the remaining dozen zombies as they walked into his trap, one by one. Once all were destroyed, the young Commander turned his attention to the orb and the Todessen maker. The enemy still had two arrows protruding from his neck and face. The robed enemy laid on the ground, his hand still on the orb. Feli walked up on him with care.

The Todessen was moving his lips, but nothing intelligible was coming out. The Elf felt physically ill, and it was intensifying as he became closer to the vile object. Swallowing the bile that rose in his throat, he resolved to continue to advance toward his objective. Feli lifted his mace and hit the orb with a crushing blow. It cracked. The sound of a demonic wail emanated from its surface as tendrils of blackness leaked outward. The eyes of the Todessen touching it widened as Feli raised his mace again. The Todessen rolled over, trying to cover the orb with a look of horror on his face. Feli never stopped his second stroke, missing the orb, but instead crushing the Todessen priests head. Blood spattered on the orb, which it absorbed greedily as if it was an offering.

"Haya, help me! What is this thing!?" Feli screamed, pulling the body off of the orb and looking at it with horror.

The young Commander began beating the crystal repeatedly. After several minutes of striking the orb with unbridled rage, it finally cracked open, like a rotten egg, emitting a blackness where no light could stand. A visage of a dark being appeared and then disappeared to nothing. The fetid stench of death and decay filled the air. Feli wretched, emptying his stomach on the fallen Todessen priest.

"Who are you Elf, to challenge my Master?" an unseen voice said.

"I am the protector of my people. Who would you be?" Feli responded, summoning his last bit of resolve.

"I will show you your fate, coward of the Draj, and the fates of those who you hold dear." The voice hissed quietly, as if it only spoke to Feli. The voice sounded as if it emanated from within his mind. He was frozen in fear as he felt cold, dead fingers across his neck, just below his gorget.

"Let me go! You will not harm those I love. I will send you back to the Underworld to rot!" Feli bluffed in fear. The demon chuckled as he continued to toy with the mortal.

The Draj's heart was racing as blind fear took hold of him, but he could not run. Visions of Torith in flames filled his mind. His love, the Princess Adenya, lain sacrificed on an altar as the enemy raised her heart above their heads, as a dark spirit rose from a void within a ring behind the altar on which his beloved lay.

"No! This is not real! You will not win, vile pretender! I am Feli, and that is my love, and I will die before you kill her!" Tears ran freely from the Elf's eyes.

Feli was surrounded in blackness. He could see nothing, but the visions before him and his own person. He groped in his blindness to find a stick, but there were none to be found. Instead, he chose to wrap strips of clothing from the dead Todessen around his mace head. Groping for a flask of oil in his pouch he broke open the container, dousing the cloth.

"You will die a fool and a coward, Elf!" the voice said laughing.

"Would that I could see in this infernal darkness! I would stifle your laugh," Feli said, focusing on the anger he felt at the vision of his beloved.

"I will kill you with my own hand, evil one!"

The Draj drew a small knife. He felt around until he felt the slate stone he had hidden behind. Finding it, the young Elf proceeded to strike the blade against the face of the gravestone. He could not see well, but he knew it to be there. Sparks showed brightly from just outside of his vision. The Draj estimated where the makeshift torch was in relation. Soon, the mace head was ablaze, and Feli had light. He drew the torch beside him in an attempt to pierce the darkness.

Outside of his visions, there was a loud screeching squeal as the darkness around the Draj fell away. The Commander could see a fading black figure that looked like a ghost. It held up its ethereal hands, as if the firelight harmed it. Feli thrust the mace in the face of his tormentor. It shrieked, fading away.

Feli stood frozen for a moment, then realized that he was alive and beside the dead Todessen priest. Quickly, the Draj found some twigs and a more substantial stick. He made a small fire to illuminate his position against the dark attacker, in the case, it decided to return. Hurriedly, he rifled through the dead adversary's belongings, finding very little, but a book and an unholy symbol. He took both.

Picking up his bow, he nocked another arrow. He was now shaking uncontrollably. Fortunately, within a few moments, he was able to locate his horse. Mounting it quickly, he rode at a gallop toward the Elfish lines. It was early morning, and the sun was beginning to rise, although moments ago, to Feli, it had looked blacker than any moonless night in history.

* * *

Puryn's messenger reached Glorin and Bogrol. They devised a plan to assist the Alliance in taking the field from the undead. Unconfirmed counts were upwards of fifteen-thousand walking dead. With scarcely four-thousand Elf, Dwarf and Human warriors, the elder races were happy that they had only one front to guard. That is when Feli returned at breakneck speed toward the unit front lines. The shield wall opened and allowed the visibly shaken and exhausted Draj to pass, and he made his way directly to where the Kings sat, readying to carry out their mission.

"Sire, I must speak to you!" Feli shouted, dismounting before the horse had even come to a stop. He ran and bowed to Glorin.

"What in the name of Haya do you think that you were doing, running out ahead of the lines like a common soldier without consulting with me first!?" the King berated loudly.

"But, Sire …," the Commander objected.

"But nothing! You are my Commander. Your loss would be catastrophic to our command structure right before a major battle. What in the Underworld were you thinking!?" Glorin was livid.

Feli stood at attention. "Your Majesty," he calmly said, "I know what people think of me, and I needed to prove them wrong."

"You are well respected by Elfish society, Commander. What do you speak of?" the King lied.

"Your Majesty, I am an Elfish man, not a boy. You do not need to cover for me. I cowered when we were so severely depleted during that war." Feli's eyes watered and reddened.

Bogrol averted his eyes and felt like crawling away. He still felt terrible for the sins of his past.

"That was a long time ago, son. All is forgiven. You have served well since that one misstep." Glorin softened his tone as he looked at the look of defeat and despair on his Commander's face.

"I have never recovered, Your Majesty." Feli snarled. "Today I am redeemed. This is my first feat of penance for my cowardice that day. I found and defeated a mage of some power, who was raising the dead in the graveyard North of us. He used a crystal orb filled with vile, black magic."

"You killed a mage?" Glorin asked concerned.

"Yes, Your Majesty, and about thirty undead—oh, and I destroyed his orb, which I believe released a demon who tormented me, but I banished that one also." Feli frowned remembering his vision.

"You did all this, and yet you frown?" Glorin spoke sincerely. "You have proven yourself, Draj."

"Wait, Sire, there is more." Feli swallowed hard. "The demon put visions in my mind of despair, destruction, and death. It told me that Torith would burn, the Elves would perish, and …"

"And what? What horror could still your tongue after uttering the first two?" Glorin asked in an exasperated tone.

"Adenya, Sire. It showed me her death. That sight did not have the desired effect, Your Majesty." Feli's countenance changed. Glorin looked at his face and could see a familiar rage. One he'd seen on another Champion's face when Adasser was threatened. Glorin smiled. His other daughter had also chosen well.

"Adenya is alive and well in Torith, hero. We will kill them all, and you will be reunited with her." Glorin said this without blinking.

Feli realized that he knew about them. They had thought that they had hidden it.

"You boys do not know the extent of a father's reach when it comes to their daughters and their suitors." The King chuckled. "Wipe that stupid look off of your face, boy. I approve. You will be allowed to court her. We just need to survive and kill these vermin first."

Feli smiled, bowing. "Yes, My King. They will all die, if I have my way."

"Commander, I need a Legion to enter, engage, and clear that graveyard of all mages and orbs. Can you handle that assignment?" Glorin inquired.

"Yes, Sire. We leave immediately." Feli saluted and turned to go, then stopped. "Oh, Sire, one more thing, the dark ones hate fire. I do not know if it is the flame or the light, but something banished that demon, and it was not my mace."

"Good to know, son! Be safe! Report in when you have secured that graveyard." Glorin saluted his Commander as the young Elf left his presence.

"Well, Bogrol, it sounds like my soon-to-be son-in-law encountered a Denir this morning." Glorin shuddered at the thought. "He is lucky to be alive."

"A Denir? Like in the Underworld?" Bogrol said as more of a statement than a question. "Gods help us, all."

The units formed up and began skirmishes on the eastern flank, as requested by Puryn. Glorin could see the Northern Alliance moving to the center of the field to form an impressive square.

"Bogrol, bring the mages from Edenyag to the front lines. If Puryn has bitten off more than he can chew, or the enemy has a hidden weapon, I wish to use everything we have to give those bastards something else to ponder, while allowing for the withdrawal of alliance troops—if necessary." Glorin nodded to Bogrol, who was nodding back.

"Good plan. The only problem, brother, is that damned girl. Puryn will be furious. Princess Elpis insisted on coming to battle, against her Master's wishes, and I KNOW that her father will be furious, as will your daughter." Bogrol wiped his brow.

"You speak the truth. There will be a hide to tan over this, but we must use everything at our disposal, and Elpis will not allow her acolytes into harm's way without being present. Takes after both of her stubborn parents." Glorin pursed his lips.

"I will pass the order, brother. See you on the field." Bogrol saluted the Elf King and rode to where the mages were encamped.

* * *

Puryn, Orus, and Harun moved their forces to the desired location, South of the Temple. On a small rise in the center of the open plains, they established two Hodan shield walls and two Draj shield walls. Spearmen and archers from Suden filled the center of the square with Puryn, Orus, Harun, and Adasser directly in the center, looking out over the field in all directions. Puryn could see close to five-hundred horsemen riding in formation, counter-clockwise around the square. As he watched the

Hodan unit ride by, the King of Yslandeth noticed a standard that he was not expecting to see. The Korinian Calvary was here, and Puryn angrily raised his eyebrow, as he noticed that his son led his unit in full dress.

Puryn's head snapped around angrily. "Why is Altwidus riding with the cavalry, Adasser?"

"Truly, I do not know, My Love. Perhaps he is his father's son, after all?" Her face reflected her husband's anger. She shook her head.

"There are trees appearing on the field, My Love," Puryn remarked, as the first waves of undead began being destroyed by the roving cavalry. "Your doing?"

"No, Puryn, they will not come to me in this place. There is only one other who could be doing this." Adasser smirked. "When I get back to that castle …" She howled in laughter.

Harun looked at Adasser with a raised eyebrow. "She is enjoying herself?" he thought. "At least someone is."

Adasser suddenly shouted. "No you did not!"

"What now, My Love?" Puryn shouted against the din of metal crashing all around him.

Sighing, she looked gravely at her husband. "An eagle tells me that Elpis leads the mages with the Elfish and Dwarfish forces. "Apparently, none of our children listen very well. They take after someone I know. Next thing I will hear is that Illari is here somewhere. He had better not be!"

The enemy was thickening rather than thinning. Puryn began to worry about their position. "This is not going as planned. We need trees, or we need more firepower. I hope that Glorin and Bogrol can see our predicament."

Adasser called to her trees, but only a few very loyal ones appeared.

* * *

Elpis watched the battle as it raged. She was dressed in red robes with a white sash. She wore the headdress of a Mistress of Magic. She taught the younger Humans and Elves the ways of basic to intermediate wizardry. Most did not realize her true potential, because she studied and practiced constantly. Her love, Adalstrum, was an adept tenth circle Master Mage. He was also half-Elf and had taught in Edenyag for fifty years. He did not know that Elpis had left for war. The Master had taught the Princess well, but she knew that he would not be pleased that she had run and put herself in danger. After several years of study, Elpis was nearly his equal in all forms of magic, but fire was her forte, followed closely by electricity.

Feli had finally returned from the graveyard with a quarter of his unit destroyed. They had found three more of the mages in the burial grounds. The enemy was prepared for the intruders this time around. The returning Draj were badly injured, and some were in need of immediate medical attention. They had paid the price, but Feli and his Draj had done the job. The undead wave had seemingly stopped for the moment, but not before the Alliance square was fully engulfed in evil.

"This will not do. You four with me," the Princess ordered her higher-level students. They all mounted Draj steeds and rode out toward the front lines.

"No, you do not, daughter of the chosen," Feli said calling out to his remaining men. "Let's go, Draj! On me!!"

The Draj quickly overtook the mages and formed a line between the undead and the magic users.

"If you see fire," Elpis said, staring at Feli with her eyes ablaze, "it would be best practice to be behind me." Her hair was floating, much like her mother's did, but the Princess looked as if her mane were composed of flame.

"Move gentlemen! Move now!" Feli shouted.

The mages formed a pentagram with Elpis at the point toward the enemy.

"My students, lend me your power. We will show this evil the power of fire," Elpis said in an eerie voice. The Draj backed up as each mage put their hands on the mages beside them. Elpis still faced toward the enemy. She was calculating the distance and area of effect.

"I think that we are good. Gods help them if I am wrong, but there is no time to play with the abacus. Prepare yourselves." Elpis began chanting.

The students bowed their heads and reciprocated, echoing their Mistress.

"Infuriar culmenas!" Elpis shouted with her fingers spread outward in a fanlike shape and fired exploded from all angles before her. The field was charred, and even the rocks sizzled for a moment after the blast. An entire army of undead was consumed within seconds. Their only remnants were the bones in piles all about the eastern front of the alliance square. Elpis could see some on the alliance front lines were patting out flames on their compatriots, while others rolled on the ground to put themselves out. "Sorry!" Elpis whispered. "Oops."

* * *

The smell of burnt hair, clothing, and rotten flesh was overwhelming, but when the wind had carried away the smoke, almost half of the undead were no longer there. Puryn and Adasser looked out over the field to see a red-robed mage and four others with her.

"That is undoubtedly your daughter, Sir," Adasser quipped.

"She's getting pretty good at that," Puryn said proudly. "Her aim needs improvement but," the King whistled, "that is almost as powerful as a dragon."

Altwidus and the cavalry had routed most of the undead rabble and were cleaning up the few on the eastern flank. Trees had begun to appear in copses, and Adasser ordered them to assist in the destruction of the undead. Before long, the alliance had contained the undead threat and within a couple of hours, re-killed all of the dead who were between them and the Temple ruins.

The heads of the fallen Alliance warriors were severed from their bodies where they fell, to avoid having to meet them in battle at a later date. The brothers and sisters in arms scowled in anger as they looked northward toward the ruins. All present knew that this was only the start.

* * *

Kairoth and the team had made their way forward to enemy contact. The main body of the Alliance was at least five-hundred yards from their position and moving forward. Kairoth was frantic to get a message to the King. The team had found Todessen regulars within a depression out of sight of the main battlefield. Puryn, Orus, and Harun were walking right into a trap, and the enemy was dug in defensively with cover. There were several hundred directly in view from the warrior's vantage point, but Kairoth could not discount the possibility of how many remained in reserve underground.

"Brynd, ride to the Alliance and warn them," Kairoth ordered.

"What about the team?" Brynd countered.

"If we lose the main body, we lose the team also, Draj." Kairoth was firm.

"I am not a Draj. I am going. I don't like it though." Brynd ran one-hundred yards and disappeared from sight.

"If you are not a Draj, fool, I am not Hodan," Kairoth said under his breath.

The team hid under cover of the stones, as Kairoth tried to figure out a plan of action.

* * *

Brynd arrived late. The unit was too close to the Todessen defenses. The battle began before the Alliance was prepared. Arrows filled the air from the direction of the temple. Catapults launched stone and pots of burning oil. The square split into four units that headed in four different directions. Puryn's unit went forward with his Lady in tow.

Adasser saw the rage and destruction of battle first hand. She was sickened. Her tears fell freely as she called to her trees. More finally came to their desperate Queen's call, but only from the field that she suspected Illari had populated. Nothing outside of the battlefield seemed to hear her call. She wondered if it was the Underlord's influence that held her in check. The High Priestess could feel the terror of her forest as they lined up between the Draj unit and the enemy. The trees were never afraid until now.

Whispering to a crow, she sent her messenger. "Tell Illari, I need more trees beside me. Tell him he must send them!"

The bird flew toward Erynseere.

* * *

Illari was watching through the eyes of the trees that dared to enter the area controlled by the Underlord's minions. The young Prince was attempting to use the local animals to aid his father and mother when he spied the Todessen secret weapon. From behind a tall, ruined wall, the Prince could see where a large, shining, black being sat. It stood thirty measures tall, with a wing-span that the Prince estimated to be over one-hundred measures wide. It had four powerful claws and a maw to match. Sulfur billowed from its nostrils as its reptilian eyelids flitted open and closed, watching intently where the Queen of Nature sat. Illari had seen enough.

The young Prince cleared his mind and meditated. He searched the open spaces through all means at his fingertips until he was able to locate his destination—the perch of the Golden Queen. She was asleep.

"Lazy old dragons," Illari complained. "Wake her again, Pine."

The pine tried using the same tactics as in years gone by, but the Golden Queen's nostrils were out of reach. The tree bounced cone after cone off of the dragon, with no success. Illari was getting angry. His mother was in danger. For some reason, the black creature keyed in on her presence. He must aid in his mother's protection.

In angry frustration, the young Prince focused directly on the dragon. In his mind's eye shouted, "WAKE UP!!!"

To his surprise, Maradwynne, the Golden Queen, jolted awake with a start, bellowing golden flame from her mouth. She almost burned down the now cowering pine in the corner of the opening of her cave.

"Who wakes me!?" the dragon growled.

"I, Illari, son of Puryn, call upon you, dragon," the Prince said with authority.

"And why should I answer your call, boy?" Maradwynne snapped, yawning and blinking.

"You should first ask yourself how I called you at will. Then we can determine why I can do these things. There must be some reason in Haya's green Ert, but know this, dragon, my father and mother stand in peril at the temple in Sudenyag!" Illari was shouting.

The fact that the young Prince was frantic was not lost upon the ancient golden dragon, who sat up and looked upon the field as directed. Strangely, she felt Puryn's aura when the boy spoke. As she gazed where the younger Elf told her to look, she could see that another battle raged, and indeed two bright white souls stood in the darkness once again.

"You are his son, are you not?" The dragon smiled. "I will go and help them once again. When will your wars cease, young one?"

"When the scourge is utterly defeated, Ancient One. Thank you! Be wary! I see one such as yourself within the walls of the temple someplace, but it is BLACK, not a metallic color such as you and your family." Illari paused. "I am sure that the Underlord has not only perverted the races of the Ert. He poisons the line of dragons also, I fear. Be aware."

"Agreed. I did feel a strange presence below. I now know what it is. It is an evil without comparison in my lifetime. I will aid as best that I can." Maradwynne swept down to intercede as she had done years ago in times of peril.

* * *

The Todessen barrage was having its intended effect, and the Alliance was taking heavy casualties, as the Todessen came over the wall toward the decimated Draj lines. Hodan was circling around to reinforce Puryn and Adasser, but Orus would not make it in time. Suden was exiting the field toward the trees. Orus looked at Harun's forces with disgust, as their horses and pikemen disappeared to the relative safety of the glens.

Sighing, Orus growled. "The pathetic coward. I despise him more now than ever."

"I agree, My King. Suden is not worth the dung I scrape from my boots." It was Faylea.

"Damn you, girl, I told you to remain with the rear guard!" Orus was worried about his little girl. He knew what was coming and did not want her around when it arrived.

"I am Hodan, father, like it or not. I am here to fight. Beat me later." Faylea winked at her father.

He shook his head. "Do not die, girl!"

* * *

While the Hodan positioned themselves and moved forward, and the Todessen Generals pushed forward to engage the beaten ranks of Yslandeth, Kairoth could see the enemy dragon hiding, biding its time.

"Somehow we must give them a chance, Salia," Kairoth said plainly. "Do you have anything in your arsenal that will deal with that!?" He pointed at the large lizard behind the wall.

"I do not know if I can take down that thing," Sal'iabac said somberly. "Maybe Safiya and I can team up on it, but I don't see how we can bring it down."

"Reynir, can you use plants or some such thing to bind and strangle that thing?" Kairoth asked.

"I don't think that my plant is quite large enough. The Queen is here and a few of her trees. Mine are here also. I will relay a message to Her Majesty and tell her we seek to engage…" Reynir took a deep breath and shuddered.

370

"We seek to engage a dragon from the Underworld. How utterly terrifying. Haya help us." He left and whispered to his two young trees. They swayed.

"Well, let's go, Salia. Blow these turds to the Underworld, and I will deal with the dragon," Kairoth said sternly.

Sal'iabac laughed as a spark popped in her eyes. "Just like old times, except with dragons added. I think we should get a bonus on this mission."

Lightning rained down upon the remaining Todessen guards. They all squealed. Many fell silent. Sal'iabac patted Safiya on the shoulder. "Your turn, sister!"

* * *

Puryn's Draj were holding the lines as they back-peddled toward reinforcements. Hodan's horns were blaring, announcing their arrival. Regardless of the reunion, the Alliance was sorely outmatched. To make matters worse, a new menace had joined the fight. In the sky above, a large, black dragon had just taken flight.

Adasser called to all life within her vicinity, and she was answered by a new strange call. Elephants. She had never spoken to an elephant before.

"We come, Queen," the head bull answered. "Our Masters ride us into battle."

"Who are your Masters, bull?" the Queen asked.

"The South men," it replied, as the Queen looked to the West and saw at least fifty elephants with spearmen riding them. In the front was Harun with his Elite guard.

Adasser looked at Orus with raised eyebrows. The Hodan King answered. "I stand corrected, Adasser. I hate him less now." Orus smiled as the elephants crushed rows of Todessen warriors. "But what of that thing?" Orus asked, pointing at the now hovering dragon. It had found something of interest to the northeast of their position, near the temple.

Orus saw him, and his jaw dropped. "What in the Underworld is that boy doing?"

Faylea's jaw dropped in abject horror, but she could not help but swell with pride, as the dragon dwarfed the visage of the tiny armored Human. "Oh, my Gods, Runnir be with you, Kairoth."

* * *

Kairoth stood in plain view of the dragon, sword and shield at the ready, as his mages killed any Todessen within range with impunity. The dragon reared back, ready to breathe fire upon the lone warrior who was now covering up with his shield and charging toward the dragon, which hovered less than ten feet above the ground.

"Salia! Now would be a good time to kill this thing!" Valtyr shrieked, readying his healing potions as he watched Kairoth charge in. "Is he mad?"

"I think so," Reynir stated. "Do not be alarmed, brother, I am going to do something that the Queen taught me years ago. I saw no need to do it until now." Reynir removed his clothing.

"Get your clothes back on! Now is not the time to commune with nature!" Valtyr protested.

Reynir smiled. "Now is a perfect time!" Reynir prayed and said some words that Valtyr did not understand, but when he was finished, there was a large tiger where Reynir once stood. It growled quietly and winked at Valtyr.

"Is that you? Scratch with one paw." The cat scratched. "Oh, my Gods, that is an excellent trick, brother. Where are you going!?"

Reynir leaped toward the Todessen, who were using the dragon as air cover, tearing the enemy to shreds as he defended Kairoth's flank from additional foes. As the druid did this, the dragon let loose with his breath. Sal'iabac muttered something quickly, throwing her hands in front of her, and the fire breathed on Kairoth was split around him. The warrior looked over his shoulder in horror to see the fire hit the mage squarely as she held the shield for as long as she could. Sal'iabac fell to the ground, badly burned and unconscious.

"Noooo! You spawn of a whore!" Kairoth shouted like the voice of Gunnir, and turned to the laughing dragon. The Hodan charged and stabbed, but the scales were too hard to break.

Valtyr hurried to Sal'iabac. She was not breathing. He prayed, but nothing happened. Valtyr sat dejected on the ground. Tears welled in his eyes, but then deep anger overtook the usually pious priest. He stood stoically and prayed a blessing upon his group, then waded through the death up next to his brother, Reynir, who was now surrounded by Todessen warriors and priests.

Valtyr scowled. "A curse be upon all of you! May Haya purge your filth from the land of the living once and for all. Be gone!" The Todessen looked up at Valtyr, who had begun speaking in ancient tongues. His person began to glow in white light. The priest turned his direct attention to Todessen, who now watched from the circle around Reynir. "I said leave or die."

"We choose to stay and fight," they responded.

"As you wish," Valtyr said in an ethereal voice. "Dei manut deax!"

When the priest said these words, twenty Todessen warriors immediately fell dead at his feet. The five remaining Todessen, seeing this, ran into the temple. Valtyr figured that they ran for reinforcements. Reynir stood nude, having transitioned back to his normal form. He was winded and injured. Valtyr grabbed his brother and dragged him back to his equipment. The dragon had taken a keen interest in one who could call to death and have it do his will. It refocused on killing the priests.

"Hello! Horse's ass above me!" Kairoth taunted. "Pay attention to me. I owe you for killing my friend! I will wear your scales as my armor."

The dragon turned its attention to the shouting below it. "As you wish, Human fool."

The black dragon reared back for an attack, as Kairoth covered behind his shield. The Hodan warrior looked for his opening, but before he could attempt his attack, a bone-shattering roar shook everything around him. The black dragon suddenly lurched to one side, slamming up against a stone wall. The Hodan warrior instinctively hit the ground and covered up. Something immense and golden had just flown by. Rolling over, the Hodan warrior shook his head to make sure he was conscious. A much larger and much angrier golden dragon was on top of the black one and tearing it to shreds.

While the two thunder lizards struggled on the ground, the smaller black one wriggled free and took to the air again, spraying black fire down on the golden one. The golden one let out a roar of pain, angrily taking flight. There, above the party, an aerial battle began. Fire erupted in the forests as Adasser's trees were mown down randomly. The Queen called out to her forests, ordering them to move to safety.

* * *

Maradwynne returned and found her mark, finally scorching the black one so badly that it lost the ability to fly, and slammed into the ground from fifty feet up in the air. The armies watched with wide eyes. Pouncing again, the golden dragon began tearing furiously at the throat of the black dragon. Kairoth could see that his delay had worked. Puryn pulled his forces back to a safe distance. The Alliance was regrouping to the West of the field. They had lost half of their forces, but were setting the shield wall to respond. The Todessen were now fighting the trees, and Adasser was exacting her revenge remotely.

The Eden mages moved under cover of Feli's unit to within range of the Todessen front lines. Using lightning, which was not the first choice of Elpis, the ten Eden mages present dispatched the rest of the Todessen without much resistance. The Draj killed any who dared to try to get within melee range of the casters.

After a drawn-out struggle, the golden dragon finally found an opening, firmly grasping the throat of the smaller black dragon. Maradwynne twisted the younger foe's head at an unnatural angle. The entire field who watched heard a loud audible "crack!" and the black dragon fell silent. Immediately after the fight, the golden dragon fell on its side, panting wildly.

Puryn and Adasser rushed to Maradwynne's side. The older golden dragon was badly injured and exhausted.

"You cannot die, Dragon Mother!" Puryn said sadly.

"It is but a scratch. Dramatic Humans!" Maradwynne bantered.

But Adasser knew differently. "You are injured, protector. I am the Holy Mother of the Forest. Allow me to heal you the best that I can."

"Please, Elf, do as you say. I am too weak to stay on this field. The evil is still here, it was not the dragon as I had suspected. It lives within the ruins before you. You must go in and root it out!"

Maradwynne laid her head down, and Adasser touched her cool scales. The Elf could feel the dragon's pain and wept silently as she prayed for healing. Slowly, over an hour or so, the dragon was healed well enough to allow her to fly. Adasser was exhausted and slept on the field under guard.

"I must go home to rest and heal, Champion." Maradwynne growled toward Puryn. "Protect your Queen. She is the avatar of Haya on the Ert. She is truly the Queen."

"I will, my protector. Please, go to your home and heal well. Thank you for your assistance. I do not think we were up for fighting a dragon this day. We will regroup and refocus on our mission. Be well, Maradwynne."

The dragon lit off up into the sky, just as she had done many years prior. Puryn's skin crawled remembering that day.

In a fog of recollection and emotion, the Yslan King called to Orus and Harun as his dragon lifted out of sight. Memories would have to wait. They needed to figure out what the next step was.

* * *

Illari was relieved. More and more trees began answering the call. He sent them to his mother, as she had requested. The forest was unaware that their Queen called to them. Illari relayed her message, and the field was now covered in small glens and copses. A tree wall formed around

Adasser as she slept. The Kings planned their next attacks.

Illari watched as his little sister destroyed entire ranks of the Todessen. He smiled proudly. "Watch after that one, trees, but be careful. She likes fire. Trust me on this."

* * *

Kairoth was in shock. He had never seen a dragon before, let alone two. He had never seen anything as powerful and intimidating as two building-sized creatures trying to kill each other. He had stood on the field against thousands of hostile enemies before, but a dragon was the definition of power and violence. The Hodan warrior looked down at the burned remains of his former lover and friend. He had no idea where Brynd was. Reynir was battered. Safiya wept openly for her sister. Valtyr was quiet and brooding. All werewas cut to the heart.

The young Hodan questioned everything he had been taught. He burned for vengeance and revenge. His hatred was complete. He wanted the corpses of the Todessen to reach Aeternum, so that Haya could smell the death that she allowed right under her nose. He wanted the Goddess to know the pain that she had caused, or at least allowed. A dark mood came over the Hodan warrior. He was fed up and ready to retire … but first he fantasized about killing Haeldrun himself.

At this rate, he did not doubt that the opportunity might present itself. The Todessen had brought everything else, why not the Underlord.

Chapter 26

After the dragon fight, and when it was determined that the Todessen front guard had been defeated or retreated, the Northern Alliance pushed its advantage. The red sun sunk behind a bluish gray horizon, its rays illuminating the field with a fiery, red tint, as if the field was not red enough with blood already. All along the dusty windswept field, corpses adorned the ground—Some new, some old. Thankfully, none of the dead stirred. The Generals surveyed the situation and advised their Kings that it was too late to mount an additional offensive. The armies needed to tend to their wounded and rest. The night would soon be upon them.

Adasser woke from her slumber. She could see the men setting immense bonfires with the wood that her trees gave willingly. A large, but thin tree ring had formed around the armies. The Queen knew that it would not stop an advancing army, but anything that tried to covertly harm the Alliance forces tonight would be in for a rude awakening. She saw her beloved directing his Generals.

"That man never stops," she thought. She spoke, "Puryn, I require water and food, please."

"At once, My Love," the King said, aiding his lady as she sat up. "Get the Queen a decent meal and some water, Squire!" the King ordered. The young man ran to the kitchen tent.

"Maradwynne stated that the black dragon was not the evil she felt from her perch. I am worried, husband. What awaits us all in that cave?" Adasser frowned.

"I have you to back my men, My Queen. The dragon has come to our aid and cleared the path to enter this evil den. I can only ask for the guidance of Haya from this point forward. Or the strength of Runnir and Gunnir." Puryn winked at the Queen, who smiled.

The squire arrived with the Queen's food, and she sat and ate, regaining her strength. She would have to be ready. She feared that the morning would bring with it, her biggest challenge to date.

* * *

Kairoth looked over at his remaining team. Brynd had survived and returned shortly before the camps were set. The priest and druid were binding wounds and eating. Safiya stood vigil over the body of her sister. She had wrapped her body in finer clothes and set a small bag of coins by her side. A staff, a small book, and a bag of reagents were also laid beside the fallen mage. Finally, Safiya draped a fine cloak over her sister. Kairoth grimaced, as if in pain. He envisioned the younger mage as tucking her in for bed. He shook his head in grief and in disgust, looking toward the skies with malice. This was all that was left of the original ten—five, and one traitor.

Valtyr stood beside the bundled sticks. Reynir had spread oil on everything. Kairoth rose, filled a tankard with mead and set it beside the mage, wrapping the stiff, burned fingers around the handle.

The Hodan warrior bent beside the body, whispering, "To keep you warm beside the fire in Aeternum, Salia. Rest well, and thank you for saving my life. I will never forget it—ever."

The warrior stood, frowning. Valtyr approached, saying the appropriate prayers and benedictions. He looked toward Kairoth. "Do we wish to say anything before we proceed, brother?"

"What is the point, priest? I used to feel as if we mattered—we were making a difference. Now, we stand beneath a silent sky and burn, yet another friend, no, even worse, someone who I loved." Kairoth made a profane gesture to the sky. "We are little more than toys to the Gods. Haya cares only for herself and her will. It does not matter who dies to make it so."

"You do not mean that, brother," Valtyr responded somberly. "You are grieving. The Goddess understands."

"She understands all right, priest. She is the reason for all of this. Why has she not raised her ass from her gilded throne and come down here and handled this brood personally?" Kairoth rose as he addressed the group. He snorted, then continued. "Because we are a means to an end, brothers and sisters, and we are of little more worth to her than the beasts of the field … if we even amount to that."

"Kairoth … wait," the priest begged.

"Save it for your proselytes, Valtyr. I am not buying the Temple stories any longer. I have seen too much that contradicts 'the truth.'" Kairoth waved his hand dismissively and grabbed a wineskin filled with mead. "I will be on the lines looking for the damned Todessen. Gods help any who I find."

Valtyr nodded as the warrior faded into the surrounding darkness. The priest looked over at the druid, who shrugged.

"Let's send her to her reward, brother," Valtyr said hopefully.

"Yeah, her reward," Reynir said sadly with a hint of sarcasm.

* * *

Kairoth drank his mead and looked at the familiar cave opening through Adasser's tree line. It was the same thing as always, except this opening was four times the size of the smaller dens. Off in the distance, he could hear the drums of Famlin's tribe. Shaking his head angrily, he thought of what he needed to do to serve his King effectively.

Finishing the last sip of mead, the warrior stood and walked to the Suden

Tribal Circle. Muttering, he said, "Salia, they will pay. You did not die for nothing. I will have my revenge."

A sentry on guard challenged Kairoth as he came within twenty yards of the camp of Basq Il Famlis. "Who are you who approaches?"

"I am Kairoth, a former friend of your Chieftain, boy. I must speak with him if he is willing."

The boy muttered a foreign tongue to two other guards who revealed their positions and came forward. Kairoth was impressed by their stealth.

"Wait here, Hodan. We know who you are. I will get the Chieftain." He left.

Kairoth waited. Within moments, the boy returned with Famlin, who was surprised to see the Hodan warrior.

"What do you want, Hodan? You smell like you have drunk a brewery. Are you drunk and seeking to fight me for the wrongs you feel that I have done? That would be unwise, because my people would tear you to shreds."

Famlin sounded strangely serious and confident.

Kairoth smirked. "You always had the heart of a bear, Suden, although I would never admit it to you before tonight."

"Enough banter, I have things to do. Why are you here, Kairoth?" Famlin demanded.

"The dragon killed her, Famlin. Salia is gone. I wanted you to know." Kairoth choked and composed himself. "We will enter that cave tomorrow as we have done in other places, many times before. You know what waits for us. This one looks to be a bit more challenging than the last couple that we all faced. Now I am down another formidable friend and soldier."

Famlin's face twisted into a frown. "Salia." His head bowed. "Who remains of the original ten, brother?"

"Brynd, Safiya, Reynir, Valtyr, and myself," Kairoth droned sadly. "And perhaps … you. If you would join us for this last push toward Gods know what."

"I am a Chieftain now, brother. I have responsibilities," Famlin stated as a matter of fact.

"Do not worry your head, Suden. We will manage," Kairoth said bowing.

"Your Excellency, I will be in our usual camp, outside the main body, where we continue to be conveniently ignored, and our existence denied. Good night."

The Hodan warrior staggered back to the party encampment and went to bed.

* * *

The sun rose. It had begun to rain lightly, and the mist gave a foreboding look to the already terrible scene around the army. Puryn stood in a small circle of Commanders, including Kairoth, Altwidus, and Elpis. Both children of the King looked at each other nervously.

"Commanders, we will send in our strike teams first. They will do their best to use stealth to weaken the enemy fortifications." Puryn looked at Kairoth and a couple of men and a woman who Kairoth did not know.

Everyone nodded. Kairoth sighed and kept his mouth shut.

"Commanders, ready the armies in shock teams of twenty-five or thirty. They must be ready to fight in close quarters. Make it so. Be blessed, my heroes. Haya is watching."

Kairoth snorted quietly, but it was not lost on Adasser, who watched his demeanor intently. She whispered to Puryn, who looked up at the Hodan man for a moment. The King looked unconcerned and shrugged, dismissing his wife's concerns. Puryn knew Kairoth and his devotion. He did not question him in the least. The Commanders left, as did the specialist team leaders.

"You two, stand fast!" Puryn commanded Altwidus and Elpis. The two sighed, closing their eyes. Here it comes.

"Father, wait," Altwidus began.

"Wait, nothing! I am here conducting operations, and unbeknownst to me, my two disobedient spawn are on the field, putting their lives in harm's way?!" Puryn was yelling. "Who in the Underworld will take the throne if I fall and then your mother also does? Do you think that this is a game?" The King leered angrily at his two children, who looked at the ground.

"I am a rancher, father. I will not dispute that fact. However, if you think that I will watch my family go into battle and sit on my throne in Korin, well then, you don't know who you raised." Altwidus was offended.

Elpis added to her brother's retort. "Would you rather I send my young apprentices to a place where I would not tread with my own boots? That is not what you told me that a leader does, father." Elpis leveled her gaze at the King, who pursed his lips.

Adasser, off near a cart, snickered at the comments, taking a sip of water from a skin.

"You, be quiet, woman. They take after you!" Puryn said to his wife, who now openly laughed at him.

"Oh yes, it's MY fault." Adasser made a face at him and then walked off to talk to her trees.

The Prince and Princess stood in front of their father. Puryn's anger was fading. In his mind, he saw them as children, and he could not separate the memories from the reality that stood before him. They were grown. They were honorable, but they were young and idealistic.

"Thank you both for your assistance. I love you both and only wish to see you safe. Your contributions both saved lives and made me proud, but please do not make my heart worry this way again. Stay with the rear guard and let us handle the rest of this." Puryn looked at the reluctance on their faces.

"But, father …," Altwidus objected.

"Wait. Let me finish. In the event that we fall, it will be your responsibility—both of you—to finish the job. I am not sending you away. You are my reserves in the case the main attack fails. Please do not die." Puryn frowned, kissing his daughter on the forehead and hugging his son tightly.

Soberly, both replied, "Yes, father."

Puryn heard activity ahead of them coming from the Todessen hive. The specialists had begun their assault. It was time. Looking over his shoulder at his children one more time, the King mounted his horse and rode to the front.

* * *

Famlin arrived at the specialist camp to the surprise of everyone present, except Kairoth. The Hodan had hoped he could inspire the thief. He knew that what the younger man lacked in prowess, he made up ten times in subtlety and subterfuge. He would be a great asset to take into the den with the team. Kairoth also knew that the thief loved his friends and held them with a loyalty akin to family. Something terrible must have gone wrong to draw him from the team. Kairoth was unsure, but put his doubts behind him as he saw the specialist packed for war.

"Is the offer still open, Hodan?" Famlin asked, smiling at Kairoth.

Kairoth nodded. "Sure, Suden. Come join us in our quest to meet the maker!"

Reynir laughed at the dark joke, watering his plant. Valtyr was unnerved by the comment, but had a strange new resolve. Brynd strung his bow and snorted sarcastically, while Safiya quietly packed her reagents off by herself. Her eyes were red, and her face blank. This was not lost on Famlin, who frowned, staring at the mage.

"We will make them pay, Safiya," the Suden said plainly.

"She will still be dead, Famlin." Safiya wiped her eyes.

They rose to enter; two other teams had entered already, and it was not going well for them.

"Damn rookies," Brynd quipped.

* * *

The team had been in the tunnels for two hours. Puryn and Orus were holding back their forces. Kairoth had no idea why. He guessed they were waiting for a messenger to tell them the way was clear. Kairoth did not intend on leaving until the head of Haeldrun's High Priest was on a stake. The Hodan was on his own personal mission.

The specialist and the ranger were as deadly as ever, setting charges and traps everywhere they were given an opportunity. The enemy was falling back and regrouping. The team had dispatched a score of Goblins, a dozen Orcs, and at least ten Todessen. So far so good. Kairoth was pleased. None of his were dead yet, but the attack was still on-going.

The thief ran down a darkened passageway toward Kairoth.

"Hey, boss, there is a larger room ahead." Famlin looked at the faces around him.

"Where is the ranger?" Kairoth demanded.

"Covering my retreat to notify you of the situation. He has cover and is doing that Draj hiding trick," Famlin said shrugging.

Kairoth nodded. "Good work. Can you use the powder to soften the room for me?"

Famlin nodded. "I have three good charges left."

"Do it," Kairoth ordered.

The thief nodded and padded away silently to where the ranger stood guard.

"Psst, it's me, don't shoot me, ass," Famlin quipped.

"Keep it down, fool," the ranger hissed, whispering.

Famlin pointed at a cask with steel coils fastened to the outside of it. "Can you still hit a moving target?"

Brynd rolled his eyes and nodded, gesturing toward the room. "Make it a good throw. We do not need back blast."

"Agreed," the thief said, hurling the cask as far as he could into the middle of the dimly lit room.

"Loosed! Hit the ground!" Brynd said, lighting an arrow on a torch in a sconce and shooting the cask.

There was commotion for a moment as the Orcs and Todessen present saw movement in the hall, then an ear-splitting explosion. Smoke filled the room and part of the passageway. Brynd stood at the ready against one side of the hallway—Famlin, armed with a short-sword, on the other. Nothing came down the hallway toward them.

"I guess we got them all?" Brynd questioned.

"Or the survivors ran," Famlin said with concern. "They are setting us up, or running interference for something else, brother."

Brynd nodded. He had suspected the same thing after an hour in the passageway.

* * *

Troops had massed outside of the entrance to the Temple. The weather had taken a major turn for the worse. Much of the army was forced to find shelter, as high winds and hail the size of apples fell at times. Many were injured while they waited for their call to enter. Adasser could see that things were getting out of hand and she knew that this was the work of evil. She did not like the look of the clouds that were moving toward their position. Lightning lit the skies nearby, striking at the ground like a serpent.

Adasser called to her favorite elm. "Please, old friend, shield these people from the weather. Thank you for your service and your sacrifices!"

The trees encircled the armies and filled in the center, setting up a thick canopy over the remaining Alliance troops who rested between their trunks.

Puryn nodded with approval. "Good solution. We have twenty Draj, and Orus is on our left flank with twenty Hodan. It is time we entered and assisted the specialists. Surely, they have cleared a space where we can establish a foothold."

Orus overheard the comment. "I agree. Let's get in there, brother. We do no good out here in this damnable weather.

The army entered, two by two. Orus insisted that Hodan lead. Puryn shrugged. He knew how the argument would go. He simply agreed. Adasser was toward the end of the procession. After navigating several twisting passageways and ninety degree turns, the Kings could hear combat ahead of them.

"Orus." Puryn nodded.

"I can hear, Puryn!" Orus rolled his eyes and smiled. "Carefully, boys and girls, do not charge in and lose your life without cause! For Hodan!"

"For Hodan," the twenty said in a subdued response.

"Luck and honor, Yslan," Orus said to his brother.

"Luck and honor, Hodan," Puryn responded.

Within moments, the Hodan Elites met up with what was making all of that racket.

* * *

The specialists entered the large room. It was a garrison post. A few tattered bodies remained on the floor, but Kairoth knew that more had to be in the area.

"Stand ready, there are not enough bodies in here. More are around here somewhere." Kairoth looked at his clean blade. "I have not drawn enough enemy blood today, but I think that things are looking up for the prospect."

Brynd had twenty arrows left. He counted them and checked his bowstring. A loud racket came from down the passage ahead of the team.

Kairoth looked at Brynd. "I may need your shield soon, brother. I am the only swordsman we have left, unfortunately."

"Twenty arrows and I will be right there beside you, brother," Brynd joked.

"Make ready, my friends, here they come," Kairoth said, pulling his shield in front of him.

The enemy came en masse. The largest entered first with huge mauls and clubs. They were Ogres. Behind the forward lines of the enemy, followed several Orcs, then a gaggle of Goblins and Todessen.

Kairoth smiled. He had fought these vermin many times in the past and he no longer feared them. They held no mystical power over the Hodan warrior. They were simply large, smelly mortals who needed to die. The Hodan would fulfill the need.

"Aw, damn, here he goes again!" Brynd shouted, looking at Kairoth. "Mage! Stand by! Priest be ready! Where is the specialist?" Brynd smiled broadly. "Doing his thing, no doubt!"

Safiya managed an abbreviated smile and said words touching her own chest. A blue coating shown over her for a second and disappeared. "Time to die, pigs."

Reynir ran forward, just behind Kairoth, and threw his potted plant against the ground. "You are on your own, friend. Destroy." The plant responded, growing as the druid nonchalantly began disrobing.

Safiya raised an eyebrow.

Valtyr smiled, then rolled his eyes, and said, "The cat will be the druid. Do not kill him! He is on our side."

"Thanks, brother, be safe! Fight well for the Goddess!" Then Reynir said words that only he understood. Soon, a tiger stood where the druid once was. Roaring, it attacked anything trying to come through the door to aid the Ogres and Orcs. The Goblins formed a shield wall in the passage. Reynir paced, looking at them. As a tiger, he was twice the size of the average Goblin, and none of the enemies seemed ready to attack of their own accord.

"You wish to block the passage? Better for me! Reynir, back up!" Safiya shouted, and the tiger backed away, watching the Goblin shield unit as he went.

Safiya glanced momentarily over at Kairoth, who had one Ogre down and had just hamstrung his second. The Orcs already lied in a pool of their own entrails. Kairoth was getting into his job again. The mage was unnerved by the shouts of rage and maniacal laughing the warrior emitted while dispatching the enemy. His vulgar terms never ceased to amaze her, as the Hodan waded through the superior numbers with apparent ease. Safiya often wondered if Runnir had claimed that one, or perhaps Gunnir. She turned her attention back to the shifting wall of Goblins. There were more, and they were getting braver by the second.

Safiya's hair floated. Electricity popped between her locks and static arcs shown in her eyes. "Move, druid," she said, raising her hands.

Reynir pounced on the back of the Ogre who Kairoth was pulverizing, moving completely out of the mage's way. The Goblin leader smelled the ozone in the air and began screeching commands, but it was too late, as bolts of lightning filled the hallway. The smell of roasted flesh and burnt hair filled the chamber.

Safiya was not the worried younger sister any longer. She was angry. She wanted them all to die. "For Sal'iabac, you vermin. Be happy it is I who you deal with, and not she."

Explosions could be heard ahead of the party as the room was cleared of combatants. Reynir stood nude near his equipment, as the Hodan forward team found the specialists. Soon, all of the expeditionary units were in the large garrison area.

Puryn's brow furrowed at the sight of a nude druid who was dressing.

"Do not worry, husband. He must have been shape-shifting. It is normal for our kind," Adasser reassured.

"Do you do this?" Puryn asked.

"Oh yes! Nothing like flying in the form of an eagle, My Love." Adasser smiled. "What is exploding ahead of us, husband?"

"That is an excellent question, My Queen." Puryn turned to Kairoth, who was still beating a dead Ogre. "Kairoth! It is dead! You cannot make it deader, boy!"

Kairoth looked up, as if waking from a dream. "Yes, My King!" he replied, shaking it off.

"What is going on ahead of us? Explosions?" Puryn asked.

"I am not entirely certain, Your Majesty, but I would wager it is Famlin of Sudenyag, killing the enemy with fire." Kairoth smiled, his gory face revealing perfect teeth.

Adasser nodded and stepped behind her husband, as a precaution. She felt a strange aura emanating from the Hodan. "Runnir?" she questioned herself and then remembered when Haya once stood by Puryn. The Queen swallowed hard. Something bigger than Todessen was happening here.

"Well done, specialists. Regroup and gather yourselves." Puryn glanced over at Reynir, who was now dressed and finishing buckling a vambrace. "We continue in fifteen minutes … unless they come for us first."

* * *

Famlin had made his way down the passageway before the Goblins became too thick. The party was handling the patrol without effort. The thief decided to scout farther ahead. He killed a couple of Goblins on his way down the long dimly lit passageway. At the end of the road, there was a large wooden door with wrought iron hinges. It was not locked or barred. The thief oiled the hinges, praying that they were not too rusty, then he opened the door toward him, just enough to peek inside.

It was another sanctuary to Haeldrun. This one dwarfed anything that he had seen to date. Off to the side, he saw troughs full of leathery orbs of some type. To the right, were the customary vats where he knew the vermin disposed of the bodies and parts of innocent sacrifices. In the center of the room, was a raised, black, stone altar with the body of a Humanoid victim on it. To the left and right of the altar, were two fifteen-measure tall statues of demons and to the rear of it all, a twenty-five-measure statue of a dark figure with burning red eyes. Famlin shuddered as he looked at the statue. The eyes seemed to pierce his soul as they appeared to follow him as he moved. The room smelled of death.

"I must tell the others," the thief thought.

As he turned to go, he could hear an enemy patrol approaching.

"One left after this. Better make it count."

Famlin lit the fuse and rolled it down the passageway with precision. He took cover as best he could. The explosion rocked the hallway and disoriented the thief, who tried to stand immediately, then fell three times before he could manage to regain his balance. The thief heard the wooden door behind him banging against a metal spike he had left in a hole in the rock, as a precaution against surprise enemy visitation. He knew it wouldn't hold for long. He ran through the tattered remains of an Ogre patrol. This was the main enemy headquarters. Famlin assumed that their Elite warriors would be in the sanctuary to Haeldrun, and now they were coming for all of them.

* * *

"I found it! I found it! To arms! To arms!" a familiar voice was yelling frantically while running full speed toward the last location of his team.

Kairoth recognized Famlin's shrieking. "Hold you fire, Hodan! That is my specialist," the gore-covered warrior stated plainly.

Famlin ran on the wall and flipped expertly over the Hodan lines, as one of the Elites looked up in wonder at the movement of the thief. Nodding, the shield man reset his gaze down the passageway. Many growls echoed in the passageway.

Reynir smiled at his plant that now covered the entrance to the room. Puryn watched as he whispered to the leaves. The plant shimmered like a wave. The druid smiled again, nodding. Adasser saw her apprentice, thinking nothing strange of his actions.

"What, husband?" she asked.

"He is talking to his plant," Puryn said plainly. "It responds to his words."

"He is my student, husband. A good student. I fear he needs no further instruction. He will ask to leave and be his own man soon." Adasser frowned, but then her smile returned. "Good for him! Watch how his simple plant becomes a formidable warrior in its own right."

The enemy consisted of eight Kvern, who led the way. Behind them, were six Ogres, five Orcs, and twenty Goblins. Two Todessen stood to the rear and directed the forces. They wore robes.

"Commanders in the rear in robes, Kairoth," Famlin shouted pointing.

"Got it. Brynd shut them up," Kairoth commanded.

"As you command, boss," the ranger said, loosing several arrows.

One of the robed individuals was hit several times, but remained alive. The second figure laid hands on him and healed the wounds.

"Kairoth, at least one is a priest! I almost killed one. The other does the same as our priest. He's a healer. Not sure if the one I hit is a ..."

Before he could answer, Brynd was hit by a barrage of energy bolts, dropping him to his knees. The ranger looked disoriented and had dropped his bow. Valtyr ran to where the ranger fell, dragging him out of the field of view of the enemy mage.

"Safiya, you have competition over there. Can you roast the one to our right?" Kairoth asked gruffly. "The ranger already damaged him pretty well. A well-placed bolt might take him out of the equation."

"I'm on it, Kairoth," Safiya said before chanting. Pointing, she released a barrage of her own bolts, knocking the enemy mage off of his feet. He did not move. The priest checked the fallen. He was not getting up this time.

"Yes!" Kairoth taunted, looking at the priest in the back row. "Here kitty, kitty! Come to Kairoth." Kairoth pointed at the dark priest and made a throat-slashing sign. The priest looked down the passageway and left swiftly.

"Priest! The condition of the ranger?" Kairoth shouted through the Hodan din as they responded to the Kvern advance.

Valtyr's long face said all that was necessary for Kairoth to know.

Looking at the floor a moment, the warrior looked at his friends and closed his eyes. "Where are you, Goddess? Is it your will that we should all perish? I am so honored to be your cannon fodder!"

Valtyr covered Brynd with a blanket. Famlin cried silently, then sneered.

"Kill them all or die trying," the thief said, caressing his last cask of thunder powder. "Kairoth, open a path for me."

There was no room to maneuver. The battle had only been going on for a few minutes when the Draj formed a shield wall and archer line. Soon, Puryn's men were killing the enemy at will, while Hodan stopped them in their tracks. No archers came to aid the darkness.

Puryn said to Orus, "It seems that they only seek to delay us, not destroy our forces."

"Maybe they do not possess the might to defeat us, but wish to take as many with them as possible?" Orus questioned.

"Maybe. Or maybe something is going on around the corner that they are hoping will deliver them." Puryn looked at Adasser who looked ill, her face was green. "Something is wrong, brother."

Puryn waved at Adasser, who waved him off. She regained her composure and tended to Reynir's plant. Soon, the vines were shooting down the hallway, and it appeared as if grass grew on the floor of the cave.

"There is a door to the sanctuary," the Queen said to Valtyr who stood nearby. "No doubt that is what the Suden was screaming about. They will be there. We need to push them out of the way, now, priest."

"Move, Hodan," the priest commanded forcefully, and the warriors locked in tight, pushing forward.

The hallway was filled with twenty to thirty Orcs and Goblins. The dead laid in the entrance to the passage, a pile of vine-covered Kvern and fallen Hodan Elites.

The priest stood behind the Hodan lines and addressed the enemy in the passageway in a loud, clear voice. "Let us pass, vermin!"

The enemy laughed.

"Move or face the consequences," Valtyr said in a deadpan voice.

Again, the enemy laughed.

"As you wish!" Valtyr glowed white once more, and pointed down the hallway at the attackers. The priest shouted, "Dei manut deax!" Half of the number fell dead. Of the remaining, half of those ran in terror. The remaining quarter of the enemy received a Hodan shield charge that cleared the passageway, all of the way to the sanctuary door. They found it barred shut from the inside.

"I have got the answer for that," Famlin sneered, cradling his keg of thunder powder. "This is it, Kairoth—the last of my stash."

"Do it," the Hodan responded. Turning to the Kings behind him, he shouted, "Everyone back around the corner. Plug your ears if you like to hear!" Kairoth waited for the thief to set the charge and they both ran back to the corner.

There was an Ert shattering explosion.

* * *

The enemy was hiding something hideous. The vats of the dead were piled high with victims. The altar to the Underlord was covered in the blood of innocents. A trough caught the blood as it ran, transferring it down a channel, into a pool. The stench of rot and death was strong in the air.

When Famlin's cask of powder blew the door from its hinges, the Hodan rushed in as they always did and set a shield wall with their remaining ten men. Yslandeth followed suit and set the edges and set a line of archers for support. Kairoth's remaining team slipped to the right of the fray, as Haeldrun's remaining minions surrounded the altar and a black-robed Todessen who was most likely the Underlord's High Priest.

Hodan and Yslan thinned the mortal shields from around the altar, but not before the High Priest directed a more sinister agent to the Alliance lines. Soon, some men were cowering on the floor in their own piss. Others had turned to run and fought like wild animals to escape. As the Kings entered the room, they could not understand why the armies of the Alliance were in terror or fighting themselves.

Adasser entered the room and the darkness. She witnessed the disorder and chaos. Scowling, she knew it had to be Denir. She had never seen one up close, but she knew all about them from the book she was given by the Holy Mother when she was a novice.

The Holy Mother of the Forest turned to the altar with her finger pointed, and said, "We need some light on the subject. Inkindus furiar culmenar!" The ring of living shields burst into flames, as fire fell on them from thin air. They screamed. Adasser turned again, this time to the vats, when she repeated the words, and they burned brightly. All around the room the men returned to their senses. Some sat shuddering, crying like children. Hideous shrieking was heard, as multiple demons skulked into whatever corner they could find where the light did not reach.

Adasser walked forward to the center of the room. Puryn ran to protect her. He looked at his bride. Her hair was white as snow, and her eyes burned like coals. He knew when the Goddess was present. Haya was here.

"You are too late, Priestess," the Todessen priest said calmly. "My Lord is here."

"As is my Mistress, fool," Adasser replied in a Godlike voice.

Valtyr approached Adasser cautiously. He looked at her in reverence, then averted his eyes. Adasser looked right at him. The priest froze in his tracks.

The Priestess smiled broadly. "Come forward, priest. You are an instrument of my glory. In you, I am well-pleased."

Valtyr inched forward in fear for his life. He looked at the priest near the altar. He had changed much like Adasser had, except his hair was jet black, and his eyes sucked the light from around them. In fact, wherever the priest moved, the light diminished greatly.

Reynir spoke. "Valtyr, something else is here, brother. Where is Kairoth?"

* * *

Kairoth had leaned up against a wall. He was in the light, so the Denir could not latch onto him, but he was away from the hypocrisy he felt was unfolding before him.

"Instrument of light who commands people to die. How pure," the warrior quipped sarcastically.

A voice answered. "Truly, you are wiser than you look, Human."

"Who are you, demon?" Kairoth responded, looking around intently. The warrior moved into a brighter light.

The voice chuckled. "Rest assured, hero, I am no demon."

"Are you on the side of the darkness?" Kairoth responded, angrily drawing his sword.

"Know this, Human, I am not of the darkness, nor am I of the light. Your sword will be of no use against me. Why do you worry? I think that you have figured things out for what they truly are. Life and light, darkness and death, they are mirrors of each other."

"True. Long have I thought that one cannot exist without the other." Kairoth began to relax. He felt comfortable, as if he spoke with a long-lost friend over an ale at the pub.

"Verily, if one becomes too strong, the other side counters equally and in an opposite manner. Otherwise, reality falls apart," the voice responded.

"Will you speak the truth to those who will not hear, Kairoth?" the voice inquired.

"Who are you, you never identified yourself," the warrior demanded.

"I will show you, hero. Do not be afraid," the voice cooed.

Kairoth could not move as something overtook his being. It was not painful, nor was it unpleasant. A voice spoke to him as he showed the warrior an overview of things past, present, and of the possible future. After it was finished, it released the Hodan warrior.

"Do you see the truth now, Human? I will let you decide. I am called in eternity by the name of Likedelir, but I am better known to the Gods and the Ert as the Conflict, a son of Haya and Haeldrun. I am the secret that no one, but the wise, discovers. I am the truth that neither side acknowledges. Follow me and be my High Priest, Hodan. A warrior-monk. I have no illusions of piety or evil deeds, only balance."

The spirit released Kairoth. The warrior agreed with everything that he had seen. "I will follow you if I can ascend to Aeternum to be with my fallen friends. Is that possible?" Kairoth asked earnestly.

"My mother needs me as much as I need her. I am sure that you will be allowed to enter the gates unhindered," Likedelir responded with surety.

"Then I accept," Kairoth said, looking with disgust at both sides preparing to destroy themselves.

"Excellent, I will give you my dispensation. You are imbued with my power. Here are my teachings, but you already know them in your heart, My High Priest. You are my first friend, Human," the God said happily. "I will speak through you to my parents. We shall be heard."

"As you say it, let it be done, My God," Kairoth stated.

* * *

"Kairoth, what is the matter, brother?" Reynir asked touching the Hodan warrior's shoulder.

Kairoth was on his knees, head bowed and had a book in his hands. Reynir sensed something odd about his friend. The Hodan man stood and turned around. His face glowed lightly and his eyes shown white. Reynir backed away, afraid.

"Fear not, druid," an unnatural voice declared. "You also know the truth, though you resist it. Let me free you from your bindings to the lie."

"What are you talking about, Kairoth?" Reynir asked coming forward. "We must serve the Goddess!"

Kairoth smiled. "You know that is not entirely true. Take my hand and see."

Reynir, out of curiosity, did take the new monk's hand. He was shown the new revelation of Likedelir. The druid thought for a moment and was disturbed by the realization that Kairoth knew the truth.

"Oh, Great God, hear me. I do not oppose you, but my Mistress is Haya. If the dark and light must equally oppose each other, then I am on the side of light. We are not in opposition, as I follow the necessity of this reality. I choose the light." Reynir smiled. "It is good to make your acquaintance,

God of Balance?"

"One way of putting it," Kairoth laughed in the God's voice.

They made their way to the altar area where Adasser spoke by the power of Haya, and the Dark Priest spoke by the power of Haeldrun. Both stood in opposition to the other, blaming their opposition for the state of things within their universe.

Haya stated, "You have brought war, pestilence, and death, My Love. You constantly seek to kill my creations. Why, why would you think that this would ever heal our rift?"

Haeldrun spat, "Once, I WAS your love, but after our children were spawned, and those two boys created these realities, you strayed from our bond. You created these adulterous relationships with your creations. You turned your back on my true love, to nurture your pets, and left me to my own devices."

Haya responded. "I stand against death and darkness, because it is the destroyer. You have become the destroyer and my adversary, My Love."

Haeldrun laughed. "A convenient point of view. You set him free so that this meeting would take place, didn't you?"

Haya feigned innocence. "Who?"

Kairoth walked up to the two mortals who spoke the words of the Gods. He was smiling. He held a book in his hand.

"Who indeed, mother. Do you think father is so dull that he does not know that I have been loosed upon the Ert once more?" The Conflict shook his head through Kairoth.

Puryn, Orus, and the remains of the specialist team sat wide-eyed, witnessing a conversation among three Gods. They stood silently, knowing that there was no place to hide from these beings. It was no use trying to run.

Kairoth looked at Adasser. "Mother, it was selfish to create life, and it was selfless in the same action. You gave rise to the growth of love and light. It is a beauty unmatched in all eternity. All good things come from that which lives."

Haeldrun scowled at the praise his son gave his mother. Adasser smiled.

"Father, you have every right to be angry and to feel betrayed by mother. For she chose another over you, just as if a wife or husband had an illicit affair with a stranger. I understand your hurt and anger. In your sadness and ire, you created the darkness as a reflection of who you became. Now, all revile you as the taker of life and the ender of all things."

Haeldrun's minion raised one eyebrow. "Where are you going with this, boy. Get on with it."

The Conflict continued. "Mother, you hate the darkness and death, yet you use death to coerce your creations to comply with your wishes. You released me from my prison to wreak havoc on the Ert. Why? To bring father back to your arms, or to unite your people under your Champion?"

Haeldrun laughed at the look of horror on Adasser's face. "Father, you state that you hate life? Yet in your loneliness, you created the Kvern, Harkyl, and Todessen to worship you, and you caused them to prosper and multiply. You brought the balance to mother's light by creating your own life within the darkness."

Haeldrun growled.

"So, mother is about life and light and uses death, and you are about death, but you use life to achieve death? Who of you two is truly pure? Neither. You are a reflection of each other. Without your polar opposites, the reality we have implodes, and all reverts back to the beginning."

"So, then, I would have my love back. He would return to me," Adasser remarked.

"And I would have her sole affection again," Haeldrun interjected.

"But once the conflict is resolved, all life and light, and all darkness and death cease to be. Both sides that join, null out to the void and all will become nothingness. I am the product of necessity. The fates deem that all things continue, because of my interference. Without conflict and opposition, this reality ceases to be. It will remain dormant until the next deviation occurs." The Conflict sat back and waited for their answers.

Neither God had a retort. Neither wished to destroy reality and cease to be who they were. They both thought about their creations. Both loved what they had made in their own ways.

"You are both halves of one being, mother and father. I am a shard of the reality that has parted you. Do we continue down the path we have set, or null it all out with a reunion? Your choice." The Conflict knew the answer.

Haeldrun scowled angrily and released his minion. The priest stood disoriented for a second and then fear gripped his face. It was short-lived as Haeldrun claimed his devoted. The priest was gone in a dark, enveloping shadow.

Adasser's hair returned to its natural color, and she swooned, buckling at the knees. Kairoth caught her and set her down gently.

"Easy, High Priestess, you have a role to play in this reality, rest assured. I will release my devoted follower. Know this, all of you who bear witness, he is my first follower, and he is my High Priest. He will be a warrior-monk, and anyone who harms him for following me, will meet me personally. I have only one follower. It is easy to hear his call." The Conflict laughed maliciously and released Kairoth, who stood stoically, absorbing everything that had just happened through him. He remembered it all. So did Adasser.

"It is never easy the first time, Hodan," the Queen said sympathetically.

"Yes, Your Majesty. You would know." Kairoth smiled genuinely at Adasser.

The group turned to go, preparing to burn whatever was left within the sanctuary, when Valtyr called out from behind the altar.

"Your Majesties! There are people in this cage. It is a prison! Please, come quickly." Valtyr could not believe his eyes.

The group made their way to the priest. He gestured to hands that reached through the bars, begging for release. They could hear women and children crying out. Puryn and Orus broke the door off of its hinges. They were nearly trampled by almost two-hundred individuals of varying racial composition, who pushed out through the door. The party stood back. Safiya readied to do her worst.

There, in the group of survivors, were Human, Dwarf, Elf, and representation of every half-race. What shocked Valtyr was that some were afraid to come out of the cage and face their liberators. The priest stepped into the prison.

"Come out into the light. You are free," the priest welcomed.

From out of the darkness a small, tusk-faced creature charged, head down. He was flailing wildly and growling fiercely, but he did not harm the much larger priest. It was a smaller half-Orc boy. A woman shrieked and ran toward Valtyr.

"Please! Do not harm him, he is but a child!" The mother was Human.

Soon, the room's occupants edged into the light. One-hundred and fifty half-Orc, half-Goblin, mixed, and full-blooded Todessen stood in the light of the torches. The Todessen were not aggressive, and this puzzled the priest. Cautiously, Valtyr backed toward the exit of the prison.

"Please wait, priest," a Todessen woman begged. She was young with striking features. Valtyr figured she was twenty years old. Her runes were gold, vice black.

"Who are you?" Valtyr asked preparing to fight.

"I am a reformed Todessen. After the invasion failed, my people ran to every corner of the Ert to escape the dragons. We were abandoned by our God and lost. Eventually, many of us turned to the light and begged the Goddess for forgiveness and a new home. She led us to the canyon northwest of here. When we converted, the Goddess changed our runes from black to gold, and we renamed ourselves the Galdruhn."

Valtyr looked with concern at the Human woman as the half-Orc child now cried, hugging her around her shoulders. The priest looked around and saw nothing that warranted aggression, but did not know what his King would do.

"Let me speak to my King. I hope he is in the mood for reason today," Valtyr offered.

"Thank you," the woman replied, and she walked over to console the upset half-Orc boy.

Valtyr walked out of the prison to a circle of onlookers.

Orus asked, "Are those Toads and Orcs?"

"Well, not exactly, Your Majesty," Valtyr responded.

"Well, they are, or they aren't," Puryn added.

"They are refugees, Sire. Converts to Haya who were being killed as heretics to Haeldrun, I am sure. They are probably what piqued his interest and brought him here." Valtyr looked at both Kings.

"We must kill them," Orus demanded.

"You must not!" Valtyr objected.

"Out of my way, priest!" Orus drew his sword.

"Your Majesty, they follow the Goddess. They are seeking refuge. They were being sacrificed. Do we follow the light in our Kingdoms, or have we given ourselves over to darkness?" Valtyr stood his ground in front of the much larger Hodan King.

"Orus, let's reconsider," Puryn suggested.

"They are Toads, Orcs and Goblins, Puryn! They are the remnant of Offlander scourge. You would allow them to live on the Ert?!" Orus shook his head.

"Think about your actions, brother," Puryn reasoned. "If they follow the Goddess and we kill them for no other reason, besides prejudice and bigotry, are we not following the darkness?"

"Oh, to the abyss with all of this foolishness! I have swallowed just about enough of this dung for my liking. If you wish to accommodate these Toads, then YOU do it, Puryn. I will not give comfort to those who killed us at will all those years ago." Orus turned and walked away angrily.

"Orus, wait!" Puryn called out, but the Hodan King ignored him and stormed out of the sanctuary.

Puryn heard him shouting down the hall. "Next we'll preserve this site in the interest of religious equality!"

Puryn shook his head. He glared at Valtyr. "Are you SURE that they are not lying to you?"

"Well, I'm pretty certain, but it is impossible to tell," Valtyr said diplomatically.

"Adasser, can you detect any evil within their ranks?" Puryn asked.

"Nothing overt, My Love. Valtyr speaks the truth." Adasser sat down and drank a bit of water. She was regaining her natural color. The sickness was leaving her.

"Bring them forward, priest," the King commanded.

The group came forward, cowering from their cages. Mothers were holding their young. Older children stood and tried to defend their mothers, but there was no aggression against them. Puryn, Adasser, Valtyr, and the rest of the remaining specialists saw them clearly. There was a new creation on the Ert—Galdruhn, and the remnants of the Offlander debauchery, which survived the war and only wished a chance to live in peace.

"I have a task for this group," Puryn ordered.

"What is your command, My King?" Kairoth responded.

"Take my new subjects to the lands North of the Raven's Pass, where the Red-Hand used to operate. I will send word to the surrounding baronies and villages not to bother them. They will be afforded an area to live and prosper like every halfling race which I protect. If they are of Haya, they will have the protection of Yslandeth."

"Valtyr, you are the priest of Haya here. Reynir, you also. I will come along for the ride," Kairoth said, relinquishing command.

"Come, let us get all of you out of this place and to your new lands," Valtyr said with a smile. The crowd sniffled and looked up hopefully.

"Your Majesty," Kairoth spoke officially to Puryn.

"Yes, Kairoth, what is it?"

"When I finish this last task, I ask that I be released from service and that my team be freed to allow them to pursue their lives in peace, also." Kairoth looked Puryn in the eye.

"After all you have accomplished, each of you will be rewarded handsomely, and released to live as you see fit upon the Ert." Puryn smiled and shook the Hodan warrior's hand. "Thank you. Thank you all."

"Thank you, Your Majesty!" the party replied, bowing.

Chapter 27

The Hodan were gone. They had followed their King out of the ruined temple. Faylea remained behind and eyed her love interest with concern. Kairoth stood in the center of his party. All of them looked at him in awe, one or two with a slight hint of suspicion. The Princess pondered the magnitude of what had just occurred. It was not lost on the young Hodan leader, that not two, but three Gods had stood in this wretched place and spoke plainly to each other and those around them. In plain sight, through the mortal conduits of their choice, they made their cases and postured for the high ground.

For many years, Faylea had given lip service to Haya, while privately submitting her prayers to Runnir or Gunnir as her first choice. Now, with the advent of this new revelation, the Conflict, or Likedelir, as he had called himself, seemed to fit her needs even more completely. She walked over to where the party was trying to put the whole event in context. Faylea could see the deep attachment that the survivors had. They were a patchwork family, vice a military unit.

"Kairoth, what was all of that?" Safiya asked, her eyes squinted, and her head cocked to the side. "Did a Denir get ahold of you, or did you get hit in the head by an Ogre? You stood beside Haya AND Haeldrun, and spoke as if you had a right to be there. Are you mad? Or simply suicidal?"

Kairoth looked over at Puryn and Adasser, who were embracing privately beside the exit to the room. The King was brushing his Queen's hair from her face, as Adasser craned her head around to see the expression on the Hodan warrior's face while Safiya lit into him. The Queen laughed loudly and leaned on her husband for support as she regained her strength.

"Keep your voice down, woman!" Kairoth said, looking over at the Queen in embarrassment. "She can hear you."

"In all fairness, I think that a bit earlier, the Queen heard much more than this from you, Kairoth," the druid replied in an offhand manner, as he bandaged a superficial wound on his arm. "Everyone did. Or least maybe, they heard 'him.'"

"Well, that was not planned, but I am not sorry." The Hodan warrior looked at the book in his hand. He opened it to page one. It was blank, save for a few pages of text written in a strange language or code. Smiling, he realized the book was writing itself, and his new God was recording their story—the God and his monk.

"What is that book?" Safiya asked with curiosity. "Is it magic?"

"Maybe, but my God has revealed to me the truth that I already knew. He reinforced the beliefs that I already have. He has reinforced the reality that I already know to exist. When he spoke to me the first time, he said that this book would contain his message to the Ert. He said that the message was already written within my heart and that I would know these words before I ever read them." Kairoth grinned like a boy at Winterfest. "It writes itself. It tells his story through our interactions and my walk upon the Ert. I am truly his warrior monk, now. There is no turning back to the foolishness of Light versus Dark. I will walk between the two and establish balance by the hand of my new Lord."

"Well, that sounds great, but what of Haya?" Reynir replied sadly.

"What of her? She is as necessary as the Underlord. All things exist, because they are two halves of the same being. For all to continue to exist, they must desire to be polar opposites. Their separation ensures and preserves the reality that we know. I have no ill will toward Haya, and unless they seek to overthrow the balance again, I have no ill will toward those of the Underlord."

"I guess," Famlin sighed. "I really don't care, Kairoth. Let's find Valtyr, get these people out of here, and burn this Gods-forsaken hole in the ground."

"Agreed. I too wish to smell the fresh air again, and there is a dragon that owes me its scales. I will collect." Kairoth sneered. "I have not forgotten what that foul creature did to Salia. If I could kill it again, I would slay it in the flicker of a candle fire."

"Valtyr!" Reynir bellowed. It echoed in the chamber. "Where in the Underworld are you?"

"Right here!" the priest waved. He was surrounded by hundreds of crying refugees, and the priest was overwhelmed. "Can you give me a hand with this?"

"I am coming, brother!" the druid replied loudly over the rising din of weeping. Turning to Kairoth, he said, "I must go, my leader. My brother needs me. Will you accompany us to their new lands?"

"Yes, definitely, my friend," Kairoth replied with a peaceful look on his face.

Reynir smiled, walking to where Valtyr was working. "That is a good look on you, Hodan."

Safiya looked at the Hodan with little emotion. "So, I guess we are walking North for a couple of weeks then?" The mage sighed with annoyance. "I should like to stop in Edenyag and resume training. Perhaps, Elpis needs an apprentice?"

Puryn overheard her question. "I assure you, mage, you will be welcomed by my daughter."

"Thank you, Your Majesty," the mage replied, bowing with respect.

"What about you, Chieftain?" the Hodan asked Famlin, who was gathering the remainder of his things. "What will you do?"

"You said it, boss. I am a Chieftain now. I will work to better the station of my people under my King." Famlin smiled genuinely. "You are my brother and are always welcome within my lands, to the end of both our lives."

"I will take you up on that, Suden," Kairoth replied shaking the thief's hand. "No longer will I utter the word, Suden, as a curse. You have regained the honor of a people. You have re-established your Kingdom. You are one of its heroes now. We would kill for that position in Hodan lore, most literally!"

"Well, boss, I've had my fill of killing! I wish to settle down and have a family. I hope a certain mage makes her way toward Sudenyag from time to time. Maybe I can persuade her to leave her scrolls and books?" He winked at Safiya, who pretended not to notice, but a hint of a smile betrayed her attempt at stoicism.

Kairoth looked to the King and Queen. They stood alone with a handful of Draj surrounding them. The Hodan warrior approached the monarchs and bowed. Puryn waved him off. "Enough of that, Kairoth. You are my chosen hero. Your team performed above all others—above every expectation. Now, you have been chosen by a God, and I will not have his new high priest bowing to me. It is not good for one's health." Puryn laughed loudly.

Adasser smirked and looked at the Hodan monk. "When did you know?" she asked.

"In this room, Your Majesty. Over there, against that wall," Kairoth pointed.

"How?" she asked.

"A voice spoke to me plainly, possessed me totally and showed me the way," Kairoth answered calmly. "Much as you must have felt the first time Haya touched your person."

"I think that your experience has been more ordered than mine." The Queen laughed. "But not more adventurous. I will hope that you do not scoff at my Goddess, priest. She is not one to take lightly, you know."

"Far from it, Your Majesty. I respect all sides and all of their views. Each has their part to play in the cosmos and in the preservation of our reality. I simply take no sides, unless the balance is skewed too much in favor of one side or the other." Kairoth bowed. "I must help Valtyr and your apprentice with our new charges. This will be an interesting trip, I am certain."

"Most assuredly, My Lord. Surely, it will prove itself to be far from boring!" The Queen smiled and hugged the Hodan warrior to his surprise. "It is good to talk to another who walks the Ert knowing what it feels like to be in my position!"

Kairoth smiled and bowed. "Be well, Your Majesties. I will travel to

Empyr once we have settled these people, and have provided for their security."

"I look forward to our next meeting, monk." The Queen smiled and bowed ceremonially.

Puryn shook Kairoth's hand. "I will remember our agreement. See you soon."

Adasser and Puryn exited the temple chambers with their Draj entourage, heading for the surface. Kairoth turned and sighed, looking at what he'd inherited. Valtyr was at his best when under unmanageable conditions. Kairoth chuckled as he watched both Valtyr and Reynir forming the mob of halflings and their parents into traveling groups. He began to walk over to the two brothers, when he was intercepted by Faylea. She had been waiting for her turn.

"Your holiness!" Faylea mocked.

Kairoth raised an eyebrow and smiled. "Really? You, too?"

"Why not me also? I know you better than most." Faylea slid in close to the Hodan warrior. "Do you love me, monk?"

"I do," Kairoth replied, touching her cheek.

Faylea's eyes opened widely at the frankness of his reply. She replied, "Will you come to Hodan and be my Prince, then?"

Kairoth looked at Faylea with an expression of sadness. "Sadly, My Love, I must pursue this path first. I must establish these people, and then establish my order. If you are willing to wait for me, I will come to you. If not, I will understand."

Faylea frowned. "I was afraid that you would say that. I will wait for a time, but you must promise to visit Warrior's Crossing from time to time. Deal?" She held out her hand to shake Kairoth's.

Kairoth pulled her close and kissed her passionately. "I would be a fool to pass up such an offer, My Princess."

"If you would have me, I would travel to Yslan with you and transport these people to their new home. I am sorry that my father was so angry, but I cannot say that I blame the man." Faylea looked the warrior in the face.

"Orus is a just man. He is unable to see beyond their appearance and into their hearts … yet. Someday, he will change his views." Kairoth seemed sure of his prophecy.

Faylea hugged him, kissing him one more time. "Let us get out of this pit and underway!"

"Agreed." The monk turned and motioned to the priest and druid, who waved back.

* * *

Orus was not pleased when he heard that his daughter had stayed behind with the Offlander scourge remnant. He figured it had to do with the boy, so he shrugged it off and saddled up with his Legions and headed back to Hodan. The King knew his Princess knew the way home. He just hoped she would find her way back there, sooner than later. Orus was tired of the status quo.

Riding back toward Hodan, the King took his boys on the scenic route through southern Sudenyag, into Cinnog and northward to the Yslandeth border. A couple of worn Hodan Legions were still considered to be a formidable and worrisome sight to anyone who might find themselves an enemy of Orus and his people. Orus did this by design. All would recognize the might of Hodan and the autonomy of the King. By the time he had reached Hodan, his trip had created the desired effect. People knew something was afoot with the Alliance and that Hodan was restless. Emissaries from all lands began arriving at the Hodan capital of Warrior's Crossing.

Cinnog reaffirmed its allegiance to the Northern Alliance. Hodan removed its troops from the northern territories of Sudenyag, as promised, and King Harun sent emissaries to Orus, settling the war once and for all. Hodan and Sudenyag were friends once again. Edenyag withdrew all troops to five miles within their own lands to avoid appearing too aggressive. King Philip, son of Cathir, sent messengers and letters of friendship to Orus, who returned the gesture, solidifying another ally to the East.

The elder races remained neutral to Hodan, although officially allied and friendly. Glorin and Bogrol both remained wary of what Hodan would do with a final peace. Prosperity was soon to follow, then, the Elves and Dwarves feared, the Hodan cycle would start again. Both the people of Torith and Dornat Al Ar stood vigilant, awaiting what they felt was the inevitable return of Hodan to its old ways. Orus knew that the elder races did not trust the Hodan. The Hodan King let them fear Hodan. If they were afraid, they would not bother him.

To the North, Orus and Puryn's friendship was strained. The Alliance held, but Orus was restless. His scouts reported that Sudenyag and Edenyag had built their own versions of great ships by using the designs of the Offlander vessels. The Dwarves had fashioned a smaller version of the Thunder Ballista and were attaching them to the sides of the tall ships. The Hodan King was impressed by reports that the Dwarves were able to sink a derelict craft in the port harbor with their new smaller weapons. It was a work in progress, but Orus began to think it was a worthy one.

* * *

The party and their charges left the temple in an orderly fashion. As they made their way out, Famlin and Valtyr made sure to burn everything behind them. Kairoth shrugged and did not seem to be moved either way with the actions. When they reached the surface, it was late afternoon. The sun was low on the horizon, and some of the armies had already left the field for home. Faylea shook her head as she noted that her father was already nowhere in sight.

"Oh, father, for the love of the Gods," she muttered.

"He's a man, Faylea," Kairoth replied. "He will come around."

"You have met him, right?" The Princess quickly kissed the Hodan monk on the cheek and went about trying to find some rations.

* * *

It began as a catcall.

The halfling Orc and Goblin children had just cleared the door to the sky with their mothers in tow. They were all smiling and hugging. Many of the refugees cried freely, but this was lost on a mob of war-weary Yslandeth Draj camped nearby. Kairoth could see that the Royal Encampment was already long gone. All that was left of Yslan was a low-level Commander and the remnants of an Yslandeth Legion. Sudenyag had several thousand of their tribal forces in the immediate area.

"Good! Captives! Let's burn them, tied to the stake!" one voice bellowed.

Several other, more descriptive suggestions were aired. The children surrounded their mothers. Some were growling madly in an attempt to show strength and intimidate their opposition. It brought about loud, raucous laughter. The armies of Yslan began to organize into small mobs as they drew weapons and advanced on the women and children of the Offlanders. Kairoth had seen enough. So had Valtyr.

The priest stood and walked in front of the terrified refugee families. Kairoth smiled as he stood behind Valtyr. The priest seemed ten times larger than normal.

"Hello, Haya," Kairoth said to no one in particular, as the priest's person began to glow slightly. The Hodan smiled and whispered. "Hello, mother."

"You will cease now!" Valtyr bellowed.

The Draj line stopped in its tracks, speechless. They all looked at each other, puzzled. Who was this man?

The Commander spoke up. "Move aside, priest. We shall finish the job."

"You will not, by Haya's order. Oh, and in case you need earthly orders, what of the orders of your King? Will you dare defy him also? Not a wise career choice, Commander." Valtyr was oddly calm and confident.

This was not lost on Kairoth, who was now nodding and smiling at the Draj lines. "If I were you, I would listen, fools. Haya has chosen this priest to be their deliverer. Will oppose the Goddess? This should be interesting." Kairoth crossed his arms across his chest. He leaned against a nearby tree that had appeared from Gods knew where.

Faylea watched Kairoth intently. She noticed that the Hodan warrior no longer carried his sword. He had a staff in one hand, a satchel over his shoulder. Somewhere along the way, he had shed his issued armor and opted for a linen tunic and pants. "Do not get yourself killed, Hodan," Faylea joked half-seriously.

Kairoth waved at Faylea, who smiled, shaking her head in disbelief. Valtyr was standing as still as a statue. His head was encircled in bright white light. His short hair stood on end, and his eyes blazed.

The priest looked at Kairoth and smiled. "What do you desire, son?" the priest asked oddly.

The monk replied, "Mother, may I handle this, please? Just once?"

"Oh, all right, but make it quick," Valtyr said in a slightly irritated tone. The glow left the priest, who remembered the conversation and felt a bit odd at being called mother. Then he realized that Haya had used him directly. He began jumping up and down happily.

"Reynir!" Valtyr said joyously. "Did you see that?"

"I did! I am jealous!" Reynir said, smiling widely at his brother's uncharacteristic display of elation.

"Excuse me, priest," the Hodan monk said in an eerie voice.

"Of course, brother," the priest said bowing.

Kairoth stood two paces from the Commander, who was clad in full Elfish mail. The Draj held a short-glaive in one hand and a shield in the other. Still, he was unnerved by the sight of the larger man, wearing only cloth and carrying a stick. The Yslan man felt an irrational fear welling up in his chest. The Hodan's eyes turned white, and his face darkened to a point where it was no longer visible beneath the hood he had pulled up over his head.

In a growl, Kairoth said to the army before him, "Do you really wish to test me today?"

"You are one man; I will test you. I will see you at the end of this glaive, if you do not move out of my way, monk." The Draj Commander stood and made ready.

"As you wish, fool!" Likedelir answered through the monk. "I wonder where your soul will fall …"

The Draj attacked with ferocity, but Kairoth was infinitely more agile, and his newfound speed made the Elite warrior look as if he stood still. The Hodan monk kicked the Yslan warrior in his face and then pounced and pummeled him with punches from various angles. The end result of the fight saw one Draj Elite face down in the dirt. He would not get up again.

"Any other challengers?" Kairoth asked, his white eyes glowing from under the darkness of his hood. "Anyone who would like to join this fool in the Underworld?"

No one stepped forward.

"I did not think so. Now, take this person's carcass away and burn him. You should offer a sacrifice to my mother for his soul. He will need it." Kairoth's face returned. He wore a disgusted look. "We are leaving with these people. My lord held back. The God of balance will not tolerate your foolishness, Yslan."

"Understood, but why protect them when they killed so many of us?" a random soldier asked angrily.

"I protect them, because they are innocents. These are your mothers, your sisters, and your daughters, Yslan. They were abused by the Offlanders, and still, they loved enough to have mercy upon their offspring. Would you reward their love and mercy with death, heroes? These have killed no man or woman, no Elf or Dwarf. They are the victims of this whole affair."

Kairoth looked at the army before him and began to preach for the first time about balance and the order of chaos in the universe. Many of those in attendance believed and began to follow his new Order that day. Likedelir was pleased with his warrior monk high priest, and blessed him tenfold. The Hodan warrior's strength, endurance, and agility began to increase gradually over time. Soon, the Hodan monk would stop using weapons altogether.

Valtyr relaxed and looked at Kairoth. "Come, sit with the rest of the clergy, Hodan!" Valtyr was laughing. He was genuinely happy. Haya had visited him, and he had found his purpose.

Kairoth responded. "I have someone I wish to spend my time with, priest! No offense intended."

"None taken," Valtyr said. "Reynir, help me boil some vegetables for these people, would you?"

"One minute, brother, I'll be right back." Reynir changed into a tiger and ran off into the woods, returning with few rabbits. He carried them back to where the priest was cooking.

The refugees looked at the tiger in fear, but their fear turned to bewilderment when the priest began talking to the tiger, and it responded with growling as if it knew him. Valtyr could see their interest and the concern of his audience. He smiled and motioned for everyone to be calm.

"It's my brother. Do not be concerned!" Valtyr said, as if it this was common knowledge. The crowd murmured nervously and sat in tight circles.

Valtyr hastily dressed the rabbits, cleaning the carcasses and putting them into a mess tent pot that he found abandoned by one army or another. Soon, the smell of a rabbit stew wafted over the area. The crew scrounged up enough bowls to allow twenty to eat at a time. All sat patiently and waited for their turn at the first real food they had seen in weeks.

The sun had dipped below the horizon, and the sky was clear and full of stars. A full moon showed low above the horizon. The undead were nowhere in sight. All that was present was the strangest fellowship of survivors and heroes that the Ert had ever seen.

"Kairoth, I'm concerned for our safety," Reynir said plainly. "We have only five to stand the watch. I am not sure where Famlin has run off to, but that is a common occurrence."

"It is a common occurrence, you tree lover?!" Famlin shouted from the darkness. He had a few young boys in tow.

"Where have you been, Chieftain?" Kairoth asked seriously.

"Setting the watch, brother. You all need your beauty rest! We have fought long and hard. We have bled the Suden soil red and black beneath our feet. You at least deserve a night's sleep before we embark on the long journey to where it all began!" Famlin smiled. "North of Hero's Rest and East of Empyr? Really?" He laughed loudly.

"It figures, does it not?" Valtyr quipped. "I must attend to them."

"By all means, brother!" Famlin responded. Turning to Kairoth, he said, "I am not saying that I follow your faith, brother, but I like what it stands for. I think that many in Suden will follow your lead! If Yslan and Hodan will not take the honor of escorting these people to their new lands, allow Sudenyag."

Kairoth extended his hand. "I accept your gracious offer. You are welcome in this flock any time, Famlin. There is plenty of room. I think we have ten in our congregation, Ert-wide!?" Kairoth laughed as they shook hands.

"Go to sleep, monk. We shall talk on the way to Yslan. Gods know we shall have plenty of time!" Famlin waved as he disappeared out in the darkness.

After Valtyr had settled the refugees and prayed for their well-being, he laid down nearby his brother, who was attending to a new plant. The druid had set up a hammock between two small trees that were not in the area earlier.

The priest smiled. "Your friends are back? Always the same with you, my brother, and that does my soul good!"

"I like my routines. They ground me in the service to the Goddess, brother! I think we have proved ourselves worthy in some small way. I think she is greatly impressed with you. Me, perhaps not as much." Reynir seemed a bit disappointed.

More trees gathered around the party as they began to bed down for the night. Valtyr noticed first.

"The Queen?" the priest asked, gesturing to the tree line.

"Most likely. They will not come if I call them." Reynir smiled. "At least I have my two friends. They are really good to me."

* * *

One of the trees rustled, as if the wind was present where there was none. A small thicket of around thirty trees formed behind Reynir as he slept. A pinecone bounced off of the druid's head. It was around midnight when the druid awoke with a start, rubbing his forehead.

"You da Masta?" Reynir heard a voice say out of the darkness.

The druid sat up in his hammock with a start and instantly fell out of it with a thud. "Who's there? Famlin, you're not funny."

The Suden watch stood in the shadows, quietly watching the show. They figured the druid must be drunk. They saw him stand and brush the dust from his tunic.

"Seriously, who is there?" Reynir asked grabbing his club.

"It us, Masta, what do you?" the voice replied. No one seemed to be alarmed within the encampment.

"Why do you keep calling me, 'Master.' I am not a master of anything," Reynir stated with the club held high.

"Da Queen uh da Light, she say, you now da Master, for dis circle." The trees all rustled violently as if declaring their allegiance to the druid, whose hair now stood up on his neck.

"Queen Adasser?" Reynir asked with a puzzled look as he put down his club. "She calls me the Master? I don't understand."

"Adasser, Queen o' Nature, but she not da Queen who call you da Masta. She da Queen of Aeternum, Masta," the voice said.

Reynir smiled as he noticed that the thirty trees had now become fifty. They all surrounded him. Tears welled up in his eyes as he now knelt.

"You speak of the Goddess? That Queen?" Reynir questioned.

"Yes, Masta," the voice answered.

"Who are you, voice?" Reynir asked to confirm what he suspected.

"We are your servants. We are your woods. We are da pines dat you saved on da hills of two mountains and in dis field. We shall follow da new Master by orders from da Queen of Life."

Reynir let out a high-pitched shriek of happiness. "Valtyr! She noticed me also, brother! Look! Look!" Reynir danced, elated that he was thought worthy by the Goddess.

"Shut up, druid!" a voice shouted in the darkness.

Reynir giggled like a child and sat in the middle of his new friends. He introduced himself to each tree, but soon he realized that they were still coming to him. He wondered when or if they would stop.

A momentary fear passed his mind. What if they all came? What will the Queen do to me!?

Chapter 28

altyr woke to the tug of a small hand on his bedroll. As the priest rolled over, the young half-Orc boy scurried backward in fear. Valtyr was startled by the lad, but quickly regained his composure, sitting up and looking at the crowd who dared not step within his encampment. They stood, dirty, tired, and cold, respectfully giving their advocate his space.

Valtyr motioned for the boy to come closer. "What is it, son?"

The young one looked up and then around with his mouth open. "The forest, Sir. Where did it come from?"

Valtyr's face twisted as if he did not understand the question, then his eyes widened as he looked at the perimeter of the encampment. The trees had encircled them completely in a tight ring. Nothing was getting in or out, unless they allowed it passage in the wood.

"Um, Reynir!?" the priest bellowed.

A faint voice off in the thick of the trees answered, "Yes, brother! What is it?"

"Can you come here for a moment?" Valtyr asked standing and nodding to the young half-Orc, who ran to his mother.

Reynir walked out of the woods. The trees parted for him. From where Valtyr sat, it appeared as if some were shrouding the young druid, bowing in their own way. The hair on Valtyr's neck stood on end as his brother entered the camp, smiling and more peaceful than he'd ever been before.

"I know, right?!" Reynir laughed.

"Not the Queen this time, is it, brother?" Valtyr asked hugging his friend.

"No," Reynir whispered choking up a bit. "They come to me, because they think that I saved them. I tried to talk some sense into them, but they are stubborn!"

"Perfect followers for your ministry," Valtyr chuckled.

"I suppose so!" Reynir agreed, laughing.

They had forgotten their audience was watching. Valtyr suddenly remembered, releasing his brother, clearing his throat, and standing up seriously. The people had knelt and bowed to the brothers with respect. Valtyr's eyes bulged in horror.

"No! No, please! Never bow or kneel to my brother or me! We are not Gods! We are only men! Rise! Rise now, please!" Valtyr cringed at the thought of being worshipped. Reynir stood by his frantic brother, stunned to silence.

"We are sorry," a woman replied, averting her eyes from Valtyr. "We meant no offense, deliverer."

The crowd murmured in agreement.

"The only Goddess who should receive your sacrifice is Haya, the Queen of Life and Light. Please, I am just a man, as is my brother, even if trees do talk to him." Valtyr smiled. "Please, come closer and let us see what we can find for food."

"I will help," Reynir said, and he walked to his tree ring and began asking for their aid.

* * *

Kairoth woke next to Faylea, who was quietly snoring. The Hodan monk smiled at her peaceful face. He hugged her gently, then kissed her cheek, letting her sleep, as he walked off alone to pray. It was a new experience for the man. He had spent much of his life calling out to Runnir, Gunnir, and sometimes even Haya, but never Likedelir. He didn't know what to say. Soon, he didn't have to worry about it.

"There are no rote prayers to me, monk, unless you make them up." The God appeared as a cloaked traveler. "Please, don't kneel. That is so unnecessary. We are friends, monk." The God smiled from below his hood.

"My Lord, I only wish to be respectful," Kairoth replied, bowing.

"Then respect my wishes! Sit, speak plainly. What do you wish?" The God sat on a nearby fallen tree.

"I don't know what I want," the Hodan replied. "A life that doesn't involve this?"

"Well, you could go with your Princess and live a posh life in Hodan, I suppose." The God sounded disappointed.

"What is your wish, My God?" Kairoth asked seriously.

"To spread the word. To build our followers. To set things right. To strike a true balance, Kairoth." The God stood and stepped closer to his High Priest.

"I will go then, Likedelir. I will do your will." The Hodan stood, bowing.

"Why do Humans always insist on making sacrifices. Stand up. I will tell you your future, Human." The God spoke plainly. "You will escort these people to the North, as promised. Then, you will be released from the King's service. At that point, you will study at the monastery in Empyr for a time. You will know when you have finished, and you will then travel to Torith and Dornat Al Ar for a bit of ancient teachings of the elder races. Finally, you will study a bit in Edenyag."

Kairoth stood stoically listening to his God's words and nodded periodically. "Yes, Lord."

"After you have a good foundation in the lore and religions of this world, you will learn to fight." Likedelir smirked, awaiting the response of his monk.

"But, Lord, I think I know how to fight already! With your blessings, I have become almost invincible! What else is there to learn there?" Kairoth wore a defensive, yet surprised look.

The God smiled openly. "You are a great warrior, My High Priest, but there is one man who you will meet outside of Warrior's Crossing on your way to claim your Princess. Yes, I approve of your selection of a wife, monk. She is a fine warrior and comes from a line of honorable people."

"How will I know who this man is?" Kairoth asked, bewildered by his God's command.

"He lives where no warrior would abide, doing work no noble would do. His hair is silver, and his bones appear brittle. He walks lame and carries a walking stick now, where he once proudly wielded his sword. You will think him a pauper and a fool, but he will show you the way. His house is humble, and his name is unknown, only because those who offend him, ne'er live to talk of the encounter."

"Where will I find him, Lord?" the monk asked again.

"I cannot give away all of the secrets. What fun is that?" Likedelir laughed then spoke quietly. "Look for him where the hawk dances and the wolf cries to the moon. It is in your book if you forget, Hodan." The God smiled sarcastically.

"I will do as you have said," Kairoth said plainly, again bowing.

Likedelir shook his head. "So bowing will be part of our worship, I see. So be it." The God turned to go. "Oh, and do not study more than a year or two, My High Priest. Her love will not wait forever. Visit her often. Stoke the fire. Do not allow it to perish for foolish, self-imposed rules. I wish balance. Remember."

"Always, My God. Thank you." Kairoth stood and waved goodbye as the God turned.

The hooded individual walked down the road, nodding nonchalantly to several passers-by who greeted him on his way. Kairoth watched him leave until he faded away into the horizon. The Hodan monk gathered his things and returned to his Princess.

She was awake, but not ready to leave her bedroll. It was still early she was only partially dressed, and she let him know by lifting her blanket briefly. She smiled mischievously and patted the spot next to her. Kairoth smiled and returned to her side. He kissed her, and she held him tightly.

* * *

It was the third hour of the morning when the horns sounded. Sudenyag had arrived. Famlin had assembled a caravan much like the others that transported goods across his nation and to markets along the way. Kairoth and the others were already packed and ready to leave. The refugees were each given a rough woolen blanket to keep warm and sandals to wear on their feet. There were about three-hundred survivors. Famlin and Kairoth estimated that half would have to walk, while half rode in wagons and on carts drawn by mules. Camels and elephants were used to carry supplies and tents. They were a ragged bunch, but Famlin did what he could.

"I have five of my best specialists and twenty of my best rangers for security," Famlin said to Kairoth.

"Where are they?" Kairoth looked around, and all he saw were herders and caravan workers.

"I said they were my best, Kairoth." Famlin smiled and patted the monk on his shoulder. "We should move now. It is getting late in the morning. Are they ready?"

"They are as ready as they'll be. Please make sure to give my team mounts. I will walk." Kairoth smiled and looked up at the clear blue sky. It was mid-morning, and he could no longer see his breath. "The planting season will come soon, I think."

"Aye, it comes very soon, my brother. Let's go!" Famlin goaded.

The caravan left the ruined temple. Smoke still filtered out of its entrance. As they passed the site of their horror, some of the survivors openly wept, remembering lost loved ones, but praising the men and women who had rescued them from certain death.

The crowd began to chant. "All hail the heroes of Haya! Praise be to the Goddess and her deliverers! Praise be to the deliverers!"

Valtyr scowled and looked at Reynir, who shook his head and laughed.

"They are praising the Goddess, are they not, brother?" Reynir was smiling.

"I suppose, but I hate when they praise me! It seems sacrilegious!" Valtyr started to chuckle.

"Haya will honor your humility, priest," Kairoth said, walking near the horse that Valtyr rode.

"Why do you walk, brother? Take my steed! Reynir and I can share. Just like the old days, eh brother?" Valtyr laughed, looking at the druid who had raised an eyebrow.

"No need, brother. I asked to walk!" Kairoth said joyfully. "I need the exercise. I will be meeting a master someday who will show me how to fight, apparently."

"Show YOU how to fight?" Reynir asked smiling. "He must be Runnir himself!"

"Perhaps! You two watch the people walking. I will also," Kairoth suggested.

"Of course, brother!" Valtyr smiled, trotting on ahead of the monk.

Six hours later, the caravan found a large clearing beside a small creek. They set up camp. Tents were erected in a tight circle around several bonfires, as was the Suden tradition. Famlin looked around and was not happy with the vulnerability of camping out in the open with so few men. The Chieftain instructed his men to keep watch, and then approached the fire around which his old team had gathered.

"Greetings, friends!" the Chieftain said happily to the group.

Safiya quietly sat eating her rations and sipping on some water. "Greetings, stranger."

Famlin cleared his throat. "I am concerned about our perimeter. We might need some help. Are you all up to helping with watch tonight? I will take the late watch so that some can get a night's sleep." The Chieftain looked over at Safiya, who managed a half smile.

"No need for that, brother," Reynir said, entering the circle with a bunch of eggs in a burlap cloth. Gingerly handing them to Valtyr, he turned to Famlin. "I have this." The druid turned to his sapling friend and asked him to relay an order to his woods. The trees swayed as if there was a strong wind where there was no breeze.

"I don't know how, nor do I want to know, how your trees brought you eggs without breaking them." Valtyr picked up the burlap gently. "I'm making a camp soup with everything in it for the refugees. At this rate, there may be enough for everyone. Be back soon." The priest walked to a fire where a large pot was beginning to boil.

"Famlin, I have been blessed with my own forest. Not as many as My Queen, mind you, but enough to protect us quite well. Do not worry, brother." Reynir pointed to the line of trees that had begun to form around the large camp.

Famlin smiled. "I am glad to have been called one of this party. You are all blessed. I must attend to my people. See you in the morning." He winked at Safiya, who winked back.

* * *

The nights were much the same for almost two weeks, as a caravan of refugees slowly traveled northward through Sudenyag and the northwestern corner of Edenyag. The terrain was mostly high desert and hard packed dirt that gave way to rolling valleys and open plains on the Yslandeth side of the border.

They avoided the settlements of Humans, for fear of persecution and retribution. Most of those fears were unfounded, as they discovered that no Human, Elf, or Dwarf would challenge anyone moving within a magic forest that was rumored to contain King Puryn's heroes. Rumors also grew from locale to locale, concerning a new religious Order that was led by a new monk, who was traveling with the survivors of Haeldrun's Temple. The new High Priest was said to be the direct representative of this new God. People were initially skeptical, but Kairoth made it a point to preach his message wherever ears were present that could listen. Likedelir occasionally obliged his priest's requests and granted a miracle or two to back his claims. The monk healed some who were sick and others who were lame. As the group moved slowly northward, the followers of Likedelir grew in number and as they did, so did Kairoth's power.

* * *

Two weeks after they had left the Temple of the Underlord, the caravan reached their destination. Kairoth prayed over the land and the people, asking for justice and protection for all of them. Likedelir, pleased with this request, made their settlement his primary concern, and over the next few months, he sped the progress of constructing mud and waddle homes for every family. Crops were sowed with seed from Empyr, and a defensive wall of trees gathered around the settlement at Reynir's request until a proper wall was finally erected.

Once the people were settled, Kairoth returned to Empyr as he had promised, and the King released his team from their service. Each member of the team was paid five year's wages in gold and given one of the finest Korinian steeds available. Every member of the band was granted lands wherever they wished within the Kingdom of Yslandeth.

Famlin returned to Sudenyag. Safiya surprised her love by changing her mind about studying in Edenyag. She decided instead to accompany her love to his homeland in the South. The two would eventually marry, and Safiya would bear her husband three sons and two daughters. Famlin named his sons Roland, Brynd and Medadel, after his fallen friends. Safiya named her daughters Sal'iabac, after her fallen sister, and Danza after Danzu, the Hodan. The couple lived a long and happy life in Suden. Their tribe recorded their leader's contributions to the reunification of Suden, and his efforts in rebuilding the nation's infrastructure in the lore of their people. Famlin is a revered name, only second to Harun the Shadow, in the Lore of the South.

After establishing a temple to the Goddess in the newly established Offlander town, which became known by the surrounding settlements as Galdsburg, Valtyr finally returned to Empyr and found that Master Donick had taken ill. The older Master was now in his late fifties and had chronic health issues that limited his ability to execute his office as a Minister to the King and High Priest of the Order of Haya's Dawn. After several years of study under Donick, Valtyr was appointed the new minister and High Priest of the monastery, by King Puryn's hand. Donick passed into Aeternum within five years of the Valtyr's arrival, but he was able to witness the fulfillment of his life's work, as Empyr's last stones were set in place only weeks before his passing.

Kairoth met Valtyr in Empyr and began his studies, traveling East to Torith within months, and then to Dornat Al Ar, eventually ending up in Edenyag within the year. He sent messages to Faylea, who waited impatiently for his return, but did not give up on their love. Eventually, she knew that he would end up by her side.

* * *

Reynir had business with his Mistress, Queen Adasser. He did not know how the conversation would go. Many times, druids were known to fight over territories in the elder days, but the Human did not want to fight his Queen, nor did he like his chances of survival if she challenged him.

Riding in on his white horse, the young druid approached the temple in Erynseere. Dismounting, he tied the horse to the post outside of the sanctuary. He could hear the Queen speaking to someone behind the door.

"Come in, Reynir!" the Queen shouted at the door. "Quit hiding like a little boy who stole a pie from the window sill!"

Reynir shut his eyes tight and muttered a prayer to the Goddess as he pushed the doors open. "My Queen, it is good to see you." Thankfully, she was dressed, thought the young man, averting his eyes.

"The Goddess tells me that you have been busy, my student." The Queen glanced at the man before her seriously. He was not a child anymore. "Have you come to challenge me? Very bold of you." Adasser did not look up from a tome that she was reading.

"No, never, Your Majesty. I would never wish to harm you," Reynir said with a look of horror on his face.

"Nor, I you, my son," the Queen replied closing the tome. "What shall we do with you, student?"

"I wish to move into Cinnog, Your Majesty. Perhaps I can establish a temple to the Goddess near the Citadel, very much South of here," Reynir offered hopefully.

The Queen smiled and laughed. "Then how will you come to visit? That is about as South as you can go, boy!"

Reynir breathed a sigh of relief. "You are not angry about the trees are you, My Queen? They came to me. I did not mean for it to happen."

"As it should be, druid. You are now a Master. You must command your own forest. Although, mine is MUCH bigger than yours," the Queen said in a purposefully childish tone, eliciting a chuckle from the now relaxing Reynir.

"You must give your old teacher a hug before you leave me forever. I will miss you. You were always such a good student, Reynir, but you are no longer a student, you are a teacher. Go forth and teach. Spread the light and love wherever you go." The Queen sniffled a bit and wiped her eyes with a handkerchief.

"It is not forever, even if I never set foot in Erynseere again, My Queen. We shall meet again in this life, or in the next. I will always consider you to be my High Priestess." Reynir hugged the Queen tightly, then turned to go. "I will come to visit on occasion, but you must come to Cinnog also! The people of Cinnog would love to see the Queen who saved Erynseere. You are a living legend, My Mistress. Until we see each other once more." Reynir bowed, exiting the sanctuary. Tears ran down his cheeks as he mounted his horse and rode southward. He had said goodbye to many already, but he knew his destiny was ahead of him in Cinnog.

The druid looked up on the hill to the West, he recognized his wood. It waited for his command. To his two original friends, he relayed the message, "We move to Cinnog."

Looking around Erynseere nostalgically, the druid frowned and spurred his horse down the road.

With all of the losses Reynir's life had brought him, there were two big additions right before his eyes. Laerwen sat on her horse beside the druid with a toddler in a cloth pack over her shoulders. They were packed and ready to go. The Queen insisted.

The young quarter-Elfish boy bounced on his mother's back, causing her to roll her eyes, but as she watched her boy's father wipe his tears away and begin to smile at her, she sighed and knew that the future was with him, not here in Erynseere.

Chapter 29

Kairoth traveled West toward Hodan, across the high desert of northern Sudenyag. As he rode at a trot, he sat up stiffly in his saddle. Rubbing his back, he looked up at the sun. It was high in the sky.

"Midday. Time to stop for a meal," he thought.

The monk who dismounted his horse to sit and eat in the shade of a tall bushy tree was a far cry from the younger, impetuous, armor-clad Hodan warrior who stormed an evil temple over a year ago. Kairoth was alone now on the road, spreading the word of his new God, and his God had blessed him with many precious things.

"Here," the monk said, pouring water into a small pan and giving to his horse. "Drink, my friend." The monk took a long swig from the water skin and hung it over the horn of his saddle. He looked around at the familiar terrain. He had ridden this road many times before.

After eating his small repast, Kairoth laid down in the shade of the tree. It was early afternoon and not too warm. Yawning, he was soon fast asleep.

Several hours later, when the weather had taken a turn for the worst, the wind had begun to blow a bit, and the rustling of the branches woke the sleeping monk. Startled, he could see the sun was now behind thick, dark clouds as large raindrops began to fall from the sky. Worse yet, his horse and belongings were nowhere in sight. Standing, he searched his satchel hanging from his shoulder. In it, he found one holy book, a preserved ration and a small bag of coins.

"Really," the monk said in disgust. "Well, I am in Sudenyag. At least the little bastards left my shoes on my feet."

The rain began to fall harder and what had begun as a planting season shower was evolving into an all-out squall. Soaked, Kairoth looked around him to gain his bearings. He estimated that he was only a couple of miles from the Hodan border. This motivated him to push harder.

"Almost home." The monk smiled. "She will kick me in my teeth for showing up at her door looking like a beggar!" The Hodan man laughed loudly, slipping and falling into the mud. Shaking his head, he chuckled again and shook his fist at the sky.

"Really, My God? What are trying to teach me this time?" Kairoth looked around as thunder rumbled in the distance. The rain was coming down in sheets, and he now resembled a larger version of a drowned Suden street urchin. Shaking his head, he trudged gingerly down the muddy road, staying to the right on the shoulder, where a small berm was dryer than the center muck.

"This would have been much easier if I had kept the horse, Lord," the monk quipped sarcastically, "but whatever pleases you." He bowed sarcastically, then slipped and fell in the mud again. "Yes, I know you are here somewhere. Only you could come up with this scenario."

Standing, the Hodan laughed again, wiping mud from his eyes. Looking to the sky, the water soon rinsed the remainder from his face.

"Onward! March!" the large Hodan man said to no one there, and march he did, toward the Hodan border.

* * *

Five miles into Hodan, it began to get dark. The rain had let up, but it was still a bit chilly in the evening. Kairoth looked at the wet wool blanket he had been using as a cloak for the past few hours in the rain. It was a muddy, soggy mess. He breathed hard and shook his head in resignation as he saw his breath mist before his face. It was going to be a cold one.

Off in the distance, an old man struggled to pull his small hand-drawn cart out of a particularly soupy spot in the road. Kairoth watched as the old man fell with a splash for the third time.

"I should go help him, eh?" Kairoth looked up at the darkening sky. "What is the matter, Likedelir? Are you angry with me for some reason? You have barely spoken to me in days."

There was silence from the skies.

"Oh well, pull this cart out and get back to Faylea before some other man wins her heart." Kairoth walked up to the old man who was sitting in the mud panting and shaking his head.

"Halt!" the old man commanded sternly. "Who are you? What do you want?"

"Nothing, Sir. I saw you in distress and wish to assist you in freeing the cart," the Hodan replied.

"Out of the goodness of your heart, I would suppose." The old man's tone dripped with suspicion and sarcasm. "I have no coin to spare. I have no work for you. I am a simple man who lives nearby. I am no one of importance."

"Ah, that makes two of us then," Kairoth said, hands up, walking toward the old man. "I have no weapons. Highwaymen stole all of my goods. I, too, have nothing to offer, but a hand with the cart, if you desire it."

The old man stood. He was covered in mud, but something about his posture struck the monk as odd. The man was a full six inches shorter than Kairoth, slightly built, and quite a bit older. Kairoth wondered how the old man managed with a cart on his good days, never mind in a mire such as this.

The old man squinted. "I am not an easy mark, young man," the old man responded calmly.

"It is a good thing that I only desire to help you with your cart then, Sir," Kairoth said, biting back a grin.

"Fine, but if you try anything, it will be your pyre." The old man huffed and turned to grab a wooden handle. "Grab that one if you would."

Kairoth grabbed the right handle, and soon the cart was pulled free of the muck and onto the better ground to the side of the road. The old man sighed and sat down on the grass next to his cart.

"Thank you. I have been fighting with that blasted thing for an hour or more. Where did that rain come from? One minute it's a fine day, the next the sky is trying to drown me." The old man stood and reached inside of his cart, pulling out a burlap bag with bread and cheese in it. Then he grabbed a skin and sat down next to the larger Hodan monk. He opened the bag and offered a loaf and a wedge to Kairoth, who gladly accepted.

"This is not necessary, Sir, but it is appreciated." The monk bowed. Then he said a quick prayer and sat up to eat.

"Are you a priest?" The old man asked with his head cocked comically to the side. "If you are, then what kind of prayer was that one?"

Kairoth swallowed. "I have been chosen to represent a new God. He is a child of the Light and the Dark. His mother is Haya and his father, the Underlord. He is a God of balance and justice, vice one of either side exclusively."

The old man's eyes widened for a second. "So if the good gets too strong?"

"Then the Dark will respond to reestablish the balance, yes. Sometimes, Likedelir works against the Light." Kairoth braced for a negative response from his host.

"Hmm," the old man said scratching his chin hairs. "So what you are telling me is that there can be too much Light or too much Darkness, so your God seeks to maintain a balance to the world?"

"Exactly." Kairoth sat up. "Have you heard my message second hand, Sir?"

"No, it's something I have long known to be the truth, even though I tend to support the Light, because I seek to live!" The old man laughed.

"My God told me that the wise come to these conclusions on their own, but that it is a rare thing to meet someone who has had the revelation!" Kairoth smiled and extended his hand. "I am Kairoth, of Hodan."

"I am Ei'nyorn. I am Hodan. I was once a serviceable warrior, as I am sure that you were also. I am old, but I am still spry for my age." The old man laughed and extended a hand to Kairoth, who could see markings on the old man's forearm.

"What are those?" Kairoth asked, looking at the image in the fading light.

"Brands from a day gone by. It is a wolf, howling to the sky." The old man looked to the ground for a moment, as if remembering something painful. "I was in one of the Wolfpack units that operated within Hodan—and from outside the borders. We fought under Jabir before Orus claimed his throne. Jabir was a fool. Orus is a good man. I fear that Hodan will soon swallow him whole if he is not careful."

"I have fought with King Puryn and King Orus on many occasions," the monk said confidently. "They are both honorable men in hard positions. Sometimes, one must be careful about what they strive for. Thrones are not for the weak-minded or those who wish a life of leisure!"

"Indeed," the old man agreed. "If you can walk another mile with me, there is an inn just up the road. I will see that you have a night out of the cold and even buy a couple of meads, if you wish to entertain an old man's stories for a few hours."

"You had me at mead, Sir!" Kairoth chuckled.

"Then let us go!" Ei'nyorn said, laughing and grabbing his cart handle. Kairoth grabbed the other.

* * *

The inn was busy when the two travelers arrived. Ei'nyorn was pleased that the smell of the dinner fare was still strong in the air. He hoped to buy himself a bowl of meat stew and some bread if any was left. Kairoth fiddled with his almost empty coin purse, but the old man waved him off.

"Call it wages for pulling me out of the mess and helping me to here." Ei'nyorn motioned for the monk to enter.

The inn was a larger establishment. It was not lavish by any means, but it was a two-story building with a common room on the bottom floor, which doubled as a tavern and eating hall. Several armored men sat drinking and loudly playing games in the corner. They were Hodan Elites. The rest of the room was filled with farmers, local tradesmen or merchants traveling from Sudenyag back to the capital city of Warrior's Rest.

"Barmaid, any dinner left?" the old man asked.

"A bit, but it's going fast. Two copper coin a bowl. One copper for mead or ale." She stuck her hand out.

"I need two bowls of stew, two meads, and two loaves of bread." Ei'nyorn handed the girl a silver coin. Her eyes widened a bit.

Ei'nyorn said in a subdued voice, "Keep the change."

"Yes, Mi'Lord." The young girl bowed and walked quickly to the kitchen, returning within moments with two trays and a pitcher of mead.

Ei'nyorn said, "I only paid for two meads."

"It's a bit watered down, and since you were so generous, my father begs you to take the pitcher." She left the food.

Ei'nyorn shrugged, looking at Kairoth. "Who am I to argue with good fortune?"

Kairoth nodded, filling his mouth with the first hot food he had eaten in days. He was content, but could feel that something was amiss in the room. The Hodan were still shouting and cursing their luck as they gambled, but the old man's demeanor seems to sour all of a sudden, and this concerned Kairoth.

"Is everything all right, Sir?" the monk asked seriously.

He sighed "Maybe," the old man responded. "We shall see."

From behind the squawking table of Hodan Elites, a slightly drunk man made his way around to where the two travelers sat. He was a large man. Kairoth looked at him calmly, estimating that he had to be almost seven measures tall and at least fifty pounds heavier than the monk had ever been at his largest. The man advancing on them wore Dwarfish plate mail and carried the standard Legion longsword and shield. They were standard issue, and Kairoth recognized them immediately. The Hodan monk began to get up from his seat.

Smiling, Ei'nyorn put his hand on Kairoth's forearm. "Thank you, son, but I am all right. Please sit. This is my problem, and I will handle it."

Against his better judgment, the monk sat back down.

"You had better sit down, priest!" the warrior said with disdain.

"What is it that you desire, Rollock?" the old man asked, standing with his walking staff.

"I want my taxes, old man, and apparently you have money to spend on traveling street preachers and mead. Pay me what you owe me. Now!" The warrior reached for his sword.

Across the room, the other five gambling Elites perked up to see what their Lieutenant was up to. They began to stand and make ready.

"King Orus will not be pleased by your extortion, Lieutenant," Kairoth quipped standing.

"You should close your mouth, or I will close your eyes permanently," the warrior threatened menacingly.

"Please, let me handle this," the old man said to Kairoth, who raised his hands and stepped back a pace.

"As you wish, but I will not let him harm you," Kairoth said in a deadly serious tone.

"Thank you, son," the old man replied grinning. "Your concern is well appreciated."

Then Ei'nyorn turned to the Hodan warrior. "Rollock, you are a piece of cow dung. If you can manage to remove the coin purse from my person, you can have it. Otherwise, you can go make love to your horse."

The room erupted in laughter, enraging the larger warrior in front of the old man.

"As you wish. I will remove your head and take your money." The warrior drew his sword.

That is when the mayhem began.

The warrior swung first, but the old man stepped out of the way of the stroke, letting it pass harmlessly to his left. Grabbing his staff with one hand, Ei'nyorn swung the weapon at the warrior's head. The Elite recovered and blocked the shot with his shield, but not before the old man had found a way to stand on its top edge.

Ei'nyorn stepped off of the shield as it crashed to the floor under his weight, springing into the air in what looked like slow-motion to the now gape-mouthed Kairoth, who was scrambling to intercept the incoming five gamblers as they made their way across the room. Ei'nyorn's next blow landed. The old man delivered a crushing two-handed overhand blow to the left side of the top of Rollock's helmet. The blow knocked the Elite to his knees. Ei'nyorn proceeded to finish the job, pummeling the much larger assailant from multiple angles, using hands, feet, his staff, and the occasional head-butt. Within seconds, the much larger man was unconscious on the floor, and the other five men who came to aid him began to exit the inn of their own free will.

The old man was panting. Sitting down gingerly, the old man grimaced as he picked up his tankard. He could see several younger lads licking their chops over what the unconscious Lieutenant had on his person.

"If any of you as much as takes a copper coin off of that man, I will beat you within an inch of your life. Do we understand?" Ei'nyorn addressed the room, but to no one in particular. You could hear a pin drop. The audience all sat back down, and soon, everyone was back to their usual activities. The only nuisance was having to step over a large unconscious man in the middle of the floor. Eventually, several men dragged the Hodan warrior over to a corner and sat him up against the wall. He would be out for a few hours if he ever woke up again.

"Aren't you worried that he'll wake up? He will not be amused if he sees us still drinking here!" Kairoth looked at Ei'nyorn with concern.

"I'm not leaving. I'm not giving him my money. He can go if he wants to. You can leave if you wish. I am not holding you here by force!" Ei'nyorn smirked.

"I will walk you back to your home. It is on the way!" Kairoth laughed, finishing his tankard.

"Barmaid, another pitcher, please," the old man asked, holding up another silver coin.

* * *

The morning came. Kairoth woke from his spot near the fire in the common room. Much to his surprise, the Hodan unit that had been in the bar had left without challenging them while they slept. The monk looked around the room and could see the old man was up, drinking tea and eating oatmeal.

"Nice of you to wake up," the old man said sarcastically.

"It is scarcely the first hour of the morning, old man!" Kairoth replied yawning.

"Well, get your things together if you want to run up the road with me a bit. I have to get home. I need to feed Rania. She will be displeased with my absence." The old man's face betrayed a bit of worry for the first time.

"Is Rania your woman?" Kairoth asked, shoveling food into his mouth and swallowing his tea quickly.

Ei'nyorn smiled. "In a matter of speaking."

Kairoth's wrinkled brow amused the old man, who chuckled and gave the girl at the counter one more silver coin.

"This is much too much, Sir," the lady said, trying to make change for the old man.

"Nonsense. It is to pay for the damages I caused last night while dealing with my 'friend.'" He smiled and closed the girl's hand around the coin.

"Safe travels, gentlemen." The girl smiled, waving to Ei'nyorn and Kairoth as they left.

* * *

About midday, Kairoth could see Ei'nyorn looking up into the sky. Shielding his eyes, the monk realized that the old man was watching two hawks off in the distance. They were hunting and apparently working together. Kairoth watched as the old man smiled.

"Oh, she is going to be very wroth with me. We should hurry! They are getting all the fat rabbits!" Ei'nyorn laughed, then began pulling the cart harder. Kairoth looked at the man as if he had lost his mind, but pulled anyway.

* * *

Up a small hill, on the rise, Kairoth saw a small farmstead with a pole fence around the entire property. It was a fair-sized piece of land. The old man was raising root vegetables in a large plot. He also had a barn with at least one horse that had escaped and was eating grass in the meadow out in front. Several chicken coops were also spotted here and there around the grounds. This old man had set himself up pretty well.

As they arrived, the sun was starting to go down. It was getting cold again. Kairoth looked at the road. He began his goodbyes.

"I should go now. Thank you for the meals on the road. They were appreciated," the monk said bowing.

"Nonsense, you should stay the night. It is cold and the night will be upon us within an hour. How far do you think that you will get in a wool blanket, on foot?" The old man motioned for the monk to enter his home. It was dark.

"Are you sure?" Kairoth was looking around, but could not see in the house.

"Of course." Ei'nyorn lit an oil lamp and covered it in a glass. The room lit.

That is when Kairoth saw her.

In the corner on a perch with a tether, was the largest hawk that the monk had ever seen. She was a beautiful bird. She squawked gently, as if chastising the old man for being gone so long. He put on a large leather glove that covered his whole arm up to his elbow, then called to her. Obediently, the hawk hopped onto his arm and shifted back and forth in an excited manner.

"I'm sorry, I'm sorry! I didn't think that it was going to rain. Give me a second, Rania, I have it!" The old man pleaded while he pulled out a small rabbit from a sack. He set it on the floor and Rania greedily pounced on it.

"Rania. I see," Kairoth said cautiously.

"Sit down, monk. She won't attack you unless you threaten her … or me. We have been friends for a while." Ei'nyorn started a fire in the small cooking pit in the kitchen. "It will take a few, but the fire will warm this whole room soon."

Kairoth nodded.

"Don't worry, she is fine. She is a good girl." The old man smiled as if he looked at his only child. "You can sleep on that cot. I like the soft chair near her perch. She will be angry if I sleep away from her tonight!"

"Thank you again, Sir. You are too kind," Kairoth responded.

The two ate a bit of bread and cheese and finished off a bottle of wine. Then both said their goodnights and went to sleep.

* * *

Kairoth woke slowly. It was warm. The smell of a smoky, smoldering fire was strong. Sitting up, he rubbed his eyes. After using the privy and washing up a bit, the monk sat, meditated and prayed. Looking around, he wondered where the old man had gotten off to. He went to find him. It was a short task.

Outside in the open field, the old man looked to the sky. He whistled loudly and waited. Kairoth didn't notice what he was looking at until she moved closer. It was Rania traveling full speed to her friend who held out his arm. The hawk took her time, climbing and descending, her head darting left and right as she scanned for a rabbit or squirrel. When she changed direction suddenly, she did it so gracefully that Kairoth thought of a dancer in a silk dress, spinning and prancing lightly upon the floor.

Kairoth reached in his satchel and pulled out his book. He opened it and read, "Look for him where the hawk dances and the wolf cries to the moon. It is in your book if you forget, Hodan.”

Kairoth watched as the bird perched on Ei'nyorn's arm. The monk approached cautiously. “Good morning!”

“Good morning! Did you sleep well?” the old man snickered.

“Very well.” Kairoth watched the bird light off to fly the perimeter of the farm. “May I see your arm with the markings on it?”

“Why?” Ei'nyorn asked defensively. “It is just a wolf.”

“May I see the top of the markings?” Kairoth asked innocently.

Ei'nyorn's face turned to a frown. “Who are you? Have you come to avenge some sister or brother?”

“I'm a passerby, but I must know if you are ‘the one’ I am looking for,” Kairoth said.

“Many have looked for me and found their death, young man,” the elderly man said gravely. “Fine, look and be satisfied.” He bared his arm to the elbow. There above the wolf was a moon.

“I knew it!” Kairoth said excitedly.

Ei'nyorn stepped back into a defensive combat stance.

“What did I say?” the monk asked with his hands up in front of him.

“Do you know what the designation of the moon means?” Ei'nyorn looked fiercely at the monk.

“I have no idea, Sir, but relax, we are friends,” Kairoth reassured.

“The moon is the mark of an assassin. I was a Wolfpack assassin for Jabir in my day. I killed many. I am the last of my band. Many were hunted and killed for their sins after Orus took the throne. Do you seek my head, because your search may be for nothing? I am not long for the Ert.”

Kairoth stood stunned at Ei'nyorn's revelation. The nice old man with the quirky personality definitely had a dark side. Regardless, Kairoth was sure that this was the man his God had sent him to find.

“Sir, I am a man who had done my share of killing. Innocents died on all sides, because of war and lesser leadership. I have no vendetta against you.” Kairoth handed him his holy book. “Take a look at this tome. It contains the orders from my God, telling me to find you and seek your training. My God sees something in you that I need to learn.”

The old man read the words and frowned. "I am no Master. I am a no good man. I am a murderer who is dying. Every day I get weaker. I cannot hold down my food anymore, and I pass blood every day. Soon, I will be gone. No one will remember me."

"Then teach me your fighting style. We can also discuss philosophy! You can tell me your story. You are changed! Your outlook on life and your actions do not show you to be evil, Sir. You could have easily killed that fool in the inn the night before last, but you did not. Why? Mercy? What cold assassin shows mercy?" Kairoth took his book back from the man in front of him.

"When I die, I have no one to take over this land. I have no one to carry on my name. At least, perhaps, someone will carry on my fighting style. I wonder if your God or someone like him used to visit me on occasion? Whoever he was, he taught me much in my time when he visited. Now, I will teach you the skills that I have honed over many years of practice." Ei'nyorn looked at the monk stoically.

"I would be honored to learn, Master," Kairoth responded, bowing.

"We must hurry. My days are numbered. I have a few months maybe." Ei'nyorn held out his arm and Rania lit down on it gracefully. "I will teach you on one condition." The old man leveled his gaze at Kairoth.

"Name it," Kairoth replied.

"I will teach you, but you must care for my partner when I am gone. She may survive in the wild now, but I do not wish to take the chance. She has been with me several years." The old man looked at the large bird and frowned. "I will miss her."

"If she will have me, I will care for her," Kairoth agreed.

"Good! Then we start in the morning!" Ei'nyorn smiled. "You will show me what he has shown you and what you have learned on the Ert. I will show you my style, and you may integrate it as you wish. What is the name of your God, monk?"

"He calls himself, Likedelir, Master, but others know him by the name, the Conflict."

"Of course, he would come to me. I have been at war my whole life."

Ei'nyorn put his hand on Kairoth's shoulder. "Let's go inside. You can tell me more over a meal."

Chapter 30

ays became weeks, and weeks turned to months. Soon, Kairoth had been with his new Master for three seasons. As the last of the leaves fell from the trees, Ei'nyorn's health began to take a sharp turn for the worse.

In the beginning of their arrangement, Kairoth's presence seemed to reinvigorate the old man. He quickly became attached to the monk, and Kairoth felt strangely at home with the old man. It was almost as if the old man had found his only son, and the fatherless son had reunited with his long-lost father.

The training sessions started out as basic lessons. Kairoth displayed his prowess to his new Master and Ei'nyorn was impressed by all that the Hodan monk already knew.

Smiling, the old man repeatedly said, "You have a solid foundation on which to build. We do not have to tear down the building, we just need to smooth out the rough-cut walls."

As the months progressed, and Ei'nyorn's health began to fade, the old man pushed Kairoth harder, as if he had too much to teach in too little time. Kairoth knew that it was true and lamented that he had taken so long to finally find this man and get to know him, but regardless of his late entry into Ei'nyorn's life, the monk knew that he was in the right place at the right time.

It was the beginning of the harvest season, called Glorus, when Ei'nyorn was unable to continue and became bedridden.

* * *

"I think today is the day, Kairoth!" the old man wheezed, sipping a hot cup of tea.

"Nonsense, you tell me that every day, old man! You are as strong as an ox!" Kairoth encouraged his Master, but inside, he feared that the old man might finally be right.

"Kairoth, you have told me of your father and mother. I tell you this, never wonder if they are in Aeternum. Never worry if they are proud of you." The old man coughed and struggled to sit up.

Kairoth helped him sit. "Be careful and take it slow. You are sick. You will be up and beating me in staff drills in no time."

Kairoth's voice betrayed him. The old man noticed. "It is well, son," the old man said, holding the Hodan monk's hand. "Pray for me to find my way out of the catacombs, monk. I have much to atone for."

Kairoth swallow hard as he looked into the misty, reddened eyes of the now-frail teacher who he had met almost nine months prior.

"You have changed your heart, Master," Kairoth sniffled a bit then composed himself. "I am sure that you will not see the catacombs."

"Ah, son, you do not know me very well. You know only the best me. Humor an old man. Please pray to your Gods for my passage. Promise me." The old man's look turned to fear.

"I will pray every day. I will pray right now."

Kairoth bowed his head, and Ei'nyorn watched. As he prayed, Kairoth felt the old man's grip loosen on his hand. He heard the shallow, easy breathing. Then, there was silence, and he knew that he sat alone.

Kairoth looked up, opening his eyes. "You were right, old man. I wish that you were wrong for just one more day, my only friend."

Kairoth looked up at a large hawk on her stand. She was looking at the monk as if she knew.

"If you will come with me, Rania, you are welcome," Kairoth said somberly. "I must prepare a pyre and send him off to Aeternum, first."

Kairoth wiped his eyes, then tossed a piece of rabbit to the bird. She jumped to the floor and began devouring it.

"I will be back soon."

Kairoth closed his Master's eyes, wrapped the body in his bedclothes and carried him out to the open field where the two practiced daily. He set his body in the cart he had helped him free all of those months ago.

"This is a good spot. I will be back soon, Sir," Kairoth said gathering wood.

* * *

"Another pyre, eh?" a hooded man said, popping up from thin air behind the monk.

"As if you did not know, My Lord?" Kairoth was annoyed with the nonchalant manner in which his God was talking about the situation.

"He was a murderer. Still, you mourn for him?" Likedelir smiled under his hood out of view.

"He was a soldier, ordered to do vile things by a vile man. Once freed from those duties, he chose to walk in the light. I would say that he embodies balance, My Lord." Kairoth's inflection in his voice bordered on disrespect.

"Are we fighting? Oh good, I have never argued with a Human before!" Likedelir was amused.

"You're a God; what good are my arguments. You will just do whatever it is that pleases you, like all of the rest." Kairoth turned his reddened eyes toward his God. "I, myself, am sick of death already. He was a good man, in the end, Likedelir. I would ask one thing, if I may."

"What is it?" the God asked knowingly.

"Spare him the catacombs. I beg you. Petition Haya to let him enter into Aeternum. Please?" Kairoth stood sadly and began walking back to where his friend laid in a cart.

"Where are you going? We are not done talking yet!" the God protested. "Come back, High Priest!" Likedelir was now grinning widely at Kairoth's rebellion.

"Come with me. Just pop up near the cart where I will burn my friend. I will entertain you," Kairoth deadpanned.

"I will!" Likedelir said almost happily, annoying the Hodan monk.

* * *

Kairoth carefully set the wood, dousing it in a bucket of oil. It was a pile at least four feet in height with a small wooden litter stand above it. Gingerly, the large monk set his Master on the pyre.

"This will not do. I must send him with provisions," the monk said entering the house.

After a short time, the Hodan monk found the old man's stash of armor, weapons, and gold. He brought out the armor and laid it on top of his Master's body. He put the sword in the man's right hand and laid his shield on top of the whole affair. Then, Kairoth poured a cup of mead and set a sack of meat, cheese, bread, and fruit beside his Master. Finally, a small bag of coin was tied to the man's belt, and Kairoth stepped back from what he had done.

"Why do you do that?" Likedelir asked, watching the ceremony.

"It is out of respect and to provide for the afterlife," Kairoth responded wondering where his God was going with the line of questioning. "We always do this when someone we love or respect dies."

"He is dead, Kairoth." The God leveled his gaze at his priest. "He is not here anymore. Do you think that anything you do for him now is going to make a difference where he is? He is not looking at this corpse."

"What is he looking at?" Kairoth responded with irritation. "Darkness or light … or neither? What is the point of life?"

"Ah, the great question of reality itself," the God said calmly. "First, I will assure you that he is not in darkness. I have petitioned successfully for his passage."

"That is a relief to me, Lord," Kairoth said penitently, realizing that he was out of line.

"Relax, priest, I am not annoyed with you! I am intrigued that you stand up for what you believe in. When I said that this was all for naught, I only meant to say to you that all of your ceremonies, all of the songs and dances that mortals do for their departed, are all for their own benefit. They do not benefit he or she who is lost. Do not feel as if anything that you do here, save praying for their souls, has any lasting effect anywhere, but in your own mind."

The God put his hand on Kairoth's shoulder, and the pyre lit without a torch being thrown into it.

"You know that I am right," Likedelir said smugly, smirking. "Live now, love now, do what is necessary while the sun still shines and green is still beneath you."

Kairoth bowed. "Thank you for helping him, My Lord, and thank you for using me to spread your message."

"We will speak again when you are King. Go to Hodan and claim your Queen. You are required in Warrior's Crossing. Take anything that you can from this place, because he does not need it and others will come to rob as soon as they see his pyre smoke rising."

Kairoth nodded and went into the house, gathering his things and everything that he could take with him. He saddled up a horse and filled the saddlebags with provisions and coin, then he gingerly approached the hawk, and she came to him without a hitch, just as her friend had taught her to do for many months.

After washing, putting on new clothes, and eating a good meal, the monk trotted off on horseback toward the main road South of the farm. Heading West, the Hodan rider looked intimidating in a long, black, cloak with a large hawk perched on his shoulder.

Kairoth looked at Rania nervously as her head darted back and forth.

"I hope you understand that I did not kill the old man, Rania. I did not want him to go either. We go to Warrior's Crossing, but I am sure that you will find a few rabbits along the way. I am not him, but I will take care of you as promised, if you wish to stay with me."

The hawk cocked her head to one side with her beak slightly open, panting. Kairoth stared back, then spurred the horse.

* * *

Faylea sat alone in the throne room. She was worried. Six months ago, her father began to think of leaving Hodan in search of the home of the Offlanders. Several very close confidents and friends loved the idea and encouraged the King to consider it seriously. The Dwarves and Suden had mastered one of the tall ships in the harbor near the Port of Valent. The prototype had been outfitted with smaller versions of the Thunder Ballista used in Cinnog against Alliance troops. The tests were a resounding success, sinking a derelict in the harbor without effort. This emboldened the King.

At first, after returning from the war in Sudenyag, Hodan was quiet. Hodan had quelled the Underlord, and the Yslandeth truce had assisted, proving that Orus was a wise diplomat and fierce warrior. But Hodan was at peace.

Slowly, over the first year without a war, the warriors became restless. Some began to murmur about the age of the King and family attachments sapping his courage and resolve. Many warmonger cliques within the ranks began to stir up discord, creating fake emergencies on the Cinnog or Suden border. Some began to pick at the scabs that remained, concerning payback for the massacre of the Legions in past engagements with Edenyag. All of their complaints fell on deaf ears. Orus was tired of war and ready to retire. The problem was, the only way he could retire was to die. He was not afraid of that. He was afraid of what the new, young victor may do to Faylea. His daughter's safety was his utmost concern.

After much arguing, Orus told Faylea of his plan. He would sail to places unknown. He promised to return, but Faylea knew that promise was a lie. Her father was a hero; a warrior who fought for those who were oppressed. He would undoubtedly die on a battlefield, but if he had his way, it would not be one that he had ever seen before.

* * *

It had been six months since Orus left. Faylea maintained the propaganda with a straight, stoic face in public, but in private, she wept for her father. Orus made his case to the people, and they cheered his pioneer spirit. They even accepted that Faylea would assume the throne temporarily until his return. That began to change, as the same dissident voices that dogged her father's reign began to question hers.

Challengers to the throne began to speak out loudly. Lawyers and wisemen for the crown rebuked the challengers. The legal decision being that since Orus was not present to fight to defend his crown, there was no one to challenge. Faylea ruled by King's decree. This argument held for the moment, but Faylea knew that her days were numbered.

In armor, and looking at her sword, she wondered if she would be able to defend the crown. She was not her father.

* * *

Kairoth trotted slowly up the road. He had released the hawk to hunt, but didn't want to get too far away until she returned to him. About twenty minutes later, a red streak appeared above him, then slowed perching on his shoulder again. She was a bloody mess and had a medium-sized rabbit in her talons. She dropped it in his lap, as she gently grabbed his leather armor.

"Nice one, girl. I suppose you want me to stop to allow you to eat it?" Kairoth rode to the side of the road and dismounted. The hawk fluttered its wings, never taking its eyes off of its catch. "Fine, fine! Go!" Kairoth laughed.

The hawk pounced as if she was elated that the Human gave her permission to eat.

"I don't know what I am going to do with you." The monk wiped rabbit innards off of his lap.

While the bird ate, a hand-drawn cart with two younger boys pulling it came up the road from where Kairoth had ridden. Both young men were about twelve years old, and pulling a couple of sacks of grain and a keg to someplace unknown. They were intrigued by the hawk eating its catch.

"Excuse us, Sir. Can we watch the bird for a bit?" one boy asked from a distance.

"Sure, but do not approach too quickly. And stay quiet," Kairoth said waving them to come closer.

The hawk eyed the two smaller Humans suspiciously and repositioned herself to keep them in sight as she ate.

"Is she yours?" one boy said in wonder.

"In a matter of speaking, but who truly owns anything that lives?" Kairoth smiled.

"Where are you headed, Sir? Are you going to the capital to watch the fight?" the other boy asked in an excited manner.

"What fight?" Kairoth questioned.

"The Princess, Faylea, fights Groma, son of Yars, for the Crown. With King Orus being gone for such a long time, the people demand that Faylea prove her prowess to maintain power. She's a woman though. I like her, but many think that a woman should not be the leader of Hodan. They say that it is an insult. I don't know about that." The boy looked at Kairoth nervously. "Are you all right, Sir? I did not mean to offend you."

"No, boy, you did not offend. I know Faylea, and she is not an insult to Hodan. Fools." Kairoth stood, startling the two boys. "I must leave immediately. Rania, come, girl!" The monk whistled.

The boys were wide-eyed at the size of the man before him. They had not realized how big Kairoth was while he sat. The hawk on his shoulder made both boys swallow hard.

"Well, Sir. The fight is tomorrow morning at dawn. You should be able to be in town in an hour or so. Good luck and be blessed by the brothers, Sir!" One boy waved to Kairoth as they grabbed their cart to leave.

Kairoth mounted his horse. "Hang on, bird. I need to move quickly."

The monk spurred his horse to a gallop toward the castle he saw plainly up the road. Hodan had not changed.

* * *

The morning was cold and bright. The blood-thirsty mobs had formed in the large coliseum where the warriors trained. Faylea stood armored and ready. The challengers had not arrived yet. Kairoth had. Grabbing his staff, he tethered his horse.

Setting Rania on the saddle, he tethered her to the horn. "You behave, girl. I will be gone for a bit."

Kairoth looked around. The shade of the area was sufficient. He tied a small metal cup to the horn by its handle. It was full of water. Rania did not look pleased as he began to walk away.

"Do not claw the horse or empty your water! Behave for once, you ornery old bird!" Kairoth smiled then tossed a piece of beef onto the saddle. Rania greedily scarfed it down and looked at the Human expectantly. "That's all for now. Behave, please?"

Up on the platform, the monk could see his love. She was in a beautiful set of Dwarven plate. She held the customary longsword and shield of the Hodan Legion. She was surrounded by guards and advisors. The guards perked up as Kairoth approached.

"Who are you and what do you want, traveler?" one burly guard asked, drawing his sword six inches out of its sheath.

"I am here to see the Princess, guard. Tell her that Kairoth is here."

"She is a bit preoccupied to speak to clergy or beggars. Come back later," the guard retorted sarcastically.

A voice from behind him said nervously. "Did that man say he was Kairoth?"

"Yeah, so what?" the guard responded to the priest behind him.

"So, that man is the one the Princess calls her beloved, fool. You would best let him through." The priest crossed his arms.

"Oh, well that is different," the guard backtracked. "Carry on, Sir."

Kairoth bowed and followed the priest. "Right this way, Sir. Please, talk her out of this!"

"You cannot talk that woman out of anything, brother," Kairoth laughed.

Faylea looked up, hearing the familiar chuckle. She dropped her sword and ran to the ragged monk. "My Gods, you are here! It has been over a year!" She slapped his face. "What is wrong with you!?"

"I had a mission that I had to complete. It is done now. I am here." The monk rubbed his cheek.

"Now, on the day that I will surely die, you show up," the Princess whispered in her man's ear.

Kairoth whispered back, "Not if I have anything to say about it. Marry me, now."

Faylea pushed him back. "Are you serious? Now you ask? Oh, My Gods, you are unbelievable."

"Trust me. Please. Do you still love me?" Kairoth batted his eyelids.

Faylea laughed. "Of course I do, you fool! I will marry you."

"Priest, come take care of this for us, would you?" the monk asked his earlier escort.

"Of course, My Lord and Lady! It would be a pleasure."

After Kairoth had kissed his new bride, he immediately took over the proceedings, as the combatants entered the coliseum to the sound to trumpets blaring. By Hodan law, the monk was now a Prince by marriage, but more importantly, a husband and the head of the household. By Hodan strict traditional law, Faylea was to obey his commands, and he was the leader now. Kairoth knew how that would be received and threw all caution to the wind.

The opponent stepped within speaking distance of the platform and made his bold declaration. "I am here for my crown, woman. Hand it over, or I will take it off of your severed head."

Kairoth's demeanor changed rapidly. "Hear me, Hodan! All present this day! I am Kairoth of Hodan, and this is my wife, Faylea, Princess of Hodan!"

The monk stopped for effect, and the crowd murmured. The monk went on. "By law, I am the head of my household, and by the same law, the rule of the land now falls to me, by the decree of the King."

Faylea interrupted angrily. "You, son of a whore. You knew what you were doing." She kicked the monk in the shin.

Stifling a laugh, Kairoth looked at his new bride. "I love you. You are a formidable warrior in your own right, but you know you cannot defeat this man. I am now the High Priest of Likedelir and trust me on this, I can handle this man."

"So, I'll fight you instead, ragged beggar man!" Groma taunted loudly with confidence.

"That you will, fool, that you will. No one threatens my family and lives." Kairoth's eyes began to glow faintly.

* * *

After the law was read, and the rules were declared, both men entered the arena. Faylea sat frowning on a small throne watching.

"Please don't die," the Princess thought.

A horn was blown to start the contest, and to Kairoth's surprise, Groma struck first, drawing blood. The cut was not serious, and Kairoth grimaced, then recovered to a defensive stance, cracking a smile. The grin caused

Groma to pause and wonder who the man before him was. The Hodan warrior decided it didn't matter and pounced in, to cut down the ragged monk before him. The warrior assured himself that this would be a quick day and the crown would be on his head by nightfall. Faylea would be his, or she would die. Either way, the problem would be solved.

Kairoth prayed sarcastically. "If ever I needed your help with a situation, it is now, Your Holiness. This man is not a slouch."

"You already know what to do. So, do it," a voice answered Kairoth in his mind.

Snorting at the response, the monk parried a sword stroke with his staff and stepped to the shield side of his opponent. Groma responded with a solid shield blow that pushed the monk backward four feet.

"Why try, ragman!? You cannot win," Groma taunted while laughing.

"Famous last words of those who are too confident, fool. Never underestimate your enemy." Kairoth quoted the Hodan code to the warrior. It had its desired effect, enraging him.

"I know that!" The warrior charged in angrily to finish the job. "Who are you to lecture me? You are not even a warrior. You are a coward," the warrior shouted.

Groma swung in a wide arc looking to get around the staff. It did not have the desired effect. Kairoth stepped inside the arc and swung his staff at the cheek plate on the enemy's helmet, delivering a crushing blow to the jaw. The hinged cheek was designed to deflect a sharp edge, but not the blunt force of a staff.

Groma staggered backward, stunned. Kairoth knew that it was now or never. He pounced on his disoriented prey before the man could regain his focus, smashing the left cheek plate this time. Blood and teeth ejected out of the helmet as the man fell to the ground. The helmet was now off of the man, and Kairoth could see his crushed face.

The old Kairoth returned. For nine months, the Master had perfected Kairoth's hand-to-hand combat skills, hardening his bones and his fists. Ei'nyorn showed Kairoth ways of increasing his power and decreasing the travel distance of the blow. The monk knew how to hit a man from one foot away and kill with his hands. Several of those blows met Groma's lifeless head, as the monk pounded the man's face to a pulp.

"No! Father!" a cry from the sidelines rang out in the silence of the arena, as Kairoth claimed his crown.

As the new King stood, a young Hodan man of about sixteen years charged the much larger monk, attempting to stab him with a dagger. The monk side-stepped the boy, slapping the knife away, as if it were just a nuisance. Then Kairoth instinctively grabbed the boy's wrist, twisted him into a bent over position. He swept the nearest leg and landed on top of the lad, who had the wind knocked out of him. Kairoth was still seeing red when he looked at the tear-stained, terrified face below him.

Regaining his composure and focusing on the moment, Kairoth realized the threat was eliminated, and the boy beneath him was only seeking to defend his father. He lowered his fist and released his grip on the boy, still sitting squarely across his chest. The assailant could not move the much larger monk and struggled frantically to break free. He could not.

Kairoth could hear someone pleading beside him. Looking to his right, he saw a beautiful Hodan woman and another child face down in the mud, begging for the life of the one beneath him.

"Please, Your Majesty. Please spare my foolish son. He is all that I have left to carry on the family name. My daughter can be your slave. I will be your slave. Do not let our family line die. I beg you." The woman sobbed.

Kairoth wore a disgusted face. He looked straight at the boy below him moving nose to nose with him. "Are we finished here, boy, or do I need to finish you and your family to ensure my love lives a life of security? Your choice, but if I kill you, I will kill them also."

The boy was shaking. "I am sorry for attacking you, Sir. My father was not an evil man. He was a patriot. He lost, fair and square, but my heart was broken when he fell. I do not seek crowns or thrones, but I loved the man, and he was my idol. Now he is gone and, in my anger, I sought to avenge him." The boy frowned. "In the end, he chose his own fate. I will swear fealty to you, and I will promise to never raise a sword against you again, if you will spare my family. You can kill me if you wish."

The muffled cries of the mother pleaded with Kairoth, who ignored her and focused on the face of the boy who was ready to die for his mistake to preserve his mother and sister. "I will not kill you if you swear fealty and do as you say. Your mother and sister are safe and under my protection. I think that you will serve me in due time, as a Commander of a Legion. I see something better in you. Your father would be proud." Kairoth stood up and grabbed the boy's hand, pulling him to his feet. "Go to them."

* * *

Faylea was miffed. "I have still not forgotten how you used my love for you to usurp my throne!" She hugged him. "Thankfully, you lived so that I can kill you later!"

Kairoth laughed and kissed his Queen. "Time for a coronation? If Orus returns, I will give the crown back to him."

"My Love," Faylea whispered, "we both know that will never happen. Father is gone." The new Queen teared up, frowning. "This is what that old man thought would happen if you ever returned. Orus even hoped for it. He would be proud of you, Kairoth."

"I only live to be with you, serve my God, and build Hodan for its people. Let's start by getting the pageantry out of the way, shall we, wife?"

Kairoth held his arm out, and Faylea took it, giggling at the formality of the gesture. Her King looked like he had walked through the gates of the Underworld to get here. Somehow, she didn't doubt it.

* * *

The coronation was full of pomp and circumstance. The line of Kings was read before the Hodan people, and Kairoth was added to the list. When messengers brought news of the new monarchs to Yslandeth, Puryn was not surprised. Orus had as much as told Puryn that he was never coming back. As a favor, the Yslan King kept an eye on Faylea, and had anyone tried to kill her outside of the challenge, Yslan had a team in position to deal with that threat. It was an unnecessary measure once the monk had resolved the issue of rule. Now, no one Hodan or without, challenged the just rule of Kairoth and Faylea.

Kairoth reaffirmed his commitment to peace. He signed treaties with Yslandeth, first to the cheers of the masses, then Cinnog, who welcomed the stability on its border. Next, emissaries contacted Sudenyag, reassuring King Harun that peace would continue with the North. Edenyag and Hodan signed a peace agreement, but the two nations continued to be wary of the other. Torith and Dornat Al Ar warmed to Kairoth and his rule. Both Kings of the elder races knew the man who they were dealing with and neither worried about his integrity.

Puryn and Adasser sighed in relief from their throne room. Even with the abrupt change in power in Hodan, the peace still held and the Alliances were solid.

This was the best case scenario that either had considered.

Chapter 31

Puryn sat on his throne in Empyr. He looked at the ornate flagstones and mosaic scenes that adorned the hall. Scenes of the Battle of Arondayre stood center stage, with lesser scenes of Swyk and Ontak holding Empyr at the end of the age. Now, he sat on the padded chair alone, contemplating the events of the first twenty years of his reign.

Shortly after the capital was completed, Donick left the Ert to join Aeternum. Not far after he departed, Puryn's father, Durn, died in his bed of old age, a farmer in the end. Puryn's mother held his hand in the end, and the family buried him on his lands near Erynseere at his mother's request. Within the year, Puryn's mother, Arla, passed and joined her husband in like manner. Elpis was by her grandmother's side when the end finally came and watched as Arla entered the gates to join her husband. She was at peace and buried beside her husband near the Erynseere forest ring.

Elpis claimed her grandparent's homestead without argument from her family. She maintained the home as it had always been and missed her grandparents deeply. Eventually, the young mage traveled to Edenyag and trained beside the greatest Human and Elfish mages the Ert had ever known. She would become their equals but return to her farm, in the end, living in peace within her lands.

Altwidus ran the Barony of Korin as he had since he was a young man. It bred the fastest and strongest steeds ever seen on the Ert. Puryn called upon his son many times to provide his expertise in husbandry and horse breeding. The Kingdom of Yslandeth outfitted all of its Elite forces and

Draj with horses from Korin. Although the Barony was remote and a bit rustic, it prospered much under the kind and wise rule of Puryn's youngest boy.

Illari was a strange case. Being the oldest son of the King, he studied without rest and stood by his father at every chance. The reality that he may be required to sit upon the throne of Yslandeth without notice terrified the young half-Elfish man. He never felt that he was ready, even though Queen Adasser assured him that he was much more prepared than either she or her beloved had been when they took over the thrones after the Great War. Illari was never assured and worked tirelessly to ensure his competency to rule.

Empyr had grown in size and glory. The treaties with the entirety of the Ert held, and peace was known throughout the lands. All who lived upon the Ert prospered according to their station and many increased their standings and wealth. Education became available to the average citizen through the petition of Elpis. Puryn finally granted her request, charging Valtyr to train up not only the clergy, but local teachers who would be sent out to the neighboring shires and villages to educate the next generation. The result was a generation of literate people. Commoners who once could scarcely read, began writing poetry and recording the events of their localities. Soon, Edenyag began to collect a patchwork of unique prose and philosophies, which was inspired by the new thinkers of the age.

Kairoth and Faylea ruled Hodan for many years, due to the mercy of their God. Kairoth knew when he married his love, that the difference in ages between he and his wife would soon send her ahead of him to Aeternum. One day, while lamenting that he had met his love too late, Likedelir heard his High Priest's prayers through his inner turmoil. The God of Balance visited the monk and promised him a long life with his lady—even a family of his own. However, Kairoth laughed, knowing that his lady, although still a beautiful woman, was nearing the end of the middle age of her life. She was well past the age of bearing children.

The God smiled and blessed his High Priest, despite his follower's doubt, granting long life to his beloved Faylea. Likedelir, in true chaotic fashion, turned back the years, righting the wrong which the God felt that his mother had cursed his High Priest with. After Likedelir's intervention, Faylea began to resemble a lass much younger than her actual age. Kairoth knew that his God had once again come through with the impossible. After the first miracle was, Likedelir delivered on the second promise. Faylea bore Kairoth a son, who she named Orus, in honor of her father, who she never saw or heard from again.

Renewed in his fervor, due to his God's favor and blessings in his life, Kairoth preached religious tolerance throughout his lands, as well as taught the masses about Likedelir. He dispelled falsehoods and debated with naysayers, deftly defending the name and the mission of his God. Over time, the Hodan King commissioned a temple to the Conflict, which was erected near his palace at Warrior's Crossing in the Hodan capital. People from all over the Ert came to worship and pay their respects to their new God, and Hodan eventually recognized Likedelir as its patron deity. Pleased, the God blessed the couple more and more.

Cinnog held fast to the worship of Haya, and the clergy within the Citadel railed against the heresy of worshipping one who switched between the Light and Dark. At times, the rhetoric would fan the flames of nationalism and religious pride so hot that some would ponder an invasion of Hodan and Sudenyag, "to quell the blasphemous activities against Haya and the Light."

Reynir, from his own temple outside of the Citadel, opposed the Temple priests openly and became the only voice of reason, in a Kingdom that was rapidly becoming a haven for fanatics. None of those fervent followers dared to challenge the druid or his followers. They knew the Goddess walked among Reynir's trees and that he was allied with Queen Adasser, the Holy Mother of the Forest of Torith and Erynseere. Many ignored what the Queen could do with her trees, but the elders of Cinnog kept the younger fools at bay, with stories of the Offlander demise at the hands of one Priestess on the day of reckoning. Cinnog simmered, but the lid was still on that pot.

Sudenyag recovered gradually. Trade resumed with the North and with the advent of seafaring, many Suden merchants commissioned ships to follow the lead of Orus of Hodan. The traders figured that if Orus could find Offlanders to kill in other places besides the Ert, then perhaps, they could find other lands to trade with and enrich the Kingdom of Sudenyag. King Harun Il Arnat lived for many years and ruled justly. He re-established the rule of law and Suden tradition. He also created the largest and most well-trained southern army the Ert had ever seen. The King believed that if peace held, they would police his lands for brigands, but if the Ert suddenly changed course, Harun vowed that his people would not be unprepared to defend themselves ever again.

* * *

"You are wise, old King," the younger Hodan King teased in reply.

"Who are you calling old, boy!" Puryn responded, laughing out loud.

Kairoth smiled. "I will leave you and your lovely wife to your castle and return to mine, my friend." The Hodan stood and bowed, extending his hand.

Puryn took his hand and shook it. "You are a great leader, Kairoth, and a good ally. If my brother had to leave me here to rule this place alone, at least he found me an excellent man to fill his shoes."

"You also, King, Chosen One. Are you ready, Faylea?" Kairoth turned to his lady, who was nursing an infant son.

"In a moment, husband. This one is hungry." She smiled and looked at Adasser, who was openly grinning.

"It has been so long since I have seen a child so close. Please, do not be offended, but you are both older parents, the Goddess, or perhaps your God, blesses you with your heir!" The Queen sighed. "I miss the time when mine were this young."

"It is true, we did have to wait a long time for the fulfillment of this blessing, but the wait was worth it, and my God blesses us with time to raise him well." Faylea smiled, as the boy began to doze off. "I believe that we are now ready, husband."

"Come by any time, Kairoth. You and your family are always welcome under my roof. We are eternal allies. May Yslandeth and Hodan stand beside one another until the end of time." Puryn stood.

"May it be as you say, my friend." Kairoth bowed.

The couple left the room with their child to return to Hodan. Puryn and Adasser sat in their throne room holding hands and looking out of a large open window. The bustle of everyday life chattered off in the distance, as the people hurried to complete the morning tasks, before the sun was high in the sky and the heat began to become oppressive.

Adasser kissed her husband on the cheek. "If Illari is not careful, husband, we, too, may have an addition to our line."

"He is not frequenting Galdsburg again, is he? What is wrong with that boy?" Puryn seemed miffed.

"Truly? You seem upset that he is interested in someone of another … race, husband, after marrying an Elf?" Adasser smirked, waiting for a reply.

"Well, no, woman, not that …" Puryn struggled to explain himself. His face was red. "It's just he's Human and Elf, and he looks to the Galdruhn for a mate? What kind of a grandchild will we see!?" Puryn made a face. "Maybe he should marry a Dwarf!"

"He is too tall. That would be an awkward sight!" Adasser laughed. "Seriously, though, husband. What if he does love a Galdruhn? What then?"

"He loves a Galdruhn then. Who can contain love?" the King replied, looking into his wife's eyes.

"Truly, husband, who can hold back love?" Adasser kissed her King.

About the Author

Austin Belanger retired from the United States Marine Corps in 2005. After his time in the military, he pursued his next career in Information Technology, graduating Summa Cum Laude from American Intercontinental University with a bachelor's degree in Network Administration.

Austin is a published poet and writes for several small online communities as a hobby. Although, he has written stories and poems for most of his life, The Champion of the Golden Queen is his first officially published offering from a series of books that will be called, "Tales of the Ert."

Austin has been married for 26 years, is a father of four sons, and a grandfather to 7. Austin grew up in Massachusetts, but moved away during his time in the military. He now calls Arizona his home.

Facebook: facebook.com/bardofthesand/

Twitter: @bardofthesand

Email: bardofthesands@gmail.com

Also by Austin S. Belanger

The Champion of the Golden Queen

The eternal battle of good versus evil is sparked by a marital spat between two gods. Now, the goddess, Haya, must defend all of creation from the evil schemes of her estranged husband, Haeldrun, who has crowned himself god of the Underworld and darkness.

As Haeldrun works on his grand scheme to snuff out the light of creation, his estranged wife makes plans of her own, enlisting the help of an unlikely band of saviors led by her chosen hero, who is the newborn son of a common man and woman.

The Light had better be on the ball, because the Darkness is bringing its "A" game!

The survival of life and light depend upon the actions and decisions of mere mortals. What could go wrong?